**Praise for *New York Times* bestselling author
Elle James**

"Jam-packed with fast-paced action and steamy
scenes, James has the whole 'sexy Navy SEALS and
the strong women they love' routine marvelously
down pat."
—*RT Book Reviews* on *Navy SEAL Newlywed*

"James picks up her Daddy Corps series with an
explosion and doesn't release the pressure valve
until the last page—and even then her cliffhanger will
leave readers begging for more."
—*RT Book Reviews* on *Cowboy Brigade*

"*Bodyguard Under Fire* is filled with riveting
suspense and some sizzling romance. Elle James
gives us another great read in her Covert Cowboy
series."
—*Fresh Fiction* on *Bodyguard Under Fire*

Elle James, a *New York Times* bestselling author, started writing when her sister challenged her to write a romance novel. She has managed a full-time job and raised three wonderful children, and she and her husband even tried ranching exotic birds (ostriches, emus and rheas). Ask her, and she'll tell you what it's like to go toe-to-toe with an angry 350-pound bird! Elle loves to hear from fans at ellejames@earthlink.net or ellejames.com.

Books by Elle James

Harlequin Intrigue

Covert Cowboys, Inc.

Triggered
Taking Aim
Bodyguard Under Fire
Cowboy Resurrected
Navy SEAL Justice
Navy SEAL Newlywed
High Country Hideout

Thunder Horse

Hostage to Thunder Horse
Thunder Horse Heritage
Thunder Horse Redemption
Christmas at Thunder Horse Ranch

Visit the Author Profile page at Harlequin.com for more titles.

ELLE JAMES

Triggered & Taking Aim

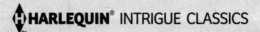
HARLEQUIN® INTRIGUE CLASSICS

Recycling programs
for this product may
not exist in your area.

ISBN-13: 978-0-373-60217-9

Triggered & Taking Aim

Copyright © 2016 by Harlequin Books S.A.

The publisher acknowledges the copyright holder
of the individual works as follows:

Triggered
Copyright © 2013 by Mary Jernigan

Taking Aim
Copyright © 2013 by Mary Jernigan

This edition published by arrangement with Harlequin Books S.A.

For questions and comments about the quality of this book,
please contact us at CustomerService@Harlequin.com.

® and TM are trademarks of the publisher. Trademarks indicated with ® are registered in the United States Patent and Trademark Office, the Canadian Intellectual Property Office and in other countries.

Printed in U.S.A.

™ www.Harlequin.com

CONTENTS

Triggered

This book is dedicated to cowboys of all shapes, sizes and sexes. These brave men and women work hard, play hard and have a sense of loyalty, decency and ethics we should all aspire to.

CHAPTER ONE

NECESSITY, BURNING CURIOSITY and a Hummer limo brought him here, but as Ben Harding sat in the leather armchair surrounded by three other men, he wondered what the heck he'd gotten himself into. He glanced around the room again. The only thing he had in common with the others was that they each wore a cowboy hat, jeans and boots.

Beyond that, he knew nothing about the men gathered in billionaire Hank Derringer's home. The Raging Bull Ranch lay in the heart of the back of beyond, South Texas, where men were tough, the drug runners were tougher and a property owner stood a good chance of getting killed riding across his own spread.

Ben had done his homework. Hank Derringer had become a recluse since he'd lost his family over a year ago in a botched kidnapping attempt. The man had made billions and continued to make more in the oil and gas industry. All facts that were easy enough to find. But why bring these men here? Why now?

Ben would have blown off the invitation to come if he'd had any other choice. His career at the Austin Police Department at an end, he'd been pounding the pavement looking for work and finding that no one, until now, wanted to hire a man who'd been kicked off the force for killing a man with his bare hands.

Did he regret what he'd done?

No.

And he'd do it again, given the same circumstances.

His gut clenched and he fought to push the rage and lingering images to the back of his mind as a tall, slightly older man joined them.

He wore a black Stetson and looked very much like the other men seated around the room. "Gentlemen, I'm Hank Derringer. Thank you all for coming to the Raging Bull Ranch." He sat near the huge stone fireplace, facing them. "I brought you here because you are the best of the best."

"Best of the best what, Hank?" The muscle-bound, blond-haired man across from Ben spoke first. He nodded toward Ben and the other two men. "And who are these guys?"

Hank tipped his head toward the man questioning him. "Patience, Thorn. I'm getting to that. For the rest of you, meet Thorn Drennan, the best sheriff Wild Oak Canyon ever had. A man the people could count on to fight for truth and justice."

Thorn's eyes narrowed. "You're forgetting—I'm no longer the sheriff."

"Precisely." Hank turned to the man with brown hair, brown eyes and a wicked scar across his right cheek. "Chuck Bolton. Your friends call you Big Tex, born and raised on a ranch near Amarillo. You know how to ride, rope and build fences like the best of them. Served two tours in Iraq and one in Afghanistan where you wiped out an entire Taliban stronghold against your commander's orders."

The man sat up straighter, his broad shoulders

straining against the seams of his chambray shirt. "Got the boot and a bum leg for that."

"A man with courage and determination to fight the good fight," Hank said.

Big Tex shrugged. "I guess it depends on your definition of 'the good fight.'"

Hank moved on to the next person, a man sitting back from the rest, dark circles beneath his eyes, an intense, haunted expression in his green eyes as he stared out the window. "Special Agent Zachary Adams, one of the FBI's best undercover operatives working to stop the drug cartels along the border. Got caught in a bad situation on the wrong side of the border. Yet you survived."

"For what it was worth." The man's gaze shifted from the window to Hank. "And, just for the record, former FBI. I quit."

Hank nodded. "Right."

Derringer turned to Ben, his smile warm, welcoming. "And then there's Ben Harding, the most highly decorated officer on the Austin police force."

"*The* Ben Harding?" Big Tex snorted. "Weren't you the guy who was fired for strangling Frank Davis to death with your bare hands?"

Ben stiffened. He'd seen what the high-powered CEO had done to that young girl in a run-down warehouse on the seedier side of Austin. He'd watched him run from the scene of the crime with the child's blood on his hands and clothing. Ben hadn't cared who he was or what big company he ran. All he cared about was making the man pay for what he'd done to the girl.

Ben's stomach roiled as he recalled the scene and

the memories of another very similar crime involving the deaths of his wife and young daughter.

His fingers balled into fists and he rose halfway out of his seat, ready to take on the world. "Yeah, I killed a man, what's it to you?"

Big Tex shrugged. "Just wondering."

"I read about it. Davis was a sick bastard into hurting little girls. I'd have done the same," the man called Zach said.

"You gave him what he deserved," Thorn agreed. "Why waste money on a system that would have turned him loose to do it again?"

The starch taken out of his fight, Ben sat back against the soft brown leather of the wingback chair. He was disappointed he wouldn't have a brawl to release all the tension balled up in his gut since he'd arrived. At least now he felt more of a kinship with the others in the room.

Hank's mouth twisted into a wry grin. "You are all highly trained in your fields, and because of your various circumstances find yourselves unemployed."

Ben snorted. "Unemployable."

"Wrong." Hank's lips spread into a smile. "I'm here to offer you a position in a start-up corporation."

"Doing what? Sweeping floors? Who wants a bunch of rejects?" Zach asked.

"I need you." Hank rose from his chair. "Because you aren't rejects, you're just the type of men I'm looking for. Men who will fight for what you believe in, who were born or raised on a ranch, with the ethics and strength of character of a good cowboy. I'm inviting you to become a part of CCI, known only to those on the inside as Covert Cowboys, Inc., a specialized team of citizen soldiers, bodyguards, agents and ranch hands who will do whatever it takes to see justice served."

"Whoa, back up a step there. Covert Cowboys, Inc.?" Big Tex slapped his hat against his thigh. "Sounds kind of corny to me. What's the punch line?"

"No punch line." Hank stood taller, his broad shoulders filling the room, the steel in his eyes indisputable. The man was on the up-and-up. "Let's just say that I'm tired of justice being swept under the rug."

Ben shook his head. "I'm not into vigilante justice, or circumventing the law."

"I'm not asking you to. The purpose of Covert Cowboys, Inc. is to provide covert protection and investigation services where hired guns and the law aren't enough." Hank's gaze swept over each of the men in the room. "I handpicked each of you because you are all highly skilled soldiers, cops and agents who know how to work hard, fire a gun and are familiar with living on the edge of danger. But mostly because of your high moral standards. You know right from wrong and aren't afraid to right the wrongs. My plan is to inject you into situations where your own lives could be on the line to protect, rescue or ferret out the truth."

Ben stood, his body tense, his first reaction to the older man's words to leave and never look back. "I'm not a vigilante, despite what the news says."

"I'm not hiring you to be one," Hank said. "I'm asking you to join CCI as a protector, a man willing to fight for truth."

"Truth, huh?" Zach said. "It's hard to find people who care about truth anymore."

Hank's lips thinned. "My point, exactly."

"Tell me, why should I work for you?" Ben asked.

The older man's shoulders straightened and he looked directly into Ben's eyes. "I care about truth and justice." He walked to the desk in the corner and lifted four folders. The first he held out to Ben. "Are you in?"

What did he have to lose? Ben had nothing to go back to in Austin. No job, no family. Nothing. Against his better judgment, Ben nodded. "I'm in."

Hank handed him the folder. "Your first assignment is on the other side of the county working undercover on the Flying K Ranch. As far as everyone else knows, you're hiring on as a ranch hand. Your job is to help get the ranch operational, but most of all to protect the woman who just inherited it."

"Sounds easy enough."

"Don't count on it. This county is in need of cleanup. I'm hoping you gentlemen will be the men to help in that effort. It's our first challenge for CCI." Hank stared at the other men. "Who else chooses to take on the challenge?"

One by one the men threw their hats in the ring and grabbed a folder.

Ben opened the file and stared down at the image of a beautiful woman with long strawberry-blond hair, green eyes and skin as pale and smooth as porcelain. His gut told him he was stepping into waters way over his head. What did he know about providing protection to a woman? He'd been a street cop, not a bodyguard. Hell, he hadn't been able to protect his own family. A knot of regret twisted in him, but he asked, "When do I start?"

"Tonight. Grab your gear and get on over there, she should have arrived today."

Ben's eyes narrowed. "You were sure I'd take the job?"

"If not you, I'd be out there doing it myself. Don't get me wrong. I won't ask any of you to do anything I wouldn't be willing to do myself."

Ben clapped his hat on his head and headed for the door. It was a job. He didn't have to like it; he just had to do it until he found something else.

"'THE COW DOG saved the little girl and became her very best friend. The end.'" Kate Langsdon closed the book and set it on Lily's nightstand. "Now it's time for little girls to go to sleep." She leaned over and kissed her daughter's forehead, her heart squeezing in her chest with the amount of love she felt for this pint-size person with the long, loose curls of silky, strawberry-blond hair, much like her own.

"Mommy?" Lily yawned and rubbed her emerald-green eyes. "Can I have a cow dog?"

"Sure, sweetie. Just as soon as we can find one as good as Jess the cow dog." Kate switched the light off on the nightstand and straightened her aching back, got up and headed into the bathroom. The past few days had been strenuous and emotionally draining, the amount of work taking the spunk right out of her. She'd driven from Houston to Wild Oak Canyon, Texas, cleaned a house that had been standing empty for two months, emptied as much as she could of the moving van she'd rented and poked through the belongings of a man she'd never known and never would.

Her father.

Tears welled in Kate's eyes. For years, she'd thought

her father dead. All this time, the man had been living in South Texas on a ranch near Big Bend National Park.

Kate dug her hand in her pocket and thumbed the key she'd received a week ago in an envelope from an attorney, including a letter, last will and testament and one corrupt video disk. The day that package arrived everything in Kate's life had changed.

She pulled the key from her pocket and tossed it into her makeup kit, stripped out of her dirty jeans and climbed into the shower. She stood for a long time as the warm spray washed down over her body, releasing the stiffness from her shoulders and tempering the ache in her lower back.

She wished all her worries could wash away with the water. As she stood in her father's house, on the ranch he'd bequeathed to her, she wondered if she'd done the right thing bringing Lily here.

She'd come to start over and to find answers. For one, what did the key fit? The video had been all static and with a brief glimpse of her father, but it cut off before her father could tell her what the key belonged to. Her father's letter left instructions for her to get help from the only man he trusted, Hank Derringer, the owner of the Raging Bull Ranch in Wild Oak Canyon. He'd help her with whatever she needed.

She hadn't called Mr. Derringer at first, taking a day to digest the fact that her father hadn't died when her mother had told her. The news had been so shocking that it took that long for it to sink in. Contacting his trusted friend was the furthest thing from her mind.

Until someone broke into her apartment in Houston while she had been at work and Lily had been at day care.

When she'd come home to find the apartment she and Lily had called home for four years looking as if the place had been tossed in a Texas-size salad bowl, she'd been angry and scared.

How dare someone break into her home? Kate knew she couldn't stay in the apartment, not after it had been violated and especially not knowing the reason. Nothing had been taken, as far as she could tell.

She'd packed up her daughter, boxed their belongings and headed west to Wild Oak Canyon and the Flying K Ranch to find the answers. How permanent this move proved to be was up to what she found, but she'd quit her job and given up her lease before she left. Either way, she couldn't go back and pick up where she'd left off.

Alone in the world except for Lily, Kate had turned to the phone number of the stranger her father had recommended.

Hank Derringer had answered on the first ring. He'd tried to talk her out of coming to Wild Oak Canyon. When she'd insisted, he'd promised to send a cowboy to her, one who could help her get the ranch back up and running and provide the protection she and Lily needed. Her cowboy would be there before they turned in for the night. Or so Hank had promised. Kate wondered what kind of protection she needed on a ranch out in the middle of nowhere.

She'd waited as long as she could to take her shower and still the cowboy hadn't arrived and probably wouldn't until morning.

When the water grew tepid, Kate turned it off and grabbed for the fluffy white towel she'd unearthed from one of the boxes she'd brought with her in the moving

van. Bent over, her head upside down to wrap her long
hair in the towel, her hands froze. Was that a sound
downstairs?

She strained to listen.

Nothing.

Kate shrugged, worried her imagination was getting the better of her. She continued towel drying her
hair when something crashed below and a low curse
followed.

Her breath caught on a gasp and her pulse raced.
She'd turned out the lights on the main floor and locked
all the doors before she and Lily had come up for the
night. Whoever was down there was moving around
in the dark. *Inside* the house.

Kate wrapped the towel around her and ran into the
master bedroom she'd planned to share with Lily the
first night until she could prepare another room just
for her daughter.

Lily lay sound asleep, oblivious to the danger, the
only light in the room the glow from the open bathroom door.

With nowhere to run, Kate quietly gathered her
daughter, blankets and all, and hurried to the closet
where she'd hung all of the clothing she'd brought
with her next to those of her father's. Kate thanked
her lucky stars that Lily slept soundly. The little girl
didn't stir as Kate laid her down in the back corner of
the closet, tucking the blankets around her, blocking
her from view.

Once she had her daughter hidden, Kate tiptoed
back to the nightstand, slid the drawer open and removed the 9 mm Glock she'd brought with her.

A board creaked on the stairs, sending Kate scurrying toward the door where she eased it closed.

Her hands shook as she alternated between holding up her towel and balancing the pistol. She wished she'd had time to dress, wishing more that she'd loaded the weapon. She prayed that the sight of it would scare a trespasser into leaving without hurting her or Lily. On second thought, she turned the gun around and held it by the barrel. Hitting the man would be better than pointing an unloaded pistol.

The doors down the hallway opened one by one. Kate held her breath as the intruder made his way toward the room she and Lily occupied. What she wouldn't give for cell phone reception.

Though, what good would it do when the sheriff wouldn't reach her ranch for fifteen to twenty minutes? She was on her own.

Where was the cowboy? Why hadn't he arrived already? Was the man moving down the hallway her cowboy? If he was, he had a lot of nerve barging in and sneaking around. He deserved the same as any thief and Kate would give it to him.

With Lily in the closet and her own hands shaking, Kate couldn't chance it. She had to divert attention and get the attacker away from the room where her daughter lay sleeping.

Kate prayed the man would give up and go away.

As she watched in horror, the doorknob turned. She wished it had a lock on it she could twist to buy her a little more time. Maybe not having a lock would work out for the better. She raised her arms and waited, her breath caught and held.

A dark figure stepped through the door. The man wore a ski mask. Anyone in a ski mask meant trouble.

As soon as his head cleared the entrance, Kate slammed the butt of the pistol down on his skull so hard the gun bounced out of her hands and skittered across the floor.

The man lurched forward and dropped to his knees.

Kate flung the door wide and leaped past the intruder.

Before she could take two steps, a large hand snagged her ankle.

Her forward momentum brought her down hard, knocking the breath from her lungs. She clawed at the carpet, kicking with all her might with her free foot, landing a couple hard heels in the attacker's face.

His grip loosened and Kate scrambled to her feet, running as fast as she could for the stairs, thankful and terrified when she heard the intruder's footsteps behind her.

She had to get the man as far away from Lily as possible. If he hurt Kate, maybe he'd leave her for dead and never find the little girl hiding in the closet.

Kate took the stairs two at a time, missing the last one, toppling to the floor and wasting precious seconds.

The man above her came crashing down the steps and leaped over the railing to land beside her.

Kate swallowed her scream, fearing she'd wake Lily. She rolled to the side, her fingers wrapping around the cord of a lamp.

She yanked the lamp toward her, grabbed the base and turned in time to see the man flying at her. He landed on top of her, knocking the wind from her.

With her hand still around the base of the lamp, Kate swung as hard as she could. The ceramic lamp made contact with the ski mask and bounced off, crashing to the wooden floor, shattering into a million fragments.

Out of options, Kate remembered the self-defense training she'd taken when Lily was little. She knew she was the only one there to defend her small daughter. With the desperation of a trapped mother bear, she freed one hand and jabbed her thumb into the man's eye.

He yelled and punched her face.

Pain radiated across her cheekbone, her vision blurred and Kate knew she wasn't going to last much longer. For Lily, she tried to hang in there, forcing the darkness back, struggling beneath the weight of her attacker.

As the intruder reeled back to hit her again, Kate squeezed shut her eyes.

Before the fist connected with her face, all the weight on top of her shifted backward.

Kate's eyes popped open.

The man in the ski mask fought against another man wearing a black T-shirt and a cowboy hat. Fists flew, and bodies banged against the old furniture. The cowboy hat flew across the room, landing in a corner.

Kate sucked in air, filling her lungs and clearing her fuzzy thoughts. She scrambled to her feet, clutching the towel around her, searching for a weapon of any kind. Her hands wrapped around the legs of an end table. She lifted it high and waited for the right moment.

The two men tumbled and flew around the room, knocking over furniture. With the lights out, Kate could barely tell who was who.

Then her rescuer hit the floor on his back and the man in the ski mask pulled a knife from his belt, the metal glinting in a ray of moonlight shining through a gap in the curtained window.

Kate's heart thudded against her rib cage.

The man in the ski mask closed in on Kate's rescuer.

Without thinking past saving the man on the ground, Kate rushed for the one with the blade and slammed the end table down over his head with enough force to break the small table into several pieces.

The attacker dropped to his hands and knees. He swung his arm out, clipping Kate in the back of her legs.

She fell hard, her head hitting the corner of a coffee table. As she landed, she heard shuffling of feet and tried to rise to see what was going on. When she lifted her head, her vision swam.

No. She couldn't give up now.

Pain radiated from the back of her head. She closed her eyes, praying for them to clear and let her get back into the fight. Lily depended on her.

Hands gripped her arms. Kate struggled, but the grasp was strong. Too strong for her to fight off.

"Shh. It's okay. I'm not going to hurt you." The voice was a deep rumble, the tone rich and warm, resonating from deep in his chest, wrapping her in a reassuring blanket.

"Bad guy?" she asked, without opening her eyes.

"He's gone." A hand brushed a wisp of hair out of her eyes. "Are you okay?" The same hand trailed softly over her cheekbone where the masked man had punched her.

Kate winced, and she opened her eyes to stare into

the bluest eyes she'd ever seen. Her breath caught in her throat, and not out of fear. "Who are you?"

"Ben Harding. Hank Derringer thought you could use my help."

Thank God. The cavalry had arrived.

CHAPTER TWO

BEN STARED DOWN at the woman, her long wavy strawberry-blond hair lying in damp ringlets against the wood floor. Wrapped only in a fluffy white towel, she looked like a fallen angel, her creamy smooth skin begging to be touched, the towel riding up her shapely thighs.

"You're staring." The woman blinked up at him, her fingers pulling the edges of the towel together over her chest. She tried to sit up, pressed a hand to the back of her head and sank back. "Must have hit harder than I thought."

"I'll call for an ambulance."

She shook her head and winced. "No. I'll be all right, just give me a minute." One arm rose to cover her eyes. The top edge of the towel slipped lower over the swell of her breasts, capturing Ben's attention.

He really needed to focus on the situation, not the female lying almost naked at his feet, which proved hard when the woman had a great figure and very touchable skin. A pang of guilt and sadness knotted his gut. He hadn't felt like touching a woman in more than two years. Not since… "Any idea what the guy was after?"

"None," she answered, the arm dropping to her side. "I'm just glad he's gone and you're here. I'm Kate

Langsdon." She held out a hand, a frown denting her pretty brow. "What took you so long?"

"I just got the assignment an hour ago."

"Well, Mr. Harding, I'm glad you came when you did. Any later and…" She shrugged and tried to sit up again. "I have to get up."

"You should stay put and let me call an ambulance."

"No, I have to get upstairs."

"Why the rush?"

"I just need to." She sat up, swayed and started to fall back. "Damn it, I can't be dizzy."

"Pigheaded woman." Ben caught her before her head hit the floor.

"Stubborn man," she whispered.

He scooped her into his arms and lifted her off the floor.

She tensed, her arm automatically circling his shoulder. "You don't have to carry me. I'm perfectly capable of standing on my own two feet."

"Not with a knot on your head and a crazy determination to get upstairs."

"Give me a minute and I'll argue this point." Her uninjured cheek lying against his chest belied her ability to put up much of a resistance. Her free hand struggled to keep the towel in place.

Ben ignored her protest and carried her up the stairs. "Which room?"

She sighed. "Last one on the landing. And really, I can get there on my own."

"No need. From what Hank told me, I'm the hired hand, here to help rebuild a ranch and protect its owner."

"Hank's words?"

"Right." His lips twisted, a frown creasing his forehead. "Let me do my job."

She chuckled, a smile curling her lips, making her face shine even with the nasty bruise turning her cheek purple. "Somehow, I don't think carrying a woman to her bedroom is part of the job description." The smile faded. "But thanks."

For a brief moment the sun had shone in the woman's face, tugging at a place Ben thought buried for good with his wife and daughter. He shook the thought from his head and turned left on the landing.

When they crossed the threshold into the room, the woman twisted in his arms, her gaze darting toward the closet.

The door was open, blankets spilled from inside, some half-dragged out on the floor. "Let me down." She pushed against his arm, her nails digging into his skin.

"I will, but I'm not dropping you."

"Let me down." She shoved harder.

He lowered her feet to the floor, his arm remaining around her waist.

She stood for a moment, swaying, and then lunged for the closet, her eyes wide, her face tense. "Lily?" Her voice was strained, desperate.

"Who's Lily?" he asked.

Kate didn't answer as she dove into the back of the closet, rifling through blankets. When her face appeared at the edge of the closet door, it was pale and pinched. "Lily?" She leaped to her feet and nearly fell on her face.

Ben was there to catch her, his arms crushing her against his chest. "Who's Lily?"

"Mommy?" A tiny voice called out from the bathroom. "Mommy?"

Kate's head came up and she fought her way out of Ben's arms, dropping to her knees in front of a little girl with a mass of golden-red curls very much like her mother's drying wispy locks. She stood silhouetted against the light streaming from the bathroom, like an angel descended from heaven.

"Oh, Lily." Kate hugged the child to her.

Sweet Jesus. Hank hadn't said anything about a little girl. Ben stood like stone, his feet rooted to the floor, unable to move, forgetting how to breathe.

The little girl was about the age of Sarah before she'd been murdered. Though his Sarah was as different from Lily as night and day, they were about the same size and age.

Before Sarah had been killed. She'd been four years old. She would have been six now, if a man Ben had captured and had subsequently been released on a technicality hadn't targeted Ben and his family.

Ben hadn't been home when his wife and daughter had been brutally stabbed to death. Had he been, he'd have killed the murderer with his bare hands, just like he'd killed the man who'd murdered fifteen-year-old Angelica Garza.

Seeing Kate Langsdon on the floor holding the little girl in her arms brought back too many painful memories. Ben's feet moved one at a time as he backed toward the door. With his heart lodged in his throat, he couldn't breathe or think. His gut told him to run as far from Kate and Lily Langsdon as he could get.

Before he reached the door, the curly-haired angel noticed him for the first time. "Mommy, who's that man?"

Kate eased her hold on her daughter and looked up at Ben, the fear of a few moments ago still evident in her pale face. "That's Mr. Harding. He's the man who came to help us on the ranch."

"Are you going to help my mommy?" she asked, her gaze open, direct, piercing the wall wrapped tightly around Ben's heart.

He yearned to run and keep running until the child's trusting eyes were erased from his mind. But he knew he couldn't leave this little girl and her mother when the intruder he'd chased off earlier might return.

"Yes, ma'am. I'm here to help your mommy." He nearly choked on *mommy*. His daughter had called his wife Mommy. His daughter had looked at him with complete trust, as if he could never let her down.

But he had. He hadn't been there when she'd needed him most. He had been all about the job, bringing in the bad guys. He'd never taken into account that the ones that got off might come back to haunt him. Until it was too late.

Kate's eyes narrowed. "Are you okay?"

No. Ben's gaze went from Lily to Kate. For a tough cop, used to facing down danger on the streets of Austin, he was more terrified of these two women than any criminal he'd ever confronted. "I'm fine." He cleared his throat. "I'll just bed down in the barn."

"No." Kate stood and swayed, her hand on her daughter's shoulder.

Before he could think through his actions, Ben was there, steadying her with a hand under her elbow, the other around her waist.

"Stay here. In the house." She leaned into him for

a moment. When she'd steadied, she pulled away and looked up into his face. "Please."

Her green eyes pleaded with him, her hand on his arm burning a path through his defenses. How he wanted to leave, but couldn't. Despite his vow to never care again, he'd proved over and over he just couldn't honor that vow after all. Killing the high-powered child murderer was evidence. Damn Kate and Lily for making him care. "I'll stay on two conditions."

Her shoulders straightened. "Anything."

He scooped up the gun she'd dropped earlier and handed it to her. "First, put this away, take it to a pawnshop or learn to use it."

She took the gun from him, keeping her body between the gun and her daughter's curious eyes. "Check. I'll learn to use it." Her chin tipped upward. "And the second one?"

His gaze swept over her, taking in the smooth lines of her shoulders, the gentle swell of her breasts and the curve of her thighs peeking out from under the terry cloth. If he had any hope of staying neutral in this situation, he had to put distance between himself and Kate. She was too damned attractive.

He forced an uninterested rise of his brows. "If I'm going to get any work done around here, you have to keep your clothes on around me."

Kate gasped, hugging the towel closer, her cheeks flaming red.

"I'll be on the couch downstairs." He stepped out into the hallway and closed the door between them with a firm click.

Kate stared at the barrier between them for a long moment, stunned at the cowboy's abrupt words and departure. "As if I planned to be standing in front of him in nothing but a towel," she mumbled.

"Mommy, why was I in the closet?" Lily's hand slipped into hers and tugged, dragging Kate's mind back to what was important. Her daughter.

She scrambled for an answer that wouldn't scare her small daughter. "I thought it might be fun to pretend to be camped in a cave in the mountains."

Lily tipped her head to the side as if debating whether or not she believed Kate's lie. Then she smiled and pulled Kate toward the closet. "Will you camp in the cave with me, Mommy?"

"Oh, baby, I don't think so. I'm pretty tired and bed sounds more comfortable. You can sleep in the closet, if you want."

Lily stared from the bed to the closet and yawned, her eyelids sagging. "No, I'm tired, too. Maybe tomorrow."

Kate grabbed the blankets from the floor and flung them across the bed as best she could, tucking Lily in on the side away from the door.

As she pulled out a pair of pajamas that would fully cover her body, she thought of Ben Harding's condition. A spark of defiance shot through her and she replaced the pajamas in the drawer, reaching for the filmy light blue baby-doll nightgown she'd bought one hot, impulsive day in Houston.

She slipped the silky garment over her head, letting the towel drop to the floor, and recalled the feeling of being held in Ben's strong arms as he effortlessly carried her up the stairs to her bedroom. Her skin sizzled where his hands had been beneath her thighs and very nearly touching the side of her breast.

Now that she had time to think beyond defending her life, she realized the cowboy Hank had sent was everything a girl could dream of—tall, dark and handsome. Add a brooding, mysterious look in his blue eyes and he was devastatingly appealing.

She hadn't felt like this since…before her husband, Troy, had been killed in Afghanistan, a month before she'd delivered Lily. Four years ago. A wave of guilt washed over her for thinking such thoughts about a man who wasn't her husband. But, then, Troy had been dead a long time, she hadn't. The man downstairs had triggered a strong physical response she thought she'd never feel again.

Kate sucked in a deep breath and let it out, the tips of her nipples tight little points poking at the sheer fabric of the nightgown. She reached for the hem, telling herself that wearing the gown was asking for trouble.

Her hands stopped before they could lift it over her head. Who was she kidding? The man wasn't interested in her any more than she should be interested in him. He was there as the hired help. Hank had promised protection for her and Lily until they could figure out who was responsible for the break-in in Houston and now at the Flying K Ranch.

As she lay down on the sheets, her thoughts drifted to the man sleeping on the couch downstairs. He'd had a strange look in his eyes when he'd seen Lily. His brows had furrowed into a fierce frown, scary in its intensity. It hadn't looked like an angry frown so much as one of great pain and sorrow. What would cause such a look on a man's face?

She didn't know. In fact, Kate didn't know much of anything about her hired gun. Hell, she didn't know anything about Hank Derringer for that matter. This area was rumored to have a big drug cartel influence. Had she asked for help from one of the local mafia?

Kate lay staring at the ceiling, wondering what she'd done by bringing Lily here. Not that she'd been any safer in Houston. Not after her apartment had been ransacked.

A yawn nearly dislocated her jaw, forcing Kate to give up trying to make sense of all that had happened. Tomorrow she'd ask the questions burning in her mind. Who the hell was Ben Harding and what kind of hired hands did Hank Derringer provide? Even more importantly, did he have any hired hands that were a little older and less attractive?

Kate rolled over and punched her pillow before settling down. Her bruised cheek reminded her of the intruder and her near miss with death. She reached out and looped her arm over her daughter, pulling her close. If anything happened to Lily, she'd never forgive herself.

Tomorrow she'd start her search for answers.

CHAPTER THREE

A KNOCK ON the door brought Ben off the couch and up on his bare feet in seconds. He must have fallen asleep after tossing and turning on the narrow couch. Every noise had kept him awake until way into the wee hours.

The sun shone through the filmy curtains, lighting his path through the boxes and furniture. From what he could see of the front porch, two men stood there in tan uniforms.

The local law enforcement.

As he pulled the door half-open, footsteps sounded on the stairs behind him.

"Who is it?" Kate descended the flight of stairs in a light blue baby-doll nightgown, pulling a robe over her shoulders that only came down to midthigh. Her creamy legs and the glimpse of her breasts through the thin material of the gown had Ben's jeans tightening.

With the door gaping, he had no choice but to open it the rest of the way.

The two men in tan uniforms stared at him, then their eyes drifted to the woman on the stairs behind him.

A flash of anger burned through his bloodstream and Ben moved to block their view as much as he could. "Can I help you?"

The bigger man stepped forward. "I'm Sheriff Fulmer, this is Deputy Schillinger. We're here to see Katherine Langsdon."

Ben's eyes narrowed. "For what reason?"

The sheriff's lips pulled up on one side in a sneer. "Now, I guess that's between me and the lady."

"It's okay, Ben." Kate laid a hand on Ben's arm and stepped up beside him. "I wanted to call on them this morning anyway. We had a break-in last night."

"Sorry to hear that. Can you describe the perp?"

She shook her head. "No, he was wearing all black and a black ski mask."

"Not much I can do to help without a detailed description."

She tipped her head to the side. "Then why did you come out?"

"Ms. Langsdon, as the only living relative of the late Kyle Kendrick, you have been served." The sheriff handed her a thick envelope, his face poker-straight.

"What?" She took the packet, her cheeks blanching, making the bruise stand out even more.

"What's this all about?" Ben slipped an arm around Kate as she opened the envelope, every protective instinct on alert in the face of the sheriff and his deputy.

"Back taxes? The will said nothing about back taxes." She looked up at the sheriff.

"Sorry, Ms. Langsdon, I only deliver the bad news, I don't create it. Your father was the one who didn't pay. Since he left the ranch to you, you're responsible now."

Ben didn't like the sheriff's tone or the way the man hit her with the notice so soon after coming to her father's ranch.

"Twenty-seven thousand?" She snorted softly. "I can't afford twenty-seven *hundred*." Kate stared at the paper in her hands. "That would completely wipe me out and then some."

The sheriff shrugged. "You might consider selling this dump. Pretty young woman like you will find it difficult to manage a place this size all alone."

It was all Ben could do to keep from punching the sheriff for his patronizing words. Ben barely knew Kate, but any woman would resent the sheriff's inference that a woman couldn't run a ranch.

"I'm not alone." Kate clutched the envelope to her chest, her chin rising. "I have Ben." She edged nearer to Ben.

His chest swelled, his arm automatically tightening around her middle, pulling her closer to him.

The sheriff's brows rose. "Hired hands don't always stick around."

"He's not the hired hand. He's…" Kate's hand waved, in search of the right word.

Afraid she'd say he was her bodyguard, Ben finished for her, "I'm her fiancé. We will be working the ranch together."

The sheriff's eyes narrowed. "What did you say your last name was?"

Ben's lips twisted. "I didn't. Now, if you'll excuse us." He moved to shut the door.

The sheriff shoved his foot in the way. "Don't cross me, cowboy."

Ben's brows rose and he stared down at the boot in the doorway. "Did you have more business to discuss?"

The sheriff stared at Ben for a long moment, then replied, "No."

"Then have a nice day." Ben glanced down at the boot and back up at the sheriff. Ben's free hand clenched into a fist, ready to take on the arrogant sheriff if the need arose. He'd seen law enforcement officers who let the power of their position go to their heads. This sheriff appeared to be one of them. He made a mental note to watch the man. He could cause trouble for himself and for Kate.

The sheriff finally moved his foot. "I'll be seeing you around Wild Oak Canyon."

Ben shut the door, muttering, "Not if I can help it."

Kate turned away, her gaze on the legal document the sheriff had given her. "Twenty-seven thousand dollars." She looked up at Ben, her eyes glazed. "That's more than I have in every savings account."

"Surely you have a thirty-day notice on it."

"Thirty days until they seize the property for back taxes owed." She shook her head. "I don't believe this. I should never have come."

"Can't you go back where you came from?" As he made the suggestion, his gut clenched. If Kate left, he wouldn't have to be around her. He could forget the way she made his body hum to life.

Kate shook her head. "No. I quit my job. They've already leased the apartment we lived in. Not that I'd go back. It's no safer in Houston than here."

"What do you mean?"

"I left Houston after my apartment was broken into and ransacked."

"In Houston?"

"Last week. The day after my father's will was read."

Ben didn't like it. Hell, she wasn't any safer in Houston than in Wild Oak Canyon. Ben resigned himself to being her protector until he could convince Hank he had the wrong man for the job. "Was your Houston apartment in a bad neighborhood?"

Kate shook her head. "I hadn't had any problems in the four years I lived there. Whoever did it tore everything apart."

"Any writing on the walls or threats?" Ben asked.

"No. They even ripped the cushions on my sofa. Every drawer was tossed, even the contents of the refrigerator."

"They're looking for something," Ben stated. "The day after your father's reading, you say? Did your father leave you anything besides this ranch?"

Kate's eyes widened. "Yes." Before Ben could question her, she ran up the stairs.

The blood racing through Ben's veins had nothing to do with whatever item she might have received from her father and more to do with the way her bottom swayed side to side and the vision of smooth, creamy skin visible along the curves of her legs. "More clothes. She damn well better wear more clothes," he muttered.

Kate paused at the top of the stairs, glancing down at Ben, her brows dipping. "Did you say something?"

"I'll get my clothes on." He strode back to the couch he'd spent the better part of the night lying awake on, thinking of the sexy legs on a woman he had no business looking at that way.

Hank Derringer was paying him to provide protection from a problem, not to become the problem or one more thing Kate had to be protected from.

He pulled his T-shirt on over his head, calling himself every kind of fool. If he had any cell phone reception at all, he'd be calling Hank and asking for a different assignment. One with a less attractive woman and…no kids.

"Hi."

Speak of the devil.

Ben's head poked through the neck of his T-shirt and he stared down at the pint-size version of Kate. Light reddish-blond curls lay in bright disarray around the child's shoulders.

She held out a brush. "Mommy told me to brush my hair."

Without thinking, Ben took the brush from the girl. He'd brushed Sarah's hair so many times he could have done it with his eyes closed. He knew just how to ease the tangles free without making her cry.

His throat closed as an image of his dark-haired daughter flashed into his memories. God, he missed her.

Lily looked up at him, her green eyes so like her mother's. "Please?" She turned her back to Ben and fluffed her mane of red-gold hair out behind her, waiting expectantly.

Just like Sarah had.

All of the air left Ben's lungs as if he'd been kicked hard in the gut. Yet his hand moved, reaching out to lift a lock of silky red-blond curls. He dropped to his haunches and ran the brush along the strand, picking out the knots with care.

He hadn't felt this emotionally wrung out since Sarah and Julia had died. But the more he brushed Lily's hair, the more his shoulders relaxed and the tightness in his chest loosened.

By the time he finished working the tangles out of the child's hair, he could swallow again. "All done," he said just like he had when he'd brushed Sarah's hair.

"Thank you." Lily turned and hugged him tight, her fresh, baby-shampoo scent filling Ben's senses.

Over the top of Lily's head he spied Kate standing on the bottom step, her eyes round. Was that a tear trickling down her cheek?

Kate ducked her head, a hand swiping at the moisture. Seeing Ben brushing Lily's hair had hit her like a Mack truck. Lily's father had died before she was born. Kate had been a single parent from day one. Seeing someone else, especially a man, brushing her daughter's hair sent a flood of longing through her, for Lily and herself.

Lily didn't know what it was to have a daddy. Just like Kate. Kate swallowed hard on the lump forming in her throat. "Lily, sweetie, go get dressed."

Her daughter's face lit. "Are we going outside to play?"

Kate smiled and patted her daughter's head. "You can play, but I have work to do outside."

"Yay!" Lily darted up the stairs, her bright curls bouncing as she went.

Kate descended from the last step and held out her hand. "My father left this key for me and a video disk."

She dropped the key and the disk into Ben's hand.

"What does the key go to?" Ben turned it over in his fingers.

"I don't know. I've tried to watch the disk, but I couldn't get it to work. The letter from the attorney had a note from my father to contact Hank Derringer for help."

"Maybe Hank can get someone to look at the disk and see if they can pull the information off."

Lily was down the stairs again, wearing shorts, cowboy boots and pulling a shirt over her head.

"Stop, young lady," Kate ordered, afraid her daughter would miss a step and tumble the rest of the way down the stairs. "You can't go out without me, and I'm not dressed."

"Please, Mommy." Lily looked up at Kate with a slight pout on her pretty pink lips.

"I'll take her," Ben offered. "We can discuss the key later." He handed it back to her, setting the disk on an end table.

Kate curled her fingers around the key. "I'll be ready in a minute. I need to finish unloading the rental van and get it back to town."

Ben smiled and raised his hands palms upward. "I'm here to help."

Kate's heart skipped several beats as the man's smile transformed his face from frowning, brooding darkness to sunshine. "You should smile more often," she said without thinking.

Immediately, his face changed back into the brooding cowboy, his forehead creasing. "I find little to smile about these days."

Kate wondered what made him so sullen and sad but didn't want to push the issue, not when he'd thrown up a no-trespassing sign in the way his body stiffened and he turned away. He took Lily's hand in his. "Ready?"

The two left through the front door.

Yes, sir, the cowboy had issues. Hell, didn't everyone?

Kate climbed the stairs, her footsteps slow at first and speeding up as she neared the top. For the first time in months, she wanted to get outside and enjoy the sunshine and fresh air. She refused to believe the hired hand had anything to do with her sudden surge of energy.

A pair of jeans, a snug-fitting ribbed T-shirt and

tennis shoes completed her outfit. After she pulled her hair up into a ponytail and settled a baseball cap over her head, she hurried out to join Lily and Ben, her steps light, eager to finish unloading and settle into her new life.

Ben and Lily squatted beside the moving van, pointing at something on the ground.

"That's a scorpion, Lily," Ben was explaining. "Don't try to touch or pick one up, they have a really bad sting."

Lily hunched over, staring at the insect crawling across the ground. She looked up and spied Kate. "Mommy, come see the scorpion."

Kate smiled and squatted beside her. With the three of them all gathered in a circle so close, her stomach knotted. This must be what it would feel like to be a family unit. Mommy, daughter and…daddy. Troy would have been a good father to Lily. He'd been so excited about the arrival of his firstborn, only to be robbed of ever seeing her.

Lily was a beautiful baby and an even prettier little girl with a grown-up sense of responsibility and a child's joy of exploring.

"The day's not getting any longer. I guess we better get this van unloaded so that I can return it to the rental center in town." Kate stood, pulled the padlock key from her pocket and unlocked the back of the van.

For the next twenty minutes, Kate and Ben worked in silence, carrying boxes and furniture into the house. Lily helped a little, then lost interest and wandered around the yard, picking flowers and investigating her new home.

Kate kept a close eye on her. After last night's break-in, she wasn't feeling exactly trusting of her new environment.

Lily had strayed to the corner of the house when Kate and Ben hauled out the sofa with the repaired cushions she'd brought with her from her apartment.

Getting the sofa through the door took them several tries, tipping it in multiple directions, before they finally shoved the item through. When the sofa cleared the door frame, Kate tripped over a throw rug and landed on her bottom, the edge of the sofa coming down hard on her ankle. "Ouch!"

"Are you all right in there?" Ben called out over the top of the sofa.

"Yes, just not very graceful." Kate stood and put pressure on her ankle and felt pain shooting up her leg. She swallowed a yelp and lifted her end again. There was no time for injuries. The van needed to be back before three o'clock or she'd have to pay for another day's rental.

Once they got the sofa settled into the living room, Kate headed toward the door, trying to hide her limp.

Ben shook his head and pointed to the sofa they'd just placed. "Sit."

"I'm fine, just a little sore. It'll work itself out." When she tried to walk past him, he grabbed her arms and made her stop.

"Let me see." His grip was firm but gentle and his tone the same.

The warmth of his hands on her arms sent shivers of awareness throughout her body. "Really, it's fine," she said, even as she let him maneuver her to sit on the arm of the couch.

Ben squatted, pulled the tennis shoe off her foot and

removed her sock. "I had training as a first responder on the Austin police force. Let me be the judge."

Kate held her breath as he lifted her foot and turned it to inspect the ankle, his fingers slipping over her skin.

"See? Just bumped it. It'll be fine in a minute." She cursed inwardly at her breathlessness. A man's hands on her ankle shouldn't send her into a tailspin.

Ben Harding was a trained professional. Touching a woman's ankle meant nothing other than a concern for health and safety. Nothing more.

Then why was she having a hard time breathing, like a teenager on her first date? Kate bent to slip her foot back into her shoe, biting hard on her lip to keep from crying out at the pain. Her head came very close to Ben's. When she turned toward him she could feel the warmth of his breath fan across her cheek.

"You should put a little ice on that," he said, his tone as smooth as warm syrup sliding over her.

Ice was exactly what she needed. To chill her natural reaction to a handsome man paid to help and protect her, not touch, hold or kiss her.

Whoa, there, girl. Kate jumped up and moved away from Ben and his gentle fingers, warm breath and shoulders so broad they could turn a girl's head. "I should get back outside. No telling what Lily is up to."

Ben caught her arm as she passed him. "You felt it, too, didn't you?"

Kate fought the urge to lean into him and sniff the musky scent of male. Four years was a long time to go without a man. "I don't know what you're talking about."

Ben held her arm a moment longer, then let go. "You're right. We should check on Lily."

Kate hurried, no, ran for the open door, her heart racing, her breathing ragged. Just as she crossed the threshold into the open breezy, South Texas sunshine, a frightened scream made her racing heart stop.

"Lily!" Kate burst out onto the porch.

The sound of engines racing up the gravel driveway greeted her. A man wearing a do-rag over his head with a bandanna pulled up over his mouth and nose straddled a huge motorcycle in the middle of the yard, holding a doll by its hair. He laughed, the sound so evil it made Kate's skin crawl.

"That's Lily's doll." Kate flew off the porch and would have scratched the man's eyes out if an arm hadn't circled her waist and yanked her back.

"Go back to the house. Now," Ben said into her ear, his voice tight around the command.

"But Lily—"

"Go." He shoved her back behind him.

Kate hesitated.

The roar of engines rose to a crescendo. An army of bikes swarmed into the yard, stirring up dust where the grass had long since died.

Kate ran for the house. Before she could reach the porch, a motorcycle cut her off. There must have been twenty bikes racing around the yard in a tight circle, trapping Ben and Kate in the center. The dust rose in a cloud, choking visibility to everything beyond.

Beyond panic, long past frightened, Kate screamed into the smoke screen, "Where's my child?"

CHAPTER FOUR

BEN HAD LEFT his Glock on top of the refrigerator inside the house while they'd been working to unload the trailer. Now he wished he had it. Two unarmed people against a biker gang weren't good odds in anyone's experience.

A rider broke the ring, circled the pair and then swerved toward Kate.

Fear for her spiked his adrenaline and he lunged toward the motorcyclist. Grabbing the closest handlebar, Ben twisted it hard toward the man astride. The sharp turn on the forward-moving bike caused the bike to flip over, rider and all.

Ben snagged Kate's hand and pulled her closer to him into the center of the circle.

The man he'd toppled pulled himself out of the dirt, his face bleeding from where he'd crashed into the gravel drive. He glared at Ben and Kate and roared, veins popping out on his forehead.

Kate shrank against Ben. "Oh, God."

They had nowhere to go; the ring of motorcycles tightened. The man with the doll eased toward them, dark eyes glaring through the slit between his do-rag and bandanna. "You need to leave, lady, before it's too late." He ripped the head off the doll and flung it at Kate's feet.

Kate reached for the doll, but Ben held her back. "When I make my move…run toward the house," he said into her ear. Anger surged and Ben threw himself at the lead man, knocking him out of his seat.

Kate ran.

Ben got one good, hard punch at the man's face before two goons ditched their rides and jerked him off their leader. Caught between two beefy Hispanic men, Ben struggled, twisting and kicking, determined to keep their attention long enough for Kate to escape.

Ben jabbed an elbow into the gut of the guy on his right.

The man loosened his hold.

Ben ducked beneath his arm. No sooner had he shaken free from his captors' hold than he was slammed to the ground from behind, a bull of a man hitting him low and hard.

The wind knocked from his lungs, Ben lay facedown in the dirt, willing his body to move. A foot in the middle of his back kept him from doing anything, especially refilling his starving lungs.

Kate screamed.

A shot of determination rocketed through Ben. He rolled onto his back; at the same time he grabbed the man's leg who'd planted his heavy boot into his back. With a hard twist, he sent the thug flying backward, landing hard on his butt.

Two more men grabbed him, hauled him up and yanked his arms behind him, hard enough that spasms of pain ripped through his shoulders.

The leader lumbered to his feet and stalked toward Ben. He hit him with a hard-knuckled fist, square in the jaw. Ben's head jerked back, hazy gray fog encroaching on his vision. Another punch to his gut would have had him doubling over, if he didn't have two big guys holding him up.

Through the torture, his gaze panned the yard, searching for Kate and Lily.

The bikers had broken the circle and raced around the yard, running over bushes, ramming into a rose trellis. One drove up onto the porch and ripped the porch swing from its hooks.

Another cut off Kate's attempt to get to the house.

Kate shot a glance over her shoulder and dodged to the left.

The biker sped past her and spun to renew his attack.

Ben planted his feet in the dirt and struggled, twisting and turning in an attempt to go to Kate's rescue, his mind conjuring his wife's last minutes on the earth, fighting to protect their daughter.

Then, he hadn't been there to help Julia. His job now was to protect Kate. If only he'd been more vigilant and not lulled into believing danger wouldn't strike during the daylight hours.

Hell, the fight wasn't over.

The gang leader swung again.

Ben jerked to the side hard enough that the guy on his left tripped. The leader's blow hit his own man in the cheekbone. The man yelled and grabbed his face with both hands, letting go of Ben.

Using the weight of the other man's body, Ben rolled into him and sent him flying over his shoulder.

Kate ran toward the road.

The biker who'd missed her straightened his bike and hit the gas. The back tire spun, then gripped the ground and shot forward.

Ben came at him sideways, plowing into the biker.

The bike and rider rolled over to the side, the rider moving sluggishly in the dirt.

One down, nineteen to go.

Kate ran on, but another bike raced after her.

Ben wouldn't catch up before the biker reached her.

A loud air horn broke through the roar of racing motorcycle engines, followed by a cloud of dust storming toward them on the gravel drive leading to the highway. Another air horn burst and a truck swerved around Kate, aiming straight for the biker in pursuit of the fleeing woman.

A shotgun's nose poked out of the passenger window and blasted a hole in the ground in front of the bike tire. As a result, the biker spun so fast, the back wheel whirled all the way around and out from under the rider.

The gang members Ben had thrown off caught up to him and knocked him to the ground. He came up spitting dirt and ready to tear into them. He swung again and again, pummeling one man in the face. When that one went down, he kicked out and sent the other sprawling on his backside.

Another shot rang out, peppering bird shot at the gang members.

One man yelped and sent his bike skittering out of the shooter's range.

The leader of the gang yelled something and circled his hand in the air, then pointed to the road.

All of the bikers revved their engines and rode out, leaving a lung-choking cloud in their wake.

Their leader left the yard, shouting, *"Dejar o te vas a morir!"*

As the dust cleared, the driver and passenger of the truck dropped to the ground.

Ben laughed, the effort making his split lip and sore rib cage hurt. He leaned against the gnarled trunk of a live oak tree, his knuckles bleeding and every muscle in his body screaming.

The driver was an older Hispanic man with a decided limp. The passenger, the one holding the shotgun, was a woman who could only be described as grandmotherly. Thank the Lord for help in all shapes and sizes.

Ben's next thought went to Kate and Lily.

Kate rounded the back of the pickup and ran back into the yard, tears making muddy tracks down her cheeks. "Lily!" she cried out.

A whimper sounded from the tree branches over Ben's head.

Hidden between the leaves was a little girl with a curly halo of hair, clutching a ball of fur to her chest, tears slipping down her cheeks. "Mommy?"

"Lily?" Kate skidded to a halt beneath the tree. "Oh, baby. I'm so glad you're okay." Kate grabbed a branch and started up the tree.

Ben snagged her arm. "Let me."

"I can do this."

"It would be better if I could hand her down to someone she knows."

Kate backed away and let Ben take the lead.

He ducked beneath the low-hanging branches and climbed upward. "Hey, Lily. How'd you get all the way up here?"

She hiccuped, her bottom lip trembling as she clutched the fuzz ball to the curve of her neck. "I followed Jazzy."

"Is Jazzy one of your toys?" He spoke in calm, soothing tones, careful not to grimace when a shard of pain rippled across his hands or ribs.

Lily shook her head. "No, Jazzy's not a toy."

A soft mewling erupted from the fur ball and little paws reached out to latch onto Lily's shirt.

"Jazzy's a kitten." Lily's eyes rounded as she stared down into Ben's eyes. "Can I keep her?"

Ben chuckled, his body hurting with every breath. He wanted to crush the little girl and the kitten to his chest and hold them there for as long as he could. He couldn't tell if the pain he was feeling stemmed from sore ribs, bruises or heartbreak. "You'll have to ask your mommy."

"Will you ask her for me?"

"You bet." Ben settled on a thick branch and wrapped his legs around it before he reached out. "Come on. I think your mother wants to fix you lunch or something."

"I'm scared." She glanced around at the ground below her. "Are the bad men gone?"

Rage burned in Ben's throat as hot as acid but he fought to keep it from his face and voice. "Yes, baby. They're gone." This child should not have been exposed to the violence of those men.

She leaned toward him and stopped, her arm around the kitten that clung to her, its blue eyes as big around as Lily's. "You're bleeding."

"It's okay. It doesn't hurt, just a little cut."

"I want my mommy," Lily whimpered.

"I'm going to hand you down to her. Come on. You're so brave to save that kitten. Now let me be brave and save you from falling out of the tree."

Lily smiled. "Silly, I'm not falling out of the tree."

"Your mother thinks you will." He winked. "But I know better. You're good at climbing trees, aren't you?"

She nodded, then let him grab her around the waist and lift her onto the branch he sat on. He hugged her to him, relief washing over him in such a rush that his eyes glazed over and he couldn't see.

"Give her to me, please," Kate cried.

Ben blinked several times before he loosened his hold on the little girl and handed her down into Kate's outstretched arms.

Kate gathered Lily into a hug so tight, Lily grunted. She sat on the ground in the dirt and hugged her some more, tears trickling from the corners of her eyes.

"I'm okay, Mommy." Lily patted Kate's face. "See?" Her empty hand pressed against Kate's face, urging her to look into her eyes. "I saved the kitten." Her smile broadened. "Can I keep her? Her name is Jazzy."

"Sure, honey. You can keep her." Kate dashed the tears from her cheeks and hugged Lily again. Then she climbed to her feet, lifting Lily to perch on her hip. "Come on, let's clean up."

Ben slid out of the tree and dropped to the ground beside the two, his hand going around Kate's waist. "You two going to be all right?"

"I hope so." Kate's eyes widened. "You're bleeding."

Lily grinned at Ben. "Told you."

Kate cupped Ben's cheek. "Come in the house and let me take care of your cuts before they get infected."

The light touch sent fire through his veins. Ben pushed her hand aside. "I'm fine. I'll just stay out here and see what I can do to clean up the mess they made." Anything rather than being close to Kate. She brought out too many feelings in him, feelings he'd thought long dead, emotions that made a man vulnerable.

The woman holding the shotgun waved her hands at them. "You three go get cleaned up and let us take care of the mess. Eddy and I can set things to rights in no time. Can't we, Eddy?"

The short Hispanic man had wandered off, picking up broken bush branches. *"Sí, señora."*

Ben stepped between the woman and Kate. "Could we at least know the names of our rescuers?" He tried to smile, his lip hurting with the effort. "I'm Ben Harding, Kate's my…fiancée."

"Oh, goodness, yes." The woman shifted the shotgun into her other hand and gripped Ben's hand in a firm, capable grasp. "Margaret Henderson. But most folks 'round here call me Ma or Marge. This here's Eddy."

"Mrs. Henderson, Eddy, glad to meet you." Ben nodded at the gun. "Good shootin'."

"No boys in my family, so my daddy taught all his girls to squirrel hunt." She grinned. "And I make a mean squirrel soup."

"I'll bet you do." Ben let go of her hand. "Thank you for showing up when you did. I think they were about to get the best of us."

"I don't know. You were holdin' yer own pretty well."

Ben didn't want to argue with the woman. He'd gotten his butt whipped and Kate would be in a world of hurt had Margaret and Eddy not come along when they did. Guilt with a hint of heartrending regret tugged at his empty belly. What made Hank think a washed-up cop was the right man for this job? It had taken an old woman with a shotgun to chase off the latest threat. Some bodyguard he'd turned out to be.

Margaret smacked Ben on the back. "Twenty-to-one odds needs a little more encouragement than bare fists. Don't let it get ya down. Question is why they were here in the first place."

Eddy stuck a long blade of grass between his lips and rocked back on his heels. "Their leader shouted *'Dejar o te vas a morir'* as he left." The man had a decided Mexican accent.

Kate shook her head. "I don't know Spanish. What does it mean?"

Eddy's gaze captured Kate's, his lips tightening for a moment before he spoke. "Leave or you will die."

KATE'S HEART SANK into her belly. Holy smokes, what the hell had she done to the bikers to warrant a death threat?

"Well, now, isn't that a nice way to welcome the new neighbors." Marge turned to face Kate, the stiff, tough persona fading with the softening of her eyes. "You must be Kate."

Kate held on to Lily, refusing to let her child out of her sight for even a moment. Her legs still shook and she couldn't keep her hand from trembling when she held it out to Margaret. "Should I know you?"

"Kate Kendrick—" the woman folded Kate's hand in both of hers "—you're the spittin' image of your father."

Kate shook her head. "I go by Kate Langsdon." She gripped the woman's hand with her free one. "Did you know my… Kyle Kendrick?" She still couldn't manage to refer to him as her father. Throughout her life, her mother had told her that her father had died in a car wreck. Growing up without a father hadn't given her any practice saying the word. And for the past four years, Lily had been without a father of her own.

"Know him? I worked for him until the day he was m—" The older woman's eyes widened and she clapped a hand over her mouth. "Sorry." Her glance moved to Lily, and her hand fell to her side. "I worked for Mr. Kendrick until he passed. He was a good man."

Kate bit her lip, wanting to refute Mrs. Henderson's statement. What man would willingly walk away from his daughter and never have contact with her? In Kate's mind, that didn't make a good man.

"Thank you for coming to our rescue." Kate smiled and turned to Ben. "Now, let's get you inside and doctored up."

The kitten Lily had been holding mewed.

An answering meow came from beneath the porch and a brightly colored calico cat stepped out of the shadows.

The kitten clawed at Lily.

"Ouch." Lily held the kitten away from her shirt.

Kate pointed to the cat. "That must be the kitten's mother."

Lily hugged the fur ball to her, her brows pulling together in a mutinous frown. "Jazzy is *my* kitty."

"Honey, you have to let her go to her mama."

"But I want a kitten."

"Jazzy will be your kitten, but you'll have to let her be with her mama until she gets bigger."

"I want her to come in the house and sleep in my bed."

"When she doesn't need her mother anymore. You can come and play with her outside until then."

The kitten dug her claws into Lily, scrambling to get to her mother.

"See, she misses her mother." Kate leaned Lily away

from her. "How would you feel if someone wouldn't let you come to your mother?"

Lily stared at the kitten and the calico mother cat, meowing over and over. "I'd feel sad."

"And the kitten is sad because you won't let her go to her mother."

Lily wiggled in Kate's arms, so she set her daughter on the ground.

Plucking the kitten's claws from her shirt, Lily settled the animal on the ground.

As soon as she was loose, the kitten ran for her mother, curling in and around the cat's long, sleek legs.

"See how happy Jazzy is?" Kate knelt beside her daughter.

"Can I play with her after lunch?"

"You sure can." If the bikers weren't back or an intruder wasn't rummaging through the only home they had to go to. Kate's chest tightened. "We'll bring food out for Jazzy and her mother."

Lily slipped her hand into Ben's and one into her mother's. "I'm hungry. Can we eat now?"

Kate almost laughed at how quickly Lily forgot the bad men on motorcycles, all her concentration on eating and getting back outside to play with her kitten. How simple to be a child and forget about all the horrible things adults could do to each other.

Ben glanced over the top of Lily's head. "She'll be all right."

The biker's warning echoed in Kate's mind. "I hope so."

CHAPTER FIVE

Kate led the way into the ranch house. As soon as she passed through the door, Lily shook her hand free and ran to the bathroom. Kate and Ben followed, filling the tiny room.

Lily stood on a small plastic step, just the right height to boost her little body up to the sink. She pumped liquid soap onto her hands and turned on the faucet, splashing water over her arms and shirt. "Do kittens like milk?"

"I suppose they do," Kate replied, her voice soft, reassuring and less shaky than it had been in the yard after being terrorized by the biker gang.

Ben's gut clenched. He should have been ready—he could have handled the situation better. He reached out and grabbed her hand. "I'm sorry."

Kate's brows wrinkled. "For what?"

"Letting it go that far."

She dragged her hand out of his, closed the toilet lid and pointed at it. "Sit."

Obediently, he did, amazed at the strength in her tone.

While washing her hands, she chewed on her lip, tears welling in her eyes. She dashed them away, apparently not wanting him to see them. Tough tone and tears didn't add up. Ben's chest squeezed. This woman had been scared out of her mind, but she refused to show it.

Lily climbed into Ben's lap. "You have a boo-boo on your mouth." She poked a finger at the drying blood.

The child felt right, her legs dangling over his knee, her feet swinging in and out. As quickly as she'd come, Lily slid off his lap and left the bathroom.

"Stay in the house, Lily," Kate called out.

"I will. I'm going to my room to play with my dolls."

The sound of footsteps on the stairs echoed through the old house.

Kate snatched a clean hand towel from the shelf over Ben's head, leaning so close, the scent of herbal shampoo wafted over him.

Her breasts brushed against his shoulder and he gasped.

Kate jerked back, towel clutched in her fingers. "Did I hurt you?"

"No," he said through clenched teeth. The pain she'd caused had nothing to do with flesh wounds. She'd stirred his heart to life and that was more painful than a broken bone or knife stabbing. He'd thought his heart was firmly locked away after the deaths of his wife and daughter.

Now he sat at the tender mercy of a woman and her daughter, reminding him with every move, every touch and soft word of all he'd lost.

She dampened the towel in the water and touched the cloth to the corner of his lip, dabbing gently to remove the dried blood.

"Lily's a great kid," he said.

"I know." Kate's gaze focused on his wounds, one hand steadying herself on his shoulder. Warmth filtered through his chambray shirt to his skin. Ben's jeans tightened and his pulse quickened.

"Some bodyguard I am," he said.

When he glanced into her eyes, he caught her staring down at him.

"You were outnumbered. You couldn't fight them all."

"I should have had my gun on me at all times," he countered.

"And they might have used it on you or Lily."

"Or you."

"I'll make an ice pack for that jaw. Any other injuries?"

The longer she stood there close enough to touch, the harder it was not to reach out. "No." He shook his head and stood, wincing, his hand automatically rising to press against his ribs.

Kate's brow furrowed. "Liar. Let me see." She pushed his T-shirt up, tucking it beneath his arms.

A bruise the size of a grapefruit was making its dark purple appearance against his skin and everything beneath the mark ached.

"Damn, Ben, you could have a broken rib." She dipped the towel beneath the faucet again, wrung it out and pressed it to his side, her fingers sliding over the bruise. "Does that hurt?"

Ben grasped her fingers and held them away from his skin. "Yes," he lied. Her touch wasn't what hurt, it was the effect she was having on him. If he didn't get away soon, he'd be hard-pressed to walk away without kissing her.

"Let me take you to the clinic in town. They must have an X-ray machine." She tugged her hand free and pressed the cool towel to his side, all her focus on his injury.

Past his level of endurance, Ben tipped her chin up. "I don't need a doctor. I'm not going anywhere."

When her green-eyed gaze met his, he realized his mistake. Her lips parted, and what she might have said next faded away on a sigh.

Ben bent and brushed his lips across hers. He'd only wanted a taste. But like water to a desert flower, the more he tasted the more he wanted.

His fingers curled around the back of her neck, tugging at her hair, tipping her head back, giving him more access to her lips, her throat and the pulse beating wildly at the base. She leaned into him. Her fingers pressed against his chest, the tips curling into his skin, not enough to hurt, but enough to ignite a flame he'd thought long burned out.

As fire spread through his veins, his arms tightened around her, his lips going from soft and gentle to crushingly hard, desperate to wipe out the stab of guilt that ravaged him from head to toe.

"I'm sorry, Julia," he said against her lips. "I'm so sorry."

The woman in his arms stiffened, her mouth moving away from his, her hands pressing against his skin.

"Let go of me," she said, her voice ragged, her tone strained.

Ben backed up, his hands dropping to his sides. "I'm sorry. That shouldn't have happened."

"Damn right, it shouldn't have." Kate's hand shook as she swiped the back of her hand over her bruised lips. "I don't know who Julia is, but I'm not her." She turned to walk out of the bathroom.

Ben caught her hand. "You're right. I had no business kissing you." Not when he still had feelings for his dead wife. Feelings that amplified his guilt for having kissed this stranger. "It won't happen again."

Without facing him, she jerked her hand free. "I don't think this arrangement will work after all."

"I understand. I'll talk with Hank about a replacement this afternoon."

"Please." Her shoulders rose and fell as if she sighed deeply, then she left the room.

Ben's fists balled. He wanted to hit something, but his knuckles were already like raw meat. He wasn't sure he could handle any more pain, both physical and emotional.

Too much about Kate and Lily reminded him of Julia and Sarah. The sooner he left the Flying K Ranch the better off they both would be.

Images of the intruder on the first night and the terror of the motorcycle gang nagged his conscience. Would Kate's next hired gun take better care of her? Would he try to kiss her and forget why he'd come?

KATE RAN UP the stairs and peeked in at Lily. Her daughter sat at her little table with her miniature tea set laid out. A teddy bear and two dolls occupied the other seats.

Satisfied Lily was okay, Kate slipped past and into her own room, closing the door behind her. She leaned against the panel and pressed her fingers to her burning cheeks.

He'd kissed her. Her bodyguard had kissed her.

What had her running scared was that she'd liked it. So much so that she'd kissed him back, practically crawling up his body to get closer.

She covered her softly swollen lips and moaned.

It had been four years since she'd known the touch of another man's kiss, the feel of big, strong hands on her skin.

Her body burned with a need she thought had been buried with her husband. Kate squeezed her eyes shut and tried to picture Troy's face, a sob rising up her throat when the only face she envisioned was Ben's.

Kate opened her eyes, her gaze darting around the bedroom to the framed photograph of her and Troy on their last vacation together. They'd gone to the coast, playing in the sun and sand as if there'd be no tomorrow. Tomorrows for Troy had ended with an improvised explosive device that detonated beside his convoy. He'd been killed instantly. One week before he was due to come home. One month before his daughter's birth. Two days before their third anniversary.

Troy smiled back at her from the photograph, his light gray eyes and sandy-blond hair so different from the dark hair and stormy-blue eyes of the man downstairs.

Kate hugged the frame to her breast, again trying to recall Troy smiling down at her as he'd kissed her goodbye. Even holding Troy's photo, Kate couldn't see him. Her mind fixated on the dark-haired, brooding man who'd come to help her keep Lily safe in their new home.

Kate set the photo on her nightstand and hurried into the bathroom. She didn't have time to worry about why her memories of Troy were fading. She had a daughter to take care of, one who needed her to make lunch.

She stared into the mirror and almost cried of fright.

Her face was smudged with dirt, her eyes red-rimmed and puffy from tears of joy at finding Lily safe in a tree.

Kate scrubbed her face with cool water, brushed her hair and secured it in a ponytail at her nape. Clean-faced and refreshed, she took a deep breath and re-solved to act as if nothing had happened. No more kisses would be exchanged and life would go on as usual.

When she passed Lily's room, her daughter no lon-ger sat at her table, the tea set abandoned.

Her heartbeat quickening, Kate hurried down the stairs.

A quick perusal of the living room found it empty. Only Mrs. Henderson in the kitchen.

Fear pushed Kate out the front door.

Ben was hanging the porch swing that had been knocked down by the gang.

As soon as he settled the chain on the hooks, Lily climbed up on the swing and patted the seat beside her. "Will you swing with me?"

"I don't know." Ben glanced out at the dry Texas landscape, only his profile visible from where Kate stood. The dark circles beneath his eyes and sad, far-away look tugged at Kate's heartstrings.

"Please?" Lily batted her eyes like a pro.

Ben chuckled and smiled. "When you put it like that…sure." He settled on the swing beside Lily and looped his arm over the child's shoulder, pulling her close.

A lump the size of a grapefruit lodged in Kate's throat and she backed away, racing for the kitchen and a hand towel to dry quickly forming tears.

Marge stood at the kitchen counter, adding lettuce

and tomatoes to thick slices of bread layered with lunch meat. "Ah, there you are. I hope you didn't mind me barging in and jumping right in. I worked here so many years, it feels more like home to me than my own house. I've missed coming out."

Kate's mouth watered. "Where did you get all that food?"

"I was the cook and I handled the grocery shopping for Mr. Kendrick. I figured with you just having moved in, you probably hadn't had time to visit the store to stock up. Eddy's a ranch hand. He wanted to check on the horses and cattle, so I asked him to bring me out after stopping for a few things at the market."

"A few?" Kate opened the pantry doors and checked in the refrigerator and gasped. "This isn't a few."

Mrs. Henderson blushed. "I'm sorry. It's kind of pushy of me, but I've been beside myself staying at home since Mr. K. passed. My husband retired last year and we just bump into each other too much. I *need* to work outside the home."

"I'm not sure I can pay you, and I don't expect you to work for free."

"Now, don't you worry none. Consider this a welcome home gift. And once Eddy gets the cattle rounded up and the fences mended, he'll give you a better idea of what this place can do to support you and your little one."

Tears filled Kate's eyes. "Why?"

"Like I said, Mr. Kendrick was a good man. Many times he'd spot me my mortgage payment when my man was out of work." The older woman sliced a sandwich in two and laid it on a freshly cleaned plate. "Now, you just sit right down there and have yourself a bite.

You could stand to gain a pound or two." Marge patted her rounded figure. "Not that you want to put on as many as I have." She laughed and moved around the kitchen like one very familiar with its contents.

Ben entered, carrying Lily on his arm. "Someone is hungry. I wonder who it is."

Lily's hand shot up. "Me!"

He swung her up in the air and caught her.

Kate's heart warmed at her daughter's giggles. Oh, to be young enough to forget so easily. Today could have turned out very badly. Any one of them could have been hurt or killed. Thank God Lily had been climbing a tree, although Kate wasn't all that comfortable with a four-year-old climbing unattended. What if she'd fallen?

If the impact on the ground hadn't hurt her, the biker gang could have.

Ben set Lily on her feet and laid a hand on Kate's shoulder. "She's all right. I won't let anything bad happen to her."

"I know that." Kate's gaze followed Lily around the kitchen, but her mind was on the hand warming her shoulder. "I was just thinking that I should be mad at Lily for climbing a tree, but I can't find it in my heart to be. If she hadn't…" Kate glanced up into Ben's eyes.

A muscle in the side of his jaw twitched. "We'll have to do a better job of keeping an eye on her. She's a very active little girl. Aren't you, darlin'."

Marge trimmed the crust off a sandwich and cut it in triangles, then set it on a plate in front of Lily. "Eat up, half-pint."

"You'll spoil her," Kate protested.

"It's my biggest fault." Marge smoothed Lily's hair

back from her forehead. "Never had any of my own. Guess I do go a bit overboard."

"It's hard not to, even when they're yours." Kate smiled at Lily. "She's all I've got."

Marge smiled. "You have Ben, too. When are the two of you lovebirds gonna tie the knot?"

Kate's face burned. She hated lying, but if it helped keep the rest of the town off her back, she'd do it, and she didn't know Marge well enough yet to set her straight on the fake engagement. "We haven't set a date."

"No hurry, huh? Too many young couples meet each other one day, marry the next and file for a divorce within a year." Marge crossed her arms. "You're smart to wait. Seems Mr. Kendrick and your mama were in that category. Young and crazy stupid in love. Mr. Kendrick never considered whether his new bride would be happy out in the middle of nowhere Texas. She wasn't suited for the rugged life of a ranch owner. Too bad she didn't stay around long enough to find out."

"My mother never talked about my father. She told me he'd died in an automobile accident."

Marge shook her head. "Nearly broke Mr. K.'s heart when your mama left him. He didn't even know you existed until after your mother died and her lawyer notified him, or I'm sure he'd have done more to get to know you sooner."

"My mother's been dead for nearly five years. Why didn't he come find me then?"

Marge shrugged. "I asked him again and again. He just said the timing wasn't right. Might have been because he'd been doing a lot of traveling." The house-keeper leaned close. "He never said, but I think he

worked for the government, secret service or something. He'd pack and leave a note that he'd be gone
awhile. Never said how long, when he'd be back or
where he was going."

"Any idea where he went?" Ben asked.

"I think he had business in Mexico. The man spoke
Spanish like a native."

Kate frowned. How sad to learn about her estranged
father from a stranger. Especially when he'd lived in
Texas all her life and hadn't bothered to get to know
his daughter even after he'd learned of her existence.

"Mrs. Henderson?" Ben began.

"Call me Marge. Please."

"Marge." Ben smiled. "What exactly happened to
Mr. Kendrick?"

"Now, that's a very good question. You'll get a different answer depending on who you ask."

"What do you mean? Didn't a coroner determine
cause of death?"

"The county coroner is a good friend of the sheriff.
He'd put whatever the sheriff wanted him to put on the
death certificate."

Kate's eyes widened. "I was under the impression
Kyle Kendrick died of natural causes."

"The coroner stated he'd died of heart failure."

"And you don't believe him?"

"Oh, I'm sure Mr. Kendrick died of heart failure,
but the cause of the heart failure, in my opinion, had
nothing natural about it."

Ben pulled up a chair at the table and sat beside
Kate. "Why do you say that?"

"The man had bruising around his throat. I'm sure
his heart failed when his lungs could no longer get air."

Kate gasped, setting her sandwich on the plate, all hunger forgotten. "Someone choked him?"

"I watch enough crime scene investigation shows to know a man with bruises around his throat didn't run into a door."

"Did you say anything to the sheriff?"

Marge shook her head. "If they couldn't see what was in front of them, either they're just plain stupid or were in on the killin'. Sayin' somethin' to them wouldn't bring back Mr. K., and it might have bought me the same demise."

A chill slithered across Kate's skin. "Who would want to kill him?"

"I can't even imagine." Marge tidied the counter, talking as she went. "Mr. K. was quiet, but well-liked in the community by the few who got to know him. He never had a bad word to say about anybody. He was kinda reclusive, but that could be expected of a confirmed bachelor like himself." She paused and stared out the window. "Could be someone involved in the troubles around here."

Kate frowned. "Troubles?"

"The Flying K is smack-dab in the middle of an area known for drug trafficking from across the border." Mrs. Henderson glanced at Lily. "Maybe Mr. K. got crossways with one of them. They found him here in this house. No sign of forced entry, but the place was a shambles. It was like someone he knew killed him, then ransacked the house. As far as I could tell, the only thing missin' was the computer out of Mr. K.'s office. Eddy thinks it was Larry Sites, though why Larry would take the computer…" Mrs. H. shrugged.

"The man could barely read, much less find his way around a keyboard."

"Larry Sites?" Kate shook her head, trying to take it all in.

"Larry was a ranch hand here at the Flying K. Worked with Eddy. But no one's seen him since the day we found Mr. K." Marge clucked her tongue. "Poor Mr. K."

A lead weight settled in Kate's belly. "The more I hear the more I'm beginning to think Lily and I need to move back to Houston."

"Oh, honey," Marge said as she laid a hand on Kate's shoulder. "I'd hate to see you go when you just got here."

"Mommy, can I go out now?" Lily asked, her hands and face covered in peanut butter and jelly.

"Sweetie, it'll have to be later. After you wash your hands and face, we're going to town. I have some business to do there."

Mrs. Henderson was there with a clean, wet washcloth before Lily could move a muscle, scrubbing the sticky jelly from her face and hands.

"What do you say to Mrs. Henderson?" Kate prompted.

"You missed a spot." Lily's tongue slid along her lips and she smacked them loudly.

Marge laughed and dabbed at the stickiness.

Lily jumped down from her chair and skipped toward the hallway. "Thank you for making lunch, Mrs. Henderson. It was delicious."

Kate pushed her plate away and stood. "Thank you for the sandwiches, Marge." She rummaged through drawers to find something to wrap hers in.

"Don't you worry about that. I'll put it away for

later. You go on. The town rolls up its sidewalks at five o'clock. If you have business there, you need to skedaddle."

"We'll find dinner in town. No need to cook anything here."

"Will do, Kate." Marge gave her a hug. "I'm glad you're here. I've missed Mr. K. and you're the spittin' image of the man, only prettier."

Kate thanked her again and hurried out of the kitchen, her mind running through all Mrs. Henderson had said.

She should have looked this gift horse in the mouth before accepting it and moving out to Wild Oak Canyon in the middle of South Texas. Now that she was here, she had to make the best of it. First things first. She wanted to know more about her father's death and the people with whom he'd done business.

BEN FOLLOWED KATE out of the kitchen. "I have a bad feeling about this."

"You and me both." She stopped at the base of the steps. "I want to freshen up a bit, then I'll be down. I assume, as my bodyguard, you'll be coming with me to town?" This last question she spoke in a whisper.

"That's right."

"In my car or your truck?"

"My truck."

"Good. I'll meet you in five minutes." She ran up the stairs.

Ben almost groaned aloud at the sway of her hips. The woman was far too distracting for him to keep his mind on the task at hand. Julia hadn't been quite as curvy as Kate. Her frame had been slight, so much so that giving birth had been especially difficult. Their obstetrician recommended that she not have any more children due to her narrow frame and complications of high blood pressure and prenatal diabetes during pregnancy.

Ben had been disappointed, wanting a whole brood of children. But he'd hidden his regret well. The sight of baby Sarah, so perfect and pink, had been all he'd needed.

Until a brutal murderer had taken her away from him.

All these thoughts stemmed from the one short glimpse of Kate's swaying fanny.

He shook his head, squared his shoulders and climbed the stairs behind her, heading for the room she'd assigned to him where he changed into a clean shirt and jeans.

Once he'd smoothed his hair into a semblance of order, he stepped into the hallway and ran into Kate.

He knocked into her, throwing her off balance. Ben grabbed her and pulled her into his arms, crushing her against his chest, his heartbeat hammering through his veins. Had he hit her any harder, she would have fallen right over the railing and down to the hardwood flooring.

Once he had her securely in his arms, he couldn't make himself let go. Her curves fit him in all the right places, so soft and tempting.

She looked up, her lips inches from his. "What are you doing?" she whispered.

"Keeping you from falling over the rail." Ben couldn't believe how cracked his voice sounded. "I promise to be more careful in the future."

Her tongue swept across her bottom lip, moistening it. "Please."

"Please what?" Why hadn't he let go of her already?

"Be more careful." She dragged in a deep breath and stepped free of his arms, straightening her shoulders while tugging the hem of her blouse. "I need to get to town. I want to run by the bank before they close."

He nodded, his hands dropping to his sides, the heat still burning within. "I need to touch base with Hank while we're there."

"Good. Then let's get going."

At least one of them had the wherewithal to get past the awkwardness Ben had instigated.

"I'll get Lily." Kate dodged past him like a scalded cat and ducked into Lily's room.

"I'll be in the truck," Ben called out, taking the stairs two at a time. He breezed through the kitchen. "You need a ride back to town, Mrs. Henderson?"

"No. I see Eddy headed this way. I'm sure he'll be wanting to get home and he promised to take me. Don't worry none about locking up. I still have a key." She patted her pocket.

Ben almost frowned, but caught himself. "Are you the only one who has a key besides Ms. Langsdon?"

"As far as I know." Marge's brows furrowed. "Why?"

"Just wondered. I'll make a stop at the hardware store to buy all new locks and keys. Just for safe measure."

She nodded. "Don't want anything bad to happen to those girls."

Ben's jaw tightened. "No, we don't." Whether it was him or one of Hank's other cowboys taking care of her, it wouldn't hurt to change out the locks on the house.

He pulled his truck around the side of the house, got out and grabbed the booster seat from Kate's car, securing it in the backseat of his truck. He tucked his 9 mm pistol into the glove box.

Lily burst through the front door and skipped across the yard, all smiles, her light strawberry-blond curls bouncing around her shoulders. She wore a sundress with a bright yellow-and-white daisy pattern. She was all sunshine and happiness, oblivious to the dangers around her.

That's how a child should be—carefree and happy.

Ben's fingers tightened around the steering wheel, memories threatening to overwhelm him. Scenes in his mind he'd tried so hard to push away.

Kate followed Lily out the door. Her pretty red-blond hair was pulled up in a loose bun at the back of her head. She wore a pastel yellow sundress and sandals, looking like spring and everything right with the world.

God, he had to get Hank to find someone else to take this job. He wasn't cut out for this. It was too soon. Every time he looked at the mother and daughter, a knife twisted in his gut. Sadly, he feared it was already too late to walk away.

Ben couldn't imagine leaving them to whatever peril the wild Texas landscape, and even wilder men who'd already threatened her, had to offer.

He opened the back door, helped Lily up into the booster seat and buckled the belt across her lap.

"I'm impressed," Kate said as she inspected his work. "You did that like you've done it before."

Ben backed away and rounded the truck, wordlessly, his teeth clenched. He'd buckled Sarah in a hundred times, careful with his precious daughter, wanting to keep her safe in case of a traffic accident. Too bad he hadn't kept her safe from her killer.

Kate climbed up into the passenger seat, her brows puckered. "Did I say something wrong?"

"No." Ben sat behind the wheel, fighting for control. Finally, he shifted the truck into Drive.

Her brow remained puckered as she sat back.

Lily fell asleep in the backseat almost as soon as they hit the highway.

Ben's grip tightened on the wheel, his knuckles turning white. His gaze panned the long stretch of road, looking for any hidden hazards, man-made or in the terrain. As knotted up as he was, he'd exhaust himself before nightfall. He inhaled and let the breath out slowly, willing himself to relax.

When they neared the town of Wild Oak Canyon, he had his control back.

Until Kate spoke, her soft tones warming him inside and out. "I believe the bank is on the next corner."

Ben shook his head. "We're stopping at the sheriff's office first."

CHAPTER SIX

KATE CLIMBED DOWN from the passenger seat before Ben could come around and open her door. He insisted on lifting Lily out of her booster seat. Still sleepy, the child stirred and lay across Ben's shoulder. Her eyelids fluttered, then closed.

The sight of Lily sleeping so peacefully on Ben's shoulder was sweet and disturbing. On the one hand the three of them gave the appearance of being a family. On the other, Ben wasn't a fixed variable in Lily's life. When they figured out what was going on and cleared the threat, Ben would be gone. Lily would wonder what she'd done to chase him off. She might even blame herself. Kate reached out. "I'll take her."

Ben turned away, refusing to give up Lily. "Let her sleep."

It only made sense. Kate wasn't too happy, knowing this was temporary. They'd made the mistake of claiming Ben was her fiancé. In a town the size of Wild Oak Canyon, that little tidbit would already have made its rounds.

Kate led the way into the sheriff's office, determined to take charge of this situation, starting with reporting the biker attack.

Deputy Dwayne Schillinger sat in a chair behind a desk, his feet propped on a stack of paper, his hand curled around a burger. "Well, well. To what do we owe the pleasure of your visit so soon?" The man let his boots drop to the floor with a thump and laid his lunch in the wrapper.

"I want to report another attack on my property and a death threat," Kate said.

"What kind of attack might that be?" Dwayne wiped his hands down the sides of his uniform, leaving a streak of yellow mustard. He finally pushed out of his chair and stood.

"A gang of bikers rode through my yard, attacked Ben and damaged property. As they left, they shouted out a death threat."

"Can you describe the men?"

"They wore bandannas around their faces and they rode motorcycles." Kate's fists clenched. "I think they were Hispanic."

"That's not much to go on. Without more detailed physical descriptions, I can't go out and arrest anyone. You have to do a little better than that."

Kate let out a frustrated huff. "Don't you know the people of this county? There can't be that many and surely you know who owns motorcycles and who doesn't."

Ben stepped up beside Kate and added softly, "One of the men had a tattoo of a snake. It wrapped around his wrist and forearm."

"Now *that* I might be able to do something with. Sounds like Guillermo Ramirez. His friends call him Snake."

A shred of relief rippled through Kate. A name for her attacker was better than nothing. "I suggest you arrest him for trespassing and assault."

"As soon as I can find him. Like his nickname, he's pretty slippery and difficult to track."

Kate fisted her hands on her hips. "I have a child living with me. I don't want this to happen again. Are you going to do your job and track down the man? Or do I need to call in the state police?"

Dwayne patted her arm. "Now, don't get your panties in a wad, young lady. We take our work seriously out here. We'll get right on it."

Kate nodded to the stack of papers on his desk. "Aren't you going to take notes, a statement or anything?"

"Don't need to." He tapped a finger to his temple. "I'll remember."

Kate dragged in a deep breath, closed her eyes and counted to three. "Thank you for caring." She turned and marched toward the door.

As she reached for the knob, the deputy called out, "Wouldn't have to be scared for yourself or your daughter if you weren't living on the Flying K."

Kate spun. "And what's that supposed to mean?"

Deputy Dwayne shrugged. "Nothing good's come of living at the Flying K. Look what happened to your father."

Kate walked back toward the man. "Are you telling me my father didn't die of natural causes like the medical examiner claimed?"

Dwayne's squinty eyes rounded. "No, ma'am. Just saying it ain't a healthy place to raise a family."

"You know something I don't?"

The deputy raised his hands. "No, ma'am. Just saying."

"I suggest you find this Snake guy and arrest him.

That would go a long way toward making the Flying K a healthier place to live." Kate left the building.

Ben followed, chuckling. "Nice."

"I don't need your patronization. I need answers." Kate stomped to the truck and yanked on the handle. Her nail bent back for her effort and the door remained closed. "Dang it!"

"Mommy?" Lily's eyes fluttered open. "Why were you yelling at that man?"

All the starch went out of Kate. "Oh, sweetie. I was just a little disappointed with him." Inside she bit hard on her tongue. "A little disappointed" was a huge understatement.

Ben clicked his key fob and the locks on the truck popped up. "Bank next?" His mouth twitched on the corners.

If Kate wasn't mistaken, the man was fighting a smile.

A shot of anger flared and died as she tried to picture her tirade with the deputy from Ben's view. Okay, so it must have been amusing to the man to see a woman dressed in a sundress and sandals rip into Deputy Dwayne with all his self-importance, attitude and mustard tracking down his shirt. "Smile and I'll serve your teeth on a platter," she warned, her own lips quirking upward. After the tension of the night and early morning, she could use a good laugh, even at her own expense.

"I wouldn't dare." Ben settled Lily in her booster seat and stepped back, allowing Kate to buckle her daughter in.

Her mood a little lighter, Kate climbed into the passenger seat and leaned back. "Not the bank yet. I want to go to the county tax assessor's office. There has to be a mistake about my father's back taxes."

Ben drove the three blocks from the sheriff's office to the county offices. When he pulled up in front of the building, he left the engine running. "I have a call to make. Will you be all right on your own for a few minutes?"

"Hopefully Lily and I will be safe inside the county offices. When we're done there, we'll go next door to the bank. Take your time." Kate climbed out, lifted Lily from her seat and took her hand, entering the cool interior of the county offices.

"Can I help you?" An older woman with gray hair and a pair of glasses perched on the end of her nose smiled a greeting.

"I hope you can." Kate pulled the letter from her purse and laid it on the counter. "I need information on the Flying K Ranch and any taxes owed on the place."

The woman grimaced. "Ma'am, I'm sorry but the computer is down and has been for two days now. The technician hasn't been able to fix it and we're waiting on someone from state to help." She pushed a form toward Kate. "If you'd like to fill out this form and leave it with me, I'll check the records as soon as I have access."

Kate sighed. "Thanks." While Lily stood patiently beside her, Kate filled out the form, then showed the woman her driver's license and a copy of the deed to the ranch as proof of ownership.

"Do you know when they'll have the system back up?"

"Not a clue. Check back tomorrow. Hopefully it'll be up then."

"Thank you." Kate left, Lily's hand clasped in hers, no less tense than when she'd entered the building a few minutes earlier. No use obsessing over a downed computer; she had only thirty days to come up with the cash, should she need it. No time like the present to see what the bank could do for her. She entered the cool, brightly lit bank lobby, her shoulders back, a smile pasted on her face.

ONCE THE TWO GIRLS were out of the truck, Ben glanced at his cell phone. Two bars. *Here's hoping.* His cell phone had been such a big part of his life in Austin. Out here in South Texas, he was lucky to use it at all.

He hit the speed dial for Hank Derringer and held his breath, not letting it out until the device sent a ringing sound back to him.

"Howdy, Ben," Hank answered.

"We need to talk."

"I take it you've met Kate?"

"I have." He inhaled and let out the breath before jumping in. "I need you to reassign me."

A long pause met his request.

"Did you hear me?" Ben prompted.

"I did. Only I've already assigned the other three members of CCI to cases." Hank cleared his throat and continued, "Is something wrong with Kate?"

"No. It's just that I'm not the right man for this particular job."

"I have full confidence in your abilities. I didn't choose you for this case by acci—"

"You didn't tell me she had a child." Ben cut him off, not wanting to hear Hank's arguments.

"Ah." That one word said it all.

"I'm not cut out to play bodyguard to this woman and her little girl. You need someone who…that… Well, damn. Get someone else."

"This has to do with Julia and Sarah, doesn't it?" Hank asked softly.

It was Ben's turn to leave dead air between the two of them. He swallowed hard on the giant lump clogging his throat before he could croak out his answer. "Yeah."

"Look, Ben, it was exactly the reason I hired you for this job. You have more of a stake in this case, more of an understanding of what's at risk, than anyone else on the team. I picked the right man."

"I can't do it."

"Yes. You can." Hank's voice softened even more. "I heard about the intruder last night and about the biker gang attack this morning. I wish I could send someone else to help you, but I just don't have the resources yet."

Ben snorted. "Good news travels fast, doesn't it?"

"What can I say? It's a small town and I have a few friends."

"In the meantime I'm stuck, is that what you're telling me?"

"You've met Kate and Lily. You've seen a little of what they're up against. At this point, could you really walk away?" Hank left a pregnant pause for Ben to respond. When he didn't, Hank went on, "I stand by my decision. I think you're the right man for the job."

"So it's take this one or resign?"

"You're not the kind of man to resign, if I read your dossier right."

Damn the man. He'd done his homework. He knew Ben more than Ben knew, or would admit to knowing, himself.

"Is that all you have?" Hank asked.

"No, can you use your connections to run a background check on Larry Sites and Guillermo Ramirez?"

"Had a check done on Larry Sites when the man disappeared after Kendrick's death. Newspapers reported that he was suspected of Kendrick's murder, that he's wanted for questioning. Otherwise, he didn't have an arrest record."

"Know anything about Ramirez? The man has a snake tattoo on his arm. He seemed to be the leader of the biker gang attack."

"I'll get an official background check on him, but from what I know, he's a thug for hire. It's rumored he works for whatever cartel will pay him the most. He's walking a thin line doing that. I'm surprised someone hasn't put a bullet in him yet. Part of it has to do with his ability to disappear. We suspect he slides across the border when it's hot on this side."

"Nice." Ben's fingers tightened on the cell phone. Kate was in a lot more trouble than just a biker gang harassing her. "Let me know when you find my replacement. Until then, I'll do the best I can."

"Thanks, Ben. Kate and Lily need you out there." Hank clicked off.

Ben sat for a long moment, staring at the street, heat waves rising from the asphalt, making mirages rise up before his eyes in wavering images of his dead wife and child.

Maybe it was the heat waves, maybe it was the tears. Ben blinked and Julia and Sarah disappeared.

He fought the urge to step on the accelerator and drive. Out of town, away from this job, from Kate and Lily. Hell, out of Texas altogether.

Instead he placed another call while he still had reception.

"Jenkins speaking."

Ben immediately recognized the voice on the other end of the connection as Detective Jenkins of the Austin Police Department. "Jenkins, Ben Harding here. I need some help."

"Ben? Is that you?" Jenkins pitched his voice low, almost to a whisper. "Man, where are you? As far as anyone knows you fell off the face of the earth."

"I'm in South Texas near a little town called Wild Oak Canyon."

Jenkins chuckled. "I guess it's true, then. You did fall off the face of the earth. What can I do for you?"

Ben jumped in. "Who's handling my case?"

"Man, you know I'm not at liberty—"

"Damn it, Jim. Who's handling it?"

Jenkins sighed. "Masters was assigned after you left."

"Anything new?"

"Not much. I think Masters tracked down the man who supplied the girls to Frank Davis. We don't have much, other than hearsay, so we haven't made an arrest yet."

"Girls?" All he knew about was the one Davis had killed.

"Apparently Davis was more deviant than originally suspected."

Ben's hand tightened around the cell phone. He wanted to kill Davis all over again. "Who was the supplier?" he asked through clenched teeth.

"You know I can't give you that kind of information. You're not on the force anymore."

Ben slammed his palm against the steering wheel. "When did you start following all the rules?"

"When you got fired." His tone was flat, final. "Why do you want to know?"

"I killed a man for killing a girl. I want to know it wasn't in vain. From the sound of it there are more women and girls being trafficked."

The silence on the other end indicated he'd gotten his friend's attention.

"Who supplied the girls to Davis? If they are victims of a human trafficking ring, it has to stop."

"I don't like going against department rules."

"Lives could depend on this." Ben's hand tightened on the receiver as he waited for his friend's response.

"Look, we know that. Masters is working the case."

"So let me help. What's it going to hurt?"

"You, me... I don't know, but I don't like playing both sides of the law."

"I'm no rogue and I doubt I could get into much trouble way down south where I am, but if there's any way I can help, I will."

After a long pause, Jenkins said, "His name is Rolando Gonzalez. He's here in Austin, but we suspect he has connections to the Mexican Mafia. As a matter of fact, he's got family in South Texas. Let me pull the file and get back with you. If you could do some looking around while you're down there, we might get more on him and who he's working for. Just don't do anything stupid."

Like killing him before they could get information out of him? Ben knew he'd gone beyond his limit on Davis. Seeing that girl lying on that cot, beaten, bleeding and past help… Ben stared out the window, his heart racing as if he was there all over again.

A movement on his right jerked him back to the present.

Kate and Lily exited the county tax assessor's office, waved at him and walked next door to the bank. If Hank got him off this case with Kate, he would have time to check out the lead Jenkins was talking about.

"I don't get reception out on the ranch where I'm working, so leave a message on my cell. If it's urgent, contact Hank Derringer." Ben left Hank's number with Jenkins. "I'll be waiting for that information."

"Will do. And Harding…stay safe. If this is as big as I think it is, you don't want to get caught in the cross fire of the Mexican Mafia."

Hell, he couldn't afford to get in the middle of the Mafia, not when he had Kate and Lily to protect. He'd wait to make any inquiries until Hank found a replacement.

"I NEED TO take out an equity loan on my father's—my ranch and open a three-thousand-dollar line of credit until I can withdraw money from a CD I set up for Lily's college." Kate leaned forward, her anger building with each time Art Manning tapped his pen to the loan application form in front of him.

"I'm sorry, Ms. Kendrick."

"Langsdon."

"Ms. Langsdon. I'll have to perform a complete credit check on you and have our corporate under-writers approve this before I can give you an answer. In the meantime I suggest you open an account here.

We can't loan money to anyone who is not a current client of our bank."

"I see." Kate stood. In the meantime, she was running low on cash and she needed money to pay Eddy and Ms. Henderson's salaries, not to mention putting food on the table and all the deposits she'd needed to get the electricity and gas switched over to her name.

"While your underwriters are thinking about it, I'll be thinking about whether or not to open an account." She gathered Lily's hand in hers.

"Ms. Kendrick."

"Langsdon."

"Without a job and a current income, I doubt the underwriters will take your application seriously."

"The land isn't enough collateral to secure a mortgage?"

"Not given the history of that particular parcel and its location."

"You mean I won't be able to get a loan?"

He shook his head. "I doubt it."

Kate breathed in and let it out before speaking again. "Thank you for your time, Mr. Manning."

She headed for the door, ready to be out in the heat, away from the stuffy air-conditioned atmosphere of the bank building.

"You look like your father." The voice belonged to a businessman dressed in a tailored suit leaning against the stand containing blank deposit slips.

Kate's steps faltered and she glanced at the man, her eyes narrowing. "Seems to be the consensus. If you'll excuse me…" Impatient and tired after a sleepless night and the fright of the morning, Kate had no intention of stopping to chat and she veered to the side.

The stranger stepped out, blocking her path to the exit. He stuck out his hand. "I'm Robert Sanders. Your father and I were friends."

To avoid being outright rude, Kate clasped the man's hand and shook it briefly. "Nice to meet you, Mr. Sanders. I'm Kate."

"Kate Langsdon." He held on to her hand longer than Kate wanted, then let go. "You have his eyes."

"I thought the hair was the dead giveaway."

"Your father's hair was much darker." Sanders raised a hand to touch one of Kate's curls.

She backed away.

The man's hand fell to his side. "But the green eyes are unmistakably his. I believe your mother had blue eyes, did she not?"

His comment took the wind out of Kate's sails. "You knew my mother?" So far, no one in town had mentioned her mother. Most people she'd run across in Wild Oak Canyon mentioned Kyle Kendrick, but not her mother, as though she'd never been there.

"No, but your father had a picture of his ex-wife on his desk. You don't look much like her at all."

That made Kate smile and her gut twist at the same time. "My mother always said I was a constant reminder of my father."

"Your mother must have been a very special woman. Your father never married after she left."

A spike of anger flared in Kate's gut. She'd loved her mother until the day she'd died. But if she had one regret in her relationship, it was that her mother had chosen to lie to her about her father, claiming he was dead, instead of alive and available if she'd wanted to meet him.

Kate suddenly felt stifled in the bank. "If you'll pardon me." She wanted out. Knowing Ben was waiting made her all the more anxious to leave, ready to get back to safe territory.

That thought gave her pause.

Damn.

After only one day, she'd come to rely on the strength and presence of Ben. If things didn't get better soon, she ran the risk of becoming too dependent on him.

Since her husband's death, Kate had been hesitant to date, unwilling to drag her daughter through relationships that wouldn't last. Not many men wanted to date a woman with a ready-made family.

Not that she wanted to date Ben. But the close proximity of a bodyguard could lead to the same outcome. Lily could become attached.

As she stepped around Mr. Sanders, the man handed her his business card. "I feel somewhat responsible for the well-being of my friend's daughter." When she didn't take his card, he lifted her hand, laid the card in it and curled her fingers around the paper. "Please, if there is anything I can do, don't hesitate to call."

Kate clutched the card. "Thank you." When she turned to leave, his hand caught her elbow.

"If you don't mind, I'd like to visit the ranch and make sure you're doing okay out there all alone."

"That won't be necessary."

"I insist."

"I'm not alone. I have my…fiancé staying with me. I'm quite all right."

Sanders's eyes narrowed fractionally, then his brows rose. "So, wedding bells are in the near future for you, are they?" He grasped her hands again. "Congratulations, my dear. I'm so happy for you."

Kate pulled free of Mr. Sanders's grip. "Thank you." She snatched Lily's little hand and turned away, hating the lies she was telling this town, but feeling more comfortable with the fact that Ben's presence would keep her safe. At least it might make others think before they set foot on her property. The more the people of the county thought a man lived there full-time, the better off she was. A lone woman on a ranch could be considered a target. Especially a ranch in cartel territory.

Houston was looking better every minute. But Kate had come too far to turn back now. She wanted to find out why her father had died. If he hadn't died of natural causes, Kate wanted to know who had killed him and why.

BEN HAD HIS hand on the gearshift ready to pull away from Wild Oak Canyon, to start a new life…elsewhere. As he flexed his arm to move the gear, Kate pushed through the glass doors, leading Lily by the hand, a troubled expression on her face.

Instead of driving away, Ben found himself climbing down and opening the rear passenger door before Kate reached the vehicle. The slump in her shoulders and the dullness in her eyes plucked at his heartstrings more than he cared to admit. "I take it that meeting didn't go well."

"County computers are down until further notice, so I struck out there."

Ben lifted Lily into her seat and buckled her belt. "We can come back tomorrow."

"Then the bank…" Kate stepped on the running board and slid into the passenger seat. "I only asked for a home equity loan to help me catch up in case I owed back taxes, and a line of credit loan to last me long enough so that I can sort through my father's will and cash in some certificates of deposit I have set aside for Lily's college fund." She snorted. "You'd think I'd gone in there asking for a fortune."

Ben didn't trust himself to comment. His insides churned. He didn't want to admit to Kate how close he'd been to leaving her and Lily in Wild Oak Canyon. What kind of coward left a woman and her child to fend for themselves?

Once they were all in the truck and belted, Ben rounded the truck and climbed into the driver's seat.

Kate sighed. "I guess the only good thing out of those two stops is this." She held up a business card. "This Robert Sanders claimed he was a friend of my father's and gave me his card in case I needed anything."

Ben reached for the card. "Let me see that."

Kate handed it over. "Looks legit."

Robert Sanders of Sanders Homes. Real Estate Broker and Construction.

Ben turned the card over, then handed it back to Kate. "Let me have Hank check him out before you get too chummy."

Kate nodded and slid the card into her purse.

Ben would keep an eye out for Sanders. If he really was a friend of Kyle Kendrick, he shouldn't be a threat to Kate. But then Kyle's place hadn't been broken into. He'd known his attacker.

Ben shifted into gear and pulled out onto the road.

"I need to stop at the hardware and feed stores for the things Eddy wanted me to get." Kate pulled a sheet of notepaper from her purse. "He handed it to me on the way out of the house." She glanced over her shoulder at Lily. "Then we can go to the diner and have supper. Would you like that, Lily?"

Lily's eyes widened, a smile lighting her face. "Do they have milk shakes?"

Kate let her daughter's happiness wash over her and she smiled back. "I don't know, but we'll find out."

"Can I have a chocolate milk shake?" Lily's feet bounced on the seat back.

Ben laughed. "We'll see when we get there."

In less than an hour, they had what they needed loaded into the back of the truck.

"Guess it's a good thing *you* drove today. I haven't had the chance to go through my father's barn and see if he had a truck. This ranching thing is all new to me."

"I can help you there."

"I thought you were a bodyguard. Were you a cowboy in your former life?"

"I grew up on a ranch." He'd loved living on a ranch, riding horses and raising cattle. But his family didn't own the ranch. Once his father's health declined to the point he could no longer handle the hard work, they'd moved to Austin where both his parents died in a multicar pileup on the interstate the week after Ben graduated from college.

"So is it true, once a cowboy, always a cowboy?" Kate's question pulled Ben back to the present.

He wasn't looking at her, but he could feel Kate's direct stare, and it made him uncomfortable. Why did she have to ask so many dad-burned questions?

He didn't respond with anything more than a shrug.

Her lips twisted. "Nice to know. You must be a

man of many talents. Anything else you'd like to share with me?"

"No." Ben pulled into the parking lot of Cara Jo's Diner. The timing couldn't have been better. He shouldn't have shared anything about his existence before Kate. None of that existed anymore. Not his parents, not his wife and child and not his work as an Austin police officer.

His slate was clean. What he did with his life now was the only thing he could do.

Start over.

A pretty young woman wielding a broom swept the sidewalk in front of the diner and smiled brightly when Ben stepped from the truck. She stopped to reach into a big cardboard box. When she straightened, there was a round-bellied puppy in her arms. "Howdy. I don't suppose ya'll want a puppy."

Kate had just set Lily on her feet and reached back into the truck to retrieve her purse, a hand holding on to the child's.

Lily wiggled free of Kate's grip, squealed and ran for the box. When she tried to step up on the curb, her sandal caught and she tripped, her little body slamming into the sidewalk.

Before Kate could reach her, Lily raised her arms for Ben to pick her up, tears streaming from her eyes.

Ben gathered her in his arms and cradled her. When he glanced up, his gut clenched at the paleness of Kate's face. He tried to pry the little girl's arms from around his neck, but she wouldn't let go. "Don't you want your mama?"

Lily buried her face in his shirt. "No, I want you."

CHAPTER SEVEN

LILY'S KNEES AND HANDS were scraped and bleeding. Her big emerald-green eyes filled with tears. "Am I gonna die?"

Ben smiled down at Lily. "No, baby, you'll be just fine."

Kate's heart skipped a few beats. A pang of jealousy tugged at her. But more than that, her chest tightened at how quickly Lily had assimilated Ben into her life. When he left, he'd leave a hole in her daughter's world that Lily wouldn't understand. She wouldn't be fine.

"Let's get her inside." The woman with the broom set the puppy down in the box and leaned her broom against the wall. "I have a first aid kit in the kitchen."

As Ben stepped into the diner, Lily practically crawled over his shoulder. "I want to see the puppies," she cried.

Kate followed Ben. "After we clean up your boo-boos, sweetheart, you can see the puppies."

"Can I hold one?" She sniffled and rubbed her arm over her nose.

Kate handed Lily a tissue from her purse. "If the nice lady says you can."

The broom lady chuckled. "My name's Cara Jo Smithson. And yes, you can hold one."

Lily grinned, her tears disappearing.

"So you're *the* Cara Jo?" Ben asked. "You're not what I expected as the owner."

Cara Jo laughed and batted her eyes. "I hope you mean that in a good way." The diner owner glanced over her shoulder at Ben, her footsteps slowing.

Kate had a sudden urge to scratch Cara Jo's eyes out for flirting with Ben. Then she had to remind herself the engagement was just a big fib. She had no hold on Ben and no right to be jealous if he flirted with the stunning Cara Jo. "The first aid kit?" Kate prompted.

"Oh, yes. This way." The woman marched to the back of the dining room and through a swinging door. Cara Jo held the door for Ben, Lily and Kate. "The washroom is at the rear of the kitchen. The first aid kit is in there under the sink."

Kate assumed the lead, stepping past shiny stainless-steel preparation tables and a huge gas stove.

"Let's get you fixed up." Cara Jo eased past Kate and Ben and entered the employee washroom, where she reached beneath a counter for a large, red plastic container with a big Red Cross sticker plastered to the top.

Ben set Lily on the countertop.

Kate moved to stand beside Ben, her hip so close it rubbed against his. A shot of awareness winged through her and she almost pulled away.

Cara Jo pulled bandages, sterile gauze and an accordion of alcohol prep pads from the kit, handing them to Kate.

While Kate dressed Lily's wounds, Ben distracted the child. He smoothed the red-gold curls out of Lily's face. "How many puppies do you have in that box, Cara Jo?"

Kate smiled, glad Ben's words captured Lily's attention, drawing it away from what Kate was doing.

"There are five, but one is already spoken for."

"What breed are they?"

Cara Jo laughed. "Purebred mutts, as far as I can tell." She opened an alcohol pad and handed it to Kate. "The vet seems to think they're a mix between Australian shepherd and border collie. All I know is that they're fuzzy and cute as can be. I'm having a hard time letting them go. But one dog in the family is enough when I'm working so much here at the diner."

Kate wiped the alcohol pad across Lily's skinned knees.

Lily grimaced and reached for the knee. "Ouch."

Ben caught her hand before she could touch the cleaned wound. "You're doing so well, Lily. I didn't know you were such a big girl. So far, not a single tear."

"Big girls don't cry, do they, Mommy?" Lily darted a look at Kate.

Kate could feel the next sentence coming before her daughter even said it.

"Big girls can take care of puppies, can't they?" Lily's eyes rounded, her head tipping up and down.

Kate's brows furrowed. "I don't know. Puppies are a lot of work. Someone has to feed them every day and take them outside a lot until they learn to go out on their own."

"I can do that." Lily's eyes widened, her bottom lip pouting outward, just a little. "Can I have a puppy, Mommy? Please."

"You just found a kitten. Isn't a kitten enough?" Kate couldn't resist her daughter's sad puppy look. And now that they lived on a ranch, not in an apartment in

Houston, she had no excuse. A puppy was a definite possibility. Still, it meant committing fully to living in Wild Oak Canyon. A puppy in a Houston apartment wouldn't work for Kate or the puppy.

"Let Mommy think about it, Lily," Ben said.

"Ben's right." Kate could have kissed Ben, the thought strangely appealing, more so than she wanted to admit. "I need to think about it."

Lily slumped.

"Hey, why the sad face?" Ben chucked a finger beneath her chin. "She didn't say no."

Teardrops shimmered on Lily's eyelashes. "She didn't say yes."

Kate shook her head, smiling. "I want to think about it."

"They'll be ready to wean from their mother any day now," Cara Jo added. "I hope they all have a home soon."

"Based on the one you were holding up before Lily fell, I'm sure they'll be snatched up," Ben said.

A bell jingled from the dining area. "If you two can handle this, I've got a customer. By the way, my special this evening is meat loaf and mashed potatoes, if you plan on staying for dinner."

"We can handle it from here," Ben reassured her. "And yes, we're staying for dinner."

Alone with Ben and Lily in the washroom, Kate's body tingled at the man's nearness. Heck, his broad shoulders practically filled the small space and his strong, capable hands dwarfed hers as he held her daughter.

Fingers fumbling, Kate applied a bandage to the

sore knee, then bent and kissed the covered injury. "There, all better."

"Not quite." Ben pulled the rubber band from Lily's ponytail that had been hanging drunkenly to one side. Strands of silky golden-red curls fell loose about her shoulders. "Can't let this brave young lady walk out of here with a lopsided pony." Carefully, he bunched the hair into his hand, smoothing all the lumps, and secured it again in the band.

Kate's breath caught and held throughout the process. Clearly, the man had done this before. She didn't know anything about Ben. For all she knew, he could be married with a little girl of his own. A family he'd soon go home to.

Her stomach flip-flopped, a sense of impending loss leaving an empty space inside. How could this be? The man was nothing more than a hired gun, a bodyguard to protect her. He'd only been around for a day.

Kate had never believed in love at first sight. Not that what she was feeling was anything like love. Respect, maybe. The man was strong, self-assured and handy to have around in a fight…or fixing a little girl's hair. That pretty much summed up her knowledge of Ben Harding. That, and he'd been a first responder for the Austin Police Department in his past life. What had made him leave to go work for Hank Derringer as a bodyguard for hire? The little bits of information she'd gleaned from the quiet man only made Kate want to learn more.

"Come on." Ben swung Lily up in his arms. "If it's all right with your mother, we'll go see those puppies now."

"I was thinking dinner would be a good idea."

The disappointment on Lily's face made Kate re-consider. "Okay, but only for a few minutes. I'll order our food while you two play with the puppies." She raised questioning brows at Ben. "Anything you'd like in particular?"

For a long moment, he stared down at her, with Lily perched on his arm. His blue eyes smoldered, his gaze lowering to somewhere south of Kate's nose.

Her pulse quickened, her mouth going dry. Kate ran her tongue across suddenly parched lips. "Food…what kind of food would you like?"

His mouth twitched. "Cara Jo's mention of meat loaf and mashed potatoes sounded great. I haven't had meat loaf in a long time."

"Meat loaf it is." Kate couldn't get out of the wash-room fast enough. Heat suffused her entire body at the thought of Ben's full lips, that blue-eyed gaze bearing down on her, reminding her she was more than just a mother. She was a young woman with needs and physi-cal desires she'd thought long gone with the death of her husband.

In an attempt to get her ragged breathing under con-trol, Kate sat at one of the empty booths and waited for Ben and Lily to step outside before she dared follow them with her gaze.

"You're one lucky lady." Cara Jo stood at her elbow, a pad and paper in her hand.

"How so?" Kate wasn't feeling so lucky. At the mo-ment, she felt trapped by her own raging hormones and latent desires.

Cara Jo spread her hands, palms up. "Why, your husband, of course."

"Fiancé," Kate corrected.

Cara Jo glanced out the big window at Ben squatting beside the box, handing Lily a puppy. "That man's hot, and he's really good with your daughter."

Kate's gaze followed Cara Jo's. "Yes, he is." Too good with her daughter and too handsome for Kate's own good.

"Let me know if you ever decide to give him up."

"Why?"

"He's just the kind of guy I'm looking for."

Kate's teeth ground together and she fought to keep from saying something stupid like *he's mine, keep your greedy hands off him.* Once again, she had to remind herself that she had no claim on Ben and that he wasn't even her fiancé. "You'll be the first to know," she said through tight lips.

Cara Jo laughed. "Lighten up. I'm not going to steal your man. He's in love with you, not me."

If only.

Kate's eyes widened and she almost jumped up from the table and ran. What the hell was she thinking? Ben wasn't her man. They'd only known each other for a day. He didn't—couldn't—love her and she'd better get such crazy thoughts from her head before she did something even more stupid, like falling for the big guy.

"Are you ordering for yourself or your family?"

"All of us." Kate had let the family comment slip right by so easily without trying to correct Cara Jo. At this point, she couldn't retract the lie without backtracking with the sheriff's office and anyone else who'd spread the rumor.

"So you're the folks who've moved onto the Flying K Ranch? I'm glad."

Kate's gaze shot to Cara Jo's. "You are? Why?"

Cara Jo shrugged with the hint of a smile. "Gets kinda lonesome out here in the middle of nowhere. There's not nearly enough women our age to talk to." Cara Jo's smile widened. "A girl could always use a friend."

Kate's eyes misted. "Thanks. I was feeling a bit overwhelmed by the acres of land between me and my nearest neighbor."

Cara Jo's sunny face darkened. "I hear you had some trouble out your way."

"Someone broke into the house the first night I was there."

"And what's this I heard about a motorcycle gang tearing through your yard?" Cara Jo shook her head. "What's with people? It's as though they're trying to scare you off or something."

"I'm getting that feeling, too. I just don't know why." Kate tipped her head to the side. "Did you know my father?"

"A little. He stopped by the diner for supper occasionally." Cara Jo gazed into Kate's eyes. "You have his eyes. I remember them being a pretty shade of green."

"So people say. I wouldn't know." Kate glanced toward Ben and Lily. "I never met the man."

"Really?" Cara Jo's pretty brow furrowed. "I think he traveled a lot. He never said much when he came in, but he was always polite and tipped well. He had a great smile, but apparently he didn't talk to anyone else about his life or what he was up to on the Flying K. He was a recluse."

"I wonder why he didn't get to know his neighbors."

Cara Jo leaned closer. "Some say he was involved in

the Mexican Mafia. I'm usually a good judge of character. I didn't see it in him."

"I wish I'd had the chance to get to know him." Her comment was no more than a whisper.

Cara Jo's frown deepened. "Yeah and if wishes were horses…"

"…beggars would ride," Kate finished.

The diner owner bent toward Kate and hugged her with her free arm. When she straightened, she swiped at moisture in her eyes and laughed. "Hey, what say we do lunch sometime?"

Warmth washed over Kate. Nobody in Houston had volunteered to be her friend. Rarely had she gone out to lunch with anyone other than Lily.

She'd been casual acquaintances with her coworkers at the hobby store where she'd been employed. Scraping out an existence for her and Lily on what little she made and the money from her husband's life insurance became an exhausting job. Spare time was spent with her daughter, going to the parks and zoo.

"I'd love to do lunch." Kate smiled up at Cara Jo. "Maybe you'd like to get out of town and come visit the ranch? I can make a mean grilled cheese sandwich." Kate glanced around the diner. "I'm not a grand cook."

Cara Jo snorted. "And you think I am? I have the usual. If I change things up, I get complaints. People can be such creatures of habit."

"Cara Jo," a gray-haired older man called out from a booth on the other side of the entrance.

"I'll be right with you." Cara Jo grinned. "Don't be surprised if I show up on your doorstep real soon. In the meantime, what's your poison?"

Kate gave her new friend their order and sat back,

admiring the tall, curvy young blonde's happy efficiency at handling her customers.

A squeal from outside drew Kate's attention.

Lily squatted on the wooden planks of the front porch, reaching out to a rambunctious black-and-white pup that nipped at her fingers. She jerked her hand away from the dog's sharp teeth and giggled.

Ben sat back on his haunches, smiling at the child. Every once in a while, his smile dimmed and his gaze grew somber.

Kate sat forward, studying the man.

The bodyguard had dark wavy hair hanging down to his collar. His square chin and lean, muscular body spoke of strength and discipline. But those smoky-blue, brooding eyes held too many shadows. Someone or something had hurt this man.

Kate closed her eyes and told herself she didn't want to know who and what had caused him so much pain. She couldn't keep them closed long. Lily squealed again and Ben's rich laughter made her want to go outside and join them.

"You should go see the puppies. They're too cute to miss." Cara Jo was at her side again. The diner owner set three glasses of ice water on the table and utensils wrapped in bright red cloth napkins. "Your food won't be ready for a few minutes. Go on before I do. That man is too yummy to be left alone long."

"No, I'll just wait here." Kate was already too aware of the man and the magnetism that pulled at her.

Lily giggled again, making Kate's heart leap.

"Have it your way, but those puppies will steal your heart." Cara Jo walked away to tend to another customer.

Lily squealed again, and Ben's laughter followed. Unable to resist, Kate rose from the booth seat and pushed through the front door out onto the porch. "Okay, you two are having entirely too much fun. Let's see what you've got."

Ben grinned up at her, the shadows gone from his eyes. "I think Pickles is her favorite."

"And which one is Pickles?" Kate dropped down on her knees and peered into the large cardboard box.

Five fluff balls growled in their puppy voices while tearing at a stuffed toy that had seen better days. Each puppy had its own unique coloring. Three were the mottled gray, white, black and red of the Australian shepherd. Two were black-and-white like a border collie.

In the corner closest to where Lily stood, one of the black-and-white pups leaped against the side of the box.

"Look, Mommy, Pickles has pretty blue eyes." She dangled her hand in the box and Pickles snapped at it, his high-pitched bark playful.

Lily laughed and hid her hand behind her back, looking up at Kate with shining eyes. "Can we take him home? Please, Mommy."

Kate lifted the puppy from the box and held him in the air. The gyrating ball of fur wiggled its way out of her hand. Kate caught Pickles before he hit the ground, her heart lodged in her chest. "You are a mess, little fellow."

"No, he's not. He's happy you picked him." Lily pointed at Pickles's long black tail tipped with white. "See, he's wagging his tail."

Kate held the puppy up to her face. The little fellow

licked the air, trying to get her nose, making her laugh at his persistent attempts.

Raised by her mother in a small condo in the city, she'd never been allowed to have a pet. No one was home to take care of it for hours and her mother thought it was unfair to animals to be left alone for so long. That and they could barely afford to put food on their table, much less buy food for a dog.

Kate hugged the puppy to her chest. Closing her eyes, she inhaled the unique scent of puppy fur and puppy breath. The defenseless pup reminded her of a time when she held Lily in her arms, alone in the maternity ward. She'd clung to her baby, after the miracle of her birth, realizing Lily was the only person she had left to love in her world.

Tears welled in her eyes and she blinked to keep them from falling. When she looked up, her gaze met Ben's.

All the pain of her own loneliness shone back to her like a mirror in his eyes.

Ben stood, his jaw tightening until a muscle jerked on one side of his face. "I'll wait in the truck."

Her heart squeezing in her chest, Kate asked, "What about supper?"

"I'm not hungry," he called out without looking back.

CHAPTER EIGHT

BEN WALKED AWAY. He would have run if he thought it would help. But no matter how far he ran, he couldn't escape the image of Kate staring at him through tear-soaked eyes.

As he dropped down off the porch, the sound of Lily's voice reached out to him, slamming another bullet into his heart. Sarah had been that enthusiastic, filled with a beautiful love of life. His daughter had been the joy of his existence.

For a few short minutes, he'd let Lily into his heart, laughing for the first time in two years. Letting her happiness revive his dead heart. Guilt swamped him, dragging him into that bottomless pit he'd crawled into after he'd discovered his wife and daughter murdered in their home.

How could he let another little girl fill that void?

And Kate's tears had touched him like nothing else since Sarah's death. He shouldn't be having these feelings. He'd lost his chance at love. He'd squandered it by not being there to protect them. Instead he'd been chasing his career as a cop, fighting to keep criminals off the street.

Ben jumped into his truck and slammed his door, then he hit the steering wheel with his palm so hard, pain reverberated through his hand and up into his arm. He welcomed it, using it to refocus on why he was there.

He had to regain his self-control or risk the lives of the people he was there to protect. No matter what, he couldn't let Kate and Lily suffer the same fate as his family.

"YOUR DINNER IS READY." Cara Jo appeared in the doorway. Her smile turned into a frown. "Where'd Ben go?"

"He's waiting in the truck. I'm sorry. We're a little tired from all the excitement last night and this morning. Could we get the meal to go?"

"Absolutely. Give me a minute and I'll bring it out."

Kate returned the puppy to the box and then fished in her purse for her wallet, extracting enough cash to pay Cara Jo for the food and a tip. "I don't need any change."

"Honey, consider it my gift to the new girl in town."

"I insist. This is your livelihood." Kate placed the money in Cara Jo's hand and closed her fingers around it. "Please."

Perhaps the other woman saw the moisture in Kate's eyes, because she didn't press the issue. "Okay. Give me a minute."

A couple minutes later, she returned with a bag filled with take-out boxes. The heady scent of hot food wafted beneath Kate's nose and her belly growled. "Thank you. And please, come out whenever you'd like."

Lily stared down into the box, her lip trembling. "Can we take him home?" She looked up at Kate, pressing her hands together like she was praying.

"Not today, sweetie. Pickles has to stay with his mommy for a few more days."

"Then can we bring him home?"

"If he's not one of the puppies Ms. Cara Jo has promised to someone else."

Lily's gaze shifted to Cara Jo. "Can I have that one?" She pointed to Pickles, who'd resumed jumping against the side of the box, barking at Lily.

Cara Jo smiled. "You're in luck. He's still available."

Lily squealed and jumped up and down.

Anxious to leave and find out what had made Ben depart so abruptly, Kate reached out and hugged Cara Jo. "Thanks for everything. I look forward to seeing you soon."

Cara Jo patted her back. "Let me know if I need to bring my shotgun out with me. You stay safe."

Kate slid her purse strap up over her shoulder. One hand held on to the bag of food while the other grabbed Lily's little fingers. "Come on, it's time to go home."

Ben stood beside the truck, his head bent, his hat tipped low, shading his eyes.

As soon as she stepped off the porch, he opened the back door and swung Lily up into her booster seat, buckling her in place. Wordlessly, he took the bag from Kate and settled it on the back floorboard, out of range of Lily's swinging legs.

Kate climbed into the front passenger seat and closed the door, unsure how to broach the subject of his sudden retreat.

When Ben slid in behind the wheel, he didn't look at her; instead he backed away from the diner and headed out of town on the highway leading to the Flying K Ranch.

"Just so you know, I asked Hank to find a replacement for me." His soft-spoken words took a moment to register.

When they did, Kate's head jerked toward him, her heart hitting the bottom of her stomach. "Why?"

"I'm not the right man for this job."

After the craziness of the day, the invasion of her home by a faceless man and the biker gang threats, Ben's announcement scared her the most. Tremors rippled through her body. A chill that had nothing to do with the truck's air-conditioning wrapped around her and she shook uncontrollably. Keeping her voice as even as possible, she remarked in a tone she hoped sounded unconcerned, "You've done pretty darned good so far."

"Nevertheless, when he's got someone else lined up, I'll be leaving."

What could she say to that? Her logical left brain said to leave it, nothing she could say would convince him to stay if he really wanted to go.

Her emotional right brain urged her to beg him to stay. He'd saved her more than once and she trusted him to do it again.

Instead, she whispered into the darkness, "Why did you walk away from Lily, me and the puppies?"

At first she didn't think he'd heard her and she let it go. Maybe she didn't want to know after all. What if he answered that he didn't like children or that he didn't like her? Nothing made sense. The way he'd been so happy and laughing with Lily led Kate to believe he liked children.

"I couldn't handle it." Ben's words broke through the frigid darkness.

Her heart already strained from his announcement that he'd be leaving; Kate wanted to know more than he was giving her. First she glanced over her shoulder at Lily.

Her baby's head dipped toward her chest, her eyes closed, chest rising and falling in deep, even breaths. Blessedly asleep, unaware of Ben's announcement that he'd be leaving.

Anger cleared Kate's head and forced her to sit up straighter. "Just what is it that you couldn't handle? Is it the constant threats out at the ranch?"

He didn't answer, ratcheting up Kate's annoyance with him for his vagueness and her desire to get to the bottom of the issues.

"Is it me? Am I too demanding?"

He shot a glance at her. "No, it's not you."

"Does Lily have you running scared? I can see that. Most four-year-old children terrify me. Especially ones who idolize me and dog my every step."

Ben's lips curled on the corners in a hint of a smile that never reached his eyes. The light from the dash didn't reflect in their dark depths. "No, Lily is a beautiful little girl."

Kate sucked in a deep breath and let it out between clenched teeth. "If it's not the situation and it's not me or Lily, what the hell had you running?"

Another long pause lasted a couple miles.

Kate turned away from Ben and stared out at the darkness. Only she couldn't see past the glass reflecting her image and Ben's behind her.

The man stared straight ahead, his eyes smoky dark, the shadows beneath them deep and disturbing.

"I lost people I loved." His voice was agonizingly

deep, and the words spoken so softly Kate thought she'd imagined it.

She turned toward him, studying his face. Had he spoken or had she imagined the words?

His hands gripped the steering wheel so tightly his knuckles had turned white. That and a tick in his jaw were the only indications of something going on more than him driving the truck.

"Who did you lose?" Kate asked, daring to believe she'd heard correctly.

"My wife and daughter. Sarah was Lily's age when she and Julia were murdered."

All the air left Kate's lungs and a weight settled on her chest that crushed the will from her. Julia. The name he'd called her when he'd kissed her. "Oh, God. I didn't know." She reached out and touched a hand to his arm.

Being with Lily had to be killing him.

Kate's worst nightmares had been those where she'd lost Lily, but every time she'd awakened to realize it had only been a bad dream.

Ben had lived it.

Her stomach roiled, the pain of loss almost as palpable as if she'd lost Lily. She swallowed hard on the giant lump choking her throat. "I'm sorry." Kate's voice caught on a sob. She looked back at Lily, counting her blessings, knowing that every minute she had with her little girl was precious.

Ben didn't have that anymore. His Sarah was gone.

Her bodyguard, the man who'd protected her and Lily, drove on as if he hadn't spoken at all. His face inscrutable, his lips pulled into a tight line.

As they turned off the highway onto the road that

led to the Flying K Ranch, movement caught Kate's attention out of the corner of her eye. Before she could react, something hit the passenger-side door with the force of a freight train, flinging Kate sideways. If not for the seat belt, she'd have slammed into Ben and possibly gone through his window.

Lily screamed from the backseat as the truck lurched sideways and skidded across the road toward the ditch.

Ben fought to keep the vehicle on the pavement, but the driver's-side tires bit into the shoulder before he could right the vehicle.

Kate barely had time to straighten before the truck was hit again. All she could see before she was tossed against the restraining belt was a dark grille and the glass of headlights that hadn't been turned on.

Ben cursed, grinding his foot to the accelerator, trying to get away from their attacker. The impact pushed them off the road and down into the ditch so fast the truck teetered on two wheels.

Her breath caught in her throat as the truck wavered, then dropped to all four tires, the jolt flinging her against the door.

Lily cried out.

"Hold on, baby," Kate called out.

Switching the truck into four-wheel drive, Ben gunned the gas pedal. The tires slipped on the gravel, then the knobby treads dug into the dirt and the truck shot back out onto the road.

The dark, steel-gray haze of dusk surrounded them.

Kate twisted in her seat, peering into the semi-darkness of a cloudy starless evening. Behind them, taillights gleamed, two specks of red racing back toward Wild Oak Canyon.

Lily cried softly in the backseat.

The danger past for a moment, Kate unbuckled her belt and crawled over the front seat into the back.

Ben flipped the overhead light on. "Is she all right?" He drove slowly toward the ranch, his gaze darting to the rearview mirror.

Kate cupped her daughter's face.

Other than silent tears trailing down her cheeks, Lily appeared to be okay. "We're okay, aren't we, baby?"

"Want me to take you two back to town?" Ben offered. "We could report in to the sheriff's office and let him know what happened."

"No. I don't want to risk being out of the vehicle if that guy returns. I just want to go home." She sat in the middle of the backseat beside Lily, holding her child's hand. Soon the tears stopped and Lily fell back to sleep.

Kate trembled in the darkness, afraid of staying where someone obviously didn't want her. She was pissed off that she was being forced out by thugs.

When they arrived at the ranch, Kate unbuckled Lily.

Ben opened the door from the outside and draped Lily's sleeping body over his shoulder.

Kate dropped to the ground, her body stiff from being hurled around the interior of the cab. Her shoulders were sore and her right breast was tender from the force of her body hitting the shoulder strap of her seat belt.

While Ben carried Lily into the house and up the stairs to her bedroom, Kate went from room to room, switching on the lights. When she reached the kitchen, her hand paused on the light switch.

A noise in the pantry captured her attention.

A moment before, she'd been so tired she could barely stand. In an instant, she was on alert. She flipped the light switch on and grabbed for the broom she'd propped beside the door early that morning.

She waited for the next sound that would indicate where the intruder stood.

Her teeth clamped down hard on her lip to keep her from screaming.

A loud click sounded from the pantry and the lights blinked out.

"Kate?" Ben called out from the staircase behind her.

Kate flipped the light switch and nothing happened.

Then something moved in the direction of the walk-in pantry. A door thumped open and footsteps scuffled across the tile.

"Stop or I'll shoot." Kate held the broom up like a shotgun. Her eyes had yet to adjust to the darkness. All she could make out was a shadowy form.

"Then shoot," a voice called out. He lunged for the back door and ran out before Kate could do anything.

And what could she have done? The broom wasn't a gun. At best she could have thrown it at him. At least he hadn't attacked her.

"Kate!" Ben's voice echoed in the living room. "Where are you?"

"In the kitchen. I'm okay."

"What happened?" Footsteps sounded on the wood floor in the hallway and Ben skidded to a halt behind her, his hands reaching out to gather her into his arms. Ben crushed her to his chest. "You scared the hell out of me. Why didn't you answer me the first time?"

"We had an intruder in here. I didn't want him to know where I was."

"Are you all right?"

"I'm fine." *Now that you're here.* She leaned back against him, wrapping his arms securely around her middle.

He turned her in his embrace and tipped her chin up.

Already her eyes were adjusting to the limited lighting. A soft blue glow poured in through a nearby window as clouds skittered across the sky, freeing the moonlight.

Kate stared up into Ben's dark eyes. "Why is this happening?"

"I don't know." He smoothed a hand over her cheek and it found its way to the back of her neck. He tugged her hair, tipping her head backward, making her lips more accessible to his...kiss.

Ben's mouth closed over hers, sending wave after wave of sensations rippling through Kate's body.

Her hands climbed up his chest, twining around his neck. She applied pressure, wanting more, needing him to deepen their connection, to warm her body with his. To chase away the shadows of fear making her tremble.

His tongue twined with hers, thrusting deep, sliding long and slow, in and out.

When his hands slipped downward, over her shoulder blades and to the small of her back, she didn't protest, couldn't tell him to stop. Not when all she wanted was for him to shove her up against a wall, wrap her legs around his waist and drive deep inside her.

How long had it been since she'd made love to a man? Since before Troy had left for war. Almost five years. More than any woman should have to grieve.

BEN'S MEMBER STRAINED against the stiff denim of his jeans, pushing against the button fly, waging a war for freedom. His hand tangled in Kate's thick, lush curls, cupping the back of her head as he bent her over his arm and took what he wanted in the form of a kiss. But it wasn't enough.

The lingering shock waves of adrenaline pulsed through his system, urging him to take action. With no enemy to attack and no imminent danger, his relief could only be derived from making mad, passionate love to this woman whose body warmed his hands and awakened desires long buried.

Kate melted against him; her hands smoothed down the back of his neck and then squeezed between their chests. Her fingers searched for the buttons on his shirt, opening one after the other until she slipped through the opening and touched his skin.

Cool, slim fingers set off a string of explosions inside Ben, sparking nerve endings to life.

Before long, she had all his buttons undone and was tugging his shirt out of his waistband.

Ben found the hem of her dress and pulled it up over her head, tossing the garment to the floor. A black lace bra was all that stood between him and her perfectly rounded breasts.

When her hands locked on the top button of his jeans, his heart skipped several beats and he sucked in a raw, ragged breath.

He closed his hands over hers. "No."

She froze and glanced up, her green eyes shadowed. Then her chin dipped and she backed away. "You're right. I shouldn't have done that. I'm sorry."

Ben's hands fell to his sides, regret burning in his

gut. He couldn't let himself be distracted, not with Kate's and Lily's lives at stake. He reached around the wall, feeling for the light switch, and flipped it.

Nothing.

"Know where the breaker box is?" he asked.

"I saw it in the pantry earlier today. The intruder must have known where to look because that's where he was hiding."

"This has got to end." Ben felt his way through the kitchen to the pantry he recalled from unloading Kate's furniture and supplies. There was a sound of rustling fabric, a drawer opened and closed behind him and a beam of light clicked on.

"This might help." Kate, now redressed, followed him into the closet-size room and shone the light on the breaker box. Her presence in the tight confines of the tiny space lined with canned vegetables and boxes of cereal only made matters worse.

He was so tense, he fumbled with the handle to the breaker box before he could get it open and find the tripped switch.

Once the switch had been returned to the on position, light poured through the open pantry door.

Kate backed out, turning off the flashlight. "Just so you know, there are several flashlights in the drawer at the end of the counter here." She slid the electric torch into the drawer and closed it, her hands shaking.

Her gaze slipped up to his, her eyes wide and haunted. "I won't attack you again. I promise."

Ben leaned in the door frame of the pantry. "You didn't attack me. If anything, I was all over you. I've never wanted to kiss someone as much as I wanted to kiss you."

Her brow furrowed. "Then why…?"

"It's wrong. I won't be here long and I don't want to lead you on in any way."

She nodded. "Good, because I'm not in the market for a man. I only need a bodyguard. I don't know what came over me. Must have been the adrenaline rush. Don't worry. I'll leave you alone."

When she turned to leave, Ben shot forward and captured her arm. "Don't get me wrong." He lifted her chin and stared down into her flashing green eyes. "I wanted to kiss you. And I still do." He bent until his lips barely touched hers.

Kate's gaze caressed his mouth, then her eyes rounded and she backed away, spun and ran up the stairs.

It took every ounce of Ben's self-control not to follow her.

CHAPTER NINE

AFTER LYING AWAKE in her bed with her eyes wide open and her mind spinning until the early hours of the morning, Kate finally fell into an exhausted sleep.

Not until Lily skipped into her room the next morning did she open her eyes and squint at the sun shining through her window.

"Oh, baby. I should be up by now to fix your breakfast."

"Mrs. Henderson fixed it for me."

Kate sat up, the T-shirt she'd slept in bunched around her. "She did?"

"Uh-huh. Can I go outside and play?"

Before her daughter finished her sentence, Kate was shaking her head. "Not until I'm up and dressed. You're not to go outside without me or Mr. Harding. Do you understand?"

Lily sighed and crawled up on the bed. "Could you hurry? I saw a lizard on the front porch."

Kate ruffled Lily's strawberry-blond curls. "No rest for the weary, is it? Okay, okay. I'm getting up. Why don't you go down and help Mrs. Henderson in the kitchen?"

"Okay." Lily rolled to the edge of the bed and dropped onto the floor.

The patter of her feet warmed Kate's heart and made her want to get out of bed and join the day.

The fear of the night before faded with the steady heat of the midmorning sun.

She quickly brushed her hair, secured it in a low ponytail at the base of her head and washed her face. A glance at her wan complexion in the mirror triggered her to dig in the drawer full of cosmetics for powder, blush and a little mascara. No sense looking like death.

Not when there was a handsome man close by. One who'd admitted to wanting to kiss her.

Excitement filtered through her body as she thrust her feet into jeans and pulled them up over her hips. A soft rose T-shirt and pointed-toed pink leather cowboy boots completed her outfit. She hurried from the room and down the stairs to the kitchen, peeking into the living room and ranch office on the way. If she were honest with herself, she'd admit she was looking for Ben.

"He's outside in the yard with Lily," Marge said as she appeared at the kitchen door.

Kate started. Having another person in the house took some getting used to. "I was looking for Lily."

"She's out there with Mr. Harding. They are too cute together. He's hangin' a tire swing for her. Eddy's out rounding up strays. We got here two hours ago."

Kate peered out the window over the kitchen sink at the man hanging from a tree branch. He expertly tied a rope to the branch, then swung out of the tree to land on his feet beside the four-year-old.

Lily grinned up at him, clapped her hands and giggled. "Do it again, Mr. Ben. Do it again," she cried, loud enough Kate could hear her muffled words through the window.

"He scrubbed an old tire he found out back with a brush and dish soap and he found a length of rope in the shed." Mrs. Henderson dried a pan as she gazed out the window, a smile lifting the corners of her mouth.

The image of the man and child made Kate's heart ache. Lily really needed a father figure. She needed a man in her life to teach her to be adventurous, to show her how to make things and climb trees.

Kate chuckled. Not that the child hadn't learned something about tree-climbing on her own. Kate's smile faded. And thank goodness she had. No telling what the biker gang would have done had they found her outside alone.

A chill shook Kate's body.

"Got a plate of scrambled eggs warming in the oven. Sit yourself down while I pop bread in the toaster."

Kate sank into a chair at the big kitchen table. "You don't have to go to the trouble."

"Now, don't argue with me. I like doin' for others. Makes me feel useful. Oh, by the way, your telephone is working now."

Kate hopped out of her seat. "Good, I want to call the sheriff."

"Oh, honey, I heard about your intruder last night. Ben— Mr. Harding already put a call into the sheriff's office reporting the incident. He said they were sending a deputy out today to look around."

Dropping down to the seat, Kate shook her head. The man was always a step ahead of her.

Marge continued talking as she scooped eggs onto a plate and set it in front of Kate. "I checked around to see if anything had been taken. I could swear I had several cans of soup and tuna I'd planned on using for lunch today. And the loaf of bread I'd laid out was gone." She shook her head. "Looked to me like someone who was hungry slipped in and took what they needed."

"Why wouldn't that person just knock on the door and ask for food? Why steal it?"

"Could have been undocumented immigrants." Marge's brows dipped. "Sometimes a steer will go missing. No telling what's been taken since Mr. Kendrick passed. Eddy said the cattle are all over the ranch. It'll take him days to account for what's left of the herd."

"I suppose I could learn to help him. Do you think Lily would be all right out riding along with us?" Kate had ridden horses a couple times, but she was by no means an expert. Lily had never had the opportunity.

"I could keep her here with me. I'm sure we could find plenty for her to play with around the house."

"I don't want to be a bother."

"No bother. I love little ones." Mrs. Henderson set a glass of orange juice beside Kate's plate. "Eat now. Better to make your decisions on a full stomach."

Kate ate the scrambled eggs and toast, enjoying being waited on for the first time since her mother died. She carried her plate to the sink and ran it through the warm soapy water Mrs. Henderson had used to clean the dishes. No dishwasher in this house.

"Look, he's got the tire up." Mrs. Henderson pointed out the window.

Lily lay on her belly through the hole of the old tire, swinging and laughing out loud.

Her happiness made Kate's heart lighter. She deserved to have a yard to play in and a real home, not an apartment in a busy city.

What would it take to find the ones responsible for trying to run them off the property? Kate wanted a place to call home, for herself as much as she wanted it for Lily. This ranch was the only thing her father had ever given to her, and she'd be damned if she let anyone take it away.

Determination and a sense of purpose flowed through her veins, giving her the inspiration she needed to fight for what she wanted for her and her baby. "Mrs. Henderson, do you know the number for Cara Jo's Diner?"

"Sure do."

Kate called her new friend Cara Jo. Then she brushed her teeth, stopped in her bedroom for her pistol and a box of ammunition. She shoved the box into her pocket. She held the pistol behind her back, then headed outside to fulfill her promise to herself.

Ben lifted Lily out of the tire and set her on the ground.

Her hair was falling out of her ponytail and she wore a thin coating of dust and a smile. "That was fun. Can we do it again?"

"After a while, sweetie." Kate dropped a kiss on her tousled hair. "Right now, I want you to go inside and help Mrs. Henderson bake cookies."

Lily squealed and ran for the house.

Kate inhaled and let out her breath in a slow, steadying release. "I want to take you up on that offer."

Ben's gaze dropped to her lips. "What offer?"

Heat spread throughout Kate's body at the thought of Ben's kiss. She shoved the image aside and squared her shoulders. "I want you to teach me to shoot my gun." She pulled the weapon from behind her back and held it out.

Ben touched a finger to the tip of the barrel and pointed it away from him. "You start by never pointing a gun at someone unless you want to shoot them."

"It's not loaded." She dug the box of ammo from her jeans pocket and held it out in her other hand.

"Trust me. Make it habit not to point a gun at anyone, loaded or unloaded, unless you intend to shoot him."

"Okay."

Ben took the weapon from her hands and inspected it. "Do you own cleaning supplies for this?"

"Yes."

"Good, it looks good for now, but after we shoot, it'll have to be thoroughly cleaned." He tipped it back and forth and weighted it in his grip. "It's a nice 9 mm Glock. Where did you get it?"

"It was my husband's." She'd almost made him get rid of it when she'd discovered she was pregnant. After his death, she couldn't bring herself to sell it. Now she was glad she hadn't. "Is it a good brand of gun?" she asked.

"One of the best." Ben clicked a button and the magazine dropped out of the handle. He caught it with his other hand. "Let me see the rounds."

Kate plunked the ammo box in his open palm, careful not to touch him, afraid to set off another bout of uncontrollable lust. That would be a disaster, considering he didn't want anything to do with her. Hadn't he said he was leaving as soon as Derringer arranged a replacement?

Ben loaded the bullets into the magazine. "Make sure your bullets are pointing toward the barrel of the weapon." He showed her how to slip the magazine into the handle and how to release it. Then he handed the gun to her. "You do it."

She didn't care how basic the lessons were, she wanted to learn and get it right the first time. When Ben left, Kate's and Lily's lives depended on Kate's ability to protect them.

Kate held the weapon, searching for the magazine release button. When she found it, she released the magazine and it fell to the ground.

"You'll want to keep your weapon as clean as possible." Ben chuckled, the sound warming Kate's insides.

As Kate bent to retrieve the magazine, a vehicle rumbled down the gravel drive, stirring up a cloud of dust.

"Must be the sheriff's deputy." Ben took the Glock from her and reassembled it, stuffing it into the back of his waistband.

The SUV pulled to a stop. The cloud of dust drifted to the ground and Deputy Schillinger climbed out. "I hear you had another intruder."

"We did," Kate responded. "He was here when we got home after dark yesterday."

Schillinger had a lump of tobacco stuffed between his teeth and his lower lip. He spit a dark stream of nasty juice on the ground at Kate's feet. "Did you see who it was?"

Kate stepped backward, her breakfast roiling in her gut. "No, he didn't happen to announce himself or show his face. He did get away with some pantry staples and bread."

"Probably illegals."

When Schillinger looked like he would spit again, Kate frowned. "Do you mind?"

The man paused, then let loose anyway, wiping a dark drop from his chin. "Not at all."

Kate stared at the mess on the ground and back at the deputy, then crossed her arms. "And let me guess... you can't do anything without a full description." Kate let out a tight breath. "I don't know why we bother to call you. I'll turn this over to the Customs and Border Protection guys. Maybe they will do something. Thank you for your time."

Another vehicle approached. It slid in beside the deputy's SUV and Cara Jo's long, lithe form stepped out. "Hi, Kate. Got a surprise for Lily." Cara Jo pushed her shoulder-length blond hair back behind her ears, opened the back door and reached in, extracting a black-and-white puppy from the backseat.

Lily burst from the house, racing toward Cara Jo. "It's Pickles! It's Pickles!" She skidded to a stop in the gravel and reached up.

Cara Jo laughed and handed her the puppy. "You have to be very careful with puppies. They're smaller than us and can be hurt easily."

"I'll be very careful. I promise." Lily clutched the squirming puppy against her chest and ran to Kate's side. "Look, Mommy, Pickles is here."

"That's great, honey. Can you take him in the kitchen and get Mrs. Henderson to help find feeding bowls? You can get one of the boxes we used to pack and use it for his bed."

Lily ran toward the house, the puppy flopping in her arms.

Cara Jo joined the group of adults. "What's happening?" She glanced at the deputy. "What are you doing here, Dwayne?"

Kate could have laughed at the way the deputy's lips thinned at being called by his first name. "I was called in on business." His chest puffed out a bit more and he looked down his nose at Kate's new friend.

Cara Jo's brows rose and she turned to Kate. "Business?"

"Unfortunately, the sheriff's department is better at serving papers than they are at finding intruders." Kate gave the lawman a pointed look. "If you're not going to dust for prints or at least write down a statement, I see no further need of your services."

Dwayne's eyes narrowed. "This isn't the place for a woman. You really should consider selling before the bank takes the ranch."

"The bank's not taking anything." She didn't know how, but she'd find a way to come up with some money.

"Then you might want to leave before anything bad happens to you or your little girl."

Ben slipped an arm around Kate's waist. "She's not going anywhere she doesn't want to."

"Besides, it's ridiculous to even consider leaving," Cara Jo said with a snort. "Give up a ranch because the sheriff's department is too scared or lazy to do anything about the growing crime rate in the county?" She hooked Kate's arm and stared at the deputy. "Why are you on the force if you can't do your job?"

Dwayne's face bloomed a ruddy red, his eyes narrowing at Cara Jo. He shifted his attention to Kate. "Think about it, Ms. Langsdon."

Ben's arm dropped from around Kate's waist and he stepped toward the deputy, his fists clenched.

Kate grabbed his hand and slipped it back around her. "He's not worth it."

Schillinger turned and marched to his SUV, climbed behind the wheel and spun out in the gravel on his way out of the drive.

"That man always has a sour look on his face," Cara Jo remarked.

Kate laughed. "I thought it was just me."

"No, it's definitely him." Ben brushed a lock of Kate's hair back behind her ear.

"Thanks for being here for me." Even if Derringer had sent him, Ben had gone above and beyond on more than one occasion. Kate couldn't imagine having to deal with everything that had happened on her own.

"I need to make a call. You going to be all right for a few minutes?" He gazed into her eyes.

Her heart flipped at the worry reflected in his eyes. "I'm fine. Cara Jo's here."

"Go on. We need time for girl talk." Cara Jo waved Ben toward the house.

Once he left them, Cara Jo faced Kate. "Now, what's this about the county foreclosing on your ranch?"

Kate shook her head. "You don't want to know."

"I wouldn't have asked if I didn't care." Cara Jo touched a hand to Kate's arm.

Cara Jo had it right, Kate had needed someone she could talk with and Ben wasn't necessarily the right person. He was the hired help. He couldn't dig her out of her financial hole. Nor did she want him to. She dragged in a deep breath and let it out. "The sheriff and Deputy Schillinger served me with papers that the county is going to seize the property for almost thirty thousand in back taxes."

"Holy moley." Cara Jo flattened a hand to her chest. "That's a lot of cash."

"Yeah." Saying the amount out loud made it sink in all the more, threatening to overwhelm Kate. "I just need time to figure things out. Hire a lawyer or something. But the local bank probably won't loan me any money to keep things going in the meantime."

"I've got a loan on my diner through that bank. But then I grew up here. They know me."

Kate sighed. "I'm an unknown and not a very safe bet." She glanced around at the barn and outbuildings. "And I'm sure the rumors about the attacks aren't giving the bank faith in my abilities to run a ranch and protect my interests."

"You can't help that someone is attacking you." Cara Jo nodded toward where Ben had been. "And you have your fiancé living here. Ben looks fully capable of handling any difficulty."

"Having Ben here didn't help me one bit in the eyes of the bank loan officer." Kate snorted. "I don't even have enough to pay Eddy and Marge until I can get my hands on my daughter's college fund."

"How much do you need?" Cara Jo propped her hands on her hips. "I can't afford thirty thousand, but I can spot you some money until you can get to yours."

Kate's chest swelled, her eyes filling. "No, I can't take advantage of you like that. You barely know me. I'll figure things out. Heck, I've only been here a couple days. Things are bound to get better."

"Sometimes things get worse before they get better. But then, don't let me be the downer here." Cara Jo hugged Kate. "The offer's open if you need it."

"Thanks." Kate gave her a watery smile. "I'll wait and see what the county assessor says when the computers come up again. No use borrowing trouble. I have enough as it is."

FROM THE HALLWAY where the phone was located, Ben could keep an eye on Kate and Cara Jo outside. He dialed Derringer.

"Hank, Ben here."

"Got the phone line hooked up at the Flying K, did you?" Hank asked.

"It's working."

"Good. Had some news on that DVD you sent to me. My contacts in the state crime lab may just be able to recover what was on it. They told me they should have it by this evening. Whatcha got?"

Ben watched as Kate and Cara Jo hugged. What were they talking about? "Can you do some digging on Deputy Dwayne Schillinger and a Mr. Robert Sanders?"

"Why?"

"Schillinger's been out here twice to investigate break-ins, and done nothing but warn Kate to leave."

"Hmm. That doesn't sound right."

"That's what I'm thinking."

"I'll get my contacts on the deputy. I take it you had another break-in last night?"

Ben's hand tightened on the receiver. "We did."

"Anyone hurt?" Hank asked.

"No, he left without attacking."

"As for Robert Sanders, he's pretty well-known in

the area, what with his ties to real estate and construction. But I'll have my folks do a little digging to see if
he's got any dirt hiding under his rug."

The pounding of horse hooves made Ben glance
toward the south. "Hank, I gotta go. Let me know if
anything comes up."

"Will do. And, Ben, be careful out there. Ranches
can be like islands. You're out in the middle of nowhere
with no one to depend on but yourselves."

"I know that. And the local authorities aren't helping at all."

Ben hung up and burst through the door as a horse
and its rider galloped across the dry grasses toward
the house.

"That's Eddy." Mrs. Henderson stood on the porch,
wiping her hands on a dry dish towel. "He's in an all-
fired hurry."

Kate was halfway to the fence, with Cara Jo following, when Ben leaped off the porch.

Eddy's mount galloped across the dry Texas pad-
dock of sparse grass and scraggly vegetation. By the
time he reached the gate, Kate was holding it open
for him.

Ben ground to a halt beside her. "What's wrong?"
Ben asked.

Eddy slipped from the saddle, his boots hitting the
ground, stirring up a puff of dust. "Found several steer
carcasses along the southern boundary."

CHAPTER TEN

"I DIDN'T KNOW if you wanted to come out and inspect, or if you wanted me to notify the sheriff's department and let them handle it." Eddy waited for Kate's response.

Kate glanced at Ben. "I don't think the sheriff will be much help. Let's get out there and see what we've got." Kate headed for the barn. "Oh, wait…. Lily." Kate performed an about-face and headed back to the house.

Just inside the kitchen door, Lily held Pickles to her cheek as she stood beside Cara Jo.

"Kate, go on, do what you have to do." Cara Jo waved Kate toward the barn. "Don't worry about Miss Lily. She and I are going to start training Pickles. Aren't we, dear?"

Lily nodded. "Mrs. Henderson's making treats for Pickles."

Kate bit down on her lip. "Are you sure?"

Cara Jo smiled. "Absolutely."

"Don't you have to be at the diner?"

"Not today. I give myself a day off every once in a while. I can do that." She smiled. "I'm the owner."

"Thanks." Kate spun and hurried to the barn where Eddy and Ben stood.

Her first time in the barn, Kate stared around at the

tack hanging from hooks on the walls. "Is there a four-wheeler or a horse I can ride?"

Eddy shook his head. "No four-wheelers, but I've got a couple horses in the stalls in the barn."

Ben captured her arms and turned her to face him. "You're not going. You need to stay and look after Lily."

"You saw what Marge is capable of." Kate nodded toward Eddy. "She wields a powerful shotgun, doesn't she?"

Eddy slapped his hat against his thigh. "Scares me, if that's whatcha mean." He slipped a rifle into the holster on his saddle.

Kate felt a little better knowing they'd be heading out with a little more firepower than her Glock, which was tucked neatly into Ben's waistband, along with the one he wore on a shoulder holster over his blue chambray shirt. She made up her mind. "Lily will be fine with Mrs. H. and Cara Jo will be there as well to entertain her and keep an eye out for trouble."

Ben crossed his arms. "Sounds like you thought this through."

"I did."

"I still don't think it's a good idea."

Her brows rose. "Why not? This is my ranch, and it's my responsibility to see to the safety of the people and animals on it." She stepped toward one of the occupied stalls. "I'm going."

Ben followed, his boots stirring the dust around her. "Have you ever ridden a horse?"

"Plenty," she lied. Well, it wasn't a lie if "plenty" meant five times in her entire life.

"Right." Ben's one-word response told Kate he didn't believe her for a minute.

Eddy led a horse from the middle stall. "This is Lucky. She's a little older and as calm a horse as we have on the Flying K."

"As compared to what?" Kate asked as she stared up at the horse, thinking the mare was bigger than any of the horses she'd ever ridden.

"She's been out roaming the pastures since Mr. K.... left." Eddy breathed deeply, his jaw tightening. "She won't be hard to ride."

Kate refused to be intimidated by the animal's size. "You'll have to show me where everything is."

Eddy led the way to the racks of saddles stored in the tack room. He nodded toward a brightly colored blanket. "If you'll toss that over Lucky's back, I'll handle the saddle."

Rather than push the point and take the saddle herself, Kate led the way back out to the horse and eased the blanket across Lucky's back.

The animal eased sideways, whickering softly.

Kate stepped away and let Eddy settle the saddle on the horse's back. She studied Eddy's moves, committing them to memory for the next time when she'd insist on doing it herself.

"When you cinch the girth on Lucky, do it a couple of times. She likes to blow her belly out. If you don't do it more than once, she'll fool you and when you get going, the saddle will slide to the side, dumping the rider."

Kate nodded. "I'll remember."

Once Eddy had the saddle securely fastened, he handed the bridle to Kate. "You can do this."

Kate nodded, trying to remember, from the five times she'd ridden at a farm outside Houston, how to slip the bridle between the horse's teeth and over its head.

Eddy walked away, calling over his shoulder, "She'll bite down to keep you from getting it between her teeth. Stick your thumb in the corner of her mouth to get her to open."

While Eddy adjusted the girth on his horse, Kate worked at sliding the bridle between Lucky's teeth. After several failed attempts, the horse stomped her feet and swished her tail, slapping at Kate like a pesky fly.

"You're going to wear this bridle," Kate said between gritted teeth.

In her peripheral vision, Kate could see Ben walking toward her. She'd be damned if she couldn't accomplish this one little task. With her teeth clenched as tightly as Lucky's, and the bridle held in one hand, Kate shoved her thumb in the corner of the animal's mouth and tugged.

Lucky smacked her lips and her teeth opened wide enough for Kate to slide the bridle between her teeth and loop the strap over her ears. "There. That wasn't so bad, was it?"

The mare opened and closed her mouth as if adjusting to the metal bit.

Kate tightened the strap beneath Lucky's chin and the one around her head. When Lucky was ready, Kate walked her to the barn door and glanced at the stirrup, wondering how in hell she was going to get her foot up that high. She glanced around the barnyard, spying a wooden step close to a hitching post. She tugged the reins, urging the horse to follow.

Lucky straightened her legs, refusing to move.

Ben had saddled a gray Arabian gelding and stood in the barnyard watching Kate struggle with the mare. "Need a hand?"

"No, I have this," she insisted.

"Lucky doesn't like the step." Eddy led his gelding out and swung up into the saddle.

Ben closed the distance between Kate and himself.

An uncontrollable surge of excitement swept over her, setting Kate's nerve endings alight.

"Let me help," he whispered. "It by no means implies you need it." Ben stooped, cupping his hands.

Kate leaned close. "I don't like relying on you." She stepped into his palms.

"Why?" He rose, lifting her high enough to toss her leg over the saddle.

"Because you won't always be there. I'll have to take care of myself and Lily." She held on to the saddle horn with one hand.

Ben nudged her calf.

His fingers touching her, even through the thick denim of her jeans, had her blood racing through her veins. She held her leg well out of his way while he adjusted the stirrup on the right and rounded the horse to adjust the left. When he had it positioned correctly, he guided her foot into the stirrup. Then he handed Kate the reins and stepped back.

Lucky danced to the side, setting loose a swarm of butterflies in Kate's belly. Now was the time to admit she hadn't ridden a horse in over ten years. But she clamped down hard on her bottom lip and held on for dear life.

Ben swung up in his saddle, turning the gelding all in one smooth motion, like he'd done this a thousand times before.

Since he'd grown up on a ranch, he probably had.

Her back ramrod-straight, Kate nudged Lucky with her heels and followed Eddy to the gate.

Ben covered the rear.

Eddy leaned down and pulled the lever, opening the gate.

Lucky bolted through and set off at a gallop.

Her heart in her throat, Kate pulled back on the reins, wishing she hadn't been so quick to say she'd ride out. No matter how hard she tugged on the leather straps, her efforts only slowed the mare marginally.

Ben and Eddy caught up to her before she'd gone far.

The ranch foreman passed her and led the way to the southwest corner of the ranch.

Ben and his gelding kept pace beside her.

"This is the first time you've been out to see what you now own?"

She nodded. The thought of all that she could see around her belonging to her seemed a bit overwhelming. "What do I do with all this?"

"That's why you hire people like Eddy to take care of the horses, cattle and whatever else you decide to raise."

"I've never been one to sit back and watch others do all the work. It bothers me to have Mrs. Henderson cooking meals and cleaning up after me. I've never had anyone wait on me. Not even my own mother." Kate stared at Eddy's back, wondering what it meant to be a working rancher and if she had what it took to do it.

"Ranching is hard work."

Kate sat up straight, though her tailbone was beginning to hurt. "I'm not afraid of hard work."

"It's twenty-four hours a day, three hundred and sixty-five days a year."

She smiled. "So is parenting."

"Lily needs a mother to take care of her."

"And I need to make this place operate at a rate that can support us. Otherwise, I'll have to find a job to support *it*. And out here in South Texas, I doubt there are jobs that pay enough to support a woman and her child, much less her ranch."

Ben touched the brim of his hat. "You have a point. Owning a ranch is a big responsibility. Are you sure you want to bite off that much?"

Kate frowned at him. "Now you're sounding like Deputy Schillinger. I'm not a quitter."

"What about the danger?"

"I'm not a quitter," she repeated, staring ahead at Eddy.

"What about Lily?"

Kate bit down on her bottom lip. That was the rub. Had it just been Kate, she'd have jumped in with both feet ready to rip into anyone stupid enough to try to run her off her land. Now she had a child to protect. And she had to give Lily a home.

Funny how, after only two days, she'd started thinking of the Flying K as home. Her home. Though she still didn't know much about the man who'd lived here, the man who'd been a big factor in bringing her into this world, she felt a tenuous connection to him and wished not once but a hundred times that she'd had the opportunity to know the man. "Lily needs a place to call home."

"Isn't home where the heart is? Wouldn't she be happy anywhere as long as she's with you?"

Anger bubbled up in her chest. "Are you trying to talk me into leaving?"

"No, I'm trying to figure out why you want to stay when all you've gotten out of it so far is threats and attacks."

As quickly as it rose, the anger ebbed away. "I've also made a new friend." She smiled. "And I met you." She glanced at him, her brows rising.

Ben's gaze remained forward as if he avoided hers. "That's not much of a bonus."

"I think so." She gave him a moment of silence before asking, "I understand we're a painful reminder of your family. But is it that bad that you still want to leave us?"

"Damn it, yes." His response startled the horse beneath him.

The gelding sidestepped, bumping into Kate's.

Ben's leg brushed against Kate's calf. He jerked the reins to the left and the horse danced away. But the brief contact had been enough to leave Kate's breath ragged, her hands shaking.

For a few long moments, Kate rode in silence, her heart hammering against her ribs. Ben wasn't afraid of evil men with guns. He feared her and Lily. It all made sense.

He'd lost his wife and daughter. Seeing Kate and Lily had to be tearing him apart. Kate's heart tightened as if someone had hold of it, squeezing mightily.

She'd lost a husband she'd loved with all her heart. Kate couldn't imagine losing her spouse and her daughter all at once. She doubted she'd be strong enough to go on living.

Ben was afraid to care again.

Eddy shouted and kicked his horse in the flanks. Black buzzards rose from the ground ahead, their huge wingspan filling the air, stirring dust into a cloud.

Relieved to have something else to concentrate on, Kate eased her horse forward, bringing the mare to a halt beside Eddy.

The stench of decaying flesh almost knocked her out of the saddle. Kate gasped and sucked in another lungful of the putrid air. She pulled her shirt up over her nose and breathed through the fabric.

Spread across the ground was the carcass of a black Angus steer, mostly picked over by the scavenger birds who'd located this meal.

Eddy and Ben dropped out of their saddles and squatted beside the dead animal.

"Whoever killed it used a knife." Ben pointed to the smooth edges of cut skin on what once had been the steer's throat.

Kate gagged and swallowed hard to keep from vomiting. She sucked in a deep breath through her shirt and let go of it. Then she grabbed the saddle horn, slipped her feet from the stirrup and slid down the horse's side, landing with a thump on her butt.

Ben was beside her, grasping her beneath her arms. "You all right?"

"I'm fine, except for my damaged pride." She stood and brushed the dirt from her hands and backside. "Who would have done this?"

"Considering they cut away the biggest chunks of meat, I'd say someone who was looking for a meal. *Madre de Dios.*" Eddy rattled off a couple sentences in Spanish before he shook his head and stood.

Ben was circling the dead animal. "There are footprints all around." After a moment he looked off into the brush to the south. "They lead toward the canyon."

"Shouldn't we follow them?"

Ben shook his head. "Only if you want to die."

A shiver rocked Kate's frame. "You think the people who killed this cow would shoot at us?"

"No, but they might slit your throat to keep you from disclosing their location."

"Oh." Kate wrapped her arms around her middle, the warmth of the day turning cool. "What now?"

Eddy looked out over the land. "We need to herd all the strays closer to the ranch house and barn where we can keep a closer watch on them."

"Doesn't that limit the amount of grazing?" Kate cast a glance at the dry land, where vegetation was sparse.

"Do you have a better suggestion?" Ben asked.

Kate stared across at Ben and Eddy. "We could call in the Customs and Border Protection and have them run interference until they get the drug trafficking under control."

"We'll report it," Ben said. "But getting the illegal activity under control won't happen overnight." He gathered his reins and led the gelding away from the dead steer. "In the meantime, we need to do like Eddy said. Otherwise you'll continue to lose cattle."

Eddy glanced at the sun tipping toward the horizon. "We can start tomorrow. It's getting late and we shouldn't be out here after dark."

Kate walked her mare a few steps away from the carnage and reached high for the saddle horn, dragging herself up enough to get her foot in the stirrup. At last she was able to sling her leg over the saddle. Proud she'd gotten up by herself, she almost cried when she noticed the reins hanging from the bit down to the ground.

A soft chuckle sounded beside her.

Ben walked across the dry ground, bent to retrieve the reins and handed them up to her without a word. That quirky smile almost made her want to kick him. At the same time it made her insides heat with want. She pushed aside her desire and focused on the next step.

The three of them rode back the way they'd come, with Eddy taking the lead again.

Halfway back to the barn, Ben shouted to Eddy, "Go on ahead. Kate and I are going to do a little target practice."

Eddy chuckled. "Can you wait until I get out of range? I prefer to remain in one piece."

"You bet." Ben reined in beside Kate and dropped to the ground. He grasped her around the waist and lifted her out of the saddle.

When she opened her mouth to protest, he covered her lips with a finger. "I know you can get down all by yourself. Just humor me. It'll be faster and you won't need to spend any more time with me than you have to."

She rested her hands on his shoulders as he let her slowly slide down the front of his body until her feet touched down. Kate clamped hard on her tongue, afraid she'd say what she really thought. That his hands on her waist had been deliciously sexy, the broad fingers spanning her middle, his muscles flexing and the ease with which he'd lifted her had left her breathless. But not nearly as air-deprived as the feel of his body against hers as she'd slid down him to her feet.

She'd do best to keep her mouth shut and get this lesson over with. The more time she spent alone with Ben, the more she couldn't imagine him leaving. Dangerous ground to be sure.

BEN REGRETTED LIFTING her from the saddle as soon as his hands closed around her. He compounded the regret by letting her body brush against his. Now all he wanted was to do it again, only this time for her to wrap her legs around his waist, her breasts pressing against his chest.

He pulled the Glock from his back waistband and checked the safety.

Kate stood with her back to him. She'd pulled the rubber band from her hair, letting it fall free around her shoulders. After she'd finger-combed it several times she gathered the long tresses in a bunch.

Ben shoved the pistol into his pocket and pushed Kate's hands aside, plucking the band from her fingers. In two quick motions he had the ponytail secured. His hands dropped to her arms, turning her to face him.

She blinked up at him, her lips parted, full and kissable. "You do that like a natural."

"Comes from having a daughter, much like Lily." His hands fell to his sides and he turned away.

He strode several feet away from Kate, needing the

distance to keep from pawing her like a teenager. His member strained against the tight confines of his denim jeans. God, he wanted the woman. Instead, he scanned the terrain, searching for a target.

"Kate," he called out.

She came to him, her hands twisting together, her brows just as knotted. "We can do this another day," she said.

"No, you need to know how to use that gun if you plan to keep it."

"Okay." Kate nodded. "Show me."

He handed her the Glock and wrapped her fingers around the grip, lacing one finger over the trigger.

Her body shook against him.

"Think of it as an extension of your arms." He helped her cup her trigger hand with the palm of her empty hand and raised her arms.

"Look down the barrel and line up the sight with the target."

"What am I aiming for?" she asked, holding the gun steady.

"See the prickly pear cactus there with the three lobes facing us?"

"Yes."

"Aim at the top center lobe. Once you have the sights lined up, press the trigger slowly."

Her pulse hammered through her veins. "Will it kick?"

"Not much."

"How much is not much?" she asked.

"Just shoot it and you'll find out."

She aimed the barrel toward the cactus, breathed in, then out, then closed her eyes and pulled the trigger.

The pop wasn't as loud as she'd expected and the kick wasn't bad at all. She focused on the cactus, noticing all three lobes remained intact. "Did I miss?"

"Yes, and you scared the crap out of me." He pushed his cowboy hat back on his head and circled behind her, his arms coming up on either side. "Let's do it again. Only this time, keep your eyes open."

Ben spooned her body with his, bringing his arms up on either side of hers. His hands closed around her fingers and he inhaled her unique scent of honeysuckle and citrus.

His groin tightened and he knew he was in trouble.

CHAPTER ELEVEN

BEN'S BREATH STIRRED the tendrils of hair hanging loose from her ponytail. Kate leaned her back against the solid wall of muscles that was her bodyguard cowboy. The warmth of his arms around her reassured and scared her all at once.

What would it be like to lie in his arms naked?

Her hands shook so badly, she thought she might drop the gun.

"Are you afraid?" he whispered.

Yes, yes, she was afraid. Afraid of falling in love with a stranger. Afraid of investing her emotions in someone who would leave as soon as the threat was neutralized. Afraid she and Lily would be heartbroken when the dust settled on the Flying K Ranch. "N-no," she lied, "I'm not afraid."

"Good. This time keep your eyes open and caress the trigger like a lover."

Holy shotgun blasts! Was he kidding her? All his words did was make her even more aware of the ridge of his fly pressing into her buttocks. She wanted to caress something, and it wasn't the trigger of her 9 mm Glock.

Perspiration beaded on her forehead. "Is it getting hotter?"

"You bet." His hand curved around her again. "Ready?"

Oh, hell, yes, but not for what he was thinking.

Focus, woman. Hell, how could she when she had the hottest cowboy in Texas wrapped around her?

Think of Lily. Images of her daughter brought Kate back to the real reason for her shooting lessons. Living alone on a ranch, she had to have the ability to protect herself and her daughter.

Her hand tightened around the grip and she forced air into and out of her lungs, focusing her concentration down the short barrel, lining up the sights with the target. Then, like Ben said, she stroked the trigger, keeping her eyes wide open.

The weapon kicked backward and Kate almost dropped it.

The acrid scent of burned gunpowder filled her nostrils and she blinked to clear her vision.

"I'll be damned." Ben leaned to her side and stared at her, his brows furrowed. "Are you sure you haven't done this before?"

"No." Dear God, his face was close enough to kiss. So much for maintaining focus on the lesson. "Why?" Her voice cracked and her body trembled.

"Take a look." He faced what was left of the cactus. The top, middle lobe had a hole blasted through it.

Kate squinted, afraid she was seeing things. Sure enough, there was a smooth round hole, dead center. A thrill of excitement rippled through her. "I did that?"

"You did." He chuckled. "I think you've taken me for a ride. How many times have you handled this gun?"

Kate shook her head, floored by her accuracy. "Other than using it to hit the intruder over the head the other night, never."

"I believe you have a promising career ahead of you as a sharpshooter or sniper."

"It was luck." Kate laughed shakily.

He nodded toward the cactus. "Do it again, only this time, aim for the right lobe." His hands fell to his sides and he backed away.

Standing alone, she didn't feel as confident or steady. But she also wasn't distracted by body contact. She looked down the barrel and lined up the right lobe in her sights.

"Remember…caress the trigger." Ben's words slid over her like melted chocolate in the dry Texas heat. Her hand tightened around the grip and the trigger and the weapon discharged.

Kate yelped. "Dang. I wasn't ready." She glanced at the cactus. "Did I hit anything?"

Ben chuckled. "The dirt in front of the plant."

Widening her stance, Kate glared at Ben. "I'm going to get this."

He nodded. "I have no doubt."

"Shh." This time her hands didn't quiver, her body didn't budge and the bullet nicked the lower corner of the lobe she'd aimed at. Her gaze shot to Ben. "Does that count?"

"If it had been a man, you most likely would have hit him where it would hurt him." Ben grinned. "That's good."

Kate couldn't look away. When Ben smiled, his entire face lit up and his blue eyes shone bright and clear. She tipped her head to the side. "I like it when you smile."

Immediately, his mouth straightened and he glanced away. "Adjust how you line up the sight based on where it hit last time, and keep practicing." Ben strode to where they'd tied the horses.

Kate took her time and fired again. The bullet bit into the top corner of the cactus lobe. Her concentration alternated between the target and Ben. He'd gone from happy to glum in seconds and it was driving her nuts.

"You know, it wouldn't kill you to smile more often." She cast a glance over her shoulder at the silent man.

He flipped the stirrup over the saddle on his horse and he tightened the girth before he muttered, "Have to have something to smile about."

"I heard that." Kate lined up the sights and squeezed off another round. The bullet pierced the center of the right lobe. Kate smiled and looked back at Ben, careful to point the nose of the pistol away from him. "How about waking up every day?"

"What about it?"

"Aren't you happy when you wake up every day?" Kate continued. "How can you be unhappy when the sun is shining?"

"The sunshine makes it incredibly hot out here in South Texas."

Kate fired off the remaining rounds in her ten-round magazine. Some of the shots went where they were supposed to, others hit the dirt in front of and behind the cactus plant, never touching it. When the last bullet was spent, she hit the magazine release button and caught the magazine before it hit the ground. The sun dipped low on the horizon, lengthening Kate's shadow.

She crossed to where Ben stood holding his horse's reins and stared up into his eyes.

The shadows were back and his jaw was tight, a muscle twitching in his left cheek.

Before she could overthink her reaction to his somber look, Kate smoothed her hand over the twitching muscle. "You must have loved her a lot."

Ben grabbed her wrist so fast, Kate cried out. "I loved Julia and I loved Sarah," he said, taking her gun in his other hand and tucking it back into his waistband. "But nothing I do now will bring them back. Nothing. They're gone."

His fingers hurt where he crushed her wrist, but Kate couldn't pull it free, nor could she back away from the intensity of his gaze.

"Julia and Sarah died, Ben." She pressed a hand to his chest. "But they never left you."

Silence settled like dust between them.

For a long moment, nothing stirred, neither one of them moved.

Then Ben yanked her hard against his chest, his lips crashing down over hers, his mouth claiming hers in a savage kiss. He let go of her wrist, one hand cupping the back of her head, the other clutching her bottom, grinding her pelvis against the hard ridge beneath his fly.

When he let her come up for air, his lips moved over hers, sliding along her chin. "I loved my wife."

"Yes, you did. But you didn't die with her."

"I know, damn it." He grabbed her arms and shook her. "I should have."

"No, Ben. You're still here for a reason."

His head whipped up. "What for? To punish me for failing to protect them?" He shoved her away from him. "I wasn't there for them."

"You didn't kill them."

"I could have stopped him."

"You couldn't be everywhere. He'd have found a way."

Ben stalked away, breathing hard, his face a ruddy red.

Kate's heart squeezed so hard in her chest, she thought she might have a heart attack. The anguish in Ben's face, the agony in his tone, ripped her apart.

"We need to go. It's getting dark."

When Ben passed her to get to his horse, Kate touched his arm.

He shook off her hand. "Don't." His glare scorched her.

Kate flinched, drawing back her hand as if he'd burned it. "I'm sorry. I shouldn't have brought it up."

He snorted and swung up into the saddle without offering her a leg up.

Kate managed to mount on her own, struggling to keep Ben's anger and withdrawal from bringing her all the way down. The man had some issues.

Hell, so did she. Only she'd had four years to work through them. Two years and a wake-up call in the form of Kate and Lily hadn't been enough time to lessen Ben's loss. He was still mourning his wife and child and nothing Kate could do or say would mend that kind of broken heart.

As Kate turned her mare north toward the house, a light blinked from the south. A shot of adrenaline raced through her system and she tugged hard on Lucky's reins, wheeling her around to face south again.

"Did you see that?" Kate glanced over her shoulder at Ben.

Lucky jerked her head and whinnied, trying to get Kate to turn back toward the barn.

Ben was already a few yards north when he reined in and twisted in his saddle. "See what?"

"A light." Kate pointed. "Out there."

Ben urged his horse around and came to a halt beside Kate. "Where?"

As dusk settled in around Kate, her eyes adjusted to the darkness. A flash of light blinked on, then off, a tiny pinprick on the horizon. "There." She gathered her reins. "Should we go check it out?"

Ben studied the light. "No."

"But—" The light grew more steady, pointed directly at them.

"No, looks like they're headed this way and we don't have time to outrun them." He spun his horse and dug in his heels. "Come on."

Kate stared at the light a fraction of a second longer. It was getting bigger. Which meant Ben was right, the vehicle causing the light was headed their way. Whether it was friend or foe, Kate had no intention of sticking around to find out.

She swung Lucky around and took off after Ben and his gelding, letting Lucky have her head.

Ben raced across the ground, dodging cactus, sage and saw palmetto. When he came to a dry ravine, he reined in so fast, Kate's horse struggled to stop in time. Tire tracks led down the banks and back up the other side.

Ben was off his horse and reaching for her reins before Kate had time to think. "Why did we stop?"

"We won't make it back to the safety of the ranch before they catch up. We have to find a place to hide." He reached up, grabbed her around the waist and pulled her off the horse. "Hurry."

Ben took the reins of both the horses and ran down the banks, following the meandering creek bed.

Kate hurried after him, slipping and sliding on the loose gravel and rocks. "Do you think whoever is out there is dangerous?"

"You want to stick around and find out?" he said over his shoulder.

Kate closed her mouth, conserving her energy to keep up with Ben's headlong race down the wash.

When he came to a point where the creek bed curved north at a huge boulder, he tugged the horses behind the outcropping and tied their reins to a scrubby root. They were a good two hundred yards from the tracks. "Stay here."

Kate skidded to a halt, breathing hard. "Why? Where are you going?"

"Back to see who's trespassing." He turned and started back the way they'd come.

Kate laid a hand on his arm. "Not without me, you're not."

"It'll be dangerous."

"It's my land. I need to see what's going on." She let her hand slip down to his.

"It's safer staying clear." The darkness was settling in around them and the stars popped out of the sky one at a time.

Kate couldn't read the expression in Ben's eyes, but she wouldn't let him go without her. She dropped his hand and crossed her arms. "If you don't take me with you, I'll follow you anyway."

Ben sucked in a deep breath and let it out. "You're a stubborn woman."

"I've been known to be. Are you going to stand

around arguing or are we going to go and find a good place to hide closer to the road?"

"I don't like it."

She snorted. "So noted."

"Then stay behind me and keep quiet."

"Yes, sir." Kate popped a salute that was all but lost on him as he turned and jogged back down the creek bed, hunkering low so that he wouldn't be seen over the banks.

Kate followed, copying his technique, her heart pounding, her breathing erratic. What was she getting herself into?

All she knew was that she didn't want to be left behind while Ben risked his life to see what was going down on her ranch.

Light glinted above them, casting a beam over the top of their heads.

Ben came to a sudden stop and flung his arm out, catching her before she barreled past him. "We hide here."

He ducked behind a boulder no bigger than a sheep and dragged her down beside him. Ben pulled the Glock from the back of his jeans and handed it to Kate. "Don't use this unless I tell you to." He removed his 9 mm from his shoulder holster and held it in front of his face.

Kate's hand trembled. Sure she'd been practicing shooting, but the thought of pulling the trigger on a person...

Her shoulders stiffened, her resolve strengthening as she thought of Lily. She'd do whatever it took to protect the ones she loved.

The rumble of an engine grew louder and the light

brighter. Then it angled down the creek bank and came to a grinding halt, dust flying all around, forming a hazy glow in front of the truck. The driver turned the vehicle off and silence engulfed the scene.

As the dust settled, Kate peered at the back of the pickup. Four men perched on the sides, wielding what looked like automatic weapons, the type used by the military.

Kate gasped, then clamped a hand over her mouth and stared wide-eyed as one man hopped out, his feet crunching as he landed in the gravel. He stretched, his gun arm rising high into the night sky. He said something in Spanish and the driver responded.

Another man, brandishing a similar weapon, dropped down and shone a flashlight in a wide beam around the pickup, turning it slowly toward the position where Kate and Ben lay.

Ben whispered, "Close your eyes."

Kate squeezed them shut and ducked her head low behind the boulder.

The crunch of gravel grew louder. Kate fought her instinct to look up and see how close the men had come, but she was afraid that if she looked, the flashlight would glint off her eyes and give away their position.

"Brille la luz aquí!" a voice shouted closer than Kate had imagined.

Ben pressed his lips to her ear. "Don't move," he whispered.

He didn't have to worry. She froze, holding her breath, waiting for the men to move away.

Light shone on either side of the boulder.

Then a loud bang blasted through the night and

kicked up dust around where Kate hovered. She bit hard on her tongue to keep from crying out.

Footsteps crunched closer and then a heavily accented voice called out. *"Serpiente para cenar!"*

Men laughed and the light bobbed skyward.

The footsteps moved away.

Kate let go of the breath she'd been holding and dared to peer around the side of the boulder.

One man had his gun slung over his shoulder and he held a long fat snake out to the side, speaking in rapid Spanish. The driver and the other gunmen laughed.

The crackle of a radio broke through their merriment and the driver responded to the call. When he finished, he waved a hand out the window. *"Vayamos!"*

The snake man dropped the reptile and leaped over the side of the pickup. The other men leaped in beside him. The truck pulled up the other side of the wash as another set of lights crested the bank behind them and dipped down into the creek.

In that one instant the light from the second vehicle illuminated the truck in front of it. Kate could see into the first truck's bed.

Huddled low and holding on to one another were several women and young girls.

One cried out.

One of the gunmen slapped the girl. *"Silencio!"*

Kate lurched forward, her heart lodged in her throat.

Ben captured her arm and dragged her back to the ground. "Don't move." He pushed her back to the ground and started to get up himself.

This time she caught his arm and held on to Ben. "There's too many of them."

"Alto!" The gunman with the flashlight shone the

beam over the creek bed for a long moment, the light hovering over the top of the small boulder.

Kate ground her teeth and fought her instinct to leap out and scratch the man's eyes out who'd slapped the girl. But even she knew it would be crazy. They outnumbered Kate and Ben and outgunned their two pistols. Taking a stand would be suicide.

After a moment, the gunman waved the driver on and the truck topped the incline and pulled away. The second truck lumbered down into the ravine and up the other side, revealing the back filled with four more gunmen and from the dark forms hunkered low in the bed, another load of people.

Ben lay still for a long time, even after the second truck exited the creek and moved off across the desert.

"Why didn't we stop them?"

"My duty is to protect you. We were outnumbered. The best we can do is get back to the ranch and report this to the Customs and Border Protection."

"But those women and the girls…" Kate stood and brushed the dust off her jeans.

"Coyotes would just as soon kill them, ditch them and save their own butts." Ben headed back down the creek bed toward where they'd stashed the horses.

Kate was left to follow, wishing with all her heart she could have done more to protect the frightened people in the back of the trucks.

Ben untied the horses, bent to give her a boost up and swung up into his saddle without speaking another word.

They hurried across the dried grasses, dodging cacti and stumpy palmetto palms illuminated by the sparkling blanket of stars in the sky.

"Do you think they could be the people responsible for killing the steer?" Kate called out over the thrumming of horses' hooves.

"Probably."

"We should have stopped them."

Ben shot a glance her way. The moon had begun to rise, reflecting light off Ben's eyes. "The only way we'd go back out there at night is with a full contingent of soldiers and the Customs and Border Protection agents leading the way. Even then, *you're* not going out there."

A chill gave her gooseflesh as she recalled the guns every one of the men carried.

Ben urged his horse into a gallop, cutting off any further conversation.

Kate dug her heels into her horse's flanks, her gaze panning the horizon, searching for the lights of the two vehicles. Her breathing returned to normal only after the glowing windows of the ranch house came into view.

They rode up to the gate at full gallop.

Eddy stood ready, swinging the gate open for them. "You two are in a hurry. Run into trouble?"

"Two trucks full of gunmen and people." Ben dropped down off his gelding. "We had to lay low until they passed."

"You did right getting back here." Eddy nodded toward his horse. "I was getting worried and was about to come out searching for you."

Kate led her horse into the barn. Before Ben or Eddy could offer to help, she'd flipped her stirrup up over the saddle and loosened the girth. Not so hard. She could get used to riding the range and checking on cattle.

When it came time to haul the saddle off the horse,

Kate tugged, expecting it to be difficult. But she pulled too hard and the saddle slid right off, the weight sending her flying back.

Ben's arms circled her waist, steadying her.

Kate leaned into him for a moment, appreciating the solid muscles and the earthy scent of a man who'd been working with horses. She could get used to having him around.

Kate pushed away. "We need to get up to the house and call the CBP." She ducked around Ben and hurried to deposit the saddle in the tack room before she did something stupid…again.

Brush in hand, Eddy stood beside Kate's mare. "I'll take care of the horses. You two head on up to the house."

"Thanks." Ben hooked Kate's arm and led her out of the barn and up to the house.

She was kind of glad to have him so close. After hiding from gunmen, the night's shadows caused her a lot more heebie-jeebies than ever before. Before she'd seen the two truckloads of coyotes and women, Kate had been more than ready to call this place home and make a stand for the land her father left for her and Lily. But now…

Kate and Ben only made it halfway across the yard when Lily burst through the screen door and raced down the steps. "Mommy!"

Ben let Kate's arm drop. "I'll make the call."

"Thanks." Kate gathered Lily up in a bear hug and swung her around. "How's my sweetie pie?" She held the child longer than normal and inhaled the scent of baby shampoo. An image of the women and girls in the backs of those trucks had been indelibly etched in her memory. She couldn't imagine being so desperate she'd subject Lily to the danger of stealing across the border in the middle of the night with men who'd just as soon take the money and leave them for dead.

"We made cookies. I found a horny toad, but it got away. Pickles piddled in the hall twice and he's asleep now." Lily glanced over Kate's shoulder at the barn. "Can I ride a horse?"

"Not now, baby."

"When?"

"Another day." A day when Kate felt more comfortable about the horse she'd be riding, and after they found the gunmen traversing her land and jailed them where they couldn't traffic humans or drugs ever again. Maybe then she could be more certain about making the Flying K their home forever.

"Come see our cookies." Lily wiggled out of Kate's arms and ran for the house.

Kate followed Ben and Lily into the house.

Once inside, Ben headed for the hallway.

Kate entered the kitchen where Lily showed her the cookies she'd made with Mrs. Henderson and Cara Jo.

Cara Jo was stacking cooled cookies in the cookie jar. "I'm so glad you two made it back when you did. I was about to call the sheriff."

"I'll tell you about it after Lily is in bed." Kate glanced around. "Where's Mrs. Henderson?"

"Her husband picked her up an hour ago."

"Thanks for staying with Lily. I owe you."

"I enjoyed it as much as I think she did."

"Now, let me see if these cookies are edible." Kate grabbed a cookie from the pile and bit into it, her empty stomach rumbling. "Oh, yes. They are wonderful. Snickerdoodles?" she asked.

Lily laughed. "How did you know?"

"My mother used to make these." Tears welled in her eyes at the memory of her mother and the weekends they'd spent making cookies and hanging out when she was little like Lily. At times like this, she missed her so much it hurt.

Kate glanced at the clock. "Holy smokes, it's way past your bedtime, young lady."

"I already had my bath. Miss Cara Jo let me stay up until you got home so that I could show you the cookies."

Cara Jo winced. "I hope you don't mind. She was so excited."

Kate shook her head. "Not at all. But now it's time for bed."

Lily danced ahead of Kate. "Can Miss Cara Jo read a book to me?"

"I'm sure she would like to get home sometime tonight and it's a long way back to town."

Lily grabbed one of Kate's hands and one of Cara Jo's and looked up at them both with her wide green eyes. "Please?"

Cara Jo laughed. "I'd love to and it'll give you a chance to wash up and have dinner."

"You're sure?"

"Absolutely." She swung Lily's arm. "Lily and I are best buds, aren't we? Why don't you grab Pickles and let's get her settled in her box upstairs."

Lily chased Pickles down the hallway and up the stairs.

Kate hugged her new friend. "Thanks, Cara Jo."

"Really, Kate. I love Lily, she's a great kid." Cara Jo climbed the stairs behind Lily, leaving Kate at the bottom.

Ben slipped up beside her. "I made the call. They're sending out a chopper to see if they can locate the trucks."

Kate faced him, her heartbeat speeding up at his proximity. Why did this man she'd only known a very short time have that kind of pull on her? "Any chance they'll find them?"

"The trucks have a big head start in the amount of time it took us to ride back to the ranch." He shrugged. "They could be just about anywhere by now."

Kate rested her hand on the banister and stared up the stairs, her heart heavy. "Do you think they're help-ing illegal immigrants or trafficking women?" Kate gazed into Ben's eyes.

His brows dipped low and a muscle jerked in his jaw. "As far as I could see, there were only women and girls in those trucks."

"Dear Lord." Kate sagged and her stomach roiled. "We should have stopped them."

"No. We were outnumbered and not as heavily armed." Ben gripped her arms and turned her toward him. "Let the Border Patrol deal with it. They have the resources and the weapons necessary to handle the coyotes. Had we intervened, we would only have made matters worse."

"Still…"

"Have faith in the CBP."

"Do you?"

Ben's lips tightened. "At this point, I have to. I have to focus on you. I can't risk your life chasing after bad guys." He turned and would have walked away, but Kate put a hand on his arm.

"Ben, what happened out there?"

"What do you mean?"

"Between us." She stopped, her gaze dropping to where her hand touched his arm. "Before the coyotes... The kiss."

He stiffened, drawing up to his full height. "What happened out there...shouldn't have. I won't let it happen again."

Kate braced her palms on his chest. The solid muscles beneath his shirt made her long to run her fingers across his naked skin. "I shouldn't have encouraged it. But..."

"It won't happen again. I'm here to protect you and Lily. Nothing more." He backed away, his tone brooking no more argument, his face set in stone.

Kate tucked her hands in her pockets to keep them from shaking. She wanted to say more, to tell him she'd felt his response, he wasn't immune to her. Instead, she turned and walked up the stairs.

IT TOOK ALL of Ben's self-control to keep from going up the stairs after Kate. He wanted her so badly it hurt and the turmoil it was causing inside him was more than he could stand.

Kate was as different from Julia as night from day. She'd already proved she wasn't afraid of anything. When the gunmen had shot so close to them, Kate hadn't fallen apart like a lot of women would have. She'd held steady and stayed low.

He wondered what Julia would have done. What she had done when she and his daughter had been...

Ben's breath lodged in his throat when he realized he couldn't even remember Julia's face. He closed his eyes, but all he could see was light auburn hair, glinting like copper in the sun.

Ben stepped out onto the porch.

Eddy was coming up from the barn. "I have the horses settled in for the night and gave them an extra section of hay."

"Thanks."

Eddy climbed the steps and stood beside Ben, staring out into the night as he rocked back on his boot heels. "Well, I'll be heading home unless you think I need to stay."

"No. Go on home. I'll take it from here."

"Think she'll stay?"

Ben didn't have to ask who Eddy was talking about. "Kate's a pretty determined woman."

Eddy nodded. "If she's anything like her father, she won't give up easily."

No, she wouldn't, but in this case, maybe she should. The situation was too dangerous.

"I'll be goin'. *Buenas noches.*" Eddy climbed into his pickup and drove away, leaving behind him a deep silence.

Darkness closed in around Ben as he crossed to the barn, checked inside, made a pass around the outside and the perimeter of the other outbuildings.

When he was satisfied there were no intruders, he climbed the steps to the house and went straight to his room. He grabbed fresh jeans and a clean shirt and ducked into the bathroom down the hall.

When he emerged, he peeked in at Lily, who lay

sound asleep, her puppy in a box beside her bed, also asleep.

Sounds from the kitchen drew him down the stairs when he should have gone straight to bed.

Kate stood with her back to him at the kitchen counter, wearing a worn T-shirt and frayed denim shorts, and she was barefoot. Her hair hung in limp, wet strands, dampening the back of her shirt. "You can wash your hands in the sink, here. Your plate will be ready in a moment."

Knowing it was a mistake, yet unable to help himself, he crossed to the sink and stood beside her. He squirted dish soap onto his fingers and cleaned his already clean hands. He couldn't resist any excuse to be closer to her.

As he dried his hands, she smiled at him.

"Sit. Cara Jo left after reading two books to Lily. Mrs. Henderson left the best roast beef and potatoes you've ever tasted warming in the oven. I'll have a plate full for you in two shakes."

Kate stood within reach and, if he was right, she wasn't wearing a bra. Dear God, he wanted her.

Ben swallowed hard and backed up several steps. "I'm not hungry." For food.

When she turned with a heaping plate in one hand and a glass of iced tea in the other, she frowned. "No argument. You need to eat." She set the plate and glass on the table and pointed at the chair. "Sit."

Too tired to argue, or maybe just too tired to fight it, he sat in the designated chair. Two candles stood in the middle of the table with a box of matches beside them. Ben struck the tip of a match against the matchbox and applied the flame to the wick.

"Sorry, forgot the silverware." Kate dived for a drawer, pulling out a knife, fork and spoon. She hit the light switch on the wall, plunging the room into an intimate hazy glow.

She returned to his side and leaned over him to place the utensils beside his plate.

He couldn't take anymore. He grabbed her around the waist and sat her in his lap. "Do you have any idea what you're doing to me?"

Her eyes widened, her mouth opened in an O, and her cheeks turned a pretty pink. She sucked in a breath and let it out, her blush deepening. "Based on where I'm sitting, I could hazard a pretty good guess."

"Damn it, Kate, I promised it wouldn't happen again."

She sighed. "Some promises were meant to be broken." Her gaze dropped to his lips.

Her words, the way she said them, and that shift of her attention was his undoing. "What am I supposed to do with you? You set me on fire."

Her lips turned upward and she smiled. "Burn, baby, burn."

Laughter rumbled up inside him. He fought the happiness, fought to control a surge of hope. In the end, he lost and grasped her cheeks between his hands, kissing her like she was the buoy that would bring him back to the surface of the sea of sorrow he'd been wallowing in since Sarah's and Julia's deaths.

Her fingers pried loose the buttons on the front of his shirt, one by one. She didn't break the kiss until the last button was freed.

Ben's hands slipped beneath her shirt and up her back. As he'd suspected, she wasn't wearing a bra.

Heat rushed to his loins, his member straining against his fly.

Kate shoved the shirt over his shoulders and down his arms.

Ben's fingers slid along her sides and upward to cup her breasts. When his fingers found the taut nipples, he paused. "Lily?"

"Will sleep until morning." She kissed his chin, her lips sliding downward to caress his neck, her breasts pressing into his palms.

Even the child conspired against Ben. With nothing but his memories standing in his way, Ben lost the fight. He shrugged the shirt off his arms and lifted the hem of Kate's T-shirt up and over her head, flinging it across the table. Then he lifted her, spreading her legs wide to straddle his hips. In the soft candlelight he gazed down at her, drinking her in like a man dying of thirst.

"Don't stop now." She raised his hand to her breast. "I'm not good at starting over. I married my high school sweetheart. I don't know how to flirt. I never had any practice."

"You're doing a hell of a job." He rolled her rosy nipples between his thumbs and forefingers.

Her back arched, her hair slipping down to her waist, curling as it dried.

"You should eat." She gasped as he took one nipple between his teeth and nipped.

"I am."

"Food, silly." Her fingers wrapped around his head and held him where he was, her thighs tightening against his sides.

"The only thing I'm hungry for is you." He stood,

bringing her up with him, wrapping her thighs around his middle.

Her arms circled his neck as she spread kisses along the column of his throat.

Ben carried her up the stairs to her bedroom, kicking the door open softly so as not to disturb Lily and Pickles.

He set her on her feet and stripped her shorts down her long legs.

Kate stood for a moment, bathed in moonlight peeking through the window. Her tongue swept across her lips, her gaze traveling over him and downward. "You're a bit overdressed." Her fingers closed around the metal rivet of his jeans. She pushed it through the hole and slid the zipper downward, slowly, her fingers brushing against his erection.

Past rational thought, he swung Kate up into his arms and, one-handed, flung back the comforter.

About to lay her against the sheets, he paused.

A movement out of the corner of his eye and a dry rattling sound shot adrenaline through him and he jumped back.

"What? Oh, my God!" Kate clung to him, her arms clamped around his neck, her gaze on the bed. "Is that what I think that is?"

Coiled against the cool white sheets was the biggest rattlesnake Ben had ever encountered. And it was angry.

CHAPTER TWELVE

KATE STIFLED A SCREAM as she clung to Ben, holding her arms and legs as far away from the snake as she could. She'd have crawled over Ben's body and run if he hadn't been gripping her so tightly. "Do something," she cried.

Ben chuckled, struggling to maintain his hold on her squirming body. "I have to put you down before I can take care of the snake." He strode to the door. "Turn on the light."

Kate flipped the light switch.

The snake on the bed rattled again, perhaps angry at having his sleep disturbed.

Kate shot a glance all around them, searching for friends of the snake in her bed. The floor appeared clear of any other slithering creatures. "Put me down."

Ben dropped her feet to the floor and steadied her. "Are you okay?"

She crossed her arms over her breasts. "No. There's a snake in my bed. A poisonous one at that."

"You can wait in the hall if you like."

"No." She didn't want to leave Ben's side. If anyone could handle a tough situation, it was Ben. "What are you going to do?"

"Get rid of the snake," he said, his tone matter-of-fact.

"How?"

He didn't answer. Instead he approached the end of the bed, careful to stay out of striking range of the big rattler. He pulled the top sheet and comforter completely off the bed and shook them.

Nothing fell out.

Kate lunged for the sheet and shook it again, before wrapping it around her body.

Ben eased the elastic corners of the fitted sheet off the end of the bed. Circling wide, he repeated the process on the other end of the bed, then he gathered the ends and pulled them together quickly before the snake could slither out and onto the floor.

Carrying the fitted sheet like a bag, he held it away from his body and descended the stairs.

Kate followed, checking the floor before she took every step. She stopped at the top of the stairs, shivering in the air-conditioning.

Ben continued down, stepping out the front door onto the porch. "I'll be back. Don't touch anything until I can check your room over."

Kate held her breath until Ben returned, letting it out as he appeared again in the doorway.

"The snake?"

He closed the door and glanced up at her. "Dead."

Kate heaved a sigh. "Thank God." Then her heart thumped against her ribs. "Lily." She dashed into her daughter's room, slapping the light switch on the wall.

Ben burst through the doorway behind Kate.

Kate gathered Lily up in her arms and held her while Ben checked her bedding and room thoroughly.

"Mommy?"

"Shh, baby. Go back to sleep."

Pickles whined in his box.

"Can Pickles sleep with me?" she asked, her voice groggy, a fist rubbing over her eyes.

"No, baby. Pickles has his own bed."

"I want Pickles to sleep—" A huge yawn interrupted Lily's protest. She snuggled down in Kate's arms and fell back to sleep.

The puppy turned around in his box three times and dropped down, his head draped over his paws.

Ben straightened the bedding and waited for Kate to lay the child down. Afterward, he tucked the sheets around Lily and pressed a kiss to her forehead.

Kate swallowed hard on a knot in her throat.

Ben had kissed Lily, the gesture so natural and right it took Kate's breath away.

When he straightened, his gaze met hers. He nodded toward the door.

Kate stepped out into the hallway, tugging the sheet up securely over her breasts, embarrassed about her behavior. She'd more or less encouraged Ben to make love to her. Hell, she'd practically thrown herself at him. Her cheeks burning, she pulled the door halfway closed and turned toward her bedroom.

Two steps in that direction and she stopped, a huge tremor shaking her so hard her teeth rattled.

Ben's hands settled on her bare shoulders. "What's wrong?"

"I can't go back in there."

"I'll check it out."

"Thanks, but it won't make a difference. I won't be sleeping in there tonight."

"I've disposed of the snake."

"Yeah, but you can't take the image out of my head."

"You can sleep in my room."

"No. You need your sleep more than I do."

"We both need sleep." He cupped her elbow with his warm, strong palm and led her past Lily's room to his.

Once inside the doorway, Kate stopped and stared at the four-poster bed, images of a naked Ben flashing through her mind. "No. I can't do it."

"I'll sleep on the couch downstairs."

"I can sleep on the couch."

"And if something happened to you downstairs, I might not hear anything."

Kate trembled. "I just won't sleep then."

"Don't be ridiculous. Take the bed." He urged her forward, stripped the comforter back and checked the sheets. "See? No snake."

A shiver racked her body yet again. "I can't get that rattler out of my mind. I almost crawled into bed with a snake." She shivered again.

He shoved a hand through his hair. "If it helps, I'll stay with you until you go to sleep."

She glanced at him, her brows pulling downward. "What we were about to do…"

"Don't worry. I'll only stay until you go to sleep. Nothing else."

"I don't know."

"For crissakes." Ben scooped her up in his arms and tossed her on the bed. "Go to sleep before I forget myself again." He turned his back on her and paced the floor.

Kate adjusted the sheet around her body and moved to the farthest side of the bed. "And I'm supposed to sleep while you pace?" She shook her head.

He stopped and shoved a hand through his hair.

The button on his fly remained undone, the zipper halfway down.

Despite her best promise to herself, Kate's gaze zeroed in on the dark hairs peeking through. The shivers of dread for the snake changed to the shivers of the kind of excitement she'd felt before the snake had come on scene.

Her gaze rose to capture Ben's, staring down at her.

He groaned. "I can't do this."

"Then don't." Kate fluffed the comforter, checking beneath it one more time before she settled in, her eyes wide. She turned her back to Ben and feigned sleep. After a moment or two, a sensation of something crawling across her leg made her sit up in the bed and drag her legs up to her chin. She shook the blanket again. Nothing fell out or slithered across the bed.

Kate peered over the top of her sheet-covered knees. "Why are you still standing there? The couch is downstairs. I don't need you." Her voice trailed off. The hell she didn't need him. It was destined to be a long, scary night.

His hand rose to the light switch. "Want me to turn out the light?"

Her hand went up immediately. "No!"

Ben sighed, crossed the room and sat on the edge of the bed.

"What are you doing?"

"Going out of my mind. What does it look like?" He swung his legs, jeans and all up onto the bed. "Come here." Ben gathered her in his arms, pulling her body up against his. "Go to sleep."

"I can't."

"Yes, you can. Close your eyes and picture Lily playing with her puppy."

Snuggled against Ben, one hand resting on his bare chest, Kate tried. Instead of her daughter, all she could imagine was trailing that hand across his taut muscles, finding and pinching the hard little brown nipples.

She closed her eyes, inhaling the fresh, clean scent of soap and man. Her hand slipped over a rib, then another, inching south to the waistband of his jeans.

Ben captured her hand. "This can only lead to one thing."

"You think?"

In a flash, he shoved her onto her back, pinning her wrists above her head. "I loved my wife, Kate. I don't need another woman in my life."

"Then why are you lying on top of me." Her gaze met his unflinchingly. She arched her back, her pelvis rubbing against the hard ridge beneath his jeans. "And why are you so aroused?"

He closed his eyes, his breath coming in short, ragged pants. Then his mouth descended on hers. His hands found the edge of the sheet over her breasts and yanked it downward, peeling it from her body, until she lay naked and trembling. Not out of fear, but in anticipation of what would come next.

She raised a hand to his zipper, sliding it lower until his erection sprang free, hard and straight.

"I didn't want this to happen," he said through gritted teeth.

"So noted." Kate's hand circled him, sliding along his length, dipping inside the denim to cup him, massaging his member. "What are you going to do about it?"

He leaped from the bed and stood with his back to her, breathing hard.

She rose behind him, her hands caressing a path, curving around his shoulders, down his sides to his narrow hips. Kate circled around to his front, beyond caring what he thought of her brazen behavior, beyond patient…ready to take him inside her.

She wanted him to fill the void she'd been living with for so long.

Kate pushed his jeans over his hips and down his legs, her hands caressing his buttocks, his thighs and the sharply defined calves.

He stepped free of the denim and threaded his hands in her hair, dragging her to her feet.

She let him, her body sliding up his, skin-to-delicious-skin. Every nerve ending burned, fire radiating from her core outward.

He cupped the back of her thighs and lifted her, wrapping her legs around his waist. "Stop me now."

"I can't." She wove her fingers into his hair, dragging his head downward until their lips met. "I need you."

His member nudged her opening, the tip sliding in. "Wait."

"Really?" Her thighs tightened around him, lifting her up.

"I have protection in the nightstand…by the bed." He groaned and lifted her off him, laying her across the bed, her legs draped over the side.

Kate reached into the drawer and removed a strip of foil-packaged condoms. She tore the packet open with her teeth and rolled the condom over him, her hand cupping him at the base.

Ben stepped between her legs, grabbed her wrists and pinned them over her head, his erection poised at her entrance. "You make me hotter than the Texas sun."

"That makes two of us, then." She wrapped her legs around his waist and tightened, driving him in.

He slid all the way inside, the smooth, slick sensations so erotic, he threw his head back and drew in a deep, steadying breath.

Then he pulled back out and slammed in again, settling into a fast, smooth rhythm.

As the friction increased, heat built and tingling sensations rippled through Kate's body. Her back arched off the bed, her thighs clenching with each thrust until she pitched over the edge, crying out his name.

His fingers dug into her hips as he plunged in one last time. Ben held steady, his face tense, his muscles bunched and his member throbbing against her channel.

As they tumbled back to the earth, Kate's legs disengaged from around his waist and dropped over the side of the bed.

Ben eased her up on the mattress and lay beside her, spooning her body with his.

"Stay with me?" she begged.

His hand rested on her naked hip. "As long as there are no regrets in the morning."

She sighed. "No regrets." Kate snuggled in his arms, feeling more safe and secure than she had since her husband left for war. If only she could count on this to last.

Sadly, she knew she couldn't.

A single tear slid down her cheek and dropped onto the sheet. How could a man come to mean so much to her in such a short time? Was she desperate for male companionship? Or was it *this* man that made her feel this way?

It didn't matter. When his replacement came, Ben would leave. She'd be on her own again.

But for now, he kept the boogeyman and the snakes away while warming her backside.

Kate closed her eyes and fell asleep.

BEN LAY FOR a long time, his arms around Kate's naked body, holding her like they belonged together. Making love to a woman had that effect on him. That had to be the explanation for his sudden desire to stay with her, to become a part of her and Lily's lives.

But that wouldn't be fair to either one of them. He'd had a wife and daughter. He'd loved them both so much it still hurt to think about them. How could he begin to love someone else as much? He couldn't. It wasn't possible. Was it?

Kate stirred against him, her bottom brushing sensitive areas, stirring desire so strong he couldn't suppress it.

He'd asked Hank to find his replacement. What if he did? Could Ben walk away and leave Kate in the hands of someone else? Could he trust that other agent to take care of Kate and Lily, to protect them from whoever was after them?

His arms tightened around Kate, his chest squeezing tight. He couldn't desert them. Not now. Not when they needed him most.

The sound of a puppy's cries pulled Ben from his thoughts. Pickles had to be missing his mother.

Ben slipped out of the bed and stood, gazing down at

Kate as she lay deep in sleep, caressed by the moonlight streaming through the window. Her long hair looking more auburn in this light as it splayed across the pillow, her lips parted as if she fell asleep whispering.

Ben brushed a strand of hair from her cheek and bent to press his lips to hers.

"Sweet dreams."

He slipped into his jeans and zipped them, then padded barefoot to the next room.

Lily lay splayed across her bed, her foot dangling over the side.

Pickles looked up at Ben, his soulful blue eyes begging Ben to rescue him from his grief and loneliness.

Ben scooped up the puppy and the box and headed down the stairs to the couch. He understood how Pickles felt. Torn from the ones he loved, but surrounded by the possibility of a new family.

In the night, everything seemed more overwhelming than during the light of day.

As he lay on the couch, his feet hanging over the arms, Ben cuddled the puppy against him and turned over the day's events in his mind.

Two things stood out, touching him with a cold hand of dread.

A gang of coyotes was using the Flying K as a place to traffic human cargo.

Secondly, that snake hadn't gotten into Kate's bed on its own. Someone had put it there.

CHAPTER THIRTEEN

KATE YAWNED, STRETCHED and glanced around her room, disoriented at first. Her tender breasts rubbed against the sheet and she remembered where she was—in Ben's bed—and that she was naked.

"Mommy?" Lily called out.

Kate scrambled to her feet, wondering where Ben had gone. She had just wrapped the sheet around her body when Lily ran by the open door.

"Mommy?"

Her frightened cry spurred Kate forward. "Lily, I'm here."

Lily stopped at the top of the stairs and looked back. "Where's Pickles? He's not in his box."

Kate smiled and shrugged, relieved her daughter hadn't asked why she was in a different room and wrapped in a sheet. "I don't know. Let me get dressed and I'll help you find him."

"Lily?" Ben's deep voice echoed up the stairs.

Kate moved to peer over the banister railing at the man.

He stood barefoot, wearing nothing but his jeans. The sight of his naked chest sent Kate's pulse skittering into crazy palpitations. An image of herself lying naked with him spread warmth throughout her body, and extra fire to one place in particular.

He shot a heated glance at her before he held the puppy up for Lily to see. "I have Pickles down here."

"Pickles." Lily ran down the stairs, her hand trailing along the railing, wild, light red hair flying out around her shoulders.

A sharp tug in the region of her heart made Kate press a hand to her chest. How like a family they were. She had to remind herself that it was nothing but an illusion. A fantasy bubble destined to pop when life returned to normal.

Ben handed Lily the puppy. "I've already taken him outside. He should play all right inside for a few minutes. Stay in the house, please."

"I will." Lily set the puppy on the floor and ran into the living room, squealing as Pickles chased after her, barking in his shrill puppy voice.

Which left Ben staring up at Kate. He stepped up one of the stair risers. "How are you this morning?"

Kate gathered the sheet around her body, a flush of warmth burning up her neck into her cheeks. "I'm fine."

He climbed two more steps, his gaze pinning hers. "Any regrets?"

Her eyes widened, her heart pounding so hard, she could hear it banging against her eardrums. "No regrets." She swallowed hard and forced herself to ask, "And you?"

When Ben cleared the top step and stood with her on the landing, Kate stepped away until her back bumped against the wall.

"None." Ben advanced slowly. When he stopped, barefoot and toe to toe with her, he reached out and touched the rise of her breasts above the sheet. "Seems you were wearing this last night."

A smile fluttered across her lips, shyness weighing on her words. "I think I need a new outfit."

"I kind of like this one." His fingers tugged on the end, untucking the edges.

Kate inhaled, her breasts rising as Ben unfolded the sheet, exposing her body to his piercing gaze.

"Oh, yes. I like this outfit." He bent, capturing a nipple between his teeth, nipping lightly.

Kate's hands feathered through his hair, pressing against the back of his neck. She closed her eyes, letting the rampant waves of desire swarm over her.

"Mommy?" Lily's voice brought her back to earth with a jolt.

Kate jerked the sheet closed, stepped around Ben and leaned over the railing. "What is it, Lily?"

"Pickles had an accident."

A chuckle rose up her throat. "I'll be down in a moment to help you clean it up." When she turned toward her bedroom, Ben blocked her path. She blinked up at him. "You heard Lily, the puppy had an acci—"

Ben lifted her chin with a crooked finger and kissed her hard, his tongue darting out to capture hers in a brief caress.

As quickly as he'd possessed her, he let her go. "I'll take care of the puppy." Then he left her on the landing and padded down the steps, entering the living room in search of Lily.

Kate stood still for several seconds, unable to get her bearings. Hell, she'd been unable to form coherent thoughts since Ben had come into her life. If she wasn't careful, she'd fall in love with a man who still loved his dead wife. And where would that leave her?

Kate eased into her bedroom, on the lookout for anything that slithered or rattled. The room remained silent as she dressed for the day in jeans, a white button-down shirt and cowboy boots. She pulled out the key her father's attorney had given her at the reading of the will and decided it was time to look for whatever it belonged to.

Perhaps when she found the lock, it would unveil the reason why someone wanted her off the property and away from Wild Oak Canyon.

As Kate gathered her ponytail in place, corralling her wild curls with a rubber band, the telephone at the bottom of the stairs rang. She decided to forgo makeup. It wasn't as if she was trying to impress anyone. Certainly not Ben. He wasn't sticking around. What had happened last night wasn't the stuff relationships were made of. Ben was a bodyguard. Kate was the job. When she no longer needed his protection, he'd be gone.

If she was smart, she'd discontinue this sex-only connection with the bodyguard. It wasn't fair to her, to Lily or to him.

With a deep breath, she hurried down the stairs and lifted the phone on the fourth ring. "Hello."

"Kate, it's Cara Jo."

"Hi." Kate's heart warmed at the sound of her new friend's voice.

"Just wanted to let you know the local church in Wild Oak Canyon has a Mother's Day Out program. Lily might enjoy playing with children her own age a couple times a week."

"Wow, that would be great. What days?"

"Tuesdays and Thursdays from nine until three o'clock." Cara Jo called out to someone on her end of the phone.

"Are you at the diner?" Kate asked.

"I am. It being Thursday, I thought I'd let you know early enough to get Lily in today, if you had a mind to." She chuckled softly. "Purely selfish reasons, I assure you. If you come to town, you could join me for lunch and do a little shopping without having to drag poor Lily around."

"That sounds good. I could run by the sheriff's office again and report the dead cattle, for all the good it would do."

Cara Jo snorted. "At least you'd have a record of it."

"Right." Kate glanced at Lily playing on the floor in the living room with Pickles. The little puppy had as much energy as the four-year-old.

Nothing like jumping into the community. And Lily was used to playing with the children she'd met at the day care in Houston. Kate made the decision. "I'll check it out today. If all goes well, I'll meet you for lunch."

"Make it around eleven-thirty. Twelve to one-thirty is our busy time and it gets hard to find a seat."

"Will do." Kate hung up, ran back up the stairs and grabbed play clothes, shoes, barrettes and a hairbrush from Lily's room.

When she returned to the first floor, the living room was empty.

Sounds of voices and laughter came from the kitchen.

When Kate entered, she was struck by how natural the scene appeared.

Lily sat in a chair on a stack of books, digging into a bowl of cereal. Ben sat beside her with a plate of eggs, bacon and toast. Mrs. Henderson busied herself at the stove, talking to both of them with her back to the room.

Kate smiled. "Good morning."

"Oh, Kate, dear. Sit. I have breakfast for you." Mrs. Henderson lifted a fry pan full of fluffy, yellow scrambled eggs and faced her. "Did you sleep well?"

Kate's face heated. "Yes. I did." *Minus the snake and the musical beds and making love to Ben.* She had slept well once she'd fallen asleep in Ben's arms. She refused to meet his gaze, but out of the corner of her eye she could see the way his lips twitched.

If he smiled now, she'd throw something at him.

Instead he shoved a forkful of eggs into his mouth and chewed.

"Lily, how would you like to make some new friends today?" Kate asked, hoping to pull attention off her red cheeks and focus it on her baby girl.

Lily set her spoon beside her bowl and lifted her cup of milk. "Yes, please."

Kate continued for Ben's benefit, "There's a Mother's Day Out program at the local church. Cara Jo from the diner suggested it, thinking Lily might like to meet some of the local children. I think it's a good idea."

Ben nodded. "Eddy had a few things he'd like picked up in town. We can take the truck."

"I'll take my car, you can follow. I think I'll be safe in town and I might want to do a little shopping while there."

Ben frowned. "Are you sure you don't want me to drive?"

"I don't think it's necessary." Kate remained firm. If Ben was leaving, she needed to get around on her own and not be afraid. "Nothing's going to happen in a town full of people."

Ben's brows didn't rise. "I'm not thrilled with the idea of taking two vehicles. Seems a waste of fuel and time. But as long as you wait for me to follow you back to the ranch, I suppose it's okay."

Kate almost smiled. For some strange reason, she liked pushing his buttons. But she understood his reasons. It was his job to protect her and Lily. "I'll let you know when I'm ready to head home."

Fifteen minutes later, she'd finished her breakfast, brushed her teeth and Lily's, and gathered her keys and purse.

Ben waited outside beside his truck, his brows dented in what appeared to be a permanent frown. He'd already switched the booster seat into the backseat of her car.

Lily ran to his arms. "Pickles cried when I put him in the box."

"Mrs. Henderson will let him out to play once we leave. He'll be fine until you get home." Ben tucked her into the safety seat and buckled the belt over her lap, then pressed a kiss to her forehead.

Kate stood back, once again amazed at how comfortable the two were together. Already, she predicted it would be hard on Lily when Ben left.

Kate climbed into the car and pulled out onto the highway bound for the little town and the church where Lily would spend the day doing what kids did—play.

The drive was uneventful and Kate relished the time alone with Lily. It gave her the opportunity to think through what had happened the night before. She never would have thought she'd be so quickly attracted to a man, and never had she dreamed she'd jump into bed with a stranger after knowing him such a short time. Having married her high school sweetheart, Kate hadn't dated as an adult. One thing was for sure, she wasn't setting a good example for Lily. Still she didn't regret the magic she'd experienced with Ben the night before.

Kate parked in front of the church.

Ben parked on the passenger side of Kate's car. He got to Lily before Kate and lifted the child out onto the ground, tucking her hand in his.

Kate took Lily's other hand and they walked into the church together.

At the administrative office, Kate filled out paperwork and let them make a copy of Lily's shot records. When it came to filling out the emergency data card, she paused. She wrote down her home phone number and her cell phone number, but the cell number was only reliable sometimes. "If you can't get me on my cell phone, call Cara Jo's diner and ask for me or leave a message with Cara Jo. I'll check in there."

"Leave my cell number, too, as backup." Ben recited his number and Kate wrote it on the form.

Kate and Ben walked with the administrator to the classroom Lily would be in. Six children ranging in age from three to five gathered around tables, wearing cute little aprons. They were elbow-deep in finger painting.

Lily was so excited, she didn't even say goodbye.

Kate left the building, happy that her daughter would have a fun-filled day with children her age.

"Now what?" Ben asked.

"I want to stop by the county assessor, do a little shopping and then meet Cara Jo for lunch." She shot a glance his way, but didn't linger on his handsome face, afraid she'd ask him to stay with her. "What about you?"

"While you're in town, I can take care of reporting the dead cattle to the sheriff's office. At least get it on record. I need to run out to Hank's and check on the status of that DVD. Then I'll drop by the hardware store for the items Eddy needed for the ranch."

Kate glanced at her watch. "Meet back here at three?"

"Three." He caught Kate's arm as she turned away. "Don't go anywhere else without notifying me first, will you?"

"I won't." Her arm tingled where he touched her. Damn. The man had her tied in knots and wanting so much more. Things she shouldn't be thinking in broad daylight came to mind more than she cared to admit. With her thoughts on her bodyguard, she wasn't focusing on what was important. The nutcase causing her grief and the human trafficking happening on her own land.

"Three o'clock." She scooted away from his grip on her arm and climbed into her car. After shifting into Reverse, she left the parking lot, cranking the air conditioner up to chill her suddenly flaming cheeks.

She stopped by the county tax assessor's office to discover no change in the computer situation. They expected someone out that afternoon to work on it.

After she left the county offices, Kate spent thirty minutes in the General Store, exploring the aisles, getting familiar with what Wild Oak Canyon had to offer.

It wasn't a huge department store, but they sold jeans, chambray shirts and cowboy hats. That and a few odds and ends in fencing supplies and plain pantry staples, fresh bread and milk. After she'd gone up and down each aisle, it was time to meet with Cara Jo at the diner across the street from the General Store.

When Kate pushed through the diner's door, Cara Jo dashed by her, carrying three heaping plates of food.

"Sorry, one of my waitresses called in sick. I have to work the lunch crowd." She set the plates on a table in the corner where three men dressed in jeans and chambray shirts sat with their forks and knives ready to dig in.

On her way back past Kate, Cara Jo gave her an apologetic frown. "Sorry. Can we do a rain check on our lunch?"

"That's fine. I ate breakfast not long ago."

"Oh, please sit, have lunch. It's on me." Cara Jo whooshed by and grabbed another two plates from the window into the kitchen.

Kate glanced around at the busy establishment. She didn't want to sit by herself, and she didn't feel like sitting with strangers.

Robert Sanders occupied a booth near the far corner, sitting across the table from the sheriff, their heads bent close, intense expressions on their faces.

Kate didn't see herself getting into a conversation with the two men. And they appeared to be discussing business. She caught Cara Jo on her next pass. "I'm going to head out to the ranch. I have some things to do out there. I'll be back in town around three to get Lily. I'll stop by then for a cup of coffee, if you have time."

"Oh, sure. Three will be our slow time. I'll see you

then." Cara Jo was off again, snatching up a carafe of steaming coffee and a pitcher of ice water.

Kate left the diner and stood outside on the sidewalk. She dug her cell phone out of her purse and dialed Ben's number. The call went straight to his voice mail. She left a message, or at least hoped she did. With spotty reception, she wasn't sure she stayed connected throughout her call.

With nothing else to do, not feeling like shopping and with nobody to talk to, Kate decided to do what she'd told Cara Jo she was going to do and head back out to the ranch.

Lily would be happily playing with her new friends and Ben was busy doing errands and updating the sheriff's deputies and Hank Derringer.

A little lonely and a bit anxious, Kate couldn't stand around and wait for someone to show up or free up to babysit her. She still had a lot of unpacking to do. Mrs. Henderson would be there and now that Kate knew how to handle the Glock, she would be just fine.

Kate jammed her hand into her jeans pocket, searching for her car keys and found the mystery key her father had left her.

She could spend time searching the house and surrounding outbuildings for the lock the key belonged to. Kate climbed into her car and headed out of town to the ranch. The wind had picked up, buffeting her little car around. With few trees or hills to block the wind, it blew through, hard and fast and filled with fine grains of sand that pinged against the windshield.

In broad daylight, Kate didn't expect to be accosted. But then she hadn't expected a biker gang to show up in her front yard the first morning after she'd arrived.

Just to play it safe, Kate kept alternating watching the pavement ahead and behind in the rearview mirrors. Anytime she passed a road connecting to the highway, she studied it carefully, looking for suspicious vehicles, lurking, waiting for her to pass by, alone and vulnerable.

She'd be glad when she got back to the ranch with Mrs. Henderson and Eddy.

Kate gripped the steering wheel so tightly, her knuckles turned white as she struggled to quell her rising fears and to maintain control of the little car being tossed around by strong southerly winds.

By the time she drove through the gate and up to the ranch house, Kate's fingers were cramping. And all for what? Nothing happened on the highway and no biker gang greeted her at the house.

As Kate climbed out of the car, her hair escaped its neat ponytail and whipped around her face and neck.

A rumbling-on-gravel sound made her turn and face the driveway she'd driven in on. Another vehicle turned off the county road onto the gravel drive far enough away that she couldn't make it out, but close enough to send a flash of fear through her.

Her brows furrowed, Kate hurried toward the house, scraping her mind for the location of the pistol and shells.

"Oh, good. You're here." Mrs. Henderson met her at the screen door, her purse hooked over her shoulder. "Mr. Henderson forgot to tell me he had an appointment at the clinic today and the Customs and Border Protection folks called a while ago to say they were on the way out to check on your reports of lights and dead cattle. I'd stick around and answer their questions, but now that you're here…"

"How long did the CBP say they'd be before they got here?" Kate asked.

"There they are now." Mrs. Henderson pointed down the drive.

The vehicle Kate had seen came into view. A big, white Hummer H2, with knobby tires and a green stripe, spit up a wide cloud of dust on the gravel drive.

"When they called about an hour ago, I thought it would be no problem. Eddy said he'd meet them at the barn when they came in. I had just pulled a pie out of the oven when David called to say he was picking me up." The older woman glanced over Kate's shoulder. "That should be Dave now. I wasn't sure what to do with the puppy when I left so it's a good thing you showed up when you did." She gave Kate a half smile. "Sorry. My husband can be forgetful. That's why I go to his appointments with him."

"Don't worry. I'll be fine without you."

Her eyes narrowed and she looked past Kate. "Where's Mr. Harding?"

"He'll be along in a bit," Kate fudged. No use detaining Marge when her husband had already driven out to pick her up.

"I can't leave you alone. Mr. Henderson will just have to go on without me." Marge let the purse slide down her arm and turned in the doorway.

"No, really. I'll be fine. Eddy's around here. The Border Protection is here. And if that's not enough, Ben gave me lessons on how to fire my pistol. It turns out I'm a pretty good shot. You go on with Mr. Henderson. He needs you more than I do."

The older woman's brows dipped. "Are you sure?" She glanced around the immediate vicinity of the ranch house as if expecting someone to be lurking in the shadows. "I don't feel right leaving you like this."

Kate rested her hand on Mrs. Henderson's arm. "You don't have to baby me. I can handle myself and Ben will be along shortly."

"Okay. But do be careful." She squeezed Kate's hand and descended the stairs. "I'll be back to fix dinner around five."

"Don't make the trip out again. I can cook, you know." Another near lie. She wasn't that good, but Mrs. Henderson didn't have to know that.

Marge patted her purse. "Well, then, I'll see you in the morning."

"Thanks, Mrs. H." Kate sighed as Mr. Henderson got out of the driver's seat and rounded the front of the car to open the door for his wife. He waved at Kate and climbed back into the car and turned it around, headed back to the highway and town.

Kate admired the way the old couple relied on each other for things. They loved each other, which was evident in the way the old man took care of Marge and she him.

When Troy had been alive, Kate had never quite pictured them growing old together. Now she supposed that she'd never had enough time on her hands to dwell on such things, what with her pregnancy occurring so close to when they'd gotten married and then Troy leaving before even Kate knew she was with child.

Kate stood in the yard as the officers stepped out of their SUV and strode across the ground to her.

One of the officers held out his hand. "I'm Officer

Mendoza with U.S. Customs and Border Protection.
Are you Ms. Langsdon?"

"Yes, that's me."

"We're here to review recent reports of suspicious
activity in the area."

"I take it the helicopters didn't find the two trucks
last night?"

"No, ma'am." The spokesman of the two pulled a
notepad out of his pocket. "Could you or your husband
show me where you saw the dead cattle?"

Kate let the husband comment pass by without comment. "Your best bet will be to have my foreman show
you where you can find the dead cattle and the ravine
where we saw the two trucks."

Eddy chose that moment to cross the barnyard, slapping his cowboy hat against his leg, dust rising and
whipping away with the wind.

Kate brought the CBP officers up to date on what
had happened on the ranch, from the attack in the
house, the home intrusions, biker gangs and dead cattle to the truckloads of people.

Mendoza shook his head. "I suggest you get a good
guard dog and a bodyguard."

"Got the bodyguard. Working on the guard dog."
Her lips curved as an image of Ben came to mind and
at the thought of Pickles being a guard dog.

Mendoza glanced over her shoulder and around the
yard. "A bodyguard isn't much good if he's not around
to guard you."

"He's on his way back from town," Kate lied, realizing she'd been stupid to leave Wild Oak Canyon without him. Without Marge as backup she only had Eddy
to protect her should someone cause trouble.

When Kate had told them all she knew, she paused, waiting for their response.

Officer Mendoza closed his notepad and slid it into his shirt pocket. "Could you show me where you found the carcasses?"

Kate turned to Eddy.

"Sí." Eddy eyed the men. "I have extra horses in the barn."

The officer smiled. "Thanks, but we'll stick with the SUV. It gets in most places the horses can go."

Eddy didn't respond, his gaze roving over the huge tires and fancy paint job of the CBP vehicle. Then he shrugged. "You'll have to follow me and my horse." He turned and walked away.

Mendoza grinned. "He always so talkative?"

Kate smiled. "He has to warm up to you."

"How long have you owned the Flying K?"

It was Kate's turn to smile. "A grand total of a week."

Eddy had mounted his horse and stood waiting by the gate to the pasture.

"Guess we better get going." Mendoza nodded at Kate. "Thank you for your time."

"Hope you find the trucks. I'm worried about the passengers as hot as it gets out here." Kate watched as the Hummer cleared the gate and Eddy closed it behind them.

Once the group disappeared across the pasture, Kate dug the key from her pocket and performed a systematic search of the inside of the house, fitting the little key into every lock on the off chance it was the right one. She checked behind furniture, paintings and beneath rugs for any hidden doors.

The attic had been particularly creepy, with spider-webs and a thick layer of dust. The hot Texas sun had heated the top of the house so much Kate had broken into a sweat as soon as she'd pulled down the attic access door and climbed to the top. After checking out two old trunks and an antique desk, she retreated to the air-conditioned second floor.

She let the attic door close on its springs. So far she'd struck out on finding the lock inside the house. She headed out the front door, letting the screen slap closed behind her.

Living in Houston had conditioned Kate to the constant noise of urban life. Here, the silence was only interrupted by the wail of wind against the windows. When she stepped out on the porch, the strong westerly breeze hit her with a heated blast, slapping her hair around her head. As far as Kate knew, she was the only person within miles of the ranch house. That gave her a kind of lonely, distant feeling. A quick glance at her watch told her she didn't have much time to check out the rest of the buildings if she wanted to be back in town on time to pick up Lily at the church and have a cup of coffee with Cara Jo.

She descended the steps, blinking the sand and grit out of her eyes. Choosing the shed closest to the house as a place to start looking, Kate kicked up dust as she trod across the dry Texas soil and flung open the door to the small building. The interior was packed with an ancient riding lawn mower, an antique car probably dating back to the 1940s, a variety of spare parts and equipment, a large rollaway toolbox and fishing poles.

After the bright sunshine, the interior was dark and deeply shadowed. She flipped the light switch beside the door and nothing happened. She'd need a flashlight if she planned to explore in the outbuildings. How long had it been since anyone had been inside this one? At least long enough to accumulate a thick layer of dust. Which, in this part of Texas, could be as little as a day. At the least, she could check out the toolboxes. They appeared to have tiny locks on some of the drawers.

The shed had no windows and only the one large door. Kate opened it wide and leaned a cement block against it to keep the wind from slamming it shut.

Then she stepped through, blocking the sun for a moment. She hugged the shadows, allowing for as much light as possible.

First, she tried the toolboxes. The key didn't fit the two locks, so she moved on. Kate squeezed between the front of the antique car and the wall of the building to get behind it. A scorpion skittered over a concrete block and down the side into a shadow.

Kate hated scorpions, having been stung more than once living in Houston. A shiver slithered across her warm skin. She'd have to warn Lily about the dangers of picking up rocks and things.

On the other side of the antique auto hung a rack of fishing poles. Below the rack, on the dirt floor was a tackle box with a keyhole on the front.

Ready to try anything, Kate stuck the key in the hole and turned it.

The lock clicked open.

A rush of excitement filled her and she dropped to her knees to better see what might be inside. The lighting behind the car was minimal, dust particles gleaming in the air. Kate held her breath as she laid her hands on the box, her pulse hammering through her veins.

Careful to look for scorpions or black widow spiders, she eased the lid back. From all she could see with the shadows and limited light, it was what it looked like. A fishing tackle box. The top compartment was loaded with dusty lures and faded rubber worms.

Kate let go of the breath she'd been holding. "Why would he leave me a key to a fishing tackle box?"

She sat back on her haunches and lifted the top compartment, exposing the bottom of the container.

Once again her breath hitched in her throat. Beneath a filet knife and a pair of pliers lay a mix of lures and lead weights. Buried among them was a slim silver thumb drive.

Was this it? Was this the item the key was hiding? Kate moved the knife and pliers aside and fished the thumb drive out of the box.

She shoved the data storage device into her pocket and stood.

The heavy shed door slammed shut, cutting off the light, throwing Kate into complete darkness. She reached out a hand to steady herself against the antique car and waited for the wind to blow the door open again so that she could see to find her way out.

The door didn't open.

Kate felt her way back around the old car to the front, her shirt catching on a nail protruding from the wall, ripping through the fabric and tearing into her skin. She screamed and nearly tripped over the forgotten concrete block the scorpion had scurried beneath.

Heart racing, afraid she'd brush against something deadly, sharp or creepy, she moved around the wall until her fingers brushed against a hinge. Finally, she'd reached the door.

Wind whistled through the cracks, a dark, lonely sound.

Kate leaned against the door and pushed. It didn't budge. She tried again, this time putting her full weight into it. The door remained closed. She stepped back, tucked her shoulder and slammed into the door. She bounced back.

As the truth dawned on her, her heart sank to her stomach. The door had been locked from the outside.

CHAPTER FOURTEEN

BEN SAT ACROSS the desk from Hank. "That's what's been happening."

"Too much for young Kate to handle alone." Hank nodded. "I'm glad you've been there to protect her." He leaned forward. "I received word from one of my connections in Customs and Border Protection. They found a dead woman on a ranch adjacent to the Flying K two weeks ago. From what they said, she was an illegal immigrant. How she got there, they would only guess. She died of exposure and dehydration."

"Damn." Ben shook his head. "A dead woman, dead cattle, intruders. You think they're trafficking humans across the Flying K and don't want Kate to interfere?"

"Sounds like it. A deadly situation if Kate gets in the middle. The immigrants aren't who she needs to be worried about. It's the coyotes who bring them across. They don't care who they have to kill to get paid."

"Hank, we only saw young women in the backs of those trucks."

Hank glanced up at Ben. "If they're trafficking young women, we have an even bigger problem. Someone stateside is harboring them and possibly selling them to underground sex dens."

Ben clasped his hands together to keep them from shaking. "Like the one we busted in Austin. I caught one of their suppliers, Marcus Mendez. The bastard got off on a technicality, then he came after my family. Think these are connected?"

"Could be." Hank leaned back in his chair. "I spoke with the regional director of the CBP. They didn't find the trucks you and Kate saw last night."

"Damn it." Ben stood and paced in front of Hank's desk. "I should have stopped them there."

"You had Kate to protect and you were outnumbered." Hank rounded his desk and laid a hand on Ben's shoulder. "You did the only thing you could. Now that you know they're running a human trafficking trade across the Flying K, you have to keep Kate from stumbling into them."

"I'll try but she was real upset by what we saw." Kate had a mind of her own and might try something dumb to help those girls. Ben blew out a long breath and dragged a hand through his hair. "I should be with her now."

"Where is she?" Hank asked.

"I left her at the diner. She should be okay there for a little while." Only now he wasn't so sure. Trouble had been following Kate since she'd arrived in this part of Texas. "Before I go, anything on the video?"

"As a matter of fact, we did make a little headway." He clicked the keyboard on his computer and then nodded toward the flat-screen television mounted on the wall behind Ben. "Look at this."

Static filled the screen, then a wavering image of Kyle Kendrick blinked into view.

"Hello, Kate. If you've received this video, something has happened to me and I'm either dead or missing and presumed dead. I couldn't leave without letting you know that of all the regrets in my life, you and your mother are my most heartfelt."

After a short pause, he continued.

"I can't say that I lived a good life. I didn't go to church, I wasn't a pillar of the community and I avoided jail on more occasions than I'd care to remember."

Ben sat back, his heart squeezing in his chest as he imagined Kate watching this video and her reaction to seeing the man on the screen for her first time.

"Then I met your mother and everything changed. I wanted to be a better man. I wanted to make her proud of me, and I thought I could. But I was in too deep. The people I worked with had me. Imagine being married to the mob. In this case, the Mexican Mafia cartels."

Ben whistled, noting the haggard expression, the dark circles around the man's eyes. Eyes that looked so much like a haunted version of Kate's. "What a life."

"I married your mother, thinking I could shake their influence. I thought I could just quit, stop running drugs and start fresh." The man in the video shook his head. "I was wrong and it almost got your mother killed." He ran a hand through his hair and tipped his head back, squeezing shut his eyes. "I had to let her go. To send her away. I didn't know she was pregnant with you. If they'd known how much I cared for her and anything about my unborn child, they'd have used it against me. I couldn't contact you, couldn't talk to your mother. I had to shut the door to that part of my life completely or risk your lives. It was the hardest thing I've done in my entire life."

Kyle Kendrick stared into the camera, his eyes narrowing. "When the DEA cornered me in Vegas, I knew it was over. They would have sent me to jail, which, in retrospect, might have been easier. Instead, they gave me a chance to redeem myself. If I would become their informant, they wouldn't lock me up." Kyle snorted. "I should have let them send me to jail." Kyle shook his head slowly.

"Once I started ratting out the leaders of the cartels, I knew my days were numbered. But I hung in there, trying to find out who the stateside head honcho was."

Ben shot a glance at Hank.

"I've come so close I might be in trouble. I'm sending this video in case something happens to me. I wanted you to know how much I loved you and your mother."

After another short pause, Kyle continued.

"In the envelope with this video is a key. It unlocks a tackle box you'll find in the shed with the old Cadillac. In the bottom of the tackle box is a flash drive. It contains all the notes I used to nail the members of the cartel and the work I've compiled leading up to the discovery of the stateside crime boss. At the time of this video, I know there are things happening in the area. I leave this information with you in the event of my untimely but fully expected death. The data is encrypted, so you'll need to hand it over to someone who can break the code. What you do with it is up to you. Toss it, ignore it or hand it off to the DEA, I don't care. Just don't get involved. I would hate to think my work once again puts you in danger."

Ben narrowed his eyes and focused on the screen.

"As I was saying, several factions are active. Drug running and human trafficking. The coyotes who run the people across the border referred to the stateside connection as *Diablo Patrón,* the devil boss. I think

I know who's responsible, but haven't accumulated enough evidence to nail him. If what I think is true…" He looked at his hands clasped in between his knees. "Let's just say, I want to verify before I call in the Feds. The stakes are high. Whatever happens to me, know that I deserved what I got. Whatever you do, don't get tangled up in this mess. And watch out for the following men…"

As Ben leaned forward, the picture on the screen tilted.

Kyle Kendrick lurched forward to catch the camera, but missed, and the machine fell to the floor with a loud crash. Then static and gray squiggles filled the video screen.

"Who?" Ben leaped to his feet. "Who was she supposed to look out for?"

Hank stood, as well. "That's the kicker. Nothing else was recorded. Or Kendrick thought he'd finished recording his message and didn't. He must have been in a hurry to get the disk in the mail."

"Holy hell." Ben paced to the end of the French doors and back across Hank's spacious wood-paneled office. He stopped and faced the older man. "She needs to leave now. Go back to Houston, get the hell out of Texas. If the cartel finds out about the flash drive, she's dead."

"Scared the hell out of me, too." Hank walked around the desk and laid a hand on Ben's shoulder. "And there's one other thing I wanted you to know."

Ben looked into Hank's eyes. What else could go wrong?

"I hired another cowboy with the skills necessary to take over for you with the Langsdon woman. You don't have to go back there. He's here on the ranch. I can send him immediately."

Ben pressed a hand to his gut as if he'd been punched. "No."

"Are you sure? He has a stack of medals and credentials almost as impressive as yours."

"No." Ben straightened. God, what was he doing? He had an out. He didn't have to go back to the Flying K and be around Kate, whose body and soul reminded him of all he had to live for. He wouldn't have to face Lily, the child who'd worked her way into his heart in such a short time and left him open to her unconditional love and the heartbreak of leaving her behind when the job was done.

"I'll see this one through," Ben said. He headed for the door before he could change his mind, or before Hank could pull rank on him and change it for him.

"What about the video?"

Ben stopped. "Do you have it in a format I can show Kate?"

"Do you have a computer?"

"Yes."

Hank dropped into his desk chair, plugged a flash drive into the side of his monitor and clicked his keyboard. A moment later he yanked the flash drive from the monitor and handed it to Ben. "Be careful out there. Don't hesitate to call me in or to notify the DEA if things get out of hand."

"Don't worry. I'll be in touch." Ben left, climbing into his truck with a sense of impending doom.

Kate had come to the Flying K with the hope of starting over, of providing a good home for Lily. She'd ended up in a hotbed of danger.

Ben couldn't get back to her fast enough. Thank goodness she'd stayed in town.

The drive back to Wild Oak Canyon passed in a flash, considering Ben broke every speed limit the whole way. Thank goodness the county sheriff couldn't hope to patrol all the roads leading into the community with so few on staff.

Once in town, he pulled into the diner, his gaze searching for and not finding Kate's car. His heart skipped several beats, but he refused to let himself get worked up. He unbuckled his seat belt, dropped down to the pavement and looked around.

Cara Jo stepped out of the diner, her brows furrowed. "Oh, thank goodness you're here."

Ben's adrenaline spiked. "Why? Where's Kate?"

"She left right before lunch to head back to the ranch. She promised to be back in time to pick up Lily, but the woman in charge of the Mother's Day Out program called and said Kate hadn't come and Lily was the last one there. I tried to call you, but you didn't answer. I tried Kate's home phone and there was no answer. I was just about to get Lily myself, but I was afraid I wouldn't be on the list of people allowed to collect her."

Ben was already back in the truck and pulling out of the parking lot by the time Cara Jo finished talking. He whipped out onto the street, drove the few blocks and skidded to a stop in front of the church.

The woman he'd met earlier stepped out the front door of the church, holding Lily's hand. She turned and locked the church.

"Mr. Ben!" Lily jerked her hand free of the woman's and ran toward him, her arms outstretched.

Ben gathered her to him and lifted her off her feet.

"Thank goodness you're here. Lily was upset and worried you had lost your way." The woman looked around Ben. "Is Ms. Langsdon with you?"

"No, she had something come up and asked me to pick up Lily," Ben lied. He held Lily close, his heart aching for the child who'd thought she was forgotten.

Lily leaned back, tear tracks dried on her cheeks. "Can we go home now? Pickles missed me."

Ben nodded. "Yes, we can." He thanked the woman and tucked Lily into the backseat of his truck, buckling the seat belt over her lap. He didn't have the booster seat, but the buckle would have to do until he got back to the ranch and found Kate.

She'd promised not to go back until he could go with her. And why wasn't Mrs. Henderson answering the phone at the ranch?

Questions swirled in his mind throughout the drive out to the Flying K. When he came within sight of the house, he spied Kate's car sitting in the drive.

Nothing moved. No one came out to greet them.

Ben shifted into Park and climbed down. He lifted Lily out of the backseat and carried her to the house. The front door was unlocked. When he pushed it open, he called out, "Kate?"

As soon as he set Lily on her feet, she ran for the kitchen where Pickles's shrill barks created such a loud ruckus, Ben could barely hear himself think.

The house was a disaster. Drawers had been pulled out of the kitchen cabinets, pots and pans lay strewn across the floor.

"Pickles!" Lily cried out. "Where's Pickles?"

A high-pitched whine sounded from behind an over-turned chair.

Ben found the puppy's box wedged between a cabinet and the chair and lifted it out, puppy and all.

Lily leaned over the box and let the puppy lick her fingers. "Oh, Pickles, did you miss me?"

Ben checked the pantry and locked the back door, then lifted Lily in his arms. "Sorry, sweetheart, we'll come back for Pickles in a minute."

He didn't want to leave the little girl alone until he was certain whoever had turned the house upside down was no longer there. He carried Lily from room to room.

The child clung to him, probably sensing all was not right. "Mr. Ben, why is the house a mess?"

Ben tried to think of something that would make sense to a child and not frighten her. "Someone must have been playing with things and didn't put them away."

"Where's my mommy?" Lily trembled in his arms and he held on tighter, anger burning below the surface. No child should be afraid to come home.

A quick look around the house, both upstairs and down, confirmed his suspicion. Kate wasn't there and not a single room had been left untouched. Even Lily's room had boxes overturned, clothes flung across the floor and pillows torn open.

By the time he got back to the kitchen, Lily was sobbing quietly. "I want my mommy."

"Tell you what. I bet I know someone who could do with some hugs."

He entered the kitchen and set Lily on the floor.

Pickles barked in his shrill little voice.

Lily ran to the box and lifted the puppy into her arms. "Oh, Pickles." She hugged his neck and held him tight until the puppy squirmed loose and tore out across the floor.

Lily laughed and ran after him into the living room.

Ben followed. Of all the rooms, this one seemed the safest for now. "Stay in the living room, sweetheart. I'll be right back."

He hated leaving the four-year-old alone in the ransacked house, but he didn't know what to expect outside. He jogged to the barn first.

The stalls were empty. He checked the number of saddles in the tack room. All were there and Eddy's truck wasn't in the barnyard. Had Kate gone with Eddy?

Ben couldn't think of a logical reason why she'd leave with Eddy.

Pulse pounding, Ben emerged from the barn and yelled, "Kate! Kate!" He made a complete circle around the barn and scanned the pastures nearby. A few horses trotted over, hoping for a treat. But Ben saw no sign of Kate.

Unwilling to leave Lily alone any longer, he ran toward the house, heart heavy and desperate to find the spitfire redhead. "Kate!"

Moving fast to get back to the house, Ben almost missed the noise coming from the shed.

He ground to a stop and held his breath so that he could hear even the slightest sound.

There it was again. A muffled cry.

"Kate?" He jogged to the shed, careful to limit the crunch of his boots on the gravel.

"Ben! I'm in here," a voice called out, followed by pounding on the wooden door.

Kate.

Ben grabbed the door and yanked. It didn't budge. A latch had been slid home after the door had closed. The wind could have closed the door, but then someone on the outside had to push the bolt through the hasp.

He slid the latch to the side and jerked the door open.

Heat hit him at the same time as Kate's body plowed into his chest.

Her face was red and she wasn't perspiring.

"Holy hell, Kate, how long have you been there?"

"I don't know. It was dark. I must have drifted off. But it seems like forever." She leaned heavily against him and smiled up at him through pale lips. "I could use a drink of water."

He scooped her into his arms. Her skin felt hot and dry. It had to be over a hundred and twenty inside the shed. If she'd been in there for several hours, the saunalike atmosphere could have killed her.

Ben carried Kate toward the house.

"Lily?" Kate's big green eyes gazed up at him.

"She's inside playing with Pickles." Ben's mouth was set in a grim line. "Why did you leave town?"

Kate nestled closer to him, shrugging. "I don't know. I didn't really feel like shopping. I wanted to find out what the key belonged to." She wiggled against him, jammed her hand into her pocket and drew out a small silver flash drive. "I found this."

Ben's eyes widened. "Ah, you found your father's data."

Kate's brows furrowed. "How do you know about it?"

"Hank's team has been busy. I have something for

you to watch as soon as we get you hydrated and cooled off."

"I'm fine. Show me."

He shook his head. "Not until I know you're okay."

When they entered the house, Lily ran past, followed by a nipping, barking Pickles. "Hi, Mommy. Someone made a mess and didn't clean up." She stopped in the middle of the floor so fast, Pickles plowed into her. "Why is Mr. Ben carrying you?"

Kate smiled at her daughter, then glanced up at Ben, her brows raised. "Why *are* you carrying me?"

Ben smiled at Lily. "Because I'm big and strong."

Lily giggled and raced off, Pickles nipping at her heels.

Kate moved against him. "You can put me down."

"I will." He glanced at the stairs, then the couch and decided he wouldn't convince her to get in a cool shower. Not when he had news about her father and with Lily playing on the ground floor. Ben laid her on the couch. "Stay."

Kate laughed shakily. "I'm not a dog." Then she looked around the room. "Holy cow."

"Yeah, and it doesn't get better."

Her shoulders sagged. "Will this ever end?"

Her sad expression was almost his undoing. "Sit tight. I'll be back with a tall glass of ice water and a cool rag. But only if you stay."

"I may not be a dog, but I can be bribed." Kate settled back against a tattered throw pillow, her skin cooling in the air-conditioned room.

By the time Ben returned, Kate was shivering, her teeth chattering together so hard she thought they might crack. "I don't know what's wrong with me."

Pain stabbed through her calf. She jerked up to a sitting position, grabbed her leg and doubled over. "Ow!"

"What's wrong?" Ben set the ice water on the table.

"Cramp." She tried to rise and fell back against the couch, too dizzy to stand. "I need…to…stretch." She pressed one hand to the cramped muscle, the other to the bridge of her nose.

"Just lay back." Ben pressed her firmly against the cushion, stretched her legs out straight, slid her shoes off her feet and pushed her toes up.

"Ow! Ow! Ow!" Kate reached for his hand, but couldn't quite get there before she fell back against the pillow. Soon, the cramp eased and she lay still, her breathing shallow, the pain gone. "How'd you do that?"

"Works on a charley horse. Figured it would help you with the cramp." He lifted the glass. "Now, let's get some fluids inside you and you'll feel better." He helped her to a sitting position and slid in behind her to hold her up while she drank.

She wanted to drain the glass, but Ben wouldn't let her.

"A little at a time. Otherwise you'll just barf it up."

She snorted. "That would be attractive."

"In between sips, you can tell me what happened."

"Before you say anything, I'm sorry." She sipped from the glass, gathering more words as the fuzziness cleared from her head. "I shouldn't have come home by myself."

"Then why did you?"

"I can't rely on you to always be here for me and Lily. I have to be able to handle things on my own."

"When we find out who's behind all the threats. Not a moment sooner."

"I know, I know." Because he was there and she couldn't lie back against the pillows, she let herself lean into the hardness of his muscular chest. "I should have waited for you. And I will from now on." As soon as the words left her mouth, she knew they were a lie. Ben wouldn't be there for her *from now on*. "Or at least until we figure out who's doing this," she added.

"My most immediate concern is getting you hydrated." He pulled her closer and urged her to take another sip.

"Don't worry. I think I could drink a bathtub full of water."

"What happened?"

"I was looking for a lock the key would fit into and had just found the tackle box in the shed and the flash drive inside it when the door slammed shut. I'd propped the door with a concrete block. Guess it wasn't enough for the gusts of wind."

Ben's arm tightened around her. "It was more than the wind. Someone closed the door on purpose and locked it from the outside."

Kate glanced up, the glass of water forgotten, another tremor shaking her. "Someone locked me in there on purpose? There weren't any windows to let any air in."

Ben's body stiffened beneath hers. "You could have died if we hadn't found you soon enough."

Kate placed the cool glass against her lips, her thoughts on Lily as she plowed through the living room, the puppy chasing after her. "I can't afford to die, Ben. I'm all Lily has," she whispered.

Ben took the glass from her and set it on the table within her reach, then he laid her back on the couch.

She wanted him to hold her longer until the chill of what had almost happened dissipated.

He stood, looking down at her with a frown pulling his brows together. "You're going back to Houston."

Kate tried to push to a sitting position. "Says who?"

"It's not safe here."

"I have nothing left for me in Houston."

"You have Lily."

She started to say something, but bit down on her lip instead. He had a good point. "I can't go back to Houston. It's not any safer. Remember? Someone ransacked my apartment there. I'll bet it has something to do with what's on that flash drive I found."

"You can't tell anyone about it. No one."

"Okay."

"And at least consider leaving here until the dust settles."

She wanted to tell him to quit telling her what to do, but before she could he pressed a finger to her lips.

"I'm not trying to be a jerk. I'm worried about you and Lily. When I came back here and couldn't find you…"

She grasped his hand and held on to it. "I'm glad you did. Mrs. Henderson wasn't due back until tomorrow morning and Eddy could be out until dark working with the cattle. That reminds me."

Ben stared down at her. "Reminds you about what?"

"The CBP was out here investigating the cattle carcasses and asking questions."

Ben's mouth tightened. "Hank says they found a woman's body on the ranch adjacent to the Flying K two weeks ago. She appeared to have been an undocumented alien."

Kate's stomach dropped. "Dead?"

He nodded.

"Wow. I really am in the middle of this, aren't I?" She sat up and waited for the dizziness to clear. "You said you got information off the DVD my father left?"

"We did." He pulled the flash drive from his pocket. "Where's your laptop?"

"It's in a satchel in my bedroom." She sat up and leaned forward, but before she could rise, Ben pressed a hand to her shoulder.

"I'll get it." Ben collected the laptop from her bedroom and returned to the living room where he booted up the system and plugged in the flash drive. "Have you had lunch?"

"No. Marge said she left a pie on the counter and to help yourself." She didn't glance his way, her eyes trained on the screen. When it came up with her father's image she drew in a sharp breath, her heart squeezing so tightly she was afraid it would stop. "That's him? That's my father?"

CHAPTER FIFTEEN

BEN ENTERED THE KITCHEN, the sound of the video barely reaching him. He figured he'd chosen the coward's way out by ducking into the kitchen while Kate reviewed her father's first and last words to her. Ben tried to block the words from his mind and Kate's reaction by keeping busy.

As he glanced around, he noted that the back door swung wide open on its hinges, the hot Texas wind blowing into the house. The countertop was empty, no pie there, only a few crumbs. Perhaps Kate had been mistaken. The pantry door also hung open. When Ben peered inside, he noted cans lying sideways on the shelves and strewn across the floor. Someone had been in a hurry to get in and get out of the kitchen. Another unauthorized entry. Since the front door most likely hadn't been locked when Kate left the house to look into the shed and barn, it wasn't a forced entry, but an entry nonetheless. The other break-ins had been just that. The doors had been locked. Whoever had come in hadn't broken a window. He'd used a key or jimmied the lock.

Could it have been the same person responsible for locking Kate in the shed? Ben had stopped by the hardware store and picked up all new doorknobs and keys for the house. He'd gotten enough copies to give Mrs. H. one and one for himself and Kate.

Maybe changing the locks in the house would keep Kate and Lily safer.

God, he hoped so.

Ben quickly made a sandwich out of bread, leftover slices of the ham Mrs. H. had cooked for breakfast and a dab of mustard. Ben didn't know if Kate liked mustard, but he added it anyway. There was a lot he didn't know about Kate.

If he was smart, he'd keep it that way. He couldn't afford to get attached.

His stomach roiled every time he thought of Kate locked in the hotbox of a shed. If he hadn't come when he had...

He wrapped the sandwich in a paper towel, grabbed a bag of chips and hurried back into the living room, bracing himself for the storm of emotions Kate might be experiencing and another chance to hold her in his arms.

Lily had crawled up on the couch with her mother and lay with her head in Kate's lap. The four-year-old's silky, light golden-red hair curled around her face, one hand tucked beneath her cheek. She was fast asleep, petal-pink lips parted.

Kate stared down at her daughter, smoothing her hand across her hair. Every so often, she'd brush a tear from her eye before it fell onto Lily.

Ben froze on the threshold of the room, holding the sandwich and bag of chips, his chest hurting so badly he held his breath to keep the pain from spreading.

Kate blinked and she looked up at him, her green

eyes darker than the deepest forest. "My father was a drug runner."

"Yes, but he wised up and went to work for the good guys."

She looked up at him, tears welling in her eyes. "He didn't abandon us."

"No. He didn't. He sent you away to keep you safe."

A single fat tear slipped down her cheek.

Another blow to Ben's insides, tearing away at the wall he'd constructed against ever falling in love with a woman or a child again.

"I wish…" Kate started, glanced down at her hand and then up at him. "I wish you'd give me that sandwich."

Ben almost laughed. She had been about to say something else, but settled for focusing on something she could control. A sandwich. A lousy ham-and-mustard sandwich.

Kate held out her hand.

Ben shook himself out of the trance and handed it to her. When their fingers touched, Kate flinched, her eyes widening. With her other hand, she twined hers around his, dragging him closer.

He leaned over her, his gaze capturing her green one.

When he was within kissing range, she stopped. "Thank you for being here for us." Then she kissed him, her hand circling behind his neck.

Barely aware of where they were, the child on Kate's lap and the near-death experience, Ben kissed her back, his lips caressing, his tongue sweeping across hers.

Lily stirred and sighed.

Ben broke it off, his lips thinning. "You don't have to kiss me to thank me. I'm just doing my job."

"Well, you're doing a darned good job, then." She tipped her chin up. "And I *wanted* to kiss you, not as payment for saving my life, although I do appreciate that you did. Thank you for helping me learn more about my father. I wish I'd had a chance to know him."

"Based on the video, he wished the same." Ben swallowed the hard knot forming in his throat. "Want me to carry her up the stairs?"

"Please." Kate brushed Lily's hair back from her forehead and pressed a kiss to her temple, then leaned back so that Ben could take Lily from her lap.

Ben lifted the child and headed up the stairs, still reeling from the kiss, more bothered by it than by having made love to her the night before.

The woman trusted him to keep her safe. What scared him most was that he didn't know who to keep her safe from.

Kate followed. "I'm going for a shower, unless you want to go first?"

"You go. I need to make a couple phone calls." He tucked Lily into bed and headed down the stairs, anxious to talk with Jenkins and Hank. When he heard the water come on in the shower, he lifted the phone from the receiver and punched the numbers for his buddy back in the Austin Police Department. A quick glance at the clock indicated the hour was late, but not too late to call Jenkins. He owed him.

"Hello."

Ben recognized the gravelly voice on the other end of the connection. "Harding here. What did you find?"

"Ben? Didn't you get my message?" The gravel left Jenkins's voice.

"No. Reception stinks out here. Give me what you have."

"Masters searched through Rolando Gonzalez's phone records. He's got a cousin he calls pretty often in your area. A José Mendez. I have an address they pulled up based on the phone number. Here."

Ben jotted the address on a notepad and ripped off the page, stuffing it in his pocket. "Any other reason Mendez could be considered a person of interest?"

"He happens to own a commercial driver's license. He drives the big trucks."

"Something big enough to transport people and drugs?"

"Yeah. Since he's in your neighborhood, I suggest you check him out. See what other connections he has."

"Will do." He'd notify Hank and let him track it down.

"Look, Jenkins, I need you to dig into anyone and everyone these guys may have had contact with."

"Hey, information flow goes both ways, you know. What do you know that I don't?"

"They are smuggling women and girls up from Mexico through here. We encountered a couple pickup truckloads last night."

"You called the Customs and Border Protection?"

"Yeah, by the time they got the choppers up, the trucks had disappeared. We need to find them before they are sold or killed."

"I'll get right on it." Jenkins paused. "Oh, and one other thing. That Robert Sanders you had me look up?"

"Yeah, what about him?"

"He was a friend of Frank Davis. Spent time up here in Austin going to social functions. The society pages have photos of them drinking together."

Ben's heart squeezed tight. "Thanks. I'll check into Sanders."

"And Harding," Jenkins began, then paused. "Be careful. The Mexican Mafia can be brutal on both sides of the border."

Ben hung up and glanced at the top of the stairs.

The door to Kate's room opened and she stepped out, wrapped in a soft pink robe, her hair up in a towel turban. Her brows dipped. "Who was on the phone?"

"I made a call to a friend of mine who has connections with the Austin Police Department."

"Why Austin?"

"I might be grasping at straws. But I hope to find something useful that will help me keep you safe and help those women."

"You'll tell me what you find, won't you?"

"You bet," Ben lied. "Want me to check your room?"

Kate stood at the doorway to her bedroom. "No. I can do it myself."

"I don't mind and I'd feel better knowing it's safe." Ben climbed the stairs, brushed her aside and entered, checking beneath the bed, pulling back the covers and sheets and opening the closet. "All clear. No snakes."

She gave him a shaky smile and touched his arm as he passed her. "Thanks."

Ben had to get away before he was tempted to kiss her again. He really wanted to and that would solve nothing and complicate everything even more.

As he descended to the first floor, a shadow passed by the front window.

If he hadn't been looking that way at that exact moment, Ben would have missed it. He focused on the window next to it and the shadow appeared again.

Ben's pulse leaped. He turned out the light in the hallway, lifted his Glock from where he'd left it on top of a bookshelf and slipped out the back door, rounding the house from the opposite direction.

As he eased his way around the side, he ducked low, careful to tread lightly and stop to listen every few steps.

When he rounded the corner near the kitchen side of the house, he paused behind a rosebush and waited, his ears cocked toward the front of the house.

A twig snapped close by.

Ben held the Glock in front of him and peered around the bush.

A dark figure hovered in the shadows by the kitchen door. He wasn't very tall, but he was barrel-chested and stocky.

Ben inched forward to a better position. If the man tried to make a run for it, Ben could head him off.

When a shadowy hand reached for the doorknob, Ben stood, pointed the gun at the man's back and said, "Don't move if you want to live. I have a gun trained on you."

The man froze.

For a moment Ben thought he'd listened, then in a burst of movement, the shadow spun and ran.

Even as he shouted, "Stop, or I'll shoot," Ben gave chase, pounding the ground behind the darkly clothed man. He could have just fired off a round and probably hit the assailant, but Ben didn't want to kill the man. He wanted answers and this guy might have some.

The intruder headed for the barn, running hell-for-leather, but he was no match for Ben, who'd been running all his life and kept in good shape.

Before the stranger disappeared around the corner, Ben threw himself at the man's legs, catching enough of a pant leg to bring the man down.

They crashed into the hard-packed dirt.

Ben leaped to his feet, pushed a foot into the middle of the man's back and pointed the gun at his head. "Don't even think about moving." With his spare hand, Ben grabbed the man's arm and pulled it up behind his back. "Get up."

The guy stood. "Let me go, please. I didn't steal anything but food. I'll pay it back, I promise."

Ben pushed the man's arm up to the middle of his back. "To the house."

"I can't. If they see me, they'll kill me."

"Who will?"

"I can't say. I know too much." The man twisted. "If they know I'm here…if I'm caught… I'm as good as dead. Please, let me go."

Ben struggled to maintain his hold on the desperate man. "Slow down. No one's going to hurt you unless you try to get away from me." Ben lifted the arm higher and shoved the man toward the back door to the house. "In the house. Now."

"Ben?" The kitchen porch light blinked on and Kate stepped out, her bathrobe wrapped tightly around her body. "Ben?"

"I'm here." He eased the man forward.

Kate's mouth dropped open for a second, then she closed it and ran forward. "What can I do to help?"

"Take the gun and hold it on him."

Kate took the weapon from Ben and held it with both hands, pointing the barrel at the stranger's head. "Who is he?" she asked.

"I haven't gotten that far." Ben pushed the man forward. "Answer the lady."

"Larry," he said, his head down. "Larry Sites."

"The man who disappeared the day my father died?" She stopped, her eyes widening in the light from the porch. "Were you there when he died?"

"Yes, ma'am," the man answered softly.

Kate jumped in front of him, her mouth set in a tight line. "Was it really natural causes? Or did you kill him?"

Sites stood still, his gaze never wavering from Kate's. "He was murdered. But I didn't do it."

Kate gasped, her hands shaking, the gun tipping wildly. "Who did?"

"Can we take this into the house?" His head swiveled from right to left, his eyes wide, scared. "I'm a sitting duck out here."

"Kate, honey, get inside." Ben glanced around the barnyard.

"You can let go of my arm. I'm not going to run. I'm tired of hiding." Sites sighed. "I might as well be dead."

Kate stepped up onto the porch and opened the kitchen door. "If you didn't do it, who killed my father?"

"I didn't have any beef with Kyle Kendrick. I just happened to be around when he was killed."

"Why didn't you tell anyone who did it?" Ben pushed him closer to the house.

"No one would have believed me, not when it was—"

A loud pop sounded and Larry's body jerked so hard he pulled free of Ben's hold.

"Kate, get down!" Ben dropped to the ground.

Kate threw herself into the house.

After a long minute, Ben whispered loud enough to be heard in the house, "Kate? Are you okay?"

"I'm fine. What happened?"

Ben inched forward to where Larry Sites lay on the ground. His hand encountered warm sticky liquid and his chest tightened. "Someone shot Sites."

"Is he…"

Ben found the man's throat and felt for a pulse. Nothing.

"He's dead." Ben crawled over the body and made a run for the door.

Kate stepped aside as he entered and slammed the door behind him. "What just happened?"

"Sites is dead. Someone shot him."

Kate pressed a hand to her chest. "I'll call the sheriff."

She hurried to where the phone sat on the table in the hallway. When she lifted the receiver, her hand shook so much she dropped it.

Ben caught the handset. "Let me." He held the device to his ear only to discover there was no dial tone. "It's not working."

Kate's brows furrowed. "It was working a few minutes ago."

"Either the phone system is down or someone cut your line."

She wrapped her arms around herself. "I don't like this. I should check on Lily."

"Do that, and get her ready to leave."

"Where are we going?" She gathered the edges of her robe closer, her body trembling.

Ben pulled her into his arms and pressed a kiss to her forehead. "I don't know, but we're not staying here. Now go. Stay away from the windows and don't turn on any lights. We don't know if the shooter is still out there." He turned and would have walked away, but Kate's hand on his arm stopped him.

"Where are you going?" she asked.

"To check outside and see what I can find."

Her fingers tightened on his arm. "Don't go."

"I'll be okay. Lock the door behind me and hold on to this." He reached up to the top of the shelf where he'd left her loaded Glock and handed it to her, checking that the safety was on. "You know how to use it. Point, click the safety off and shoot. Just make sure it's not me. I'll call out when I want back in. Otherwise leave all the doors locked. If you have to…leave them locked until morning when Mrs. H. arrives." He kissed her lips this time. He couldn't resist. She looked so vulnerable in her pale pink robe. "Relax. I'll be all right."

Her hand trembled as she cupped his jaw. "What if you don't come back?"

"I will." He kissed her again, this time his tongue pushing past her teeth to slide along hers. It was a lot harder this time to break away, but he did. He needed to know if the shooter was still out there. If he was and he planned to target Ben and Kate, they were pretty much trapped inside the house.

Kate followed him to the back door. When Ben slipped out, she closed the door behind him and locked it, her heartbeat pounding against her rib cage. "Please be okay," she whispered. Then she turned and hurried up the stairs to get ready for whatever happened next.

Fumbling around in the dark, her pulse racing, Kate dressed and grabbed a bag out of her closet. She shoved in a change of clothes for herself, her brush and toothbrush.

In Lily's room, she gathered an outfit, shoes and Lily's favorite doll, shoving them all into the bag and zipping it closed.

Pickles stood, stretched, then leaned up against the side of the box and whined.

Afraid he'd wake Lily, Kate lifted him from the box and cuddled him beneath her chin, inhaling the warm sweet scent of puppy and drawing comfort from the creature. "It's going to be okay. Ben will be back and we'll all be fine."

The minutes stretched by. Kate set the puppy in the box, looped the bag over her shoulder and carried it down the stairs, placing it by the front door. She returned to Lily's room and carried the box with Pickles down the steps. On her last trip, she carried Lily down and laid her on the love seat out of view of the windows. Her little girl barely stirred throughout the process.

Sounds of an engine drew Kate to the living room window. She peeked around the edges, careful not to provide too much of a silhouette should a shooter decide to fire at her.

Ben's truck pulled up right in front of the porch and stopped, the lights glaring out into the side yard. Ben dropped out of the driver's seat and rounded the front of the truck, leaping up onto the porch.

Kate was there, unlocking the door even as he knocked.

He burst through and closed the door behind him.

"Did you see anything?"

"Nothing. I found fresh motorcycle tracks, but whoever rode in on it was gone. Ready?"

Kate nodded. "What about Sites?"

"There's nothing we can do for him but report the murder. We have to get you somewhere safe first. Then we can notify the police."

Ben lifted Lily from the love seat and cradled her in his arms.

Kate slung the bag and her purse over her shoulder and hefted the box with the puppy.

Ben's brows dipped. "You have all that?"

She smiled. "I'm a mother."

"Okay, straight out. I'm right behind you."

Kate sucked in a deep breath and let it out. It did nothing to calm her nerves, but she stepped out onto the porch and down to the pickup, sliding the box onto one side of the backseat floorboard. She tossed the overnight bag onto the other side and climbed into the passenger seat, sitting low.

Ben came out half a minute later, carrying Lily. He settled her into her booster seat, tightened her straps and fumbled with the box containing the puppy. Finally, Ben climbed into the driver's side and shifted into Drive.

Before he'd gone ten feet down the driveway, headlights flashed on directly in front of them and the red and blue of a law enforcement vehicle whirled like circus lights.

Ben had to stop or risk running into the vehicle.

"It's the sheriff." Kate reached for her door handle. "We can tell him about Sites and the shooter."

Ben grabbed her arm. "Stay put and don't say anything."

"Why?"

"Trust me."

"Please step out of the vehicle," Sheriff Fulmer called out, service weapon drawn. He approached the driver's side of the truck while Deputy Schillinger came up on Kate's side.

"Sheriff, what's this about?"

"We had a report of gunshots fired. Please step out of the vehicle and keep your hands where I can see them."

Ben got out slowly, his hands held high. "Your report was correct. Someone shot Larry Sites. His body is lying on the ground outside the kitchen door."

To Ben, his gaze narrowed. "Cool your heels, cowboy."

The sheriff nodded toward Ben, his gun trained on Ben's chest. "Up against the truck and spread your legs."

Kate could barely breathe as she slid down out of the truck. "You're worrying about the wrong man. Whoever shot Sites might still be out there."

Schillinger jerked his gun toward Ben. "Look out, sheriff, he's got a gun."

Kate stepped in front of the deputy's weapon. "He's licensed to carry one."

"But he's not licensed to kill." The sheriff nodded to the deputy. "Check it out."

Sheriff Fulmer removed the Glock from Ben's waistband and tucked it into his belt. While the deputy rounded the house to the kitchen, the sheriff patted Ben down, running his hands up Ben's legs and into his pockets, emptying them of their contents. He opened Ben's wallet and checked the driver's license. "Says he's Ben Harding from Austin." Fulmer tossed the wallet onto the hood of the truck and continued his search. When he delved into Ben's front pocket, he pulled out a small silver flash drive and held it up to the light. His hand closed around the tiny device and he slid it into his pocket.

Kate leaned forward. "Hey, that's not yours."

"And you're wrong." The sheriff continued to search Ben's other pocket. "It's evidence."

"It's mine," Kate said. "You have no right to take it."

"It's on a man who might have committed a murder."

"He didn't!"

"Leave it, Kate," Ben warned her. "We'll get it back when we clear up this mess."

Two minutes later, Deputy Schillinger returned. "It's Sites, all right, and he's dead as a doornail. Gunshot wound."

Kate bit down on her lip, wanting to say more, to stop what was happening to Ben and get back the data storage device her father had placed in her possession.

Sheriff Fulmer grabbed Ben's wrist and pulled it behind him, then the other and zip-tied them together at the base of his spine.

"Am I being arrested?" Ben stood tall. "I know my rights."

"You're being arrested on suspicion of a homicide. You have the right to remain silent and I suggest you do and get into the car." Fulmer shoved Ben toward the sheriff's vehicle.

"Sites tried to break in and when I stopped him, someone shot him."

Kate stepped forward. "Ben didn't kill Sites. Someone else did."

Schillinger waved his gun in her face. "Don't get in the way or you'll be going with him. In which case, we'd have to place your little girl in the care of child welfare services."

As the sheriff pushed Ben into the car, Ben called over his shoulder, "Kate, get Lily to somewhere safe."

Kate's shoulders sagged, her eyes filling with tears. The only person she'd felt safe with was being hauled off in a police car. "Where?"

"Ma'am." Deputy Schillinger stepped between Kate and Ben. "I suggest you climb into the truck and drive into town in front of us. You can't stay here, since this is now officially a crime scene."

"But Ben didn't do it," Kate insisted.

The sheriff stopped in front of her. "Are you admitting to the crimes?"

"No, of course not." Kate's head spun, her vision clouding. What the hell was going on? Had the entire world turned upside down?

"Kate," Ben called out. "Go to town. Get help, call a lawyer, just don't argue with them."

"For a murderer, he gives good advice." Schillinger gripped her elbow, dragged her around the truck and shoved her up into the driver's seat. "Drive."

With no other choice and Lily to consider, Kate did what she was told and drove into town, the rotating lights from the sheriff's vehicle filling her rearview mirror.

She held on to her sanity, her resolve strengthening

as she reached the city limits. First stop for her was Cara Jo's Diner where she hoped Cara Jo was home above the restaurant and had a phone she could use. She had to get in touch with Hank.

CHAPTER SIXTEEN

BEN LEANED OVER the backseat, his gaze on the tail-lights of his truck as Kate turned left into the diner parking lot. Good, she was going to her only friend in town, Cara Jo, where she could use a phone and contact Hank with the number he'd given her earlier. Hank would help clear up this mess and send reinforcements to protect her and Lily.

Ben could kick himself for not getting Kate to safety faster. He swiveled in his seat as the sheriff's SUV passed the diner and continued on to the sheriff's office. "If you'll look at the gun, you'll note that it hasn't been discharged."

Sheriff Fulmer ignored him, pulling to the side of the road a block away from the diner. "Schillinger, you're to stay here and keep an eye on Ms. Langsdon."

"Why?" Schillinger asked. "I thought we had our killer."

Fulmer glared at him and said in a deadly tone, "Get out."

Schillinger muttered beneath his breath as he climbed out of the SUV.

The sheriff shot down the road, sliding into the parking lot at the sheriff's station. He got out and left Ben in the backseat as he unlocked the door to the office. Apparently the offices were only open during the day.

Ben waited for the sheriff to come back and lead him into a jail cell.

Fulmer didn't even glance back at the SUV as he entered the office and closed the door behind him.

After a few minutes, Ben frowned, working the zip tie around his wrists, trying to free his hands. Unfortunately, the sheriff had cinched it good and most likely the back doors of the SUV were locked from the driver's control panel. Even if he got the zip tie off his wrists, he'd have to break the window or cage separating the passenger from the driver. Why would the sheriff leave a murder suspect sitting in the back of a vehicle?

A moment later the sheriff stormed out of the office, flinging the door so hard it cracked against the wall. "Where is it?" he yelled, his face red, his eyes round, angry and maniacal. Fulmer yanked open the back door of the SUV, grabbed Ben by the front of his shirt, hauled him out and slammed him against the vehicle. "Where the hell is it?"

"I don't know what you're talking about."

"The database. The information Kendrick left to his daughter. Where is it? And don't tell me you don't know. You spoke to Derringer on the telephone and said you had a flash drive." He shook Ben and flung him against the SUV again.

Without his hands to balance, Ben tripped and fell to the ground.

Fulmer kicked him in the side. "Tell me!"

Pain shot through his side where the sheriff's boot crashed into his ribs. When the sheriff pulled his leg back to deliver another kick, Ben rolled to the side to avoid it. "Why? What's on it that you'd accuse me of a murder I didn't commit?"

"I need that damned data. My wife's life depends on it." Fulmer reached down and dragged Ben to his feet. "Please, tell me. Tell me where it is."

Ben shook his head. "I don't have it."

"Sheriff," a voice called out. "Sheriff!" Deputy Schillinger ran toward them, sweating, red-faced and breathing erratically.

"I thought I told you to watch the girl."

"She went into the diner...with the kid." Schillinger dragged in a deep breath. "Then she left the diner." The deputy doubled over, wheezing. "I couldn't...follow her...without a vehicle."

"Damn! Which way did she go?"

"West on Main."

The sheriff held Ben by the collar of his shirt. "If she has it, I'll get it. If she doesn't, you'll get it for me before you get your precious fiancée back." He slung Ben away from the SUV. "Don't let him out of your sight."

Fulmer climbed into his vehicle and spun the vehicle around, burning a trail of rubber against the pavement.

His heart racing, Ben's gaze followed the sheriff. "What did he mean, his wife's life depends on that data?" Ben asked the deputy.

"I shouldn't be saying this, but the best I can tell, the drug cartel kidnapped her when she went down to visit her family in Monterrey, Mexico." Deputy Schillinger hooked his hand through Ben's elbow and started toward the sheriff's office.

Ben dug his heels into the pavement. "Why didn't he call for help?"

"They threatened to kill her if he told anyone." The deputy tugged on his arm. "Come on. I've got a cell with your name on it." He led him toward the building.

Ben went along with him, every escape scenario he could imagine racing through his head.

When Schillinger dropped his hold on Ben's elbow and reached for the doorknob, Ben stepped back. "I'm sorry, but I can't go with you." Ben ducked his head and rammed into the deputy's back, sending him flying headfirst into the metal door.

He hit with a sickening thud and crumpled to the ground.

With no time to spare, Ben ran back toward the diner, his wrists still bound together.

When he reached the restaurant, he raced around back and kicked the door until Cara Jo peeked out the window, then threw open the door and came out on the landing above him. "Ben? Oh, thank God." Wearing a robe and flip-flops, she rushed down the stairs.

Ben's heart squeezed in his chest and his rib ached where the sheriff had kicked him. "Where's Kate?"

"She brought Lily and the puppy inside, then went back out for her overnight bag. Next thing I know she's driving off without telling me where she went."

Cara Jo pressed her hands to her cheeks. "From what I could see, there was a man in the passenger seat."

"Who was it?"

"I don't know. All I saw was his silhouette as the truck sped out of the parking lot. I called 911 and the dispatcher said she'd get word to the sheriff."

Ben gripped Cara Jo's hand. "Where's Lily?"

"She and Pickles are sleeping in my bed upstairs."

"I need a phone."

"Come up and use mine."

Ben pushed ahead of Cara Jo and raced up the stairs. The living quarters above the diner were small but decorated tastefully. "Where?"

"By the kitchen counter." Cara Jo pointed to the telephone. "You're not going to be able to do much with your hands tied behind your back." The diner owner pulled a butcher knife out of a drawer and sliced through the zip tie.

Ben rubbed his raw wrists for a second to get the feeling back into his fingertips, then dialed Hank.

The man answered on the first ring. "Derringer speaking."

"It's Ben. I need help, ASAP. Someone has Kate and I don't know who it is or where they're going."

"Slow down and tell me what happened."

Ben gave his boss the abbreviated version of what he'd learned that day. "Someone wants that data file and they're willing to kill to get it."

"Does Kate have it?"

"No."

"They'll use her as leverage to get you to give it to them."

"I figured that." Ben leaned his head against the wall. "The sheriff was with me when someone else took Kate. Larry Sites is dead and I have no idea where to start looking for Kate."

"Ben, hold on." Sounds of keyboard clicks echoed across the phone, then Hank was back. "I had a tracking device placed on your truck. If she's in it, we can find her. I have my IT guy pulling it up as we speak."

"Thank God." Ben sagged against the counter. "Hey, this might be small, but my guy in Austin said Robert

Sanders was photographed at a fund-raising event in Austin with Frank Davis."

"The man you killed?"

Ben winced. "Yeah. Did you find anything else about Sanders? He approached Kate the other day, claiming to be a friend of her father's, which doesn't make sense since most people around here claim Kate's father kept to himself. He didn't have friends, just acquaintances."

"From what I'd known of Kyle Kendrick, he didn't talk much to anyone and was always on the road, traveling from here to Mexico and back."

"You think Sanders could be the U.S. link between Mexico and the human trafficking?"

"Could be. Be careful. If he is, he has a lot to lose and he'd gladly take down anyone who gets in the way of his enterprise." Keyboard clicks sounded on Hank's side. "My IT guy says the truck's headed out County Road 949. From what we can see on the satellite map, there's not much out there but a diesel mechanic shop and some storage buildings."

Ben's hand froze on the receiver. "Would the address of the mechanic's shop be 1421 Highway 949 West?"

"Looks like it. Why?"

"My Austin contact said the man who supplied Frank the woman he killed had a cousin who lives at that address."

"Ben, I'm calling in the Border Protection and Texas Rangers. Don't try to go in there without backup. You could be stirring up a rattlesnake's den."

"Hank, they have Kate. She was my responsibility."

"Ben!" Hank shouted.

Ben hung up and sprinted for the door.

Cara Jo stood there dangling a set of keys. "You can't get there without a vehicle. Take my Mustang and bring Kate back safe."

"Lily?"

"I'll take good care of her."

"Do you have a gun?"

"I do and I know how to use it." She lifted a 9 mm Beretta from a shelf in an antique cabinet. "Girl can't be too careful when she lives alone."

"Don't let anyone in. Not anyone until I get back here with Kate. As a matter of fact, hit Redial and get Hank to send someone out to stand guard."

"Will do." She shoved him out the door. "Now go. I want my new friend back. Alive. Oh, and there's another one of these—" she waved her gun "—under the driver's seat and it's loaded."

Ben ran to the bottom of the stairs and leaped into a vintage 1967 Mustang. Seconds later he'd skidded out on Main Street and turned onto County Road 949 headed west, having flashbacks of when he'd gotten home too late to save Julia and Sarah. History could not repeat itself. He wouldn't let it.

His hands tightened around the steering wheel and he jammed the accelerator to the floor. The car was old, but it packed a lot of power. He hoped it was enough to get him there in time.

"YOU NEVER WERE my father's friend, were you?" Kate stared straight ahead, her hands clutching the steering wheel, thankful she'd unloaded Lily and the puppy first before she'd come back down to the truck for her overnight bag. At least they were safe from this latest threat. She risked a quick glance at the man beside her.

Robert Sanders sat in the passenger seat with a pistol pointed at her side. "We were business partners. He helped me find the drugs in Mexico and I sold them."

Kate's heart sank into her gut. The fact the man was admitting all this to her was a sure sign he planned to kill her when all was said and done.

Tears threatened, but Kate wouldn't let them fall. She didn't plan on dying today. Lily needed a parent to raise her. She'd already lost one. Kate would be damned if she lost another.

"I'll ask you again. Where is the flash drive your father left you?"

"I told you. The sheriff took it from Ben when he arrested him for murder."

"Then you'd better hope the sheriff doesn't decrypt the data before your fiancé gets it back."

"I suppose the information on that thumb drive implicates you in the human and drug trafficking going on around here."

"Amongst others who'd rather not be named."

"What are you going to do with me?"

Before they got too far out of town, Sanders punched buttons on his cell phone one-handed and hit Send. "I have Kendrick's daughter and I know you have the thumb drive. If you don't want your wife to die, you'll meet me at the shop, immediately." Sanders paused. "Ten minutes. Be there or I make the call."

Kate shot a glance at Sanders. "I'm not Ben's wife."

"I wasn't talking to Ben." He slipped his cell phone into his shirt pocket and steadied the gun on Kate. "Faster."

Kate eased her foot onto the accelerator. Sanders had called her on her ploy to slow down enough for someone to catch up. The farther away from town, the less likely Ben would find her.

Although how he'd get free from jail, she didn't have a clue. She hadn't even had a chance to call Hank and let him know what was going on. When Cara Jo discovered her missing, she'd call the police. A lot of good that would do.

After what felt like a very long time, Sanders leaned forward. "Turn left at the next driveway."

Kate slowed as the headlights from Ben's pickup reflected off several large metal buildings and an old barn.

"Stop."

Kate slammed her foot on the brakes.

Sanders shot forward, hitting his head on the dash. "Damn you, woman. You should have left when Snake warned you."

"My father left me that ranch. I wasn't going anywhere." Kate shifted into Park.

"You're going to wish you had." Sanders grabbed her by the hair and dragged her out of the truck through the passenger side, tossing her to the ground. "Get up. And don't try anything. I'd just as soon kill you as look at you. You Kendricks have been nothing but a thorn in my side."

He kicked her in the ribs.

Pain radiated through her rib cage as Kate staggered to her feet, reluctant to stay down where the man could kick her again.

A man with a bandanna and a tattoo on his arm stepped out of the shadows. *"Buenas noches, Patrón."*

"Did Sites spill the truth before you shot him?"

"No, amigo."

"I asked you to take care of him weeks ago."

"He was a slippery one."

"Where are the other men?"

"Moving the first shipment. They will be gone all night."

Sanders pushed Kate toward the man. "Put her with the others."

"Con las putas?"

"Sí. Do as I said."

The man with the snake tattoo grabbed Kate's arm and hustled her toward the derelict barn.

Before they'd gone two yards, headlights swung into the driveway.

Guillermo stopped and stared back toward the road.

Kate tried to wiggle out of his grip, but his fingers tightened on her arm.

Sanders held his pistol out and waved it. "Get out of the car, Sheriff."

The sheriff remained inside.

Sanders shot out a headlight and held up his cell phone. "I'm dialing now. Your wife is as good as dead."

Fulmer climbed out of the SUV with his hands raised. "Don't. Delia is all I have. Don't hurt her."

"If you didn't want me to hurt her, why were you snooping around the Flying K?" Sanders asked.

"I'd heard Kendrick had a flash drive full of the names of the people he'd been working with on both sides of the border."

"Heard? As in, bugged the phone?"

The sheriff shrugged. "I figured Kendrick's daughter might have learned something from her father."

"Her father is dead and we'd been all over the house and found nothing. Even in his computer."

"It didn't hurt to be aware, so I bugged the phone." The sheriff took a step closer. "When I heard Harding talking about a flash drive, I knew you wouldn't want it to get into the wrong hands."

"Wrong like yours?" Sanders held out his hand. "Give it to me."

The sheriff pulled out his pockets. "I don't have it."

"Kate here tells me you picked it off her fiancé."

"I confiscated a flash drive but it wasn't the right one. It didn't contain the data, only a video message from Kendrick to his daughter telling her of the drive and where to find it."

"You lie!" Sanders shot at Fulmer's feet.

Kate flinched.

The tattooed man seemed as reluctant as Kate to leave the little scene unfolding.

"I wouldn't risk my wife's life over a data device. I want her back. Alive."

Sanders shook his head. "You're a stupid fool. Your wife doesn't *want* to come back."

Fulmer's face blanched. "What do you mean?"

"She left you and returned to her family."

"She went back for vacation. Someone kidnapped her. Her parents were beside themselves when they told me."

"They told you what she wanted them to tell you. She's been working for me on the other side of the border making good money sending me the goods."

"No." Sheriff Fulmer backed away a step. "She wouldn't do that to me. Delia loves me."

"She loves money more." Sanders's lips twitched. "And the beauty of it is, you've been working for me to keep her safe. Ironic, don't you think?"

"You bastard!" Sheriff Fulmer lunged at Sanders.

A shot rang out as Fulmer reached Sanders.

The two men staggered, the sheriff falling to the ground, a hand clutched to his chest.

Kate dived for the man, but came up short when her captor jerked her backward.

Blood dribbled from the side of the sheriff's mouth and he stared up at the night sky. "I loved her...."

Kate choked back a sob. The man had to have loved his wife very much to have risked his career and his life to save her.

Her thoughts turned to Ben. If something were to happen to her, he'd blame himself for failing to reach her in time. She refused to be the next victim on his watch. Ben deserved a chance to love again. He was a good man and he'd be a good husband and father again, if only he could believe in himself.

"Guillermo!" Sanders jerked his head toward the barn. "Get her inside and burn the building."

As the tattooed man dragged her away, Kate prayed she'd live long enough to tell Ben...

Tell him what?

That she loved him? After knowing him such a short time? Could it be love? Her father said he'd fallen in love with her mother the moment he met her. Could it have been the same for her?

Love or not, she wanted the chance to get to know Ben better, to see if what she felt for him was love. She'd never thought she'd love another after losing Troy. But Ben...he could be her second chance. Her heart was big enough to love again.

Guillermo unlocked a padlock securing a heavy chain to the door of the barn and pulled the chain through the handles. Before he could shove her in, she backed up sharply and jerked out of his grip, then plowed into his side, sending him sailing through the open doorway. Several female, frightened cries erupted from within.

"Mierda!" the big man shouted.

Before Guillermo could regain his balance, Kate ran for the shadows.

A shot rang out, spitting dust up beside her, but she made it to where the moonlight cast a deep shadow next to the big old barn.

"Get her!" Sanders shouted.

Footsteps pounded on the gravel behind her.

Her pulse banging against her eardrums, Kate ran as fast as she could, tripping over objects hidden in the dark. When she cleared the back of the building, a wide-open field loomed in front of her, illuminated by the moon.

If she stepped away from the barn, she'd be found. If she stayed where she was, she'd be caught.

The whirring of a helicopter sounded in the distance and a long beam of light moved toward the barn and building complex.

It had to be the cavalry. Kate dropped to her knees and choked back a sob. Ben must have escaped.

An arm circled her neck and yanked her up.

Kate cried out, struggling to get her feet beneath her.

Headlights blasted into the compound and sirens blared in the distance.

Guillermo hauled Kate out into the open and shoved her toward his boss. He flipped a switchblade out, the smooth metal glinting in the beams of the car's headlights.

Sanders grabbed her hair and jammed the gun into her cheek. "Move and I kill her."

"Don't hurt her." Ben's voice washed over Kate like a cool balm in a blazing desert. He climbed out of an older model Mustang, carrying a gun aimed at Sanders. "I have what you're looking for."

He was there. Ben had come, against all odds.

"You give me Kate. I'll give you the device." Ben reached into his pocket with his left hand.

"Why don't I just shoot you and get the device myself?"

"You could do that, but then you might not have time to find it and destroy it before that helicopter arrives, and what would your friends on both sides of the border do to someone who let that kind of information get out?" Ben tipped his head toward the sky. "You only have a few seconds."

"Put your gun down," Sanders demanded.

Ben didn't budge.

"Do it—" Sanders shoved Kate in front of him "—or I put a bullet through her pretty head."

BEN SUCKED IN a breath and let it out slowly, praying for the right move, the right decision, the one that ended with Kate going home to Lily and raising her daughter in peace.

"Don't, Ben." Kate's voice shook. "He's going to kill me anyway. And you, too."

"Shut up." Sanders jerked her hair back hard.

Kate whimpered but didn't cry. "No," she said. "You shut up." In a flurry of movement, Kate slammed her elbow into Sanders's gut and dived for the dirt.

A shot rang at the same time Ben fired, clipping Sanders in the shoulder.

Sanders staggered backward into Guillermo, knocking the other man to the ground. When Sanders rolled over and staggered to his feet, clutching at his belly, Ben was there, his gun drawn, ready to kill the man.

Overhead, the helicopter moved into position, a spotlight filling the yard with blinding light.

Ben held his gun steady. He bent to touch Kate's shoulder. Her face was down in the dirt, but he felt for a pulse. After a second or two a strong, rhythmic thump beat against his fingers and he let the air he'd been holding out of his lungs.

Cars with rotating blue and red lights and sirens screaming whipped into the yard.

Kate stirred, then sat up with a jerk. "Ben!"

"I'm here."

"Oh, thank God." She threw herself into his arms and hugged him so tight she almost knocked him over. "I thought he'd kill you."

As the Texas Department of Public Safety swooped in with guns drawn, Ben lowered his weapon and gathered Kate in his arms, his hands weaving through her hair. He inhaled the scent of her shampoo, a huge weight lifting from his shoulders. "I wasn't too late."

She laughed and captured his face between her palms. "No, you weren't. And you saved more than me." She grabbed his hand and dragged him toward the barn.

The lawmen stepped in front of her, blocking her way.

Hank Derringer appeared beside the lawmen. "It's okay, they're the good guys." He swept past the men in uniform and stuck out his hand to Kate. "I apologize for not coming sooner. I'm Hank Derringer. And you're Kate. You have your father's eyes."

"I know." Kate smiled. "Your timing was good. And thanks for assigning this cowboy. I wouldn't be here shaking your hand without him."

"I knew he was the right man for the job." The older man winked at Ben. "Convincing him was the hard part."

"I'm convinced and glad you put me up to it." Ben touched a finger to Kate's cheek.

"You're not done yet." Kate took his hand and resumed her march toward the barn. "There are people in that barn."

As the words left her mouth, women and young girls peeked around the edge of the open doorway with dirt-streaked faces.

"We found them." Kate smiled up at Ben. "You're a hero. You saved these people."

"No, you did. I just came as backup." He hugged her to him and swung her off the ground. When he set her on her feet, he took her hand in his. "Let's go home."

Kate's smile faded. "I'd love to, but now that the bad guys are caught, you don't have to stay."

"The hell I don't." He slipped an arm around her and walked toward the Mustang. "I know a little girl who'd miss me, even if her mother won't."

She batted his arm with a light pat. "You're growing on me, cowboy. Given time…who knows…a woman could fall in love with a man like you."

He stopped and turned to face her, cupping her cheeks in his palms. "That's what I'm counting on." Then he kissed her.

EPILOGUE

KATE SAT WITH Ben on the porch swing, Lily between them, holding a very wiggly Pickles. The sun was setting on the horizon after a hard day's work on the ranch.

"Eddy and I got all the cattle rounded up and accounted for," Ben said, his hand twirling through a strand of Kate's hair.

Kate relaxed for the first time in a long time, content with her life and the direction it was going. "Think we'll have any more trouble with traffickers on the Flying K?"

"With the information Hank pulled off the flash drive, the Border Protection officers rounded up the gang of coyotes on this side of the border and the Mexican authorities claim they did the same on their side. I reckon they won't be hauling people across your spread anymore. You'll be happy to know that the women and girls found in the barn have been returned to their homes."

Pickles leaped from Lily's lap and scrambled across the porch.

Lily squealed and shot after him.

Ben scooted closer, pulling Kate into his arms.

Kate snuggled against him, pulling one foot up beneath her. "Did my father list the name of the kingpin on the U.S. side of the border?"

Ben shook his head. "No. But he left notes that he'd been working on. Hank will follow up on those. He's keeping the information close to his chest because your father mentioned a leak in our government."

Kate sighed. "At least they cleaned up around here, for now."

"You and Lily should be okay here on the Flying K."

Kate sat up straight and gave Ben a crooked smile. "That reminds me. I had some good news today."

"Did you stop by county records?"

"Yes, I did. The taxes were all paid up. The sheriff was just trying to scare me off the land so that Sanders's trafficking operation would go undiscovered and unimpeded. That's good news, but not *the* news."

Ben turned to her, his eyes narrowing. "What is it, then?"

"My father's attorney called. Seems the package I received in Houston wasn't all that my father left me. The attorney's been busy collecting all my father's bank information and sent me a detailed listing of the money my father had put away."

"Drug money?" Ben asked.

"That was my first thought. I wouldn't want any of that, not when people die every day in that business." Kate leaned into Ben, resting her head on his shoulder. "He received a salary from the FBI for his work with them and he set it all aside. Not to mention the FBI also carried a life insurance policy on him and I was named the beneficiary."

"Enough to get the ranch up and running?"

"More than enough." Kate tipped her toe on the porch, setting the swing in motion. "If I manage it well, Lily and I won't have to worry about money ever again."

Ben hugged her to him. "I know you were worried. I'm glad it's working out for you. You and Lily deserve to be happy."

She backed away enough to stare up into his eyes. "The point is… I can afford to hire ranch hands. You can continue working for Hank if you like."

Ben frowned. "Trying to get rid of me?"

"No, but I know deep down you're a cop and fighting for justice is what you do best. If working for Hank is what you want, then Lily and I will be here for you when you're not out on assignment."

Ben shook his head. "You're amazing. I think you know me better than I know myself."

She shrugged. "You're a good man, Ben Harding."

He leaned back and drew her against him. "And to think I didn't want this job in the first place."

Kate smiled up at him. "So what's keeping you?" She pressed a kiss to his lips.

"That, for one." Ben captured her face in his hands and deepened the kiss. "I never thought I could love another woman as much as my first wife." He paused, looking down at her. "I was right."

Her heart squeezing tightly, Kate's smile drifted downward. "What do you mean? You don't like us?"

"On the contrary. I love you more than I could imagine ever loving any woman." He brushed a kiss to the tip of her nose. "You're brave."

"Not where snakes are concerned," she argued.

"You're resourceful." He kissed her right cheek.

"A girl has to be, to get by these days." Kate's blood thickened, spreading warmth slowly across her body.

"And you make a great mother to Lily." He kissed her left cheek.

Kate laughed, her chest swelling with emotion. "What's not to love about Lily?" She clasped his cheeks between her palms. "Get to the point, cowboy."

"I think I'm going to love you for a very long time... if you'll let me."

"I'm counting on it, cowboy." Kate sealed her promise with a kiss.

* * * * *

Taking Aim

This book is dedicated to
the brave men and women who risk their lives daily
fighting for truth and justice.

CHAPTER ONE

Zachary Adams sat with his boots tapping the floor, his attention barely focused on the man at the center of the group of cowboys. This meeting had gone past his fifteen-minute limit, pushing twenty now.

The wiry, muscular man before them stood tall, his shoulders held back and proud. He was probably a little older than most of the men in the room, his dark hair combed back, graying slightly at the temples.

"I'm here to offer you a position in a start-up corporation." Hank Derringer smiled at the men gathered in the spacious living room of his home on the Raging Bull Ranch in south Texas.

"Doing what? Sweeping floors? Who wants a bunch of rejects?" Zach continued tapping his foot, itching for a fight, his hands shaking. Not that there had been any provocation. He didn't need any. Ever since the catastrophe of the Diego Operation, he hadn't been able to sit still for long, unless he was nursing a really strong bottle of tequila.

"*I* need you. Because you aren't rejects, you're just the type of men I'm looking for. Men who will fight for what you believe in, who were born or raised on a ranch, with the ethics and strength of character of a good cowboy. I'm inviting you to become a part of CCI, known only to those on the inside as Covert Cow-

boys Incorporated, a specialized team of citizen soldiers, bodyguards, agents and ranch hands who will
do whatever it takes for justice."

Zach almost laughed out loud. Hank had flipped
if he thought this crew of washed-up cowboys could
help him start up a league of justice or whatever it was
he had in mind.

"Whoa, back up a step there. Covert Cowboys Incorporated?" The man Hank had introduced as Chuck
Bolton slapped his hat against his thigh. "Sounds kind
of corny to me. What's the punch line?"

"No punch line." Hank squared his shoulders, his
mouth firming into a straight line. "Let's just say that
I'm tired of justice being swept under the rug."

Ex-cop Ben Harding shook his head. "I'm not into
circumventing the law."

"I'm not asking you to. The purpose of Covert Cowboys Incorporated is to provide covert protection and
investigation services where hired guns and the law
aren't enough." Hank's gaze swept over the men in
the room. "I handpicked each of you because you are
all highly skilled soldiers, cops and agents who know
how to work hard and fire a gun and are familiar with
living on the edge of danger. My plan is to inject you
into situations where your own lives could be on the
line to protect, rescue or ferret out the truth."

One by one, the cowboys agreed to sign on with
CCI until Hank came to Zach.

"I'm not much into joining," Zach said.

Hank nodded. "To be understood. You might not
want to get back into a job that puts you in the line of
fire after what you went through."

Zach's chest tightened. "I'm not afraid of bullets."

"I understand you lost your female partner on your last mission with the FBI. That had to be tough." Hank laid a hand on Zach's shoulder. "You're welcome to stay the night and think about it. You don't have to give me an answer until morning."

Zach could have given his answer now. He didn't want the job. He didn't want any job. What he wanted was revenge, served cold and painful.

With the other cowboys falling in line, Zach just nodded, grabbed his duffel bag and found the room he had been assigned for the night. The other men left, one of them already on assignment, and the other two had places to stay in Wild Oak Canyon, the small town closest to the Raging Bull Ranch.

Zach hadn't been in the bedroom more than three minutes when the walls started closing in around him. He had to get outside or go crazy.

The room had French doors opening out onto the wide veranda that wrapped around the entire house.

He sat on the steps leading down off the porch at the side of the rambling homestead and stared up at a sky full of the kind of stars you only got out in the wide-open spaces far away from city lights.

Zach wondered if the stars had been out that night Toni had died. No matter how often he replayed that nightmare, he couldn't recall whether or not the stars had been shining. Everything seemed to play out in black, white and red. From the moment they'd been surrounded by the cartel sentinels to the moment Toni had died.

Zach's eyes squeezed shut, but no matter how hard he tried to erase the vision from his mind, he couldn't shake it. He opened his eyes again and looked up at the stars in an attempt to superimpose their beauty and brilliance over the ugly images indelibly etched in his memory.

Boots tapped against the planks of the decking and Hank Derringer leaned against a wooden column. "Wanna talk about it?"

"No." Zach had suffered through days of talking about it with the FBI psychologist following his escape and return to civilization. Talking hadn't brought his partner back, and it had done nothing to bring justice to those responsible for her senseless rape, torture and murder.

"Do you have work lined up when you leave here?" Hank asked.

"No." Oh, he had work, all right. He had spent the last year following his recovery searching for the cartel gang who'd captured him and Toni Gutierrez on the wrong side of the border during the cartel eradication push, Operation Diego.

The operation had been a failure from the get-go, leading Zach to believe they had a mole inside the FBI. No matter who he asked or where he dug, he couldn't get to the answer. His obsession with the truth had ultimately cost him his job. When his supervisor had given him an ultimatum to pull his head out of his search and get on with his duties as a special agent or look for alternative employment, Zach had walked.

Out of leads, his bank account dwindling and at the mercy of this crackpot vigilante, Hank Derringer, Zach was running out of options.

Zach sighed and stared down the shadowy road leading through a stand of scrub trees toward the highway a mile away. What choice did he have? Crawl into a bottle and forget everything? Even that required money.

"If I take this job—not saying that I've agreed—what did you have in mind for my first assignment?"

JACIE KOSART AND her twin, Tracie, rode toward the ridgeline overlooking Wild Horse Canyon. The landmark delineated the southern edge of the three-hundred-and-fifty-thousand-acre Big Elk Ranch, where Jacie worked as a trail guide for big-game hunting expeditions.

Tracie, on leave from her job with the FBI, had insisted on coming along as one of the guides, even though she wasn't officially working for Big Elk Ranch. "Don't let on that I'm an agent. I just want to blend in and be like you, one of the guides, for today."

Jacie had cleared it with Richard Giddings, her boss. Then Tracie had insisted on taking on these two guys with short haircuts and poker faces instead of the rednecks from Houston.

Happy to have her sister with her for the day, Jacie didn't argue, just went with the flow. Her job was to lead the hunting party to the best hunting location where they stood a chance of bagging trophy elk.

Instead of following behind, the two men rode ahead with Jacie and Tracie trailing a couple of horse lengths to their rear.

"I was surprised to see you," Jacie stated. Her sister rarely visited, and her sudden appearance had Jacie wondering if something was wrong.

"I needed some downtime from stress," Tracie responded, her words clipped. She flicked the strands of her long, straight brown hair that had come loose from her ponytail back behind her ears.

Not to be deterred by Tracie's cryptic reply, Jacie dug deeper. "What did Bruce have to say about you coming out here without him?" Jacie had to admit to a little envy that Tracie had a boyfriend and she did not. Living on the Big Elk, surrounded by men, she'd have thought she'd have a bit of a love life. But she didn't.

"I told him I needed time with my only sibling." Tracie gave her a tight smile that didn't quite reach her eyes.

Jacie gave an unladylike snort. "As thick as you two have become, I'm surprised he didn't come with you."

Tracie glanced ahead to the two men. "I wanted to come alone."

Tracie might be telling the truth about wanting to come alone, but her answer wasn't satisfying Jacie. Her twin connection refused to believe it was just a case of missing family. "Everything okay?"

"Sure." She glanced at Jacie. "So, how many guides are there on the Big Elk Ranch?"

The change in direction of the conversation wasn't lost on Jacie, but she let it slide. "There are six, plus Richard. Some of them are part-time. Richard, Humberto and I are the full-timers. Why?"

"Just wondered. What kind of process does Richard use to screen his guides?"

Jacie shot a look at her sister. "What do you mean?"

Tracie looked away. "I was just curious if you and the other guides had to go through a background check."

"I don't know about any background check. Richard offered me the job during my one and only interview.

I can't vouch for the rest." Jacie frowned at Tracie. "Thinking about giving up the FBI to come guide on the Big Elk?" She laughed, the sound trailing off.

Her sister shrugged. "Maybe."

"No way. You love the FBI. You've wanted to join since you were eight."

"Sometimes you get tired of all the games." Tracie's lips tightened. "We should catch up with them." She nudged her horse, ending the conversation and leaving Jacie even more convinced her sister wasn't telling her everything.

Tracie rode up alongside the men.

Jacie caught up and put on her trail-guide smile as they pulled to a halt at the rim of the canyon. "This is the southern edge of the ranch. The other hunting party is to the west, the Big Elk Ranch house and barn is to the north where we came from, and to the east is the Raging Bull Ranch." Jacie smiled at the two men who'd paid a hefty sum to go hunting that day on the ranch. Richard, her boss, had taken the guys from Houston west; these two had insisted on going south, stating they preferred a lot of distance between them and the other hunting parties.

Jacie and Tracie knew the trophy bucks preferred the western and northern edge of the spread, but the two men would not be deterred.

Supposedly they'd come to hunt, based on the hardware they'd packed in their scabbards. Each carried a rifle equipped with a high-powered scope and a handgun in case they were surprised by javelinas, the vicious wild hogs running wild in the bush.

Jacie cleared her throat, breaking the silence. "Now that you've seen quite a bit of the layout, where would you like to set up? It's getting late and we won't have much time to hunt before sunset."

Jim Smith glanced across at his buddy Mike Jones.

Mr. Jones slipped a GPS device from his pocket and studied the map on it for a long moment. Then he glanced at Jacie. "Where does that canyon lead?"

"Off the Big Elk Ranch into the Big Bend National Park. There's no hunting allowed in the park. The rangers are pretty strict about it. Not to mention, the border patrol has reported recent drug trafficking activity in this canyon. It's not safe to go in there." And Jacie discouraged their clientele from crossing over the boundaries with firearms, even if their clients were licensed to carry firearms as these two were. All the hunters had been briefed on the rules should they stray into the park.

Jacie's gelding, D'Artagnan, shifted to the left, pawing at the dirt, ready to move on.

"We'll ride farther into the canyon." Mr. Jones nudged his horse's flanks, sending him over the edge of the ridge and down the steep slope toward the canyon.

"Mr. Jones," Tracie called after him. "The horses are property of the Big Elk Ranch. We aren't allowed to take them off the ranch without permission from the boss. Given the dangers that could be encountered, I can't allow you—"

Mr. Smith's horse brushed past Jacie's, following Mr. Jones down the slope. Not a word from either gentleman.

Jacie glanced across at her twin. "What the heck?" She pulled the two-way radio from her belt and hit the talk switch. "Richard, do you copy?"

The crackle of static had D'Artagnan dancing in

place, his head tossing in the air. He liked being in the lead. The two horses descending the slope in front of him made him anxious. He whinnied, calling out to the other horses as the distance between them increased.

The answering whinny from one of the mares below sent the gelding over the edge.

Tracie's mare pranced along the ridge above, her nostrils flared, also disturbed by the departure of the other two horses.

"I'll follow and keep an eye on the two," Tracie suggested.

"Richard, do you copy?" Jacie called into the radio. Apparently they'd moved out of range of radio reception with the other hunting party. Jacie switched frequencies for the base station at the ranch. "Base, this is Jacie, can you read me?"

Again static.

They were on their own and responsible for the two horses and clients headed down into the canyon.

"You feeling weird about this?" Tracie asked.

"You bet."

"Why don't you head back and let Giddings know the clients have left the property? I'll follow along and make sure they don't get lost."

"Not a good idea. You aren't as familiar with the land as I am." Jacie glanced down the trail at the two men on Big Elk Ranch horses. "If they want to get themselves lost or shot, I don't care, but those are Big Elk Ranch horses."

Tracie nodded. "Ginger and Rocky. And you know they like being part of a group, not off on their own." She shook her head. "What are those guys thinking?"

"I don't know, but I don't want to abandon the

horses." Jacie sighed. "I guess there's nothing to it but for us to follow and see if we can talk some sense into those dirtbags."

"I'm not liking it," Tracie said. "You should head back and notify Giddings."

"I don't feel right abandoning the horses and I sure as hell won't let you go after them by yourself. We don't know what kind of kooks these guys are." Jacie nodded toward the saddlebags they carried on their horses, filled with first aid supplies, emergency rations and a can of mace. "Look, we're prepared for anything on two or four legs. As long as we keep our heads, we should be okay."

Each woman carried a rifle in her scabbard, for hunting or warding off dangerous animals. They also carried enough ammo for a decent round of target practice in case they didn't actually see any game on the trail, which they hadn't up to this point. Tracie had the added protection of a nine-millimeter Glock she'd carried with her since she left training at Quantico.

"Whatever you say." Tracie grimaced at her. "My rifle's loaded and on safe." She patted the Glock in the holster she'd worn on her hip. "Ready?"

"I don't like it, but let's follow. Maybe we can talk them into returning with us." Jacie squeezed her horse's sides. That's all it took for D'Artagnan to leap forward and start down the winding trail to the base of the canyon.

"Hey, guys! To make it back to camp for supper, we need to head back in the next hour," Jacie called out to the men ahead.

Either they didn't hear her or they chose to ignore

her words. The men didn't even look back, just kept going.

D'Artagnan set his own pace on the slippery slope. Jacie didn't urge him to go faster. He wanted to catch up, but he knew his own limits on the descent.

The two men riding ahead worked their way downward at a pace a little faster than Jacie's and Tracie's mounts. At the rate they were moving, they'd have a substantial lead.

Jacie wasn't worried so much about catching up. She knew D'Artagnan and Tracie's gelding, Aramis, were faster than the mare and gelding ahead. But there were many twists and turns in the canyon below. If they didn't catch them soon, they stood a chance of falling even farther behind. It would take them longer to track the two men, and dusk would settle in. Not to mention, it would get dark sooner at the base of the canyon where sunlight disappeared thirty minutes earlier than up top.

As Jacie neared the bottom of the canyon, the two men disappeared past a large outcropping of rock.

D'Artagnan stepped up the pace, stretching into a gallop, eager to catch the two horses ahead. The pounding of hooves reverberated off the walls of the canyons. Tracie and Aramis kept pace behind her. If the two clients had continued at a sedate rate, they would have caught them by now.

The deeper the women traveled into the canyon, the angrier Jacie became at the men. They'd disregarded her warning about drug traffickers and about entering the national park with firearms, and they'd disrespected the fact that the horses didn't belong to them. They were Big Elk Ranch property and belonged on the ranch.

At the first junction, the ground was rocky and disturbed in both directions as if the men had started up one route, turned back and taken the other. In order to determine which route they ended up on, Jacie, the better tracker of the twins, had to dismount and follow their tracks up the dead end and back before she realized it was the other corridor they'd taken.

Tracie stood guard at the fork in case the men returned.

Jacie climbed into the saddle muttering, "We really need to perform a more thorough background check on our clients before we let them onto the ranch."

Her sister smiled. "Not all of them are as disagreeable as these two."

"Yeah, but not only are they putting themselves and the horses in danger, they're putting the two of us at risk, as well." Jacie hesitated. "Come to think of it, maybe we should head back while there's still enough light to climb the trail out of the canyon."

Tracie sighed. "I was hoping you'd say that. I don't want you to get hurt out here."

"Me? I was more concerned about you. You haven't been in the saddle much since you joined the FBI."

"You're right, of course." She smiled at Jacie. "Let's get out of here."

"Agreed. Let them be stupid. We don't have to be." Jacie turned her horse back the way they'd come and had taken the lead when the sharp report of gunfire echoed off the canyon walls.

"What the hell?" Jacie's horse spun beneath her and it was all she could do to keep her balance.

Aramis reared. Tracie planted her feet hard in the

stirrups and leaned forward, holding on until the gelding dropped to all four hooves.

More gunfire ensued, followed by the pounding of hooves, the sound growing louder as it neared them.

Tracie yelled, "Go, Jacie. Get out of the canyon!"

Jacie didn't hesitate, nor did her horse. She dug her heals into D'Artagnan's flanks, sending him flying along the trail. She headed back the way they'd come, her horse skimming over the rocky ground, his head stretched forward, nostrils flared.

Before they'd gone a hundred yards, Rocky, the gelding Mr. Jones had been riding, raced past them, eyes wide, sweat lathered on both sides, sporting an empty saddle, no Mr. Jones. Rocky hit the trailhead leading out of the canyon, scrambling up the slope.

Jacie dared to glance over her shoulder.

Mr. Smith emerged from the fork in the canyon trail, yelling at Ginger, kicking her hard. Both leaned forward, racing for their lives.

The distinct sound of revving motors chased the horse and rider through the narrow passage. An ATV roared into the open, followed by another, then another until four ATVs spread out, chasing Mr. Smith, Tracie and Jacie.

Jacie reached the trail climbing out of the canyon first, urging D'Artagnan faster. He stumbled, regained his footing and charged on.

Tracie wasn't far behind, her horse equally determined to make it out of the canyon alive and ahead of the ATVs.

Mr. Smith brought up the rear on Ginger.

As Jacie reached the top of the slope, she turned back, praying for Tracie to hurry.

Her sister had dropped behind, Aramis slipping in the loose rocks and gravel, distressed by the noise behind him. Just when Jacie thought the two were going to make it, shots rang out from the base of the canyon.

One of the ATVs had stopped, its rider aiming what appeared to be a high-powered rifle with a scope up at the riders on the trail.

Another shot rang out and Mr. Smith jerked in his saddle and fell off backward, sliding down the hill on his back.

His mount screamed and surged up the narrow trail past Tracie and Aramis.

Three of the ATVs raced up the path, bumping and slipping over the loose rocks.

From her vantage point at the top of the ridge, Jacie stood helpless as the horror unfolded.

Aramis reared, dumping Tracie off his back. She hit the ground and rolled, sliding down the slope back toward the base of the canyon.

Jacie yanked her rifle from its scabbard, slid out of her saddle and dropped to a kneeling position, aiming at the man at the base of the canyon.

The man was aiming at her.

Jacie held her breath, lined up the sights and pulled the trigger a second before he fired his gun.

His bullet hit the ground at her feet, kicking up dirt into her eyes.

For a second she couldn't see, but when her vision cleared, she saw the man she'd aimed for lay on the ground beside his ATV, struggling to get up.

One down, three to go.

Ginger topped the rise, followed by Aramis, spooking D'Artagnan. He pulled against the reins Jacie held on to tightly. She didn't let go, but she couldn't get another round off while he jerked her around.

When he settled, she aimed at the closest rider to her. He was halfway up the hill, headed straight for her.

She popped off a round, nicked him in the shoulder, sending him flying off the vehicle. The ATV slipped over the edge of the trail and tumbled to the bottom.

The other two riders were on their way up the hill. One split off and headed back down the side, straight for where Tracie lay sprawled against the slope, low crawling for her Glock that had slipped loose of its holster. The other rider raced toward Jacie.

Jacie aimed at the man headed for Tracie.

D'Artagnan pulled against the reins, sending Jacie's bullet flying wide of its target.

She didn't have time to adjust her aim for the rider nearing the top of the hill. He was too close and coming too fast.

Jacie let go of D'Artagnan's reins, flipped her rifle around and swung just as the rider topped the hill. She caught him in the chest with all the force of her swing and his upward movement. Jacie reeled backward landing hard on her butt, the wind knocked out of her.

The rider flew off the back of the vehicle and tumbled over the ridge.

Jacie scrambled to the edge and watched as the rider cartwheeled down the steep slope, over and over until he came to a crumpled stop, midway down.

The last rider standing had reached Tracie before she could get to her gun. He gathered her in his arms and stuck a pistol to her head. *"Pare o dispararé a mujer!"*

Even if she couldn't understand his demand, Jacie got the message. If she didn't stop, he'd shoot her sister.

Two more ATVs arrived on the canyon floor.

Jacie had no choice. She didn't want to leave her sister in the hands of the thugs below, but she couldn't fight them when they held the trump card—her sister.

She eased away from the edge of the ridge and scoped her options.

D'Artagnan and the other horses were long gone, headed back to the safety of the Big Elk Ranch barn.

The ATV she'd knocked the rider off stood near the edge of the ridge. If she hoped to escape, she had to make a run for it.

Jacie ducked low and ran for the ATV, jumped onto the seat, pulled the crank cord and held her breath.

The two new ATV riders were on their way up the hill. The man holding Tracie fired off a shot, but his pistol's range wasn't good enough to be accurate at that distance.

The ATV engine turned over and died.

Jacie pulled the cord again and the engine roared to life. She gave the vehicle gas and leaped forward, speeding toward the closest help she could find. The Raging Bull Ranch.

She had a good head start on the other two, but they didn't have to know where they were going; they only had to follow.

Jacie ripped the throttle wide open, bouncing hard over obstacles she could barely see in the failing light.

The sun had completely dipped below the horizon, the gray of dusk slipping over the land like a shroud. Until all the stars twinkled to life, Jacie could only hope she was headed in the right direction.

After thirty minutes of full-out racing across cactus, dodging clumps of saw palmetto, lights appeared ahead. Her heartbeat fluttered and tears threatened to blind her as she skidded up to a gate. She flung herself off the bike and fell to the ground, her legs shaking too badly to hold her up.

Dragging herself to her feet, she unlatched the gate and ran toward the house. "Help! Help! Please, dear God, help!"

As she neared the huge house, a shadow detached itself from the porch and ran toward her.

On her last leg, her strength giving out, Jacie flung herself into the man's arms. "Please help me."

CHAPTER TWO

Zach STAGGERED BACK, the force with which the woman with the long brown ponytail hit him knocking him back several steps before he could get his balance. He wrapped his arm around her automatically, steadying her as her knees buckled and she slipped toward the floor.

"Please help me," she sobbed.

"What's wrong?" He scooped her into his arms and carried her through the open French doors into his bedroom and laid her on the bed.

Boots clattered on the wooden slats of the porch and more came running down the hallway. Two of Hank's security guards burst into Zach's room through the French doors at the same time Hank entered from the hallway.

The security guards stood with guns drawn, their black-clad bodies looking more like ninjas than billionaire bodyguards.

"It's okay, I have everything under control," Zach said. Though he doubted seriously he had anything under control. He had no idea who this woman was or what she'd meant by *help me*.

Hank burst through the bedroom door, his face drawn in tense lines. "What's going on? I heard the sound of an engine outside and shouting coming from this side of the house." He glanced at Zach's bed and the woman stirring against the comforter. "What do we have here?"

She pushed to a sitting position and blinked up at Zach. "Where am I?"

"You're on the Raging Bull Ranch."

"Oh, dear God." She pushed to the edge of the bed and tried to stand. "I have to get back. They have her. Oh, sweet Jesus, they have Tracie."

Zach slipped an arm around her waist and pulled her to him to keep her from falling flat on her face again. "Where do you have to get back to? And who's Tracie?"

"Tracie's my twin. We were leading a hunting party on the Big Elk. They shot, she fell, now they have her." The woman grabbed Zach's shirt with both fists. "You have to help her."

"You're not making sense. Slow down, take a deep breath and start over."

"We don't have time!" The woman pushed away from Zach and raced for the French doors. "We have to get back before they kill her." She stumbled over a throw rug and hit the hardwood floor on her knees. "I shouldn't have left her." She buried her face in her hands and sobbed.

Zach stared at the woman, a flash of memory anchoring his feet to the floor. He remembered his partner, Antoinette Gutierrez—Toni—in a similar position, her face battered, her hair matted with her own blood, begging for her life.

The room spun around him, the air growing thick, hard to breathe.

Not until Hank ran forward and helped the woman to her feet did Zach snap out of it.

"We'll help," Hank promised. "Where is your sister?"

The woman looked up and blinked the tears from her eyes, her shoulders straightening. "Wild Horse Canyon."

"Joe." Hank addressed one of his bodyguards. "Wake the foreman and tell him we need all the four-wheelers gassed up and ready to go immediately."

Joe jammed his weapon into his shoulder holster and ran out the open French doors.

Hank turned to the other bodyguard. "Max, grab the first aid supplies from the pantry, along with one of the blankets kept in the hall closet. Meet us at the barn in two minutes."

"A woman needs our help." Hank turned to Zach. "Are you coming or not?"

The woman in question's eyes narrowed as she stared from Hank to Zach. "I don't care who comes, but we need to get there fast. If they take her hostage, the longer we wait, the harder it will be to find them."

"Understood."

Zach stared at the woman, his pulse pounding against his eardrums, his palms damp and clammy. "I'll come." The words echoed in the room, bouncing off the walls to hit him square in the gut. He'd committed to helping an unknown woman when he'd failed to help the partner he'd been with for three years.

Hank steered the woman toward Zach. "Find out what you can while I call the sheriff and let him know what's going on."

When Hank left the room, the woman glanced at Zach. "Are you coming or not?"

Having committed to the task at hand, Zach hooked

the woman's arm, ready to get the job over with as quickly as possible. "It would help if we knew who you are."

"Jacie Kosart. I work on the Big Elk Ranch. It's a three-hundred-fifty-thousand-acre spread bordering the Raging Bull and the Big Bend National Park."

"Jacie." He rolled the name on his tongue for a second, then dove in. "What were you doing out this late?"

"My sister and I were leading a big-game hunting party for my boss, Richard Giddings. The two men who'd commissioned us didn't want to hunt on the normal trails the deer like to travel." Jacie explained how they'd come to the canyon, the subsequent shootings and her escape. "We have to get back. I think they killed the two hunters. If not, they need medical help." She gulped, tears welling again. "Tracie has to be all right. She just has to."

"We'll do the best we can to find her and bring her home." Zach tried to sound confident when he felt nothing like it. If the men in the canyon had anything to do with the drug cartels, Jacie's sister was as good as dead.

The sound of engines revving outside signaled the end of their conversation and the need to move.

Zach cupped Jacie's elbow and led her through the French doors and out to the barn where five ATVs idled in neutral. The man Zach assumed was Hank's foreman sat astride one of them giving the engine gas.

Hank, dressed in jeans, a denim jacket and cowboy boots, jogged down from the house flanked by his two bodyguards, each carrying an automatic assault weapon. Hank carried two, one of which he tossed to Zach. "In case we run into some trouble."

Zach dropped his hold on the woman's arm and

caught the high-powered weapon, slipping it into the scabbard on one of the four-wheelers.

"You all right?" he asked Jacie.

She nodded. "Yeah. I just want to find my sister."

The two bodyguards mounted a four-wheeler each and Hank took another, leaving only one left.

"The girl can ride with you. I don't want her falling off and injuring herself. This way you can keep an eye on her and lead the way."

Zach frowned but mounted the ATV and scooted forward for Jacie to climb on the back.

She balked, staring at Zach and the space allotted to her. "I can take the one I rode in on."

"We don't know how much gas it has in it, and given that you've passed out once, you're better off riding with one of us."

Zach sucked in a deep breath and let it out. "Get on."

Jacie flung her leg over the back and slid in behind Zach, her thighs resting against his, her chest pressing into his back.

He revved the engine and shot out of the barnyard headed south.

With Jacie looking over his shoulder, directing him, he raced across the dark earth, dodging clumps of prickly pear cactus and saw palmettos.

The woman held on lightly at first, her grip tightening as Zach swerved in and out of the vegetation with nothing but the stars shining down on him from a moonless sky.

As they neared the edge of the canyon, Jacie pointed and yelled over the roar of the engine. "There!"

Zach pulled up short of the edge of the canyon. On the slim chance the assailants were hanging around at the bottom of the canyon, he didn't want to provide them with a target at the top. He cut the engine.

Before he could dismount, Jacie was off the back and scrambling toward the edge.

He caught her as she lunged for the trail, yanking her back from the edge and out of line of sight from the bottom. "Are you trying to get yourself killed?"

"My sister was down there. We have to save her." She struggled against his hold.

"For all we know they could still be down there."

She fought to free her arm. "Then let's go."

The other riders had pulled to a halt and dismounted.

Zach dragged Jacie over to Hank. "Hold on to her while I check it out."

"Take Joe with you in case you run into trouble."

"I do better on my own." Zach crouched low and dropped over the rim of the canyon, slipping down the trail as quietly as possible. In the light from the night sky, he could make out where the trail was disturbed, one edge knocked free. Probably where a horse, a motorcycle or a four-wheeler had run off the side.

The bottom of the trail was bathed in shadows, making it hard to distinguish the boulders from crouching thugs waiting to pounce.

Careful not to fall off the edge himself, Zach moved swiftly down the trail, reaching the bottom. The shadows proved to be boulders and one wrecked ATV, crumpled among them. Nothing moved. Zach explored among the boulders to the other side of the ATV and found the body of a man lying at an awkward angle, facedown, his leg bent, probably shattered in the fall. The ground beside him sported an inky-black stain.

Zach didn't have to guess that the stain was a drying

pool of this man's blood. This guy hadn't died from the fall, based on the dark bullet-sized circle in the middle of his back. If Zach turned him over, he'd likely be a mess on the other side where the bullet exited his body.

Zach searched the area around the base of the cliff and shouted up, "Clear!"

Five four-wheelers inched down the narrow trail, lights picking out the way.

Joe led the pack followed by Hank, Max, the foreman and Jacie.

Zach frowned and met her as she cleared the trail. "You should have stayed at the top."

"Did you find her?" Jacie glanced around, her eyes wide, hopeful. Then her shoulders sagged and she slumped on the seat of the ATV. "That's Mr. Smith, one of the two hunters we were escorting." She sucked in a deep breath and let it out slowly. "Tracie's not here, is she?"

"Believe it or not, that's a good thing." Hank left his four-wheeler and crossed to Jacie. "If she's not here, it's a good chance that she's still alive."

Jacie's jaw tightened. "Then come on, let's find her."

Zach shook his head. "It would be suicide to continue searching in the dark. If the attackers are in the canyon still, they would have the advantage and pick us off from above."

"We can't leave her out there."

"Zach's right. We have to wait until daylight." Hank stood beside Zach. "Going in at night wouldn't be doing your sister any favors."

"Then I'll go on alone." As she pressed the gas lever, Zach grabbed her around the waist and yanked her off the bike.

"You're not going anywhere." Zach slammed her against his chest, his arms wrapping around her waist. "One captive is enough. We don't want to risk another. Besides, your sister most likely wouldn't want you to risk it."

Jacie struggled against him. "Let go of me. My sister is my responsibility."

"Then take your responsibility seriously and do what's smart. We need to wait until daylight before we risk going into that canyon."

The woman stopped. "I guess you're right."

When she quit struggling and seemed to settle down, Zach released her. In the next second, she shot across to the four-wheeler she'd left running, hopped on and took off on the trail leading into the canyon.

"Damn, woman." Zach ran after her, catching up as she entered the narrow trail flanked by high cliffs.

As she slowed to negotiate around a boulder, Zach jogged alongside her and jumped on the back. "Stop, damn it!"

"Not until I find my sister." She goosed the accelerator lever on the handle and nearly unseated him.

Zach grabbed around her middle and held on.

They slid around a corner, the starlight barely reaching them at this point.

About the time Zach steadied himself, Jacie hit the brakes and jerked the handles, sending the machine sliding sideways, and the tail end with Zach slipping around to the right.

JACIE COULDN'T LET the search end. Not when her sister's life hung in the balance.

When she saw the cowboy boot, she slammed on

her brakes. In a random patch of starlight, a jean-clad leg peeked out from behind a large boulder.

Her heart skipped several beats and then hammered against the wall of her chest. Jacie threw herself off the four-wheeler and scrambled up from her hands and knees to run toward the leg, sobs rising from her throat, echoing off the canyon walls.

Footsteps crunched behind her. Probably Zach, but she didn't care. If this was Tracie… *Oh, dear God, please be okay.*

The other four-wheelers entered the canyon at a more moderate pace, coming to a halt behind Jacie's.

She dropped to her knees beside a body, relief washing over her as soon as she saw it was a man.

"It's Mr. Jones." She felt for a pulse, her hand still for a long time before she glanced back at Zach, a glimmer of hope daring to make an appearance. "I have a pulse. It's weak, but I have a pulse." She leaned into the man's face. "Mr. Jones, can you hear me?"

Nothing. Her hopes dying, she tried again, patting the man's cheek gently. "Mr. Jones, please. Can you hear me?"

A muscle twitched in the man's leg.

Encouraged, Jacie spoke louder. "Mr. Jones, we're going to get you some help, but can you help us?"

The man's eyes fluttered open. "Set…up." He closed his eyes again.

"Mr. Jones!" Jacie wanted to shake the man but was afraid to add to his injuries. "Please, did you see where they went? Where did they take my sister?"

His eyes never opened, but his lips moved.

Jacie leaned in closer, tilting her head to hear what he whispered.

"Not Jones."

Jacie leaned back. "What do you mean?"

The man whispered again.

Leaning close, Jacie caught what sounded like letters.

"D... E... A." As if it had taken everything he had left, the last letter ended on a raspy exhale.

Mr. Jones, or whoever he was, didn't draw another breath.

Jacie felt for a pulse. Not even a weak one thumped against her fingertips. "No pulse. He's not breathing." She clamped his nose with her fingers and breathed for him.

Zach dropped to his knees on the other side of him and leaned the heel of his palms into the man's chest five times. "Now breathe," he instructed.

Jacie blew into the man's mouth. His lungs expanded, pushing his chest up.

Zach resumed his compressions. For every five, Jacie breathed one breath.

Hank and the bodyguards scoured the vicinity while Zach and Jacie worked over Mr. Jones.

When they returned, Jacie glanced up at Hank. "Any sign of my sister?" She knew the answer, but she had to ask.

"None."

Rather than let the news cripple her, Jacie renewed her efforts to save Mr. Jones.

After fifteen minutes, Zach quit pumping the man's chest and he touched Jacie's arm before she could breathe into the man's mouth.

"He's gone."

"No." Jacie sat back on her haunches. "He might have told us where they went."

"I doubt it. From what you said, he was hit before they grabbed Tracie." Zach rose to his feet and held out a hand to Jacie. "Come on, let's get you back to the ranch. We'll start the search in the morning."

"She has to be okay." Jacie let him pull her to her feet, where she leaned against him, pressing her forehead against the solid wall of his chest. "She's all I have."

Hank patted her back. "We'll find her. Don't you worry."

Zach stood beside her. "I saw his lips moving, but I couldn't hear him. What did Jones say to you before he died?"

"I'm not sure." Jacie shook her head. She'd never had someone die on her. Hell, she'd never seen someone get shot in all the years she'd been working on the Big Elk Ranch. She'd never seen someone die of a gunshot wound. She pushed the image of the dead men from her mind and concentrated on the only clue she might have to find her sister. "At first he said what sounded like 'set…up.' Then he said 'Not Jones… D… E… A.'"

Zach stiffened against her, his hands gripping her arm. "Are you sure?"

She glanced up into his face. "As sure as I can be. The man was barely able to whisper. I could have gotten it wrong. Why?"

"Damn. These men most likely were agents with the DEA."

Hank ran a hand through his shocking-white hair and looked around the canyon walls. "Think they were set up?"

"Sounds like it."

Jacie froze. "Oh, dear God." She didn't, she couldn't have… "My sister is an FBI agent here on vacation to visit me."

Zach still held her.

Jacie was sure, if he weren't still gripping her arms, she'd have fallen to her knees. "Do you think she was working undercover, as well?"

"If so, and it was a setup…" Zach's jaw tightened. "Apparently, there's some bad blood in both agencies."

Hank sighed. "Holy hell. I was too late, then."

Zach dropped his hold on Jacie. "What do you mean?"

"I'm sorry, Jacie. I've failed your sister." Hank reached out for one of Jacie's hands. "You see, Tracie came to me yesterday asking for my help."

"I don't understand." Jacie's head spun. Had she been walking around in the clouds since her sister arrived? "My sister only got here two days ago. Why would she come to you?"

"She wanted help finding out who was the leak in her agency and she didn't want to go through official channels." Hank's gaze shifted back to Zach. "Since you are former FBI, this was to be your first assignment."

CHAPTER THREE

ZACH RODE BACK to the Raging Bull Ranch, a knot the size of Texas twisting his gut.

Hank couldn't be serious. To ask him to take on the FBI as his first assignment? The organization that had left him and Toni to die in the godforsaken hell of the Los Lobos cartel in the Mexican state of Chihuahua?

Captured in Juarez on assignment, drugged and transported to a squalid compound in Mexico, Zach and Toni had been tortured and starved in the cartel's attempt to attain information from them about who in the FBI was supplying military weapons to their archrivals, La Familia Diablos.

He'd been forced to watch as they raped, mutilated and finally killed Toni. Bound and gagged, he'd been helpless, unable to do anything to save her.

When another gang stormed the compound, they'd crashed into the concrete building where Zach had been held, giving him the opportunity to escape under cover of the night. But it had been too late for Toni.

Wounded, dehydrated and barely able to see through swollen eyes, he dragged himself out of the compound and hid in the mountains, stealing food from a farmer until he could make his way back to the States.

Two years, surgery, rehab and psychiatric treatment

had healed the external scars, but the internal ones festered like a disease.

Jacie rode on the back of the four-wheeler, her arms circled around Zach's waist.

Hank wanted him to help her and her sister, who was certain to be experiencing exactly what Toni had been subjected to, if not worse. If she wasn't dead, likely she would be wishing she was soon.

No. Zach couldn't do this. He couldn't commit to finding Tracie, not when he knew the outcome wouldn't be good. Her twin would expect him to come back with a woman intact, healthy and cared for.

The arms around him tightened, reminding him that the woman on the back of the vehicle was already counting on him to help her.

As he pulled into the barnyard of the Raging Bull Ranch, he mentally prepared his exit speech. "Hank, I'd like to talk with you privately."

No use bringing the woman in on his cowardly departure. She wouldn't understand, and seeing the desperation in her eyes would only drive another stake through his heart.

Red and blue flashing lights shone from the road leading into the Raging Bull Ranch.

"Zach, we'll talk as soon as I've had a chance to bring the local law enforcement up to date on the situation. Meet me in my office in five minutes." Hank and his two bodyguards left. The foreman rode one of the four-wheelers to the back of the barn, leaving Zach alone with Jacie.

He glanced away from her, the look of worry and sadness in her eyes more than he could handle.

A hand on his arm precluded ignoring the woman.

"Zach, what are we going to do now? How are we going to find my sister?"

"There is no *we*." His words came out sharper than he'd intended.

Jacie snatched her hand away from his arm as if she'd been bitten. "What do you mean? I thought Hank said you were the one assigned to help Tracie."

"If I chose to accept the assignment and go to work for Hank in his insane business." Zach snorted. "Truth and justice. There is no truth and justice when a gun's held to your head or a whip's lashed across your naked skin. I won't be a part of Hank's fantasy."

"You mean you're going to turn your back on my sister and leave her to die?"

Her words struck him where it hurt most. Square in his gut where guilt ate away at his insides. "I can't do anything for your sister." He turned his back to her. "She's as good as dead."

"No! She's alive. She's my twin. I can feel her presence." Jacie grabbed his arm and jerked him around. "You can't just walk away. My sister needs you. I need you. I can't do this on my own. I will if I have to. But I wouldn't know where to start."

"Don't worry, Hank will find some other cowboy to ride to your rescue. It just won't be me. I'm not the right man for this job."

"You're not a man at all," Jacie spat out. "What kind of man would run away rather than help save a woman's life?"

Zach rounded on her and grabbed her arms in a vicious grip. His heart slammed against his ribs, and rage rose up his neck to explode in his head. "That's right! I *can't* help your sister. I *can't* save a woman from the cartel. I couldn't save Toni and I refuse to watch it happen all over again. I. Can't. Help. *Got that?*" He shook her hard.

Tears welled in Jacie's gray-blue eyes, her long, rich brown hair falling down over her face. "I get it. You have your own issues. Fine. I'll do this without you." She struggled against his hold. "Let go of me. I don't want or need you or any of Hank's hired guns. I'll get my sister back. Alive! Mark my words." She shook free of him. "In the meantime go find a bottle to crawl into or see a shrink. Whatever. I don't give a damn." She spun on her booted heels and marched away from him.

The farther away she moved, the more Zach's chest tightened. If Jacie went tearing off after her sister, she'd end up captured and tortured, as well. What kind of fool would throw herself at the cartel and expect to survive?

The rage subsided, leaving Zach cold and empty.

Jacie was a fool. But she was a fool who loved her sister enough to sacrifice her life to save her twin.

Zach had begged his captors to torture him and leave his partner alone. Instead they'd tortured her in their efforts to drag information out of *him*. Sadly he didn't have the information they'd wanted and Toni had paid the price for his ignorance. His captors had wanted the name of the agent feeding their rivals information about upcoming sting operations. While the Los Lobos cartel took hits, losing some of their best contacts, La Familia Diablos got away with all their people and goods intact.

Heartsick by his own agency's betrayal, Zach had returned to the States, healed his wounds and quit the FBI. Tired of the politics, the graft and corruption.

If Tracie had been after the same person...the one disloyal to his country and fellow agents...she was crazy. The traitor kept his hand so close to his chest. No one knew who he was.

As Jacie disappeared around the corner of the ranch house, Zach started after her. Jacie, unskilled in the art of spying and tactics, wouldn't last two minutes going up against a drug cartel.

His footsteps sped up until he was jogging. Since he was on the outside looking in, he might discover who the mole was in the FBI, the man who'd sacrificed his own people to line his pockets with blood money.

Jacie had almost reached Hank when Zach caught up with her. "Wait."

The woman kept walking. "Why should I? I told you, I don't need you or anyone else to help me find my sister."

He snagged her arm and spun her toward him. "Look. Despite what you're saying, you won't last two minutes out there. The cartel employs trained killers. What kind of training have you had in shooting and dodging bullets?"

Her shoulders were thrown back, her chin held high. "I'm a damned good shot."

"At game. Ever shot a person?"

Her eyes narrowed. "Not before tonight."

"You have to be willing to shoot before you're shot."

"I'll do whatever it takes to find my sister and bring her back alive." She swallowed hard, her chin rising even higher. "Even if it means killing a man to do it. And I might just start with you if you don't let go of me."

He dropped his hold. "You were also right that I

have issues. I won't go into it, but they involved the cartel. I've been on both sides of the border. I know what to expect."

"So? You just said you wouldn't help me."

He sucked in a breath and let it out slowly before capturing her gaze with a steady one of his own. "Though I think the effort is futile, I'll help you find your sister."

Jacie snorted. "No, thanks." She turned away and would have walked off.

Zach grabbed her hand and steeled himself to reveal a piece of his soul he hadn't revealed to anyone. "I watched someone I cared for tortured and killed by the Los Lobos Cartel. It's not something I want to do again. I promise to do my best to find your sister before she meets the same fate."

Jacie's eyes flared wide, then narrowed again. "How do I know you won't flip out on me again?"

"I'm a good agent." He paused. "I *was* a good agent. I know when to focus and I'm driven to get the job done."

"Then why did you quit the FBI?"

"For the same reason your sister asked for help from Hank. I was betrayed by someone on the inside. My partner paid with blood. If I can find your sister and, in the process, find the mole, my partner will not have died in vain."

Jacie's eyes narrowed even more and she chewed on her bottom lip. Finally she stuck out her hand. "Okay, then. Let's go find my sister."

JACIE SHOOK ZACH'S HAND, her fingers tingling where they touched his. She wasn't completely convinced

Zach was her man, and she didn't like the way her pulse quickened when he was near, but she didn't have a whole lot of choices. Going searching for the people responsible for her sister's abduction would be hard enough on her own.... Hell, it would be impossible. Having a former FBI agent on her side would be a step in the right direction. He might still have connections and contacts.

Hank led the county sheriff over to join them. "Zach, this is Sheriff Fulmer from Wild Oak Canyon. He'll be working with the FBI and DEA on this case."

Zach shook the sheriff's hand.

Jacie refused to, knowing the man's track record since he'd taken office a year ago. He tended to look the other way rather than stop the flow of drugs through his county. "When will the DEA and FBI be sending someone out to assist?" And hopefully take over the operation.

"I spoke to the regional director of the FBI a few minutes ago. They're as concerned as you are to get your sister back. As for the DEA agents, the county coroner and the state crime lab are on their way out as we speak. If you could show me where the bodies are, I'll cordon off the crime scene until they arrive."

"My foreman will take you out there," Hank said. "If I need to sign any statements, let me know."

"From what Mr. Derringer says, I'll need a full statement from you, Ms. Kosart, as you're the only eyewitness."

"I'll provide one in the morning. Right now I need to get back to the Big Elk Ranch and notify my employer of the situation and check on the horses." She hadn't even thought once about the horses since Tracie had been taken. Now she focused on them to keep from going crazy with inaction.

"I'm going with you." Zach glanced at Hank. "I'm in."

Hank nodded, ignoring the raised eyebrows of the sheriff. "Keep me informed, will ya?" was all he said; then he turned his attention to the sheriff. "Scott, my foreman, and I will show you where we found the two agents." He led the officer away.

"Give me a minute while I get my keys." Zach pointed toward a black four-wheel-drive pickup standing in the circular drive. "You can wait by my truck."

"Okay, but hurry. I'm worried about the horses." Jacie was worried about a lot more than just the horses, but she trudged toward the vehicle, taking her time, while Zach ducked into the ranch house.

Jacie recognized the truck as a model produced a couple of years before. It wasn't new, but it shone like a new truck with only a thin layer of dust coating the shiny wax finish. The man had some issues, but taking care of what was his wasn't one of them.

He returned in two minutes, carrying a small duffel bag in one hand, wearing a black cowboy hat and a light leather jacket. When it flapped open, the black leather of a shoulder holster was revealed with a pistol nestled inside.

Jacie had spent her life around men and guns, working for the Big Elk Ranch. Leading hunting parties required a thorough knowledge of how to shoot, clean and unjam weapons of all shapes and sizes. Knowing Zach carried a pistol and was former FBI gave her a small sense of comfort that she wasn't the only one who could handle a gun going forward in the search for her sister.

Before he reached her he clicked the door lock release.

Jacie climbed into the truck and buckled herself into the passenger seat.

Zach stashed the bag in the backseat and settled behind the steering wheel. "You'll have to tell me where to go. I'm new around here."

She gave him the directions and sat back, staring ahead where the headlights illuminated the road, keeping an eye out for the wildlife that skirted the shoulders looking for something to eat. Too many times she'd had near misses with the local deer.

In her peripheral vision, she watched the way Zach handled the truck with ease, his fingers gripping the steering wheel a little tighter than necessary, his face set in grim lines. She wanted to know more about him; what made his eyes so dark and caused the shadows beneath? Had his experience with the cartel left such an indelible mark he couldn't separate that chapter of his life with a possible future?

"Toni was your partner?" she asked.

The fingers on the steering wheel tightened until the knuckles turned white. For a long moment Zach didn't answer.

About the time Jacie gave up on getting a response, he spoke.

"Yes, Toni was my partner."

"I'm sorry. You two must have been close." Jacie dragged her gaze from the pain reflected from his eyes. "Did he leave behind a family?"

"*She* wasn't married. Her father was her only relative."

Interesting. So his partner had been female. Which would explain his reluctance to go after another female when he'd failed the first. Jacie chewed on that bit of information. "Were you in love with her?"

As soon as the question left her lips, Jacie could have smacked herself. The man was torn up enough about losing his partner. Bringing it up had to be killing him. Her curiosity didn't warrant grilling him about his past. "I'm sorry, this must be painful. I'll shut up."

"Yes."

"Yes that you want me to shut up or yes that you loved her?"

His lips twitched, the movement softening his features to almost human. "Both."

Jacie sat back, her gaze back on the road, her chest tightening. "Turn left at the next road."

Zach nodded.

"Did she know you loved her?" Jacie closed her eyes. "That was too personal. You don't have to answer. I'm sorry. While Tracie went into the FBI, I knew I couldn't because I can't keep my mouth shut unless I'm out hunting."

"Pretend you're hunting." Zach turned where she'd indicated. "And no. She didn't know." He pulled up to a closed gate attached to six-foot-high fencing. "Game ranch?"

"That's what I do. I didn't go to Quantico or study to be a doctor. I got my marketing degree from the University of Texas and came back here to work as a hunting party coordinator, a fancy title for trail guide. It allows me to be where I love to be, outside, and working with horses and people." She couldn't help the defensive tone in her voice.

"I'm not judging."

"I love my sister and I'm so proud of her, but part of me feels as though I didn't push hard enough, that I'm not living up to my potential. I went on trail rides while my sister ran off to be an FBI agent working for the good of her country."

"And look what it got her." Zach's lips thinned. "Betrayal by that country she's fighting for."

"I don't believe that. One bad apple, and all that, doesn't mean everyone will turn traitor. I still believe in the FBI and the other branches of service dedicated to protecting our freedom. And I'm sure Tracie feels the same. If she knew there was a mole in the organization, she didn't run from it, she went looking for it. Especially since she asked Hank for help."

Zach nodded toward the gate. "I take it the gate doesn't open without a remote."

Jacie's face heated. She slipped from the truck and ran to the gate, punching in a code, triggering the automatic gate opener arm to swing out.

Jacie climbed back into the truck and sat quietly as Zach drove the winding road that led to the lodge at the Big Elk Ranch.

The lights shone bright, unusual for the earliest hours of the morning.

Before the vehicle came to a halt, Richard Giddings leaped off the porch and opened the passenger door to the pickup. "Oh, thank God." The tall man with the slightly graying temples reached out. His hands circled her waist and he lifted Jacie to the ground. "I'd been so worried about you. When your hunting party never returned, I had everyone out looking until midnight. When Derringer called to say you were on your way, I was relieved and sick all at once." He wrapped an arm around her shoulder and led her toward the house. He'd taken a couple of steps before he stopped and stared down into her eyes. "I'm so sorry about your sister."

Despite the exhaustion threatening to overwhelm her, Jacie planted her feet in the ground and threw back her shoulders. "Tracie will be all right. We'll get her back."

Richard smiled down at her with his warm green eyes. "She's a fighter, just like her sister."

"Damn right." Jacie backed away from her boss. "Richard, I'd like you to meet Zach." She stopped, realizing for the first time she didn't know Zach's full name. She tilted her head and raised her eyebrows, hoping he'd take the hint.

Zach stepped forward and held out his hand. "Zach Adams."

Richard's eyebrows V'd over his nose. "Should I know you?"

"Not at all." He glanced at Jacie and smiled. "Jacie and I go way back to college, don't we?"

"Y-yes. We do."

"We dated for a while, lost touch, but I just couldn't forget her. And since I was in the neighborhood, I planned on reconnecting in the morning, once I got my bearings." He shook his head. "Imagine my surprise when she found me first at Hank's place."

Richard held out a hand and shook Zach's. "You picked a really bad time."

"No, actually." Jacie crossed to Zach's side. "I'm glad he's here. With Tracie being gone and all, it's nice to have the support of…friends." She hooked her arm through his. "Do you mind if he stays in the Javelina Cabin? I know it's empty." And it was the closest one to the tiny cabin she'd called home since she came to work full-time at the Big Elk Ranch.

"Sure." Richard nodded. "You can show him the way. I'll have Tia Fuentez make up a plate of food since you missed dinner. How about you, Mr. Adams? Hungry?"

"Call me Zach. And no, thank you. I had my supper." He pulled Jacie close. "But I'll use that time to get a shower and hit the rack."

"Make yourself at home. The ranch is big, but the people are friendly."

"I've noticed that." He smiled again at Jacie. "I'm looking forward to catching up with Jacie, and maybe we'll hear something about her sister soon."

Jacie steered Zach toward the line of cabins leading away from the lodge. As soon as they were out of listening range, she whispered, "Why did you lie to my boss?"

"I'd just as soon everyone in this part of Texas think that I'm here as an old college buddy or boyfriend, rather than an agent searching for your sister. In this case, we don't know who are the good guys and who are the bad guys. So we play it neutral and I blend in. The best undercover agents are those who blend in."

"Okay, then. When do we start looking for my sister?"

"Was that a helicopter I saw out by the barn?"

Jacie frowned, taken off guard by the change in subject. "Yes, Richard has a helicopter he uses occasionally for the big game hunts or flight-seeing tours over Big Bend."

"Think he'll take us up so that we can fly over the canyon?"

Her heart fluttered with excitement. "I'm sure he will. I'll ask." Maybe they'd spot the people holding Tracie.

"Good. It would be better coming from you, since it's your sister and you work here. Remember, I'm just a boyfriend."

Her cheeks warmed at the thought of Zach as her boyfriend, even if it was pretend. "I'll get right on it."

"I'm gonna hit the sack for a few hours of sleep. We have a busy day ahead of us. I suggest you do the same."

She nodded, staring out at the night sky, wondering what her sister was going through and if she was okay. "We're going to find her."

When he didn't respond, Jacie's fists tightened. "We *will* find my sister."

"I promise you this." He faced her, capturing her cheeks in his hands, his gaze severe, his lips pressed into a firm line. "I'll do the best I can."

A shiver rippled across Jacie's skin as she gazed into his brown-black eyes. The intensity of his stare and the tightness of his grip on her face gave her a sense of comfort and commitment. This man had lost someone he loved to terrorist cartel members. He wouldn't let it happen again if he could help it. They would get her sister back or die trying.

CHAPTER FOUR

JACIE SHOWED ZACH to the cabin and left him to get a shower.

After retrieving his duffel bag, he checked his cell phone, surprised that he had reception. Out in the boonies of south Texas, he hadn't seen much in the way of reception outside the small town of Wild Oak Canyon. The Big Elk Ranch must have a cell tower of its own.

Glad for the ability to use his own phone, Zach didn't lose time in contacting an old buddy from his Quantico days back on the East Coast.

"Hello?" a gravelly voice answered on the fifth ring.

"Jim, Zach Adams."

"Zach?" James Coslowski paused. The sound of something falling in the background, followed by a curse, crossed the airwaves. "Do you realize it's only three in the morning?"

"Sorry for the late call, but I need a favor."

"And it couldn't have waited until morning?"

"No. I need to know everything about Special Agent Tracie Kosart that you can find, and as soon as possible."

"I repeat…this couldn't wait until I've had a gallon of coffee, say after a more reasonable hour like seven?"

"She was abducted tonight by what appears to be a Mexican drug cartel."

"Damn." The gravel had been scraped from Jim's voice. "You know I'm not supposed to release any information—"

"I know. I'm asking as a huge favor. I'm working this case as a private investigator, but I need to know why they would have abducted her. Anything you can find out and share would help."

"Still, you're no longer with the agency."

Zach snorted. "Since when are you a rule follower?"

"Since I got married and have a wife, and a baby on the way."

Zach's chest tightened. "Sorry, man. I didn't know. Congratulations."

"There's a lot you don't know, having dropped off the face of the earth for the past two years." Jim sighed. "I'll do the best I can. Just don't go all vigilante and get yourself into trouble."

Zach's fist tightened around the cell phone. "What difference would it make? I didn't get any help from my employer last time. I certainly don't expect any better this time."

"Just stay safe. Some of us care what happens to you."

His heart pounding against his ribs, Zach ended the call, grabbed a towel from the bathroom closet and hit the shower.

So much time had passed since he'd been gone from the FBI. Jim had been a good friend and Zach hadn't even acknowledged his wedding. The invitation had likely been tossed with all the mail he'd ignored for so long.

About time he rejoined the human race and pulled his head out of the dark fog he'd sunk into.

JACIE HURRIED TO the main lodge and entered through the back door. Richard had only left them a few moments before; surely he hadn't gone straight to bed. Not with members of his guest list dead and Jacie's sister missing.

As she'd expected, she found him in the resort's office, surrounded by rich wood paneling and bookshelves filling two walls from floor to ceiling.

Richard sat behind his desk, scrubbing a hand over his face.

Jacie cleared her throat.

Her boss glanced up, his eyes bloodshot, the lines beside his eyes and denting his forehead deeper than she'd remembered. "Come in, Jacie." He rose from his chair and rounded his desk, opening his arms to her.

She fell into them, pressing her face against his broad chest. This man had been like a father to her since she'd come to work full-time for him. "Will we get her back?"

"Damn right we will," he said, his voice gruff, his arms tightening around her for a moment. He then pushed her to arm's length. "I've been thinking. Tomorrow at sunup, we'll take the chopper up and do our own search for her. To hell with waiting for the government to get out there. I figure the more people looking, the better."

Jacie stared up at her boss, blinking the tears from her eyes. Richard wasn't good around emotional women, and Jacie made certain she didn't put him in a position to deal with female emotions. She forced a smile, though her lips quivered. "Thank God. I was just coming to ask you if we could use the helicopter."

"I'll do everything in my power to find your sister, Jacie. This should never have happened. I should have done a better background search on those DEA agents."

"You can't blame yourself."

His hands squeezed her arms. "That could be you out there."

She hadn't thought of it that way, and she couldn't now. "But it wasn't."

"Still. I might have lost my best PR woman and trail guide. Do you know how hard it is to find someone like you?" He dropped his hands from her arms and stepped back, running his fingers through his graying hair. "We'll find her. Mark my words." His voice was thick and he appeared to be on the edge of a rare emotional display.

"Thanks." Jacie touched her boss's shoulder. "You and I better get some sleep. We have a long day ahead of us."

He nodded without speaking.

Her chest tight, emotions running high, Jacie left the lodge and returned to her cabin with her first glimmer of hope.

Once inside, with the door closed behind her, she felt the walls press in around her. She paced the inside of her tiny cabin, her heart alternating between settled and crazed. Her sister was out there with terrorists and she could do nothing about it until daylight. The canyons were dangerous enough without the cloak of darkness hiding the animals and drop-offs. It would be suicide to ride back out there. Yet every fiber of her being urged her to do just that.

A woman of action, she felt the inaction eating at her like cancer. Jacie entered the little bedroom, determined to shower and try to rest. Tomorrow would be a long day spent in the canyon. Hopefully they'd find something that would lead them to Tracie.

And to think Tracie had come here to get away from the stress of her job. Some stress relief. Or had she come for an entirely different reason?

Jacie glanced at the phone on the nightstand. Hank had promised to contact the FBI and DEA, but what about Tracie's boyfriend, Bruce Masterson? Granted, he was an FBI agent himself, but large federal agencies like the FBI didn't always communicate to all persons involved.

She hesitated.

Her sister hadn't admitted to any trouble between the two of them, but she hadn't been as excited as she'd been about Bruce the last time Jacie spoke with her on the phone. Still, the man had been Tracie's boyfriend for the past year and had moved in with her six weeks ago. He deserved to know his girlfriend was missing.

Jacie pushed aside her misgivings and reached for the phone, dialing the number Tracie had given when she'd moved in with Bruce.

On the fourth ring, a male, groggy voice answered, "Masterson."

"Bruce?" Jacie asked.

"Tracie?" The grogginess disappeared. "Where are you?"

Bruce's response told Jacie a lot. Tracie hadn't informed him of her destination. "No, Bruce, this isn't Tracie. It's Jacie, her twin."

"Oh." He paused. "Is Tracie with you?"

"No."

"She's not here, if that's what you wanted to know."

"I know." Jacie dragged in a deep breath. "That's why I'm calling."

"What's wrong?" Bruce demanded. "Is it Tracie? Is she okay?"

A sob rose in her throat and threatened to cut off Jacie's air. "I don't know," she managed, her voice shaking.

"What happened, damn it?" Bruce's voice rose.

"She came to visit the night before last and insisted on coming with me on a hunt." Jacie told Bruce what had happened, her voice ragged, emotion choking her vocal cords. "She's gone, Bruce. Captured by what appears to be members of a Mexican cartel."

For a long moment, Bruce didn't say anything. When he finally spoke, his voice was deadly calm. "I'm coming out there."

"I'm not sure who will be involved. The local law enforcement plans on a search party as soon as it's daylight. We notified the DEA and the FBI and—"

"You notified the FBI already?" Bruce asked. "Why the hell didn't I get word?"

Jacie shrugged, then remembered Bruce couldn't see her. "I don't know. Maybe they're still trying to organize a recovery team. All I know is that my sister is missing and I want her back. Alive."

"Don't worry. I'll be there by morning." The phone clicked in Jacie's ear.

She set it back on the charger, and let out a long steadying breath. The more people she had looking for her sister, the better.

If Jacie planned to be one of the search team, she

had to be at her best. A shower and sleep would help her maintain her strength through what looked like a long day ahead.

After thoroughly scrubbing her hair and body, she toweled dry, slipped into a tank top and soft jersey shorts she liked to sleep in and blew her hair dry.

All her movements were rote behavior, her mind on her sister, not the tasks at hand. By the time she stepped out of the small bathroom and into the bedroom, she knew she wouldn't sleep. Her imagination had taken hold and spun all kinds of horrible scenarios Tracie could be enduring. She'd gone over and over all the events of the day, hoping to find one grain of information that might help her locate her sister. And nothing.

The walls closed in around her, and her heart beat hard in her chest, forcing her toward the door and outside, where she felt closer to her sister than anywhere else. She didn't have any other family. Her father and mother had died in a car wreck five years ago, shortly after Jacie finished college. She had no one to turn to, to hold her and tell her it would be all right.

Jacie stared up at the stars, their shine blurred by the rush of tears. Overcome by the events, she sank down on the porch steps and buried her face in her hands, letting the tears flow.

A COOL SHOWER went a long way to waking Zach and clearing his mind, as well as dousing the craving for a strong drink to dull his wits. He lay on the bed, settling on top of a quaint, old-fashioned quilt, not ready to sleep, but hoping he'd find comfort in the reclining position.

The air conditioner struggled to reduce the heat inside the cabin after being off during the hottest part of the day. After fifteen minutes of trying, Zach gave up and rose from the bed. He checked his phone, knowing it hadn't rung and probably wouldn't until the following day.

He wished it was morning already so that he could get started on the search for Jacie's sister. Inaction drove him nuts.

Zach stepped out on the front porch in nothing but his jeans.

The cabin beside his had a soft light glowing through the window. But it wasn't the window that drew his attention.

A shadowy figure hunkered low on the steps leading up to the porch. Soft sobs reached him across the still of the night.

Careless of his bare feet, Zach left his porch and crossed the short distance to the cabin where Jacie lived.

She didn't hear his approach and Zach took a moment to study her.

Jacie's long, deep-brown hair lay loose about her shoulders, free from the band that had secured it in a ponytail for the hunt. Starlight caught the dark strands, giving her a heavenly blue halo.

Unable to stand still any longer, he climbed the steps.

Her head jerked up and she gasped, her eyes wide, the irises reflecting the quarter moon. "Oh, it's you." She sat up straighter, her hands swiping at the tears. "Shouldn't you be getting some rest?"

"I wanted to know if your boss agreed to using his helicopter."

Jacie sniffed and glanced away. "I didn't have to ask. He volunteered its use. We will leave at sunup." She glanced back at him as she rose. "If that's all, I'll be calling it a night."

Zach should have let her go, but he couldn't, knowing she'd go on to her bed and probably continue her tears into the early morning hours. He reached out and grabbed her arm before she made it to the door. "Your sister is tough. If she's still alive, we'll find her."

Jacie whirled. "Not *if*. My sister is alive. I know it. Either you believe it, or leave." Her chin tipped up and she glared through tear-filled eyes.

A smile tugged at the corners of his mouth. "You two are twins in more ways than one. I wouldn't be going after her if I didn't believe there was a chance of bringing her back alive." He brushed his thumb across her cheek, scraping away an errant tear.

"She has to be." Jacie's lips trembled. "I've gone over and over everything I saw and heard since Tracie got here. There has to be something. Some indication as to what happened. I feel like she came here for a reason."

Zach gripped her arms. "What do you mean?"

"She's never shown up unannounced until last night. Tracie has been all about the bureau since she trained at Quantico. I thought she really missed me, but the more I think about it, the more I realize she wouldn't have come without telling me ahead of time."

"Did she say anything about anyone? Was she working undercover?"

"I asked her why she'd come. She only said to get a break from work and stress." Jacie's eyes narrowed. "What worries me is that when I called her boyfriend, the man she lives with, he didn't know where she'd gone." She glanced up at Zach. "She didn't even tell him where she'd gone."

Zach didn't like it. Something wasn't right about what Jacie was telling him. "Did she say anything about the men you were guiding? Did she give you any indication that she knew them?"

"No and no." Jacie dragged in a deep breath and stared up at the sky. "I wish I'd been more persistent. But she wasn't being very forthcoming with her answers. I didn't want to butt in if she wasn't ready to talk." A single tear slipped free and trailed across her skin. She swiped at it, a frown marring her brow. "Damn it, I never cry."

"It's not a crime." Zach pulled her into his arms and held her, stroking his hand across her hair, the silken strands sifting through his fingers, the scent of honeysuckle wafting around him. She fit perfectly against him, molding to his body, her soft curves belying the strength it took to lead a hunting party into the dry, dusty terrain of Big Bend country.

She wasn't wearing a bra and her breasts pressed into his chest, the material of her shirt providing little barrier between her naked skin and his.

His gut tightened, and without realizing it, his hands slid lower, pulling her hips against his.

After a while, she looked up, her lips full and far too luscious for a tough hunting guide, her blue-gray eyes limpid pools of ink tinged with the reflection of the stars.

Zach fought the urge to bend closer and capture her lush mouth, his hands tightening around her waist.

Finally he gave in and cupped her cheek. "I'm going

to hell for this…but I can't resist." He claimed her lips—gently at first.

When her hands slipped around his neck and drew him closer, he accepted her invitation and crushed her mouth, his tongue pushing past her teeth to slide the length of hers. He wove his fingers through her hair and down her back. Capturing the soft curve of her buttocks, he held her hard against his growing erection.

Her mouth moved over his like a woman starved and hungry for more.

When breathing became necessary, he dragged his lips away and sucked in a deep lungful of air. He dropped her arms and stepped back. "I don't know what the hell just happened, but that was totally unprofessional on my part."

Jacie raised a finger and pressed it to his lips. "Don't. It takes two." She backed a few steps, inching toward the cabin's front door. "I'd better get to bed. Morning will come soon and I want to be awake and alert." She touched a hand to her swollen lips. "Thanks for being here."

Zach pushed his hand through his hair. "Right, I'd better go." He turned, paused and faced Jacie again. "You gonna be all right?"

"Do I have a choice?" Jacie squared her shoulders. "Good night." Then she entered the cabin and closed the door behind her with a soft click.

For a long moment, Zach stood on the porch, his lips tingling from the unexpected kiss and the desire urging him to repeat it.

What the hell had he gotten himself into?

CHAPTER FIVE

THE ALARM CLOCK blasted through the nightmare Jacie had been having, saving her from falling over a cliff in the canyon. She sat straight up and blinked. No sunlight shone through the windows, and a glance at the clock proved it was early.

After lying awake for hours, she must have fallen asleep…for what it was worth. Her dreams had been horrifying, leaving her drained and fatigued more than ever. Used to getting up and going before dawn, she hauled herself out of bed and, in less than five minutes, pulled her hair back into a ponytail, washed her face and ran a toothbrush over her teeth.

Pausing for a brief moment, she stared at her reflection, wondering why a guy as gorgeous as Zach would kiss a woman who didn't wear makeup or fix her hair. She touched a finger to her lips, the memory of Zach's kiss sending shivers across her skin.

"Get a grip," she muttered, and dressed quickly in jeans, a T-shirt and her well-worn cowboy boots. Ready for the day, she grabbed her cowboy hat and stepped outside onto the porch. The eastern horizon showed signs of the predawn gray inching up the sky. It wouldn't be long before the sun rose and they could take the helicopter over Wild Horse Canyon and hopefully find her sister.

"Sleep much?" A deep, warm voice spoke to her from the corner of her porch.

Jacie gasped and stepped backward, her face heating as the object of her musings chuckled nearby.

Zach's amusement had the opposite effect of setting her heartbeat back to normal.

After their kiss, just being around him took her breath away and made her pulse hammer through her body. What was wrong with her? She hadn't been this aware of a man...ever.

"Did you spend the night on my porch?" she asked, her voice a bit more snappy than she'd have preferred, but then he'd startled and...unnerved her.

He leaned against a thick cedar beam, his arms crossed over his chest, his boots crossed at the ankle, cowboy hat tipped down over his forehead, shadowing his eyes. He appeared relaxed, yet poised to move in a flash. "No. I slept." He tipped his hat back and studied her. "You don't look like you slept at all."

"I take that to mean I look like hell. Gee, thanks." She stepped down one step and stared out at the road leading into the ranch compound. A plume of dust rose in the distance, moving closer at a fast rate. Jacie stepped down one step. "Wonder if that's the FBI or DEA. I thought they'd be basing out of Hank's ranch headquarters since it's closer to the canyon than here."

Zach faced the oncoming vehicle. "I spoke to Hank a few minutes ago. He said both agencies called and are on their way from El Paso but not expected until around noon."

As the vehicle neared, Jacie noted it was a dark pewter pickup with no noticeable markings, and it was coming fast. She dropped down the last two steps and made her way toward the lodge.

Zach followed, his boots crunching in the gravel.

As Jacie rounded the side of the lodge to the front, she noted Richard, Trey, the helicopter pilot, and Richard's other full-time guide, Humberto, standing on the front porch. She and Zach joined them as the truck skidded to a halt in the gravel.

"Expecting someone?" Richard asked.

"No." Jacie's eyes narrowed as a tall man with short-cropped brown hair dropped down from the driver's seat. "Wait, that might be Tracie's boyfriend, Bruce Masterson. He said he'd get here as soon as possible." She glanced at her watch. "He must have broken every speed record between here and San Antonio to make it so quickly. It's okay, he's another FBI agent. Can't hurt having more help finding her."

Zach stood beside Jacie, his bearing stiff, his face unreadable.

The man approached Jacie, frowning. "Jacie?"

"Yes, I'm Jacie." She held out her hand. "And you are?"

"You look so much like your sister, it's uncanny." He climbed the steps and took her hand, staring down into her face. "Bruce Masterson. Tracie's fiancé."

Jacie's eyes widened. "Fiancé? She failed to mention that part. I thought you two were just living together to save on rent."

He gave her a lopsided grin. "Her words. I asked her to marry me before she moved in. She wanted to wait on the engagement, claiming she wasn't ready to settle down. Something about proving herself in the bureau." The smile faded. "Heard anything yet?"

Jacie shook her head. "Nothing."

As if finally aware he and Jacie weren't alone, Bruce glanced at the men gathered. "I assume you're the posse."

Jacie introduced Richard, Humberto and Trey, leaving Zach for last. "And this is my…boyfriend, Zach Adams." For now, it was easier for Bruce to assume Zach was her boyfriend versus her bodyguard. She didn't want any of the focus to shift to herself when her sister was the one who needed to be found.

Bruce tipped his head. "I don't recall Tracie mentioning that you have a boyfriend."

Her skin heated at Bruce's intense stare. "Apparently Tracie needs to work on her communication skills."

Zach shook Bruce's hand. "Don't worry, it's almost as new to you as it is to us. I just showed up recently in the hope of rekindling our college romance." Zach hooked an arm around Jacie's body, pulling her against him. "Seems the feelings are mutual." He pressed a kiss to the top of her head.

Tracie's fiancé's eyes narrowed. "Zach Adams. The name sounds familiar."

Jacie's heart clambered against her ribs. The FBI community was big, but agents ran into each other often. Would Bruce recognize Zach? Did it matter if he knew? Zach hadn't mentioned it to Bruce, so Jacie kept her mouth shut.

"My name's pretty common." Zach's arm dropped from around Jacie. "Our main concern right now is getting Tracie back, safe and sound."

"Right." Richard clapped his hands together. "The chopper has seating for four."

"Chopper?" Bruce's glance shifted to Richard. "The FBI requisitioned a helicopter for the search already?"

"I don't know about that, but we're not waiting." Richard nodded toward Trey. "We have a helicopter we use for scouting out game. Trey is our pilot."

"I'd like to get on board if possible." Bruce glanced from Jacie to Richard.

Jacie shook her head. "Sorry. I'm going."

"Which leaves one seat," Bruce pointed out.

"No, it doesn't." Zach claimed Jacie again by draping an arm over her shoulder. "I go where she goes."

Bruce frowned. "Wouldn't you rather a trained operative help in the search?"

"I've explored canyons before," Zach said. "I know my way around."

"With a weapon?" Bruce argued.

Zach's jaw tightened. "I know how to shoot."

Richard turned to Humberto. "Humberto, you'll take the truck and trailer loaded with two four-wheelers over to Hank's and take off from there." He faced Bruce. "If you're set on going, you can ride with Humberto." Richard pointed his finger at Trey, Zach and Jacie. "You three ready?"

Jacie nodded. "The sooner the better." She pushed aside the horror she'd envisioned of what Tracie was enduring and focused on finding her. "Let's go."

Zach cupped her elbow and led her to the back of the house to the landing pad beside the barn.

"Do you recognize Bruce from your days at the FBI?" Jacie whispered.

"No. But that doesn't mean he didn't recognize me."

"Will it be a problem if he does?"

"We don't know until he comes forward."

Jacie nodded. "In the meantime, you're just my boyfriend from college. By the way, I went to Texas A and M."

He grinned. "Good to know. Have to have our stories straight in case someone asks."

"By the way, where did *you* go to school?"

His mouth twisted into a mischievous hint of a smile. "Now, that would blow my cover if I told you, wouldn't it?"

Richard turned toward Jacie. "I'll take the front with Trey. You two can look out the side windows. We'll head for the ridge overlooking Wild Horse Canyon and go from there."

Jacie nodded. Any effort toward finding her sister was a step in the right direction. She had to focus on that and not on the evasive answer Zach had given her.

She didn't know much about him, other than that he was former FBI and now worked as a cowboy for hire with Hank.

Jacie bit her lip to keep from pressing for more answers and climbed into the helicopter.

Trey handed her a headset and one to Zach.

They tested the communication devices as Trey started the helicopter engine, the noise of the rotors drowning out any attempts at conversation without the headset.

With her seat restraints fastened securely around her, Jacie curled her fingers around the straps and closed her eyes. As she sent up a silent prayer for a safe takeoff and landing and finding her sister, a hand nudged hers.

She opened her eyes.

Zach pulled her fingers free of the belt and wrapped it in his big, warm hand. He didn't say a word but squeezed gently as the helicopter left the ground.

The man didn't even flinch or exhibit any measure

of anxiety, as if he'd been up in helicopters on many occasions. Which Jacie wouldn't know, given that he hadn't shared much of his background with her. He was a stranger, yet their kiss made her feel closer to him than the other two men in the helicopter. Jacie had worked with Richard and Trey over the years; Richard was more of a father figure and Trey, an acquaintance with a wife and family waiting for his return in the little town of Wild Oak Canyon.

The helicopter skimmed past the barn and house, rising into a bright blue sky with big fluffy clouds dotting the heavens. It was like any other day, except two men were dead and Jacie's twin was missing.

She concentrated on the ground below, practicing her ability to recognize features before they reached the canyon when it would count.

The truck with the trailer loaded with two four-wheelers flew down the highway below toward the Raging Bull Ranch, making good time.

As they passed to the southeast of Hank Derringer's spread, Jacie made out a gathering of vehicles in the barnyard. True to his word, Hank was on it, organizing locals into a search party. The FBI and DEA would arrive soon and add to the number.

God, she hoped they found Tracie and that she was alive.

ZACH HELD JACIE's hand throughout the flight.

In less than fifteen minutes, he could make out the ragged edges of a canyon, spreading out below him.

"That's Wild Horse Canyon ahead," Richard's voice crackled over the headset. "Where exactly did you enter the canyon?"

"Farther to the east." Jacie's hand tightened around Zach's fingers as she leaned toward the window, staring at the ground. "There. Right below us. A trail leads down the side of that slope into the canyon. You can see the four-wheeler at the bottom, flipped upside down. The attackers came in from the southwest."

Trey eased the controls to the right and down. The helicopter dipped to the side, swinging toward the narrower fissures in the canyon walls.

"There are so many places to look," Jacie said, her voice staticky in Zach's ear. He recognized the tone of despair the vastness of the canyon must be infusing in her.

"Just look out your window. I'll look out mine. With four people in the air and more following on the ground, we'll cover a lot of territory."

Her fingers squeezed his and she shot him a grateful look.

Zach would rather continue to stare at the fresh-faced woman than at the ground, but he pulled his attention back to the task at hand. Getting involved with the client went against his training as an agent. He knew the risks. He'd learned his lesson when he'd fallen in love with Toni. Don't get involved. It led to heartache. In his line of work, he was better off remaining aloof, impartial and alone.

He glanced at the hand he held and almost let go.

At that exact moment, Jacie's fingers tightened. "What's that?"

"Where?"

"Down there," she said, her voice tight, strained. "In that J-shaped curve. I thought I saw a reflection of light off something metal." Her gaze didn't waver as Trey circled around and brought the chopper closer.

Zach peered out his side of the aircraft as the chopper banked back to the left. "I see it. We won't get any closer in this. We'll have to find a clearing to land."

Trey rose again, his head turning back and forth. "I can't land here. I'll have to take it back the way we came a bit."

Jacie rocked in her seat. "It might be her. Oh, dear Lord, let it be Tracie."

In the middle of making a wide circle, a loud bang caused the helicopter to lurch to the side.

"Holy crap! Our rudder's been hit." Trey's urgent announcement riffled through Zach's headset. "I'm losing directional control. I have to land now, before I lose it all. Brace yourself."

As the chopper started a slow spin, Jacie stared at Trey struggling with the controls. Then she looked at Zach.

He turned toward her and cupped her face. "Hold on. I gotcha." He let his fingers slide down her arm and he clutched her hand again, bending forward, and urging her to do the same.

The helicopter rotors turned, easing the aircraft down between the tight walls of the canyon.

If they tipped even slightly to either side, the blades would hit the rocks and that would be the end of their search and possibly the end of their lives.

Zach wanted to pull Jacie into his arms and protect her from the rough landing, but they were better off trusting the seat belts. He'd save the embrace for when they landed safely.

The ground seemed to spin up to meet them faster

than Zach liked. At the last moment before the skids hit the uneven surface, he prayed the first prayer he'd made since Toni's death.

The chopper hit the ground, jolting Zach so hard his teeth rattled. The scent of aviation fuel filled the air. He waited several seconds for any shifting before he flung off his belt and reached for Jacie's.

"I can't get it to unbuckle." Her hands shook as she fought with the release clamp.

Zach brushed aside her fingers and flicked it open, then dragged her across the seat and out into the open, away from the damaged craft.

Trey shut down the engine and scrambled out of the pilot's seat. Richard joined him beside Zach and Jacie.

Everyone tugged their headsets off and stared at the downed helicopter.

"What happened?" Richard asked.

"I'd get closer to investigate, but with fuel leaking, it's best to stay back until we're sure it won't create a fire." Trey sucked in a deep breath and let it out, visibly shaken by the experience. "I've never had that happen here."

"Why did the helicopter shake so hard before it lost the rudder?" Jacie asked.

"We were hit by something, hard in the tail."

"What? A bird?"

"No, more like a rocket."

"Who in the hell has rockets out here?" Richard demanded.

Zach's body grew rigid. "Maybe we shouldn't stand so close to the helicopter and seek some cover. The cartels have this kind of ammunition. Either provided illegally by the black market or stolen from the Mexican

Army. Whatever, we're in hostile territory and should treat it as such." He grabbed Jacie's hand and dragged her toward an outcropping.

The woman dug her heels into the rocky soil. "No. We can't give up the search now. What about the metal reflection? It could be a vehicle. They could be holding Tracie nearby." She jerked her hand free and headed back the way they'd come in the chopper. "We have to check it out."

Zach sighed. She was right. Though he didn't like the idea of being trapped in a canyon with the possibility of being shot at, he had to either catch up with Jacie or risk her being taken as easily as her sister, or killed like the DEA Agents.

"Will you at least wait over there in the shadows until I get some more firepower?"

She frowned. "You can't go back to the chopper. It might explode."

He smiled. "I'd rather risk an explosion than walk off into a desert canyon underarmed."

She bit her bottom lip for a moment. "Okay, but hurry."

Zach nodded to Richard. "Get her over there, will ya?"

The Big Elk Ranch owner's brows furrowed. "Let me get the guns. No use you losing it on my chopper."

"Please, just make sure she's under cover."

"I'm coming with you," Trey insisted.

Zach rushed back to the chopper, grabbed four weapons hooked over the backs of the seat. He tossed two rifles to Trey and checked the other two. Each was fully loaded, safeties on. With the weapons slung over his shoulder, he and Trey ran back to where Richard and Jacie stood in the shadows of the overhanging cliffs.

Zach handed Jacie a rifle. "Know how to use one?"

She snorted. "You have to ask?"

"She's a better shot than I am," Richard admitted, taking the rifle Trey handed him. "Let's go."

On the alert for any movement, high or low, Zach took point. If they'd been shot down by a rocket, no telling what other armament the cartel had in their arsenal. He didn't like being at the bottom of the canyon, basically sitting ducks for anyone standing guard on the rim. They didn't have much choice if they wanted to get to the point where Jacie had spotted the metal reflection.

"Up ahead," Jacie called out in a husky whisper. "That's the lower end of the J-shaped crevice. What I spotted was just on the other side of that curve." She hurried to catch up with Zach.

His arm shot out and clotheslined her at the chest. He pressed a finger to his lips and waited until she made eye contact with him. "I'll take lead. No use all of us charging in and getting shot. Let me scout ahead and see what's up there. I'll whistle if all's clear."

"But—"

Zach held up his hand. "One person can move silently. Four have less of a chance."

Richard's hands descended on Jacie's shoulders. "He's right. In fact, maybe we should wait and let the FBI or DEA go in. They are better trained and equipped to handle a situation like this."

"I can do this," Zach reassured him.

Jacie nodded. "Let him. He knows what he's doing. I'll stay until you whistle."

Zach took off, the rifle slung over his shoulder, his handgun in his right hand, safety off, ready for whatever lay ahead.

He eased through the shadows, careful not to disturb the loose rocks and gravel as he rounded the corner of the rocky escarpment. On the ground beside him, he noted tire tracks. Whoever had come this way had come on what looked like an ATV. One larger than the four-wheeler back at the canyon rim.

Zach stopped several times to listen. Not a single noise reached him or echoed off the walls of the canyon. He moved forward and finally rounded the curve leading back the other way. An all-terrain vehicle with seating for four stood smashed against a rock. Two bodies lay motionless, one slumped over the steering wheel, the other crumpled down in the passenger seat.

Without making a sound. Zach stood so still he could have blended in with the rocks themselves, his gaze panning the immediate vicinity and the rocky ledges above. Nothing moved; nothing made a sound. Several vultures circled high above.

Zach stepped out into the open, crouched low, ready to duck and run if shots rang out. He eased over to the vehicle and checked for a pulse. Both men were dead, their bodies stiff, skin purple and eyes sunken. Rigor mortis had set in. These men had been dead for at least four hours.

Zach climbed halfway up a slope and stared around. As far as he could tell, he was alone.

As he puckered to whistle, a movement caught his eye at the base near the corner he'd just come around.

He reached for the rifle and stopped when he real-

ized it was Jacie, doing as he'd done, easing around
the base of the canyon walls, sticking to the shadows.

Zach's jaw tightened and he slipped quietly down the
slope coming up behind Jacie as she worked her way
toward the vehicle, her attention on the bodies within,
not the world around her.

Zach waited between two rocks until she came within
range.

"Bang. You're dead," he said.

CHAPTER SIX

JACIE GASPED AND swung her rifle around.

Before she could point it and pull the trigger, the man hiding in the crevice knocked the weapon from her hands, spun her back around, twisting her arm up between her shoulder blades. He cinched his arm around her neck, limiting her air.

"Let me go." She bucked against his hold, her body stiff, her feet kicking outward to throw him off balance. "Or I'll—"

He held her steady, as if she were nothing but a child. "Or you'll what?" he whispered against her ear. "You're in no position to threaten or bargain."

"Zach?" She froze, all the fight left her and she sagged against him. "Damn it, Zach, you scared the crap out of me."

He turned her in his arms, refusing to release her yet. And frankly Jacie was glad. She hadn't liked it when he'd walked away and stayed gone for so long she thought he'd fallen over a cliff or had been captured. His strong arms around her brought back that feeling of safety at the same time it spelled danger of a completely different kind.

"I could have been one of the drug runners." He brushed his thumb over her cheek, pushing a strand of her hair that had escaped her ponytail behind her ear. "You could have been shot and killed or worse—taken in by the same terrorists who have your sister."

Her breath hitched in her throat, and her blood rushed through her veins like the Rio Grande in flood stages. His body pressed to hers, warm, sexy and overwhelming. "You've made your point. I should have stayed put."

"Yes, you should have."

"I couldn't stand waiting, not knowing whether you were all right, or if you'd found Tracie." She stared up into his eyes.

He kissed her, a brief brush of his lips, and set her at arm's length. "She's not here."

JACIE'S LIPS TINGLED and she fought back the urge to cry. Instead she squared her shoulders. "So, what's all this?" She waved her hand toward the abandoned vehicle and the dead men. "What can we learn from what we found? There has to be a clue as to who took her." She moved toward the four-by-four, bracing herself for what she'd see. The two dead men last night had been partially cloaked in darkness and still looked fairly normal. These two had been dead longer and were a waxy zombielike purple. "How long do you suppose they've been here?" Her gag reflex threatened to choke her.

"At least four hours. Maybe longer."

"Not long after they took Tracie," Jacie noted. A shiver shook her from head to toe. She had to remind herself that Tracie might not be here, but at least she wasn't one of the bodies left behind.

"Holy hell, Jacie, don't ever do that again." Richard burst into the open, huffing and puffing, followed by Trey. Behind them Humberto and Bruce emerged.

"We brought reinforcements," Trey offered.

Bruce stepped forward and studied the two bodies without touching them. "Looks like members of La Familia Diablos."

Zach stiffened, his face going pale beneath his tan.

Had Jacie not looked at him at that exact moment, she'd have missed his reaction to Bruce's words.

"How do you know?" Jacie asked.

Bruce pointed to the tattoo on the driver's right shoulder, the tail of a dragon dipping below his T-shirt sleeve. "The Diablos all have a dragon tattoo on their right arms. If you push the other man's sleeve up, you'll likely find one similar to this one."

"I'll take your word for it." Jacie had no intention of touching either of the two dead men. Instead she inched toward Zach, taking comfort in his presence. "Why would they kill their own people?"

"Who said they did?" Bruce glanced across the dead man at Jacie. "There are two crime families in this area—Los Lobos and La Familia Diablos. Any chance they get to kill each other off, they'll take it. My bet is the Diablos took Tracie and the Los Lobos ambushed them. Since Tracie isn't here among the dead, thank God, they must have her in the Los Lobos camp."

Humberto stood to the side, his eyes narrowed, his face grim. "The Diablos will avenge their *compadres'* deaths."

"Will they attack Los Lobos?" Jacie's hand reached for Zach's.

"Probably," Bruce responded. "It'll be a bloodbath."

Her fingers tightened around Zach's. "Then we have to get to Tracie before the Diablos do."

"It's not that easy," Zach said quietly. "I've heard

they have tightly guarded compounds on the other side of the border. No one gets in or out without running a gauntlet of killer guards."

"But we can't give up now." Jacie stared toward the south as if she could see the camp from where they stood in the canyon. "Tracie's still alive. I just know it. But for how long…" She turned back to Zach.

His face was set in grim lines and his lips remained tightly shut.

"There's nothing you can do but let the FBI and DEA handle this." Bruce touched Jacie's shoulder. "I'll get with them and explain my assessment. They'll decide whether or not to launch an attack and when. But as far as you and the members of the Big Elk Ranch are concerned, you should step back and let the pros handle it from here."

Zach's fingers tightened painfully around Jacie's.

"But—" Jacie couldn't let it go. She just couldn't stand back and do nothing.

"Jacie." Zach tugged her hand and forced her to face him. "He's right."

Bruce took charge. "You guys can double up on the four-wheelers to get back to the truck. Humberto and I can stay until two of you can come back to get us."

Zach raised a hand. "Jacie and I will stay back."

"I'd rather get her out of the canyon. If there was even a chance either of the gangs is still here, she'd be in danger. It's bad enough one of the Kosart women is already a captive." Bruce turned to Humberto. "You're okay with staying, aren't you?"

"No," Richard said. "The men killed last night and Tracie were my responsibility. I should be the one to stay with Mr. Masterson. Besides, Humberto needs to lead the way out of the canyon."

"I'd rather keep Humberto. No offense, Mr. Giddings. He's probably faster on his feet."

Richard's eyes narrowed. "You might be right about that. I'm not getting any younger." He turned to Zach and Jacie. "Come on, the sooner we get the two of you out of here, the sooner I can get back down here and retrieve these two gentlemen."

Jacie wanted to argue, but she didn't know what else they could do without horses or additional four-wheelers to track the men responsible for kidnapping Tracie. She climbed on one of the ATVs and pressed the start button.

Zach slung his leg over the back and sat behind her, his arms circling her waist, holding on tight.

Without a word, she twisted the throttle and the cycle shot forward.

Zach's arms tightened, his hard, muscled chest pressing against Jacie's back. It wasn't long before they climbed the narrow trail out of the canyon and came to a stop beside the truck and trailer.

Jacie waited for Zach to dismount before she got off.

Richard and Trey topped the rise and pulled up beside them. Trey climbed off.

"I'm going back for Humberto," Richard said.

"I'm going with you." Jacie turned the four-wheeler in a tight circle.

When she came to a halt, Zach grabbed her handlebar. "Let Trey." His stare was intense.

She'd hoped to check out the murder scene one last time before she gave up and called their search a failure. "No, I want to go."

"Jacie." Richard pulled up beside her. "Trey can handle this. You stay here." It wasn't a request. Her boss meant business.

She got off the bike.

Trey mounted and the two men rode back down into the canyon.

As they disappeared over the ridgeline, Jacie's vision blurred, and she fought back tears of anger and frustration. "I thought you were supposed to help me."

"I am." Zach gripped her arms and turned her to face him. "There's more to this than either of us can handle on our own."

"But she's my sister!" Jacie pounded her fists against his chest. "I can't just stand by and do nothing."

"We won't. We can do some work behind the scenes. There has to be people on the ranch or in the town who know what's going on and can help us find your sister."

"You think we can learn anything back there?" Jacie waved at the canyon. "Tracie disappeared there."

"But she knew enough to follow those men into the canyon. She knew something, and we need to find out what it was. It might be the key to who took her and where they might be holding her." Zach pulled her into his arms. "Hank hired me because he had faith in my abilities as an agent. He trusted me to do the job." Zach tipped her chin up and stared into her eyes. "I need you to trust me too."

This man hadn't shown her much of anything yet. How could she trust him? She knew nothing about him. For a long moment Jacie stared up into Zach's dark gaze. Something about the way he held her and the sorrow buried deep in his liquid brown eyes made her say, "I trust you."

For several long seconds, he held her, his gaze unwavering. Then he bent his head and kissed her.

Jacie should have pushed him away, but that rational idea didn't even enter her head. Instead she wrapped her arms around his neck and dragged him closer, needing the comfort of his arms, the pressure of his mouth on hers, if only to chase away the fear of losing her only sister.

But it was more than that. This man had known suffering. His heart still bore the scars, and despite his apparent effort to hide them, he wore them on his sleeve.

All thoughts melted away as the kiss deepened. Jacie's tongue pushed past Zach's teeth and slid along his, thrusting and tasting the hint of coffee and mint.

His fingers dug into her buttocks, smashing her against him, the evidence of her effect on him pressing into her belly.

Jacie didn't know how long they stood, locked in the embrace. The world around them faded away, leaving them alone, until the sound of a hawk crying out overhead dragged her back to the real world.

She forced her hands between them and pushed against his chest. "What are we doing?"

Zach ran a hand through his hair and sighed. "I'm sorry. That shouldn't have happened...."

"Again," she concluded. "Why can't I keep my hands off you?" She stared down at the offending digits. "This effort isn't about you and me. It's about bringing my sister back alive."

"And the sooner we get back to civilization, we can work on that."

A hole the size of Texas opened in Jacie's heart

and she looked across at Zach. "We will get her back, won't we?"

"We will." Zach's gaze bore into hers, his dark brown eyes so intense they appeared black. If anyone would fight to free her sister, Zach would. But he'd do it his way. Not ride off without a plan.

ZACH SAT IN the backseat of the king cab pickup with Jacie beside him. Richard drove, Humberto rode shotgun and Bruce and Trey sat in the truck bed. Since the others had returned, Zach hadn't spoken a word, his mind churning over what he'd learned and the information he still required to determine the whereabouts of Tracie Kosart.

As Bruce had said, the dead men in the four-by-four had been members of the Diablos. As soon as Zach had seen the tattoos, he'd known. He'd studied the gangs prior to taking the assignment to infiltrate the Diablos gang area in the border town of El Paso. He and Toni had crossed into Juarez as honeymooning tourists. Only someone in the bureau must have leaked the fact that they were undercover agents. Within twenty-four hours, they'd been captured and the rest was the awful history he would never forget.

His hands clenched into fists. If Los Lobos knew Tracie was FBI, she'd be in for the same treatment as Toni.

Zach's gut knotted. He vowed to himself to find her before they went too far. He glanced at Jacie. She was better off not knowing what her sister faced. It would only make her more reckless and determined to go to her sister's rescue. One lone woman against an army of thugs.

She sat quietly staring out the window as if she might see her sister walk out across the dry Texas land. Her forehead was creased with worry lines.

As soon as they got back to the ranch, Zach would start asking questions. If there were cartel members crossing the border nearby, there were cartel members on the U.S. side aiding them.

As soon as the truck pulled up to the Big Elk Lodge, Zach jumped down and rounded the truck to assist Jacie. She'd already slipped from her seat and stood beside the truck. "What next?"

Zach cupped her elbow and turned toward the other men. "If you need us, we'll be in town." He gave half a smile. "Seems I left home in such a hurry I forgot a few things I hope to pick up at the local stores."

"We have shaving cream, razors and toothbrushes in the lodge, if that's what you're missing," Richard offered.

"Thanks, but I'd rather go to town." Zach winked at the owner of the Big Elk. "Getting away will help keep Jacie occupied while the FBI and DEA do their thing."

Richard nodded at Jacie. "Don't worry, darlin'. They'll get her back."

Jacie's lips formed a tight smile. "I know." Her entire countenance read *failure is not an option*. Zach could have kissed her again. She was strong and tough. The few tears she'd shed had been more out of frustration and real fear for her sister's life.

"Come on, honeycakes." He led her away from the group toward the tiny cabin where she lived. "We'll take my truck. It's not as well known around town."

"Where are we going?"

"To Wild Oak Canyon."

She let him open her door as she turned to face him. "Why are we really going to town?"

"Your sister came to visit, and from what it looks and sounds like, she had an idea that something was going to go down last night, or she wouldn't have insisted on riding out with you and the two DEA agents."

"So what does that have to do with going to town?"

"How did she find out about who and what might be happening?"

"Through her contacts at the FBI?"

"It might have started there, but she wasn't the only one around here who knew something was going to happen. Those DEA agents wouldn't have gone down into that canyon without backup if they'd thought they were in danger."

"You think they were expecting to meet someone who wasn't going to be shooting at them?"

"Yes." Zach rounded the truck and climbed up into the driver's seat. "There have to be other people nearby who knew what was going to happen. Cartel members like to brag about their kills and ambushes." He paused with his fingers on the key in the ignition. "If we find the right people, we might discover who knows something, like who's responsible and where they're holding your sister."

Jacie's eyes lit. "Then what are we waiting for? Go!"

Zach twisted the key and set the truck in motion, heading down the long, dusty gravel driveway. "Now, don't get your hopes up. Cartel members tend to be pretty close-lipped around strangers."

Jacie slammed a fist into her palm. "Then we'll beat the information out of them."

Zach chuckled. "That's my girl. Tough as nails and soft as silk."

Her cheeks flamed. "I'm not your girl," she muttered. "And I'm not soft." She stared at her work-roughened fingers. "And 'honeycakes'? Really, was that all you could come up with?"

Zach chuckled, betting she was soft in all the right places, and "honeycakes" was perfect.

He shook himself and forced his attention back to the road, headed into Wild Oak Canyon.

"Where does everyone go at one point or another to talk or share a cup of coffee?"

"That would be Cara Jo's Diner," Jacie said. "She's a friend of mine. Everyone has dinner there at least once a week to catch up on everyone else's business."

"Good. We'll start there."

CHAPTER SEVEN

JACIE ENTERED THE diner first, her nostrils filling with
the comforting smells of meat loaf, roasted chicken and
fried okra. Once Zach passed through the door and it
closed behind him, Jacie paused, closed her eyes and
inhaled deeply, letting the aromas calm her.

"Smells like home."

Jacie opened her eyes and tipped her head toward
Zach.

A smile tugged at the corners of his lips.

This was perhaps the first clue he'd given her about
his life outside his work. "Did your mother make her
kitchen smell that good?"

"Always. She loved to cook and we always had great
food." His smile faded. "I miss her."

"What happened?"

"She and my father had me late in life. And all that
good cooking clogged their arteries." He sighed. "They
died within months of each other. Mom couldn't imagine life without Dad." Something about the grim set of
his lips spoke more than his words.

"Where were you during all this?" Jacie asked.

"I wasn't there when Dad had his heart attack."

"Were you working for the FBI then?"

He nodded.

"Undercover?"

Again he nodded. "I didn't know until it was almost too late to see my mother before she passed too."

Jacie's chest tightened. She and Tracie had lost both their parents to an automobile accident. "At least you got to say goodbye to your mother," she said quietly. Then she squared her shoulders. "How about that booth in the corner?"

"I'd prefer to sit at the bar. We might learn more there."

"Right."

As she strode across the floor, Cara Jo, the diner's owner, pushed open the swinging door to the kitchen with her hip and carried a large tray full of steaming entrees to a table of cowboys. "I'll be with you in a minute. Seat yourself," she called out.

Cara Jo's shoulder-length, light brown hair swung as she spun around in her cute little waitress outfit. The retro-styled dress that hadn't fazed Jacie in the least in the past suddenly made her more aware of her dusty jeans and even dirtier shirt. Her face probably had the same layer of grime and her hair… "We'll take a seat at the bar," Jacie said.

"Suit yourself." Cara Jo laid out one full plate at a time in front of the cowboys. No sooner had she set a plate on the colorful gingham tablecloth than a cowboy practically stabbed her with a fork, diving into the vittles.

Jacie chuckled. "Cara Jo has the best food in the county."

"Isn't this the only diner in the county?"

"Only one that's stayed in business. People come back when the food's this good." She stopped at the bar. "I'm going to wash up. I'll be right back."

"Me, too. I can still smell aviation fuel and dead men." Zach wrinkled his nose. "Back in two shakes."

While Zach headed for the men's room, Jacie pushed through the door of the ladies' room.

What she saw in the mirror was worse than she'd imagined. Brown hair stuck out of the loosened pony-tail, in complete disarray, windblown, not in a good way, and tinged gray with dust. Her face had a layer of fine Texas sand over it, giving her a sun-dried, tanned look that wasn't any more appealing than it sounded. When she patted her shirt, a cloud rose from her and she coughed.

Holy hell, you'd think she had more pride than to show up in town looking like...well, like one of the cowboys. People expected the men to look wind-worn and filthy. But a woman was supposed to have more pride.

She squared her shoulders and stared into the mirror. "Why do I care? My sister is missing and no one really cares about how I look." Except herself. She yanked the ponytail out of her hair, bent over, her long brown hair hanging down, and ran her fingers through the thick tresses, shaking out the dust. When she flipped it back, it was better. Not great, but better.

She patted her shirt, flapped it to get the dust to fly loose, then slapped at her jeans. The light in the room grew hazy.

"This is crazy. It's not like the man sees me as any-thing more than the job." She sighed. "Oy, but that kiss..."

Jacie splashed her face with water from the sink, wishing she had a little lip gloss to coat her dry lips. Who was she kidding?

Semisatisfied that she didn't look like a complete loser, she stepped out of the bathroom and ran into a hard wall of muscle.

Zach caught her in his arms and steadied her. "Do you always talk to yourself in the bathroom?"

Her cheeks burned and she grimaced up at him. "Are the walls that thin?"

He nodded.

Mortified, she couldn't bring herself to ask how much he'd overheard. "Well, then, we should start our investigation." She hurried past him, hoping he'd only heard her mumbling.

"Just so you know, you're not just the job," he called out softly behind her.

Jacie was sure her face couldn't get any hotter. She plopped into a bar stool and gave Cara Jo all her attention. "Could I get a glass of ice water?"

"You bet. Guess it's getting pretty hot out there already." Cara Jo snagged a full, frosty pitcher, poured two glasses of ice water and set them in front of Jacie and Zach. "Jacie, sweetie, who's your handsome friend?"

Jacie stiffened at Cara Jo's flirty query. "Zach Adams."

"Her boyfriend from college," Zach interjected.

Cara Jo's eyebrows furrowed, a smile playing at her lips. "You never told me you had a boyfriend from college." Still holding the pitcher of water, she planted her fist on one hip and looked down her nose. "Come on, tell all."

"Not much to tell." Jacie hated lying to her only friend outside the Big Elk Ranch. "We met in college."

"Well, it must have been more than a chance meeting for him to show up here after all these years."

"I missed her." Zach slid an arm around Jacie's

waist, his breath stirring the hairs around her neck, making gooseflesh rise on her arms.

Jacie couldn't continue the lie and she had more important things on her mind. She sucked in a long, steadying breath. "Cara Jo, Tracie's missing."

Cara Jo plunked the pitcher on the counter. "Oh, my God. How? When?" She reached across the counter and gathered Jacie's hands in hers. "Oh, baby, you must be beside yourself. And to think, she was just in here the day before yesterday."

"That's when she got in town." Jacie gave her the bare-bones details of what had occurred since.

"Holy hell, Jacie, you were almost killed." She rounded the counter and hugged her friend. "What about Tracie? Do you have any idea where they might have taken her? Have the FBI and DEA arrived? Have they mounted a search and rescue?"

Jacie gave a wry chuckle. "Slow down, will ya? We have no idea where they took her and yes, the FBI and DEA are on it. But I can't just sit around and wait for them to find her. I have to do something."

"Honey, what *can* you do? You're not trained to fight the Mexican cartel. Hell, even the soldiers and agencies who *are* can't seem to slow them down." Cara Jo stopped talking when she looked Jacie in the face. "Sorry. I'm not helping, am I?" She squeezed Jacie's shoulders and stepped back around the counter. "What can I do? Want me to join the search party? I will."

"No." Jacie shook her head. "They want me to stay out of it. What I need is to find out anything I can about when my sister came to town. Did she talk to anyone? Meet anyone here in the diner? Say anything?"

Cara Jo pinched the bridge of her nose. "She asked

for directions to the Big Elk Ranch…. Think, Cara."
For a long moment she said nothing. Finally she looked
up. "I seem to recall her talking to a man outside the
diner."

"Did you see him? Who was it?"

"I don't know. He was dark haired, maybe Hispanic.
Not very tall." Cara Jo's eyes widened. "Wait a minute. If I remember correctly, someone was sitting at
the window booth staring out at the same time Tracie
was talking to the man." Cara Jo's lips twisted into a
grimace. "Oh, yeah. It was Bull Sarly. Maybe you can
get that cantankerous old man to tell you who it was."

Jacie bit her lip. "All we can do is try. Maybe if he
knows how important it is to find her quickly…"

"Yeah." Cara Jo snorted. "Good luck with that."
She raised a finger. "If you're planning on going out
there, I have something you'll need." She hurried into
the kitchen and emerged a minute later with a wad of
white butcher paper. "You'll need this."

Jacie smiled. "Thanks."

"Cara Jo, can you remember anything else?" Zach
asked. "A conversation, maybe not between Tracie and
anyone else, but one that might have to do with a meeting in Wild Horse Canyon?"

Cara Jo shook her head. "Nothing like that. I'll tell
you what, though, the whole time your sister was here,
she kept fiddling with her cell phone. She'd press a
button, put it to her ear and then take it down and end
the call before it even had time to ring. I thought it
was weird at the time but figured the line was busy
or something."

"Cara Jo." A pretty blonde with a miniature version

of herself sitting beside her in a booth waved her hand. "Can I get a cup of milk for Lily?"

Jacie's friend smiled at the woman and called out, "Got it." Then she focused on Jacie again. "Hey, would you like to meet Kate and Lily? They just moved into the old Kendrick place."

"Maybe next time I'm in town." Jacie liked meeting people, but her sister took priority over socializing.

"I understand." Cara Jo pulled a carton of milk out of a refrigerator under the counter and poured a plastic cup full, snapped a lid on it and stuck in a straw. "It was good to meet you, Zach. I'd hang around and chat, but I have to work. My waitress called in sick. Let me know if I can do anything to help. I can shut down the diner in a heartbeat and be ready."

"Thanks, Cara Jo. I'd appreciate it if you'd keep your ears open." Jacie reached across the bar and squeezed Cara Jo's hand. "If anything comes up in a conversation that might relate to Tracie's disappearance, call me."

"You bet I will."

While Cara Jo waited on the tables, Jacie swallowed some of the ice water and stood. "Let's go find Bull Sarly."

"I take it you know the man." Zach cupped her elbow and escorted her from the diner as if she were dressed in a fine dress at a cocktail party instead of wearing jeans and a dusty T-shirt.

Jacie hated to admit it, but she liked it. After working at the ranch for the past few years, she'd almost forgotten what it was like to be treated like a lady. She'd made it a point to be one of the guys. The men trusted her as a guide more if she looked like one of them. For a long time, it had seemed like an asset, her ability to blend in with the menfolk. Since she'd met Zach, the ability seemed more a liability.

ZACH PULLED OUT onto Main Street. "Where does Mr. Sarly live?"

Jacie blew out a breath. "On a small plot of land west of town. Out by the dump." She glanced at Zach. "Let me warn you, he's a cranky old geezer. Never has anything good to say about anyone. We'll be lucky if he tells us anything. Hell, we'll be lucky to get past his rottweiler, Mo."

"We'll manage." Zach had been shot at, beat up and tortured in his line of work. What kind of grief could one cranky old man give him that he hadn't already overcome?

Five miles west of the town of Wild Oak Canyon, Jacie motioned for him to pull off the road onto a rutted track that looked more like a shallow ravine than a road. It wound through clumps of saw palmetto and prickly pear cactus, the vegetation like so much concertina wire strung along a perimeter.

"I take it Mr. Sarly doesn't get many visitors," Zach remarked, bracing himself for a meeting with the man.

"He doesn't want any. He's said as much."

"Sometimes a man might push others away to keep from being hurt. Perhaps Mr. Sarly was hurt by a woman or lost someone he loved and hasn't gotten over it."

"Uh-huh. Or he's just plain cranky and doesn't like people at all. I always give him the benefit of the doubt. But he always gives it right back in my face." Jacie shook her head. "You can't please all of the people."

"True." As they rounded a patch of scrawny mesquite trees, a tired, gray-weathered wooden house came into view. Sitting on the porch with a shotgun in his lap was a big man wearing only a faded pair of blue jeans and old brogan boots. His gut hung over his waistband and his long gray, shaggy hair blended into an equally long and shaggy beard, neither of which had been combed or cut in at least a decade. A husky red-and-black rottweiler lounged on the porch beside the man's chair, seemingly unconcerned by the approach of a strange vehicle.

Zach pulled to a halt out of range of the shotgun's blast.

When Jacie moved to open her door, Zach held out a hand. "I'll handle this."

"But—"

"Please."

Jacie shrugged. "Here, you might want this." She handed him the package wrapped in white butcher paper he'd all but forgotten.

With a frown, Zach held up the package. "What's this for?"

She grinned. "The dog."

As soon as Zach's boots touched the ground, the dog leaped off the deck and raced toward him.

"Throw the package," Jacie yelled.

Without thinking, Zach did as Jacie said and threw the package at the dog.

The rottweiler ground to a halt, sniffed at the offering and then clamped his teeth around it. He then trotted off into the brush.

"Damned good-fer-nothin' hound," Bull Sarly grumbled from the porch.

After the dog left, Zach headed for the porch. "Mr. Sarly."

"Ain't no mister up here."

"Bull Sarly?" Zach continued toward the man with the shotgun.

"That'd be me. Ya got twenty seconds to state yer piece. Take that numbskull that long to rip into whatever you brought for him. And I'll be shootin' whatever's left after the dog's finished with ya."

"Then I'll speak fast." Zach never let his gaze drift from the old man's. He studied the way the gnarled fingers tightened around the worn wooden stalk of the gun in his lap, anticipating any aggressive move on the other man's part.

"Tracie Kosart was kidnapped yesterday by Mexican cartel."

"So? I ain't no Mexican cartel. Get off my property."

"You were at the diner day before yesterday when she came in."

"Man's got a right to eat." He held up a hand. "You can stop right there."

Zach halted at the base of the steps, directly in front of the old man, his jaw tight, his knees bent slightly, ready to spring. "Before she came into the diner, she spoke with a short Hispanic man. You sat in the booth staring out at them. Can you identify the man?"

"I could…" The old man stuck a straw in his mouth and sneered. "If I gave a rat's behind."

Zach's blood boiled. While this man lorded himself over them, Tracie Kosart could be suffering horrible torture. Frustrations of the past day, no, the past two years exploded in one flying leap.

Zach climbed the steps, grabbed the shotgun, jerked

it out of the curmudgeon's hands and flung it across the yard. Then he lifted the man to his feet and slammed him up against the wall of the house. "How about right now?"

The man's eyes bulged, his face and body breaking out in a sweat. "You ain't got no right to push me around on my own property. I'll have your job for this. Let me go," he gasped, scratching at the fingers pressing into his windpipe.

"You're assuming I care about my job." Zach pushed the man higher up the wall until his feet dangled. "I don't. However, I do care about finding a woman who could very well be raped, tortured and killed. Preferably before all three of those things happen." He shook the man. "Now, are you going to tell me something that will help me find her, or do I make you sorry you didn't?"

"Zach. Don't." Jacie's voice called out behind him.

"Listen to the girl," Sarly whined. "Won't do you no good if you knock me out or kill me."

"Please." Jacie's hand touched Zach's arm.

A blast of calm washed over Zach's raging nerves. Still, he wanted to beat someone's head in, and Bull Sarly was just enough of a pain in the butt to deserve it.

The hand on his arm tightened. "He's not worth going to jail over," she whispered.

"And your sister's not worth saving?" Zach rasped.

"Yes, she is, but this isn't going to help."

"Sister?" Bull stared from Zach to Jacie. "You didn't say nothin' 'bout that woman being yer sister. Let me down. Maybe I know somethin'."

Zach held him there a second longer, then let go so

fast the man slid down the wall before his legs engaged and held up his bulk.

"Talk fast. A woman's life depends on us finding her sooner than later."

Jacie stepped up to the man and touched his arm. "Mr. Sarly, the cartel took my sister. We think she might have spoken to someone the day she came to town who might know where they would have taken her. Please." Her eyes filled with tears. "She's my only living relative. I'd do anything to save her."

A growl sounded behind Zach.

As Sarly had indicated, once the dog had finished the treat, he was back and ready to take up where he'd left off.

Zach pulled the pistol from his shoulder holster and aimed it at the dog. "Call him off or I'll shoot him."

"Don't." Sarly raised a hand. "Like your sister, Mo is the only family I have." He gave the rottweiler a stern look. "Sit."

A long moment passed as the dog growled low in its throat, knowing a threat when he saw it and ready to launch an attack to the death.

Zach's weapon remained trained on the dog.

"Sit, damn you." Sarly pushed to his feet and took a step toward the dog.

Mo squatted on his haunches, his lip still pulled back in a menacing snarl.

"Good boy." The older man patted his leg. "Come."

The dog trotted up the steps to his master and sat at his feet.

Zach let out the breath he'd been holding. He liked dogs and hadn't wanted to shoot the creature. But he would have, if it was Jacie's or his life over the dog's.

"Look, I don't want nothin' to happen to yer sister, any more than you do." Bull scratched his beard. "I seem to recall her lookin' just like you and I really thought it was you until she asked for directions to the Big Elk." He snorted. "Didn't even know you had a twin."

Jacie gave him the hint of a smile. "Not many people do."

"Did you recognize the man she spoke to outside the diner?" Zach pushed. The clock was ticking and they hadn't gotten any closer to finding Tracie.

"I thought it strange that you—" he nodded toward Jacie "—would be talking to a man from the wrong side of town. What with you working out at the Big Elk with yer hotshot clients."

Zach stepped toward Sarly. "Get to the point."

Sarly glared at Zach. "Back off and I will." He faced Jacie, his features softening. "I had a sister once." He sighed. "The guy she was talkin' to was Juan Alvarez. I know that 'cause he used to work at the feed store with Henry Franks. Franks fired him when he didn't show up for two days. What with all the traffickin' goin' on round here, he figured Juan was involved, and Henry didn't want no part of that."

"Juan Alvarez." Jacie glanced across at Zach. "I know who that is."

"Then let's go." Zach was already off the porch and halfway to the truck when he realized Jacie wasn't right behind him.

She stood on the porch with Mr. Sarly, shaking his hand and smiling. "Thank you, Mr. Sarly. You don't know how much I appreciate your help. If ever there's anything I can do for you, let me know."

His ruddy older face reddened even more. "Well, now. Next time you come bring ol' Mo some of whatever you brought this time. He seemed to like it right plenty."

Jacie patted Bull's hand and hurried toward the truck, climbing in without a word.

As they pulled away, Zach glanced in his mirror at the man retrieving his shotgun.

Zach's first instinct was to slam his foot to the accelerator. But the man just held it in one hand, patted the dog with the other and watched as they pulled out of sight.

The truck bumped along the rutted track to the highway, where Zach stopped and turned toward Jacie. "Where to?"

"The south side of Wild Oak Canyon. From what I know, Juan lives in a not-so-safe neighborhood on the edge of town. You'll want to make sure your gun is loaded and you're ready to fire."

CHAPTER EIGHT

JACIE'S HEART RACED as they sped toward town. "Is this what FBI agents do? Follow clues, one step at a time to find a missing person or apprehend a suspect?"

"Yes."

Her hands twisted in her lap as she studied Zach, hoping to catch a glimpse of the former agent in him. Perhaps that would help her to understand what drew her sister to join the FBI. "Doesn't it get tedious and frustrating?"

"Yes." The word was short, with no telltale expression or anything a person could read in to.

Jacie frowned. "Anyone ever tell you that you don't talk much?"

His lips twitched. "Yes."

Jacie's stomach flipped. When he wasn't looking all fierce and deadly, the man was downright handsome.

"Are you always so forceful when you question people?" she pressed.

The hint of a smile disappeared. "Only when I'm out of time and patience."

A heavy weight pressed down on Jacie's shoulders. "Do you think we'll be too late?"

His foot lifted from the accelerator and he stared across at Jacie, his lips thin, his eyes narrowed. "No." Then he jammed his boot on the gas and the truck shot forward, faster than before. "At this point, we go all or nothing. Doubt can't be a factor. Got that?" He shot a stern frown at her, his nostrils flaring.

"You're right. My mother used to tell us not to borrow trouble." She sat back, the intensity of his stare making her glad he was on her side.

They blew into town, exceeding the speed limits, but Jacie didn't care.

"Turn left at the next street," she said.

Zach took the corner a little too fast. The bed of the truck skidded around behind them, leaving a trail of rubber in the hot pavement.

They passed houses along the road, the exteriors diminishing in care and upkeep the closer they got to the edge of town, until all that was left was a smattering of crumbling shacks and even seedier mobile homes.

"Next right." Jacie pulled her cowboy hat low on her forehead and tucked her hair beneath.

Zach nodded his approval. "You're learning."

Men sat on porches or lounged in old lawn chairs; some stood around the shade trees. A small child played in the dirt, his hair shaggy, his clothes unkempt.

As Zach passed, narrowed gazes followed the shiny pickup's progress.

Jacie squirmed at the attention, not at all comfortable. "Is it safe to stop here?"

"If Juan is here, we need to find him. Safe or not. Maybe I should take you back to the Big Elk before I conduct business."

"No." Jacie sat up straighter. "I'm not afraid for myself."

Zach's lips twisted. "Don't tell me you're afraid for me?"

She shrugged. "Maybe." She was, but she wouldn't admit it. The man had a death wish, based on the way he walked up to Mr. Sarly, an angry bully holding a gun, as if he had nine lives to spare.

A young, dark-haired, dark-skinned man stepped out on the metal stairs leading into a ramshackle mobile home.

Jacie's heart fluttered. "That's him." She nodded toward the trailer. "That's Juan." She recognized him from one of her trips to Cara Jo's Diner.

"Let me do the talking and stay in the truck with the doors locked."

"No way." Jacie reached for the door handle. "You can't go out there alone. You need backup."

He snorted. "Like you're my backup? Please."

Anger bubbled up in Jacie's veins. "Some backup is better than none."

Zach grasped her hand in a tight clamplike hold. "Just do it. If I'm worrying about you, I might not see what's coming, like a fist or a bullet."

Jacie let go of the door handle and bit her bottom lip, torn between wanting to help and hurting the situation. "What are you going to do?"

"I'm going to ad-lib and get some information."

ZACH PULLED IN FRONT of the trailer, shot the truck into park and climbed down. "Alvarez," he called out.

Alvarez leaned against the door of his trailer. "Lost, *gringo?*"

"You owe me and I'm here to collect." Zach marched toward the Hispanic.

Juan's eyes narrowed. "I don't owe you nothin'. Never saw you before."

A couple of the men who'd been lounging against

beat-up cars pushed away and ambled toward Alvarez and the ruckus Zach was stirring.

"I asked for good stuff and you gave me shit." Zach marched up to the steps. "I want what I paid for, and I want it now."

Alvarez leaped to the ground and flipped out a switchblade. "I don't know who the hell you are, but I don't owe you nothin'."

Before the other two men could get close enough, Zach whispered low and without moving his lips, "You spoke to a woman two days ago in front of the diner."

Alvarez froze.

Zach went on. "I need to know what you said. Come with me and you won't be hurt." Louder he said, "Do I have to beat my stuff out of you?"

Juan lunged, his knife aimed at Zach's heart.

Zach ducked, grabbed Juan's knife hand and twisted it up and behind the man, pushing it high between his shoulder blades.

"Dios!" The knife fell from Juan's grip. "It's not here. I'll take you there, just don't break my arm."

"That's more like it." Without loosening his grip, Zach scooped up the knife and held it to Alvarez's throat. "Now tell your *compadres* to back off or I use this on you. And I warn you, *entiendo español.*" *I understand Spanish.*

Juan spoke to the men in rapid-fire Spanish.

Zach understood enough of the language to gather that Juan told his buddies he'd be okay, not to interfere, he'd take care of this.

With Juan as his shield, Zach moved toward the pickup.

Inside, Jacie unlocked the door and slid to the center.

Zach pulled his pistol from his shoulder holster and handed it to her. "Point this at him and shoot if he so much as breathes wrong."

"Will do." She aimed the gun at Juan.

"In the truck," Zach ordered.

When Juan glanced into the truck, Jacie raised her head and stared straight into his eyes.

For a moment, Juan's eyes widened and he blinked. Then he ducked his head and climbed in without further argument.

Zach slammed the door shut, then rounded the truck and climbed into the driver's seat. "Just so you know, she's actually a better shot than I am, so do yourself a favor and behave."

Juan sat silent, staring at the pistol Jacie held in both hands, her finger caressing the trigger grip.

Back through town, Zach drove, his attention alternating between the road ahead, the rearview mirror and the woman holding the gun on the man beside her.

She held it steady, her face a mask of intensity.

Once he was certain he hadn't been followed, Zach shot out into the country, far enough away from town he could be certain no one was behind him.

Juan nodded toward the pistol in Jacie's hand. "She can put that down. I won't try to run or hurt you."

"If it's all the same to you, I'll keep it right here," she said.

Zach's chest swelled at her calm, clear and determined tones. She wasn't shaking, she hadn't hesitated to take the weapon and she probably was a better shot than he was, given that she hunted for a living.

Zach pulled off onto a side road and traveled another quarter of a mile before he parked beside a large clump of prickly pear cactus.

"How do you know my sister?" Jacie started.

"I don't know you and I don't know your sister," Juan muttered. "And I don't have your stuff, because I never sold you none."

Zach nodded to Jacie. "Keep the gun on him." Then he got out of the truck and rounded the front.

"You better answer our questions. My friend gets really cranky when he has to use force," Jacie warned, loud enough Zach could hear her.

He almost smiled, but that wouldn't be effective in what he planned next for Juan Alvarez.

Zach yanked open the passenger door.

"I don't know nothin'," Juan insisted.

"Maybe I can jog your memory a little." Zach grabbed Juan by the collar of his shirt and yanked him out onto the ground, then slammed him against the truck. "The woman you spoke to the day before yesterday was kidnapped last night. Which I suspect you already knew."

Juan shook his head but didn't voice a denial.

"Think real hard before you deny it. Next I will use that pretty little gun my assistant is holding to blow each one of your fingers off, one at a time."

Jacie slid down out of the truck, her eyebrows raised. "He's not kidding. But if you want to play Russian roulette with your hands, we can oblige." She lifted the nine-millimeter pistol. "I want my sister back and I'll do anything to get her."

Juan's eyes bulged. "La Familia Diablos *es muy loco.* They'll kill me if they know I said anything."

"So, were you the one to set my sister up to take

the fall in Wild Horse Canyon?" Jacie stepped closer. "Maybe I'll start with the trigger finger. Hold it out."

Zach's chest swelled even more at Jacie's ability to follow his lead. He knew without a doubt that she would never shoot another living being without deadly provocation, but Juan didn't know that.

Jacie was so convincing at her role, Zach could almost believe she would start shooting. Zach shoved Juan to the ground and stepped on his hand, splaying the fingers wide. "What did you tell the woman?"

"I'll tell you whatever you want to know," Juan squealed. "Just don't shoot."

"Start talking." Jacie squatted next to the man.

"She got my name from my cousin in San Antonio. She came to me asking when a shipment was going down with the men from the DEA. She paid me five hundred dollars and promised not to tell La Familia who told her. That's all. Now are you going to let me up?"

Zach snorted. "I'll think about it."

"I didn't do anything," Juan insisted.

"Did you inform La Familia Diablos that my sister was coming?"

"No. I hate La Familia. They killed my brother, Roberto. I owe them no allegiance."

"Let him up," Jacie demanded.

Zach removed his foot from the man's hand, grabbed his shoulder and hauled him to his feet. "Don't try anything," he warned Juan.

Jacie's eyebrows furrowed. "You knew the woman you'd spoken to was captured?"

"Sí."

Her gaze narrowed. "How?"

He shrugged, rubbing at the hand Zach had stood on. "News travels fast in the barrio."

"Then you also know Los Lobos killed the men who captured her and took her."

Juan's lips clamped shut and he stared from Zach to Jacie.

"Maybe you even know where Los Lobos are keeping her?" Jacie prompted.

"No." Juan looked away.

"Liar." Zach's lips thinned and he stepped toward Juan, fists clenched. "Either you know or you know someone who does." He held out his hand for the gun Jacie still held. She slapped it into his open palm.

Zach's fingers curled around the handle, warm from Jacie's touch. "Save us the crap and tell us what you do know."

Juan stared from Jacie back to Zach. "You aren't going to shoot me." He straightened his shoulders. "You don't have it in you."

"Try me," Zach said, his tone, low and dangerous. His hand rose with the gun pointed at Juan's forehead.

Juan stared down the barrel. At first Zach thought he would succeed at calling his bluff. To hell with that.

Zach pointed the nine-millimeter at Juan's foot and fired off a round.

"Madre de Dios!" Juan grabbed his foot and hopped in place before he fell to the ground and pulled off his shoe. Blood oozed from the side of his foot. "You shot me!"

Jacie stood with her mouth hanging open. Then she swallowed hard, her throat working in spasms. She shook back her hair and stared down her nose at the wounded man. "A flesh wound. The next one will count." She held out her hand. "My turn."

Zach passed the weapon back to her, his eyebrows rising.

"Did I mention I'll do just about anything to get my sister back alive?" She aimed the gun at Juan's kneecap. "I want answers now, not after she's dead."

Juan held his hands over the knee, as if they would have any effect stopping a bullet. "They'll kill me."

Jacie shrugged. "Us or them? You choose."

"Okay, okay." Juan stood. "Los Lobos might have taken her into one of the caves they use to stage drug runs. In Wild Horse Canyon."

"Guess who's taking us on a little trip into the canyon?" Zach's mouth quirked upward.

Juan's eyes rounded into saucers. "No. I told you what you wanted to know. Let me go."

"Sorry. That's not an option." Zach nodded to Jacie. "Let's go. We're burning daylight." The quicker they got to the canyon, the better for Tracie. Even a trained agent didn't hold up well under torture.

Zach shoved Juan into the truck.

Jacie got in beside their captive and took Zach's gun from him.

Without uttering another word, Zach slid into the driver's seat and spun the truck around, heading toward Hank's Raging Bull Ranch.

When he passed the turnoff to the Big Elk, Jacie looked at him with a frown. "Shouldn't we go back to the Big Elk and get horses?"

"Shouldn't you take me back to *mi casa?*" Juan whined.

"No," Zach answered. "You'll be showing us exactly where this cave is."

Juan pointed at his foot. "But I'm injured. I can't walk."

"You'll be on horseback," Zach said.

Juan didn't look any happier. "I don't know how to ride."

"Can I just shoot him now?" Jacie asked.

Juan sat in silence for a moment, glaring out the front windshield. "What if I don't remember?"

"Then we'll shoot your knees and leave you out there for the four-legged coyotes to clean up." Jacie waved the gun. "Enough excuses."

Zach fought the smile. Jacie was getting into her tough-girl role, maybe a little too much. She was tough, but Zach knew the real woman beneath the attitude. She wouldn't shoot.

Zach, on the other hand, wouldn't suffer a stubborn fool. If the man knew something, Zach would shoot one digit at a time until he got the information out of him. He wouldn't let Tracie go through what Toni had suffered. Not if he could help it.

He drove the rest of the way to the Raging Bull without speaking another word, his mind running through the task at hand. Hopefully, the FBI and DEA would prove some kind of help storming the cave. Zach couldn't do it on his own. Not as heavily fortified as the Los Lobos had proved by shooting down the helicopter. Assuming the Los Lobos had done the shooting.

An operations tent had been set up in a field beside the barn on the Raging Bull Ranch. A phalanx of rental cars and dark SUVs lined the fence railing, where people milled about, pressing handheld radios to their ears.

Zach pulled into the front drive, weaving through the cars to find a place to park among the government vehicles.

Hank met them with a frown denting his forehead. "Glad you made it."

Jacie let herself out of her side of the truck. She handed Zach the gun. "I think he'll behave as long as he's surrounded."

Zach took the Glock. "Thanks." Then he turned to Hank. "What's the latest?"

"The FBI and DEA have joined forces in the search and rescue efforts. They have boots on the ground and birds in the air in Wild Horse Canyon, tracking from the point where you found the four-by-four and the dead members of La Familia."

Jacie stepped up to Hank. "Any sign of my sister?"

Hank shook his head. "Sorry. None."

Her shoulders sagged for a moment, then she straightened and turned to Zach. "Well, then, what are we waiting for?"

Hank stared from Zach to Jacie and then to the man standing behind them. "You two find out something?"

"Yeah." Zach jerked his head toward their informant. "This is the man who told Tracie about the op going down in the canyon."

Hank's eyebrows dipped. "What's he doing here?"

"He knows where the Los Lobos hole up in a cave in the canyon when they're making a drug run." Zach gave the informant a pointed look. "He's going to show us where that is."

Juan grumbled, "If I don't, you'll blow my knees off."

Hank laughed and pounded Zach on the back. "A man after my own heart."

"Not man." Zach jerked his head toward Jacie. "Woman. She's the one who threatened to blow his knees apart and, what was it you said?"

"Leave me for the four-legged coyotes to finish off." Juan glared at Jacie. "She's an animal."

Jacie shrugged and repeated her mantra. "I want my sister back."

Hank hooked Zach's elbow and he led him away from Juan. "Are you going to let the operations center know what you found?"

Zach sucked in a breath and let it out. "I don't know."

Jacie joined them. "Don't. We don't know who is bad in the group, possibly in both agencies, given the two DEA agents weren't on orders."

"Probably a wise decision." Hank nodded. "However, going up against Los Lobos alone is suicide."

"Not if they don't see you." Zach glanced at Jacie. "Which means I can't allow you to go."

"Like hell you can't." Jacie stuck a finger into his chest. "Look, mister, that's my sister out there. I'm going to get her back. And I know those canyons better than any of you."

"I'll have to trust our friend there to get me in and out at night. I'm sure he's had practice."

"You're waiting until dark?" Jacie asked.

"Can't go any sooner without alerting Los Lobos and the team of rescuers." Zach glanced toward the western sky, where the sun made its way toward the horizon. It would be dark before long and the air rescue units would be called in, as would the ground teams.

"Are you sure you don't want to let the FBI and DEA know what we found out?" Hank asked.

Zach raised his eyebrows. "What exactly do we know?"

"Los Lobos have a cave hideout in the canyon," Jacie offered. "Not that I'm condoning asking for FBI or DEA help on this."

"Do we know for certain they do or is Juan leading us on?" Zach shot back at her.

Jacie swallowed hard on a rising knot forming around her vocal cords. "My sister might be in that cave."

"If she is, we'll need more than just you and me to bring her out. We need to recon and see what we're up against."

"Right." Jacie's back stiffened. "You said 'we.'"

"I really meant me." Zach pointed at the Hispanic lounging against his truck. "Juan is only showing me where. I'd go it alone if I knew where. As it is, I don't trust Juan any farther than I can throw him."

"All the more reason to take me," Jacie insisted. "I can watch your back."

Hank laid a hand on Jacie's arm. "Zach's right."

"Oh, please, you can't take sides. You put him on this case to help me, not replace me."

"He's trained to do this stuff. You'll only—"

Jacie held up her hand. "Slow him down, right? And what do you expect me to do while you go fight the terrorists? Stay home and knit?" She waved at her dusty clothes. "I'm not the stay-at-home kinda gal, in case you haven't noticed."

Zach grinned. "No, you're not." His smile died.

"You can stay and lurk around the operations tent with the FBI and DEA and see what they've come up with," Hank suggested. "Maybe you can figure out who our mole is in the bureau."

Jacie snorted. "Like I'd have a clue."

Zach turned to Hank. "I'll need a couple horses."

"I'll have my foreman set you up. For now, get to the kitchen and grab a bite to eat. You might need it, if you get lost in the canyon."

"Good point. I'll be sure to take a flare with me."

Jacie stood with a frown drawing her eyebrows close, her arms crossed. "Glad you two can joke about this."

"Come on, you could use some food too." Zach hooked her arm and urged her toward the house, calling over his shoulder, "Juan."

Juan sneered at him.

"If you want food, join us."

For a moment Juan remained stubbornly leaning against the truck. Then he pushed away and followed in a deliberately slow swagger.

JACIE SAT THROUGH a meal quickly prepared by Hank's housekeeper. She could barely swallow, her throat muscles clenching each time she thought of her sister and how long she'd been held captive by notoriously vicious gangsters. She tried not to think about it, but her only other thoughts strayed to Zach and what he was about to undertake.

Riding horseback through the canyon was treacherous enough during the day. At night it was deadly. If Juan didn't know exactly where he was going, they could end up lost and another rescue mission for the local authorities.

As dusk descended, dread threatened to weigh Jacie down.

She walked with Zach and Juan to the barn and

stood back as Zach tied a saddlebag loaded with provisions onto the back of his saddle.

Juan's gloomy countenance didn't help to ease Jacie's mind.

"Well, that's it." Zach patted the horse's hindquarters and led him toward the rear entrance to the barn.

Jacie walked alongside him, her head bent. "I don't like this."

"I know." Zach faced her and tipped her chin with his finger. "We'll do our best to locate your sister and get back here as quickly as possible. Maybe even before sunup."

"What if you get in trouble?" She stared into his face, wishing he'd reconsider and take her along. "What if you're hurt?"

He smiled, his hand cupping her cheek. "Worried about me?"

Jacie stiffened and had a retort ready on her lips, but stopped short of delivering it when she realized she was worried about him. "I haven't known you long, but damn it, I am worried about you. I kinda got used to having you around." Her hand covered the one he'd used to cup her cheek and she pulled it lower, pressing a kiss into his palm.

"Stay safe for me, will you?" His eyes dark in the dim lighting from the overhead bulbs, he leaned close and captured her lips in a soul-stealing kiss.

For what felt as long as a lifetime and as short as a moment at once, the world around Jacie faded away, leaving just her and Zach.

Their tongues connected, thrusting and caressing.

When Zach broke away, he smoothed his hand over her hair. "Stay here. I trust Hank to keep you safe."

She laughed, the sound lacking any humor. "I'm not the one who needs to worry about being safe."

Zach smiled, chucked her beneath her chin and strode out of the barn, leading his horse.

The men had agreed not to mount, but to lead their horses quietly away from the barn, walking close to the animals so as not to be spotted by the agencies working the case.

The activity at the operations tent increased with the search teams reporting in.

During all the confusion of agents and law enforcement personal converging, no one seemed to notice the two horses walking across the pasture. Eventually the two faded into the distance.

Jacie remained in the shadows, every nerve ending screaming for her to follow.

CHAPTER NINE

HANK APPEARED AT Jacie's side. "I asked Ben Harding to accompany you until Zach returns from the canyon."

"Thanks, but I don't need a babysitter." Jacie glanced one last time into the darkness. "What I need is a ride back to the Big Elk Ranch. Zach didn't leave me his truck keys."

Hank shook his head. "Zach wanted you to stay here where you'll be safe."

"From what?" Jacie raised her hand. "I didn't get kidnapped. I'm not the one being tortured. No one is after me. Unless you know something I don't."

Hank smiled. "You and your sister are very much alike. When she came to me for help, she didn't mince words and didn't stand for any fluff." He patted her arm. "Ben should be here in less than fifteen minutes. As soon as he arrives, I'll have him take you back to the Big Elk."

"Thank you." Guilt forced Jacie to add, "I'm sorry I bit your head off."

Hank's smile disappeared. "I understand. It's hard to lose someone you love. Even harder to know that they might still be alive."

Jacie had heard about Hank's wife and son disappearing a couple of years before. She laid a hand on his arm. "Still nothing about your family?"

"Nothing."

"Mr. Derringer, Grant Lehmann's here to speak with you," Hank's foreman called out.

"If you'll excuse me. Lehmann's an old friend and a regional director of the FBI."

"Good, maybe he can get things moving on finding my sister."

Hank left her standing in the barn's rear doorway.

Jacie wandered over to the operations tent and peeked in.

Agents and sheriff's deputies were finishing up with their reports. Everyone said the same thing. No sign of Tracie Kosart, or anyone else for that matter. The ground-tracking team had followed the trail until it disappeared. They suspected the kidnappers knew enough to drag a branch or something from the back of their vehicles to smooth away their tire tracks.

"Stopping in?"

The voice behind her made Jacie jump. She spun to face Bruce Masterson, wearing black chinos, a black polo shirt and a headset looped over his head, currently pushed back from his ears.

He held out a hand, inviting her to precede him into the portable ops center. "You look so much like your sister it takes me aback every time I see you."

Jacie stepped beneath the lights strung out between tent poles before responding, "That happens with identical twins." She halted just inside and faced him, something gnawing at her since she'd first called him. "I have a question for you."

He grinned. "Shoot."

"You sounded surprised to hear that Tracie had come to see me. Why? I thought you two were living together." Jacie tilted her head to the side. "Wouldn't you know when she'd left and where she was headed? Or have your living arrangements changed since the engagement?"

The man shrugged. "She left without telling me. I assumed she was called out on a job."

"Were you two having a fight or anything?"

Bruce shook his head. "No. At least not one I was involved in."

"She didn't leave a note?"

"No. Her suitcase was gone, so I assumed she was on assignment. It was too late to call the office and double-check." Bruce fiddled with the headset, staring over Jacie's shoulder. He waved at someone behind Jacie. "I have to admit I was a little worried, but happy to hear from you to know she was with you. Until you told me she'd been kidnapped. I had to beg to get special permission to join the search and rescue mission."

His answers sounded legit; still, Jacie couldn't imagine her organized sister taking off without informing her fiancé of her whereabouts. Jacie had opened her mouth to say just that when a voice called out her name. She turned, looking for the source.

Bruce glanced around the tent. "Where'd your boyfriend go?"

Jacie hesitated, the truth the first thing that wanted to pop out of her mouth. She bit down hard on her tongue and thought before answering. "He got called away on business."

"I thought I just saw him here. Isn't it late to be called in to work?"

"Apparently he didn't think so. He headed into... El Paso to find a business center."

"Is he coming back?"

"Um, yes. Of course." Jacie sent a silent prayer that what she'd said wasn't yet another untruth.

Zach would be back, and hopefully with news of her sister. In the meantime, she had to wait.

"What exactly does your boyfriend do?"

Irritation flared in Jacie. She didn't like lying, but Bruce's barrage of questions left her no choice. "I'm not exactly sure. I think he's into security work, something high-tech. When he talks about it, I glaze over."

She forced a fake smile. To handle the guilt, she told herself she was on an undercover mission and the lies were only to protect herself and her partner. Not that Zach considered himself her partner. Still, no one, other than herself and Hank, needed to know he was out scouting the canyon for the Los Lobos cave. Not even Tracie's fiancé, who for some reason Tracie hadn't seen fit to inform of her plans.

A man wearing a black cowboy hat ducked beneath the tent. "Jacie?" It had to be the guy Hank had promised, Ben Harding.

Jacie raised her hand, relieved she didn't have to answer any more of Bruce's questions. "I suppose that's my ride."

Bruce frowned. "Headed back to the Big Elk? And here I thought you'd stick around awhile."

"I'm of no use here."

"I wouldn't say that. It's like having Tracie here." Bruce slid a finger along Jacie's cheek. "You two are so much alike."

Jacie frowned. Zach had just touched her cheek before he'd left, and this man was wiping away that warm fuzzy feeling she'd gotten the first time.

An icky sensation crept into Jacie's gut. Was Bruce coming on to her? She shook her head. No. She was reading too much into his touch and comment. "We're only alike physically. We're completely different when it comes to tastes, likes and dislikes." She added a little emphasis to the last statement as if telling Bruce *back off, you're not my type.*

The cowboy stepped through the crowd and stopped beside Jacie. "I take it you're Jacie?"

She gave him a tight smile, relieved he'd come to take her away. "That's me. Let's go." Jacie hooked his arm and led him out of the tent. Okay, if she was honest with herself, she dragged the unsuspecting man out.

Once outside in the darkness of night, Ben laughed. "Hey, what's the rush?"

"I'm not a secret agent and my sister's boyfriend was asking questions about Zach and where he was." She slowed to a stop and gave her rescuer a smile. "Sorry, that was rude of me." Jacie stuck out a hand. "I'm Jacie Kosart."

The cowboy removed his hat and took her hand. "Ben Harding. Nice to meet you. I understand I'm here to take over for Zach while he's busy."

Jacie's hand dropped to her side and she continued toward the makeshift parking lot. "No, you're just here to take me to the Big Elk Ranch, where I live."

"Oh, that's not what I had understood from Hank."

"Apparently Hank worries about the wrong people. Which vehicle did you drive?"

Still carrying his hat, Ben scratched his head. "Hank's a pretty smart guy. The dark gray pickup on the very end." He pointed to the one.

Jacie lengthened her stride, eager to be on her way

before anyone waylaid her with unwanted questions. "Maybe so, but I'm not the one who's missing. I don't need a babysitter and I told him as much."

Ben chuckled. "Okay, then. Let's get you home."

"Thank you." Jacie climbed into the passenger seat and leaned back, her mind miles away from the interior of the truck, far across the Texas landscape, near the edge of the canyon with Zach and Juan. She hoped Zach kept a close eye on his informant.

Jacie hadn't trusted the guy and worried he'd try something, injuring Zach or setting him up to take a fall with Los Lobos.

Ben drove the length of the Raging Bull Ranch driveway before speaking again. "Which way?"

Jacie gave him the directions.

"Hank tells me it's your sister lost in the canyon. I'm sorry."

"Not lost…kidnapped."

"Right." Ben nodded. "I don't know much about Zach, but from what I've learned about Hank, he's a good judge of character. If he's assigned Zach to help find your sister, I'm sure he'll get the job done."

"Thanks. I just wish he'd taken me."

"Hank says you work as a trail guide at the Big Elk. I can see where that would come in handy out in the canyon. Why didn't he take you?"

"Zach gave me some crap about stealth. I think he's crazy going in alone."

"He's trained as an FBI agent. He knows the risks. And from what I've heard, he's not afraid to take them."

"As long as he doesn't get himself killed."

"There is that." Ben glanced across at her, his eyes reflecting the light from the dash. "He knows the stakes and he signed on anyway. I guess most FBI or law enforcement types understand there's always a chance you might not make it back from a mission."

Jacie sat up straighter. "Not helping."

Ben chuckled. "Sorry. I forgot your sister was— is—FBI."

"Yeah, she is and I'm not." Jacie turned sideways, facing Ben. "What is it that drives someone into a job like that? Are they adrenaline junkies or something?"

Ben shook his head, his gaze on the highway in front of him. "Maybe for some. For most, it's a need to fight for truth and justice."

Jacie snorted. "At the risk of your own life?"

His gaze captured hers for a moment. "Don't tell me you wouldn't give your life for your sister."

"In a heartbeat. But she's not giving her life for me, she's sacrificing it for nameless, faceless people."

"No, she's sacrificing for the good of a lot of people. What about for the next child that could be molested if she didn't fight to get the child molester off the streets? Or the families with small children or young teens that live in terror while a serial killer stalks their neighborhood? Those people have faces. They are real."

Jacie slumped in her seat. "You're right. I'm just mad she didn't tell me everything when she came out here to supposedly visit. Now she's got herself in a bind and Zach could well be walking into a trap." She flung out her hands. "I hate not knowing and not doing anything."

"Understandable. Just have faith he'll be okay and we'll find your sister."

Jacie couldn't leave it up to faith. She was a doer. By the time they arrived at the Big Elk Ranch, she'd worked herself up into a silent lather. No sooner had Ben pulled up in the parking lot of the lodge than she was out of the truck. "No need to stay, I'm just going to wait in my cabin until I hear from Zach or my sister."

Ben's brow furrowed. "If you're sure you'll be all right?"

"I will." She waved. "Thanks, Ben." Then she slammed the door and took off for her cabin. Wait in her cabin, ha!

She waited as long as it took for Ben to back up, turn around and head back the way he'd come, before she made a sharp turn toward the barn.

"Jacie?" Richard Giddings called out from the front porch of the lodge. "Is that you?"

Jacie swallowed her irritation and answered, "Yes, sir."

"What's been happening? I haven't seen or heard from you since this morning."

"Rich, I don't have time to fill you in. I need to get back out there."

He dropped down off the porch. "Out where?"

"The canyon."

"At night?" Her boss shook his head and looked around her. "That's insane. Where's Zach?"

The secrecy of the mission Zach was on required Jacie to keep the truth from her boss, but she didn't have to lie. "He had business to attend to."

"All the more reason for you to stay put. No one in their right mind should be out in that canyon at night."

Jacie stopped herself from snorting out loud. She couldn't agree with him more, but she also wasn't at liberty to say why. Not that she didn't trust Richard with her life and that of her sister, but what if someone overheard their conversation? Someone who would inform Los Lobos they had a visitor on his way to spy on them?

"Tracie's been gone over twenty-four hours."

Richard pulled her into a big bear hug. "Then come up to the lodge and stay with me until Zach gets back."

She considered it. But she'd rather go out to the canyon and follow Zach.

"No, you're not going out to the canyon tonight. I won't allow you to make use of any of the Big Elk assets to commit suicide." Richard set her at arm's length.

She stared up at him. "How do you know what I'm thinking?"

"As long as you've been working here, I think I'd know you by now. You're a doer and it's eating you up not to be doin'." He slung one arm over her shoulders. "Now, are you coming to the lodge for a beer or going to your cabin to wait?"

"Thanks for the offer, but I think I'll sit it out in my cabin. I could use a shower."

"Have it your way, but the offer remains open. I'm here if you need a shoulder."

"Thanks." Tears lodged in Jacie's throat. This man had been more than good to her. He'd been the father she missed so badly, the friend she'd needed on more than one occasion. Jacie tamped down the urge to ride off into the canyon and did as Ben had suggested and had faith that Zach would return unharmed. And with news of her sister.

Jacie trudged toward her cottage. A quick glance behind her confirmed Richard remained where she'd left him, watching her as she made her way home.

Once inside, she went through the motions of stripping off her dirty clothes. In the corner, her sister's suitcase lay on its side, just as she'd left it over a day ago.

Jacie dropped to her haunches and unzipped the case, feeling like a sneak looking through her sister's things. Maybe buried among Tracie's pajamas and blue jeans, she'd find a clue that would help her understand why she'd left Bruce without telling him and what she thought she'd find following the DEA agents into the canyon.

The suitcase was just like Tracie, neat and organized, each T-shirt folded precisely the same, the socks rolled military-style, a habit probably learned at Quantico.

Jacie unzipped a side pouch inside the suitcase and found Tracie's wallet with her FBI identification and her cell phone.

Her heartbeat picking up, Jacie recalled Cara Jo saying something about Tracie staring at her phone the whole time she'd been in the diner. Had she tried to call Bruce and he hadn't answered? Or had she been calling another contact to verify whatever she'd found?

Jacie hit the on button and waited. The screen flickered to life; a battery with a red line blinked into view. Great. Low battery. The screen warning cleared, replaced by another screen requiring a four-digit pass code.

Stumped, Jacie stared at the little boxes and rows of numbers. What would Tracie have used? She keyed in the month and day of Tracie's birthday. That didn't open it. She keyed in the month and year. Another failed attempt. The little battery indicator in the top corner indicated eleven percent.

Her heart racing, Jacie dug through her sister's belongings, searching for her phone charger. When she didn't find one, she slipped on her shirt and jeans, grabbed Tracie's car keys and ran out to the little economy car she'd driven up from San Antonio. Surely she had a charger in the car.

Once again, she struck out and her own cell phone charger didn't work on her sister's model. When Jacie emerged from the little car, she trudged back to the house. She probably only had a few more tries before either the phone locked up or the battery died.

As she stepped up on the porch, the sound of gravel shifting brought her out of her intense concentration on her sister's phone, and Jacie glanced around.

The moon shone down on the lodge and cabins, casting long shadows at the corners and sides.

Jacie listened for the sound again. Perhaps a raccoon was on its way through to the barn to get into the feed, or one of the ranch dogs had scampered into the shadows. With a shrug, Jacie entered the cottage quickly and closed the door, locking it behind her. Never had she felt unsafe at the Big Elk Ranch. All this cloak-and-dagger stuff had her spooked and she found herself wishing Zach was there with her.

How could one man become so much a part of her life in so short a time? Jacie stared at her sister's cell phone she'd laid on the bed. Maybe she'd think of the code while shampooing the dirt out of her hair.

Once again, she slipped out of her clothes, grabbed a towel out of the linen closet of the tiny cabin and stepped into the closet-sized bathroom. At least the bathtub was a normal size. Opting for a bath instead of a shower, she filled the tub and added some of the bath salts Tracie had given her for Christmas. She realized this was the first time she'd used them and she wanted to cry.

When the tub was full, she sank into the steamy water, sliding low to immerse her hair. She came up, blinking water from her eyes, and squirted a healthy dose of shampoo into her hand. Jacie went to work washing away the dust from her nearly fatal helicopter ride of earlier that day. Had it only been that morning? So much had happened since then. And yet so little.

Jacie slipped beneath the surface again, rinsing the bubbles out of her hair. A dull thump sounded through the bathtub water.

She sat up straight, water splashing over the edge of the tub, her ears perked.

A soft scraping sound reached her ears and sent her flying out of the tub, wrapping a towel around her middle as she emerged from the bathroom. "Who's there?"

The scraping had stopped and nothing but an eerie silence surrounded Jacie. She reached for the nine-millimeter Glock she kept in her nightstand, fully loaded.

"I have a gun and I know how to use it," she called out. Normally she'd feel silly about saying that out loud. But nothing about the past two days had been normal. A shiver rippled down her spine.

She rushed through the little cabin, turning off the lights. If someone was out there, he wouldn't be able to see a shadow moving around inside, and she might possibly see his figure moving around the outside. Jacie dressed in clean work clothes instead of her pajamas.

Unable to sleep and seriously afraid, she pulled the mattress off the bed and laid it on the floor, then wrapped her mother's quilt around her body. Propping her back against the wall, she pointed her gun at the only door into and out of the house. She waited for morning and the return of Zach and her sanity.

CHAPTER TEN

ZACH FORCED JUAN to take the lead as they found their way through the twists and turns of the canyon. The horses picked their way carefully over stones and around boulders, sliding in some places.

By the light of a near-full moon, Zach studied the walls, rock formations and crevices, memorizing them in case he ended up finding his way out of the maze on his own.

He still wasn't sure Juan knew where he was going or if the man was leading him straight into a trap. Without much else to go on, Zach had to take his chances.

The crevices narrowed and widened, but they were always wide and cleared enough to allow a four-wheel-drive ATV access.

After they had traveled for nearly an hour, the walls loomed higher, the path narrowed and the shadows made it more difficult to see.

Zach shifted in his saddle to ease the aching muscles of his inner thighs and give his sore tailbone a break. Hopefully they'd get there soon. He didn't know how effective he would be if he was too stiff to climb off his horse.

Juan halted his gelding at a giant outcropping of boulders and dismounted.

Zach rode up beside him. "Why are you stopping?"

he asked, careful to keep his voice low. Sound bounced off the canyon walls, echoing up and down the length.

"This is as far as I go on horseback." He tugged his horse to the side, into the deepest shadows.

"How much farther ahead is it?" Zach dismounted as well.

"I will show you. But we'll go on foot. The horses will make too much noise and alert the lookouts."

Zach tied his horse to a stunted tree, wedged in the crevice between giant boulders. Juan did the same, then led Zach around the outcropping, hugging the shadows along the base of the canyon walls.

They'd gone the equivalent of four football fields when Juan stopped and pointed to a dark spot ahead and on the left. "That's the cave and this is as far as I go."

Zach studied the location, the possible areas he could use as cover and concealment. "Okay." He nodded.

"I've done what you asked. Now you can let me go, no?"

Zach shook his head. "Sorry, buddy. I want to make sure you didn't lead me on a wild-goose chase, *and* I can't risk you alerting the gang in the cave. You get to stay here and wait for me to return."

Zach pulled a wad of zip-ties from his back pocket, grabbed Juan's wrist and whipped it up and behind him. He grabbed the man's other hand and slipped the zip-tie around Juan's wrists, tugging it tight.

"What are you doing?" Juan danced around, tugging his hands against the bindings. "You can't leave me here tied up. I am not a member of Los Lobos. If they knew I led you to them, they would kill me."

"Then you better keep really quiet so they don't find you. When I get back, I'll cut the ties and we'll mosey on home." Zach crossed his arms. "Now, are you going to sit so that I can bind your legs, or do I have to knock you down?"

Juan shook his head. "I promise I won't go anywhere."

"Since I don't know you well enough to stake my life on your word, you'll have to go with the zip-ties. I figure it'll take you at least as long as it takes me to get up there and back to find a rock to break them on."

"What about coyotes and snakes? Look, amigo, don't leave me like this."

"You'll be okay for the short time I'm gone." He pointed to the ground. "Sit."

With his hands tied behind him, Juan sighed and dropped to his knees and then to his butt, kicking his feet out in front of him. "You're one tough hombre. If I had my knife…"

"But you don't, and I might have some discussions with you if this is all a waste of my time." Zach slipped the plastic strap around Juan's ankles. Then he pulled a small roll of duct tape from his other back pocket and slapped a piece over Juan's mouth.

With his guide secured from running away or running his mouth, Zach proceeded around the bend and along the base of the canyon toward the dark shadow that was the mouth of a cave. He didn't hurry, careful not to scuff gravel or trip over unseen rocks. When he came within twenty yards of the entrance, he stopped and scoped the surrounding area. So far he hadn't sighted a single guard. Nothing and no one moved in and out of the cave or anywhere else around it.

Zach held his weapon in front of him. From where he stood to the entrance, there were no shadows to hug, no boulders to dive behind. He'd have to make a mad dash in case a sniper spotted him and started taking potshots at him.

With a deep breath, Zach ran toward the entrance, zigzagging so that he didn't provide an easy target for someone who could halfway shoot a gun.

He climbed a rise and ducked into the cave, slipping into the shadows. Deeper inside, a single light illuminated a small area. Having met no resistance, Zach took the time to let his eyes adjust to the limited lighting before he moved closer to the glow. Voices carried to him, and by the sound of them, they were in Spanish.

Two men sat in front of a fire, one holding a stick at the end of which was some dead, skinned animal, roasting in the flame. The other smoked a cigarette. Both men had weapons, but they lay on the ground beside them. Apparently they weren't expecting company or anyone else.

Besides the men and the fire, there were small wooden crates and cardboard boxes lining the walls. Zach passed one after the other. Most of them were empty.

As he neared the fire, one of the men spoke in rapid-fire Spanish telling a raucous story about a woman and her mother. The other burst out laughing.

Zach stepped forward, his weapon drawn. In Spanish he asked, "Are you Los Lobos?"

The men reached for their weapons.

Still speaking in Spanish, Zach warned, "Reach for your guns and I'll shoot you. Hands up."

One man looked at the other and dove for his gun.

Zach shot him in the shoulder, knocking him backward into a wall.

The man grabbed his shoulder and slid to the ground, moaning.

"Don't shoot," the other man said in halting English. He kicked both weapons toward Zach, his hands still in the air.

"Are you Los Lobos?"

"No."

Zach pointed at the downed man's other shoulder. "No lies."

The bleeding man raised his good, bloodied hand. "*Sí, señor.* We are Los Lobos."

"Where is the woman?" Zach asked.

Both men looked at each other, their foreheads wrinkled in frowns.

The man who was still standing shook his head. "What woman?"

"The one the Los Lobos murdered two La Familia Diablos guys to get."

Again the standing man shook his head. "Los Lobos didn't take a woman. With the FBI and DEA all over the canyon, we couldn't leave our stuff here. The boss had us move it. We stayed to clean up the last of it." He blinked, glancing over Zach's shoulder.

Before Zach could spin, a hard poke in his back made him think twice.

"Drop your gun," a heavily accented voice demanded.

Zach had no intention of giving up his weapon. In a lightning-fast move, he ducked to the side and knocked the barrel of the rifle the man held downward, causing the stock to lever up and hit his attacker in the jaw.

The man pulled the trigger and a bullet ricocheted off the floor, disappearing into the shadows.

The unarmed men dropped to the ground.

Zach jerked the rifle out of the man's hands and

pressed his Glock into the guy's cheek. "Are there any more of you hiding or coming?"

The man with the gun in his cheek shook his head, his eyes wide. *"No comprende."*

The other man translated and received a response in Spanish. The translator faced Zach. "There are two more on their way to help move the rest of the stuff."

"Then let's get down to business." Zach nudged the gun deeper into the man's face. "Where's the woman?"

A thin sheen of sweat broke out on the man's face and he fired off his answer in such garbled Spanish Zach couldn't make heads or tails of it.

"What did he say?" Zach demanded of the translator.

"Los Lobos didn't take the woman. La Familia Diablos did."

Zach shook his head. "Then Los Lobos killed the two Diablos who took her, and now Los Lobos has her."

The man with the gun in his cheek shook his head and rattled off more Spanish.

"That is not the truth, *señor.* La Familia still has her. Someone made it look like Los Lobos killed those men."

"How about I shoot one of you at a time until someone tells me the truth?" Zach said.

All three men held up their hands. The man who understood English best spoke. "We are telling you the truth. Ramon just returned to pick us up. News from the boss is La Familia Diablos set it up to look like Los Lobos took the woman so that the Federales would look in the wrong place for her and cause troubles for Los Lobos."

For a long moment Zach continued to hold his weapon to the man's cheek. In his gut he knew what they were saying was most likely the truth. Finally he eased away from the trio, backing toward the cave entrance. He scooped up the other two weapons and slung all three over his shoulder while still holding the Glock on them.

"I'll let you live this time. Believe me when I say, if what you've told me is all lies, I'll find you and I'll rip your limbs off one at a time and make you wish you were dead long before you are."

Without waiting for them to respond, Zach slipped out of the cave and ran back across the wide-open space, weighed down by the three extra guns. When he reached the relative safety of a large boulder, he removed the bolts from the Los Lobos rifles and tossed the weapons on the ground.

A shout sounded behind him. He leaned around the boulder. The three men emerged from the cave, headed in his direction.

Zach fired off a round, kicking up the rocks at their feet. They hurried back to the cave entrance.

With no more time to play around, Zach ran back to where he'd left Juan. With Juan's switchblade, he severed the zip-ties. "Let's go."

Juan ripped the tape off his mouth. "Did you find the woman?"

"No. If you want to live, you'll get moving." Zach didn't wait for Juan; he ran back the way they'd come, reaching the horses before Juan.

The sound of engines revving echoed off the canyon walls as Zach and Juan mounted the horses.

Now that he knew that most of Los Lobos had vacated the canyon, Zach wasn't as concerned about noise as he was about getting a bullet in his back. He urged his horse to a trot, praying the animal wouldn't break a leg on the rocky terrain. They maneuvered through the maze of canyon corridors until they emerged at the base of the ridge where Tracie had been taken.

AFTER SITTING IN the dark on the floor for what felt like an hour, Jacie glanced at the clock. Thirty minutes? It had only been thirty minutes? That's it? She refused to wait around her cabin another moment. She had to get back out to the canyon. Zach could be in trouble. Maybe he'd found Tracie and they were fighting their way out and needed an extra gun to even the odds.

Jacie dressed in clean black jeans, a black T-shirt and her black leather jacket. She knotted her long hair in a rubber band and shoved it under a black baseball cap Richard had given her. After loading her rifle and her Glock with rounds, she shoved a box of bullets in each jacket pocket and shoved the chair away from the door.

If someone was out there, she was loaded and wouldn't hesitate to shoot. She switched on the porch light and flung open the door.

The porch was empty and nothing moved as far as she could see into the shadows past the illumination. When she turned to lock the door, she noticed that the oil-rubbed bronze door lock had fresh scratches in it.

Her gut tightened. Someone had definitely been trying to get in. On instinct, she went back inside, closed the door and grabbed her sister's credentials and cell phone. She shoved them beneath a plastic bag of moldy tomatoes in the bottom of her miniature refrigerator. No one would bother them there.

Having hidden the only two things she considered of any interest to anyone, she locked the front door and slipped across the compound to the barn, weapon drawn and ready.

Once inside the barn, she fumbled in the tack room for a flashlight, switching it on and shining the light around the interior for good measure. She'd had that creepy, being-watched feeling since she'd come back to the Big Elk.

Satisfied she was alone, she led D'Artagnan, her bay gelding, from his stall and tossed a saddle over his back. Once she had the saddle cinched and the bridle settled over the horse's head, she turned to lead him out the back of the barn.

A hinge squeaked and the overhead lights blinked on. Richard leaned in the doorway, fully dressed and ready to ride. "Wondered when you'd make a run for it."

"Oh, Richard, I'm sorry. My head tells me I should stay and wait for Zach to return, but my gut says he's in trouble and might need some help. The least I can do is cover his back."

"Thought you'd feel that way. I guess it wouldn't do me any good to tell you not to go."

She shook her head, her fingers tightening on the horse's reins. "I have to go."

"You're not going by yourself."

"I don't want to put anyone else in danger."

"Too bad. You're not going by yourself. My horse is ready and waiting out front. You have to put up with me in this crazy midnight rodeo."

"You could be shot at."

"Heck, I get shot at all the time by these darned fool weekend hunters who can't figure out the business end of a gun." Richard chuckled. "Come on. Let's you and me go for a ride in the moonlight. It's a mighty fine night for it."

Jacie choked back her response, afraid her voice would shake with her gratitude. Richard had always told her he appreciated her ability to avoid the feminine hysterics most women were prone to. It was one of the reasons he'd hired her. She was a straight shooter and not at all froufrou.

Her heart a little lighter, Jacie led her gelding out into the barnyard where, sure as he'd said, Richard had his black quarter horse saddled and ready to go.

He had a rifle in his scabbard and an old-fashioned revolver in a holster slung around his hips. The man could have been a gunslinger in a former life, he looked so natural. They left the ranch compound without speaking and nudged their horses into a gallop as soon as they cleared the last gate.

If all went well, they'd be at the ridge of the canyon in less than an hour. Then Jacie would have to decide what next. She didn't know where the Los Lobos hideout was in the maze of canyon trails. Hell, she'd cross that bridge when she came to it. Right now anywhere closer to the canyon where her sister disappeared and Zach had gone to find her was better than waiting around her cabin with someone trying to break in.

ZACH AND JUAN raced back to where the trail led up out of the canyon. As Juan started up the narrow trail, two motorcycles emerged from the shadows Zach had just left. Two more shot out close behind.

Zach turned on his horse and fired at the lead cyclist. His bullet went wide of its target and the cycle continued straight for them.

Four to one wasn't the best odds. Zach could take them, but then he'd waste time. Time was something he couldn't afford to give up. The longer Tracie remained in the clutches of the cartel, the more torture she'd have to endure. And the longer he was in the canyon, the longer he was away from Jacie.

He spun his horse, aimed at the closest pursuer and fired.

The rider jerked off the bike and landed on his back on the ground. The next rider swerved to miss him and slid sideways on the rocky surface. Two down, two more to go. Without cover and concealment, Zach would be at a disadvantage defending himself and if he tried riding up the trail to the top, he might as well paint a target on his back and Juan's. The two pursuers at the bottom only had to dismount and take aim.

Out in the open and out of options, Zach leaped off his horse and slapped the animal's hindquarters, sending it up the hill after Juan.

Zach dropped to the ground, drew his weapon and aimed at the nearest man. When he pulled the trigger, nothing happened.

The men on the motorcycles drew steadily closer.

Zach pulled the bolt back and ejected the bullet inside, then slid it home, aimed and pulled the trigger again.

Nothing.

On the ground, his gun jammed, Zach lay still, hoping to surprise the two men with the only other weapon he had on him. Juan's switchblade.

CHAPTER ELEVEN

JACIE AND RICHARD neared the ridge at a trot, glad for the full moon and the near-daylight conditions in which to maneuver the Texas landscape.

The closer she got to the canyon, the faster Jacie's heart beat. She sensed trouble. A nudge to her gelding's flanks urged the animal into a gallop.

Almost at the edge, her horse ground to a halt and reared, his whinny filling the sky. Up over the top of the ridge sprang another horse and rider, charging straight for them.

The horse and rider skirted Jacie but didn't make it past her boss. Richard headed him off, leaned over and snatched the reins out of his hands, jerking the horse to a stop.

A string of Spanish curse words rolled out of the rider's mouth, and Jacie recognized him as Juan, the man who'd been with Zach when they'd taken off on their reconnaissance mission.

Jacie calmed her gelding and joined Richard and Juan.

"Where's Zach?" she demanded.

"I don't know. He was behind me."

The sound of engines carried up to her from the canyon below.

A feeling of déjà vu washed over Jacie and she

whirled her mount, heading for the canyon. Before she reached the edge, another horse topped the trail and headed her way. This one was riderless.

Damn. Damn. Damn. Jacie sank her heels into the gelding's flanks, sending him hurtling over the edge and down the trail. Below on the floor of the canyon, two motorcycles were nearly at the base of the path leading upward.

Zach was nowhere to be seen.

Then a shadow sprang up from the ground beside the first motorcycle and the rider was yanked off his seat, landing flat on his back.

The trailing bike veered straight for the two figures grappling on the ground.

Jacie pulled her rifle from the scabbard and, one-handed, fired off a round above the head of the attacker. It didn't deter him a bit. Either he couldn't hear over the roar of the motorcycle engine or he wasn't fazed by gunfire.

Now that the second motorcycle was practically on top of the tangled shadows of the men on the ground, Jacie didn't dare shoot at him for fear of missing and hitting Zach instead.

The rider leaped off his bike and joined the fight.

Jacie let her horse pick his way down the treacherous trail, while her heart hammered against her ribs. She prayed she wouldn't be too late to help.

A shot rang out from below.

Jacie's gelding sidestepped, nearly taking them both over the edge.

One of the shadows fell, lying motionless on the ground. The other two continued the struggle. One of them had to be Zach.

Jacie reached the bottom and charged toward the dueling pair, leaping out of the saddle before the horse came to a complete stop. Still holding her rifle, she pointed it at the pair.

Zach knocked the man to the ground and staggered back, bleeding from a gash on his cheek. The man on the ground rolled to the side, grabbed his fallen weapon and rolled to his back, aiming at Zach.

Jacie fired off a round, hitting the man square in the chest before he had a chance to pull the trigger. His gun fell to the side, and he lay still, his eyes open, staring up at the full moon.

Zach dropped to his knees, breathing hard. "I thought I told you not to come," he grumbled.

"And if I hadn't, you might be dead." Jacie laid her rifle on the ground and knelt beside him. "Are you okay?" She studied the gash on his cheek and searched him for other signs of injury, wishing she had a flashlight to work with.

"I'm okay." His lips twisted, then straightened into a smile and he shook his head. "Thanks."

"Now, was that so hard?" She pulled his arm over her shoulder and helped him to his feet.

"I'm really okay, just winded."

"Shut up and let me help." She led him to her horse. "Take the saddle. I'll ride behind."

Zach dragged himself up into the saddle.

Jacie assisted with a firm hand on his rear, shoving him upward. She couldn't help thinking that he had a nice behind. Some kind of thought to have when she'd just killed a man.

Holy crap. She'd just killed a man.

Her knees wobbled. The finality of her actions hit her, and her heart nearly stopped.

Zach moved his foot out of the stirrup and reached down for her hand. "Come on. We have to get to Hank's place."

Jacie didn't have time to go soft on him. So she'd killed a man. A man who would have killed Zach if she hadn't. And her sister was still missing.

She straightened her shoulders, dragged in a steadying breath and put her hand in Zach's, her foot in the stirrup.

As he pulled her up, she swung her leg over the horse's hindquarters and landed neatly behind the saddle and Zach, wrapping her arms around his waist.

Zach reined the gelding around and sent it up the trail at a slow, steady pace, letting the horse choose his steps, given that it was carrying double the burden.

Jacie leaned into Zach's back and inhaled the heady scent of dust, denim and cowboy, letting his strength and courage seep into her. She didn't look down, just closed her eyes and let the horse and the man get her out of the hell she'd just experienced.

Richard waited at the top of the hill with the reins of Juan's horse tied to his saddle horn. "I would have come down, but you had it all under control before I could. I take it we need to report a couple of deaths?"

"We'll hit the ops tent on the Raging Bull and let them handle things." Zach glanced around. "Have you seen my horse?"

"He's halfway back to the barn by now."

Jacie couldn't be sorry about that. It meant she didn't have to drive. It gave her an excuse to hold on to Zach a little longer without revealing how needy she actually felt. What was it about this man that made her want to be strong for him at the same time he turned her knees to jelly?

Richard rode ahead with Juan.

Zach and Jacie allowed the gelding to take his time. Moonlight streamed over them and they were alone in the stark Texas landscape.

After a few minutes, Jacie swallowed her disappointment and bucked up the courage to confirm, "I take it you didn't find Tracie?"

"No." The word was terse, almost angry.

"What did you find?"

"Juan was correct in that Los Lobos had a rendezvous point in a cave in the canyon, but they were in the process of relocating because of all the activity in the canyon with the FBI and DEA looking for Tracie and the people who killed their agents."

"Did you find out where they moved Tracie?"

Zach shook his head, staring straight ahead. "Every man I questioned said the same thing. Los Lobos didn't kidnap anyone and they didn't kill the two La Familia Diablos men."

"If not Los Lobos, who?"

"They think that whoever killed the men wanted it to look like Los Lobos to throw the FBI and DEA off the trail of the real killers and to stir up trouble for Los Lobos with La Familia Diablos."

Jacie leaned her forehead into Zach's back. "Then we're back to square one. We don't have a lead and we don't know who took Tracie or where."

His hand rested over hers, warm and gentle. "We'll find her."

"Are you thinking it's someone internal to the FBI or DEA who set this all up?"

"I can't be certain, but I'd bet it is."

"Where do we go next?"

"I'm not sure. First, I need to talk to Hank and an old buddy of mine I trust from the FBI."

"No. First we need to have your wounds tended." Her arms tightened around his middle for a second before she realized he might have been hit in the ribs. She loosened her hold.

"I'm fine. I just need a shower. I can get that back at the Big Elk and you can get some rest."

They rode into the Raging Bull compound and were immediately surrounded by the agents and local law enforcement personnel manning the night shift.

Richard and the groggy ranch foreman took their horses. Richard would borrow one of the Raging Bull trailers to get the horses and himself back to the Big Elk.

After reporting on the two dead men and filling them in on what Zach had discovered, Jacie was so tired she could barely stand.

"Out and about again?" Bruce appeared at Jacie's side. "I thought you'd given up and gone back to the Big Elk." Her sister's boyfriend stood close behind her, his breath stirring the stray hairs resting against her neck.

"Couldn't sleep." Jacie took a step away from Bruce, tucking the loose strands of hair behind her ear and praying Zach would wrap up what he was doing. She was too tired to talk with anyone, especially Bruce.

"Your sister always pushes her hair behind her ear like that."

"What has the FBI come up with so far?" Jacie

changed the subject, her gaze still on Zach, willing him to look up.

Several feet away, his head tilted toward the sheriff who'd been giving him the lowdown on retrieval of the two bodies in the canyon, Zach glanced across at her and frowned.

"Not as much as I'd hoped. Whoever took Tracie didn't leave much of a trail."

"At least we can rule out Los Lobos. And if it wasn't Los Lobos, either La Familia has some inside traitors or someone else took my sister. Any guesses?" Jacie finally pinned Bruce with her gaze, her eyebrows rising up her forehead.

Bruce shook his head, his eyes shadowed. "You are a lot like your sister. Get down to the business at hand. That's what I love about her."

"Where is she, Bruce?" Anger fueled by frustration and exhaustion bubbled up inside her. "You have two federal agencies and the local law enforcement on this rescue effort and what have you found? Nothing."

An arm slipped around her waist. "You ready to go, darlin'?"

Zach's resonant baritone washed over her like a soothing warm wave. The tension that had held her upright for the past hour slowly seeped out of her and left her oddly boneless and ready to collapse. Her chin tipped upward and she gave him the hint of a smile. "Yes. I'm more than ready to go."

Zach pulled her against him and stared across at Bruce. "If you don't mind, I'm going to steal my girl away and get her home to bed."

Heat flared in Jacie's body at Zach's words, the images they generated making her tingle all over. Her nipples hardened into tight little buds rubbing against the lace of her bra.

"Take me home," she whispered, leaning into him, grateful for the added support when her knees turned to jelly.

As he drew her away from Bruce, Jacie whispered, "Did you talk to Hank about our next steps?"

"He called it a night an hour ago. I hate to wake the man when there's nothing more we can do tonight."

"Good point."

"We can do that in the morning. Right now I need that shower and some shut-eye." He glanced over at the young Hispanic seated on the ground beside a parked vehicle, his head in his hands. "Come on, Juan. We'll take you home."

Juan scrambled to his feet and followed Zach and Jacie.

Jacie was past exhaustion, and the worry about her sister weighed so heavily she wanted to burst out crying. But that wasn't the way she worked. The thought of going back to her cabin and collapsing into bed sounded wonderful.

Except her mattress was still on the floor and someone had tried to break in while she'd been in the shower.

She glanced at Zach. No, she wouldn't put that on him, not after all he'd just been through. Jacie could handle a gun and take care of herself for what remained of the night.

Zach promised the sheriff he'd fill out a police report the next day, then he grabbed Jacie's arm and led her to his truck, Juan following.

Without uttering another word, they left the Raging Bull and headed for Wild Oak Canyon then the Big Elk Ranch.

ZACH'S RIBS HURT and the gash on his cheek stung from where one of Hank's employees had cleaned and applied antiseptic ointment to his wound. He'd passed on a bandage, but now was second-guessing that decision.

"Dude, you're one crazy son of a b—"

"Please." Zach cut him off. "I owe you an apology for dragging you into that. But thanks. At least it ruled out Los Lobos as the people who kidnapped Tracie."

"Can I have my knife back now?" Juan asked over the backseat.

"I might be crazy, but I'm not stupid." Zach chuckled. "I'll give you back your knife when I drop you at your home."

Juan leaned back against the upholstery. "Whoever killed the two from La Familia must have wanted this woman really bad. No one messes with La Familia without retribution. As many as there are, someone will pay soon."

Jacie turned sideways and peered over the back of the seat. "If you know anyone around here associated with La Familia, now would be the time to tell us."

"What? Or you'll shoot me?" Juan shook his head. "*No estoy loco.* If I tell you who, everyone will know it was me. I'd be a marked man."

"Give us a hint?" Jacie begged.

"No." Juan stared at Zach in the mirror. "Your woman can shoot me dead, but it would be better than what La Familia would do to me."

Zach nodded. La Familia was known for its brutality with public beheadings and hangings. Los Lobos was no better, a fact Zach knew from experience. "Leave him alone. He's done enough."

Jacie settled back in her seat, her lips tight. "What about Tracie?"

"I have a contact that might be able to help. And I'll get Hank on it, as well."

Zach dropped Juan at his trailer and handed him his knife. "We're square now?"

Juan peered through the truck's open window at Jacie. "For what it's worth, I didn't know your sister would be a target. She asked when the next shipment would be handed off. All I did was tell her. She gave me five hundred dollars for that information." He snorted. "I should have asked for a lot more."

Jacie's mouth twisted. "And I shouldn't have let her go on the trail that day."

Zach drove out of the little town of Wild Oak Canyon in silence.

The back of Jacie's head rested against the seat, her profile one of natural, wholesome beauty. Unfettered, unblemished beauty that went deeper than skin. "Do you think Juan really knows someone in La Familia?"

Zach drew his attention away from Jacie's profile and back to the road before answering, "Yes."

"Then why didn't you make him tell us who it was?"

"I've seen what these cartels do to the people they deem traitors or informers. Juan did what we asked of him today. We put him in enough danger just associating with us. Besides, I don't think he's involved in what's going on with your sister."

"If he knows who we can ask…"

"He'd be dead by morning if we moved on his information."

"What about Los Lobos? Won't they be after Juan?"

"Maybe, but they didn't see me with him in the canyon. Not where they would recognize him."

Deep in thought, Zach didn't see the other vehicle until it broadsided his truck, metal slamming into metal, forcing him to swerve and bump through the gravel on the roadside. "Hold on!" He gripped the steering wheel with both hands and fought to get it back up on the road.

Jacie grabbed for the handle beside the door and held on, the seat belt tightening, bracing her against the rough terrain.

Zach veered back up onto the road, only to be hit again. This time the truck careened off the road and down the embankment into the ditch and back up on the other side.

The vehicle on the road slowed and the window slid downward.

"Duck!" Zach cried, hitting the accelerator, sending the truck back down into the ditch and up onto the road.

At the same time, the dark older-model SUV shot forward, catching Zach's truck bed.

The back end swung around, but Zach corrected and hit the gas again, propelling the truck forward.

The vehicle behind him raced to catch up.

In the rearview mirror, all Zach could see was the dark silhouette of the vehicle whose headlights were blacked out.

Something rose above the top of the vehicle behind him, and dread filled his gut. Zach jerked the steering wheel with one hand as he shoved Jacie's head down with the other.

The back windshield exploded inward with a spray of bullets. One zipped all the way through and smashed into the front glass, sending out a spider web of fissures, making it difficult to see.

Zach couldn't outrun the SUV, and the turnoff to the Big Elk Ranch was still several miles away. "Jacie, you're going to have to return fire."

"Are you kidding?"

"It's that or one of us isn't going to make it to tomorrow, maybe both. Use my rifle."

"I'd rather use mine."

She grabbed her rifle from where it rested on the floorboard, removed her safety belt and turned in the seat, steadying the gun's barrel on the back of the headrest.

"What do you want me to aim at?"

"Start with the shooter on top. Hell, just shoot at the whole damn vehicle. It'll be hard enough to hit anything on these bumpy roads."

She fired once.

The vehicle behind them swerved, then straightened.

The next round caused the man on top to duck inside.

Her third round forced the driver to drop back.

"That's my girl." Zach grinned. "You're pretty good riding shotgun."

Still sitting backward in her seat, Jacie smiled. "Knowing how to handle a weapon comes in handy sometimes, besides on the hunt."

The vehicle behind them dropped back farther until it spun around and headed in the opposite direction.

"Thank God." Jacie turned and settled back down in her seat and took stock of the truck. "I'm sorry your truck took the worst of that. And you kept it so nice and shiny."

Zach could have laughed. "To hell with the truck. You could have been hurt."

She glanced his way, one hand clasping her left shoulder. "Uh, actually…" Jacie moved her hand.

Because Jacie had been wearing a dark shirt, Zach hadn't noticed the blood until the light from the dash glanced off the liquid.

"Damn. We're going straight to the doctor." He slowed, ready to do a U-turn in the middle of the highway.

"It's only a flesh wound and I have no desire to enter into another game of chicken with the SUV that attacked us back there." She pointed to the road ahead. "I have a first aid kit in my cabin. A little disinfectant and a bandage ought to fix me right up."

Zach's foot hovered over the accelerator. "Are you sure?"

"I've lived on a ranch long enough to know a serious wound from a not-so-serious wound. I just want to go home. Please."

Still not fully convinced, Zach gave in and hit the gas, sending the truck shooting forward. He pulled onto the dusty road into the Big Elk Ranch, anxious to get there and assess the damage himself.

The trailer from the Raging Bull was parked beside the barn, empty. Apparently Richard had arrived earlier, taken care of the horses and called it a night.

If need be, he'd take Jacie to the lodge and call an ambulance if her wound was more than just torn flesh.

After parking in front of Jacie's cabin, Zach leaped down and rounded the truck in a jog.

Jacie had the door open and was stepping down.

He grabbed her around the middle and eased her the rest of the way down to the ground.

For a moment he stared down at her, appreciating that she wasn't crying. She hadn't burst into hysterics at the sight of her own blood, and she was staring back up at him, the moon reflected in her eyes.

"Anyone ever tell you that you're an amazing woman?" Zach said.

"No, but you can say it again. It sounds nice." She smiled, and then grimaced. "I'd better get this cleaned up. And you need a bandage on your face."

"We're a pair. We look like we lost the fight."

"The hell we did. We've only just begun." She led the way up the steps to her cabin and fumbled in her pocket for the key.

Before she could find it, Zach pushed the door and it swung open. "Did you lock this door?"

Jacie frowned. "Yes, I did."

When he moved to enter, Jacie held out a hand to stop him.

"Wait," she whispered. "What if someone's inside?"

Zach pulled her to the side and lifted the rifle to his shoulder. "Stay here." He gave her a steady, stern look.

She nodded.

Zach stood to one side of the door, edged it open wider with the barrel of the rifle and peered inside.

Furniture had been upended and papers and clothes scattered across the floor. "I think whoever did this is gone," he said, his voice so low only Jacie would be able to hear him.

Ducking low, he entered the cabin, keeping out of the moonlight streaming through the windows. He worked his way around the cramped interior, checking in the bathroom and closet before he was satisfied that it was no longer occupied.

"It's clear," he called out.

Jacie came inside, closed the door behind her and flipped on the light. The tears welling in her eyes, which she'd refuse to let fall, were Zach's undoing.

He crossed the room and opened his arms. Jacie fell into them, wrapping hers around his waist. "I'm just too tired to deal with this."

"Then don't. All we need is that first aid kit, and we're out of here."

"It was in the bathroom." She leaned away from him and he slipped into the bathroom. "And we don't have to leave. I'm okay."

He stayed in the bathroom longer than necessary to retrieve the kit under normal circumstances.

"Find it?" Jacie asked.

"Most of it." Zach emerged with the kit, stuffing bandages and tubes of ointment into the plastic container. "I have enough to work with." He glanced around the bedroom. "Was your sister staying with you?"

"Yes."

"Did she leave anything here that might explain why she came? Maybe something that would be worth ransacking this place for?"

"I went through her suitcase and discovered her cell phone and FBI credentials. I hid them before I left to find you."

Zach frowned. "Why did you hide them?"

Jacie looked away. "Someone tried to get into the cabin while I was in the bath."

Zach blew out a long breath. "Not good news."

"You're telling me." She stared at the mattress, recalling the cold chill of dread she'd had as she sat on the floor, her gun trained on the door.

"Where did you hide the cell phone and credentials?"

Jacie's lips quirked upward. "In the fridge beneath the rotting bag of tomatoes."

Zach's mouth quirked. "Smart move. Let's hope the intruder didn't figure it out." He picked his way across the floor to the refrigerator, pulled it open and rummaged around inside. He came out with the cell phone, credentials and a tight smile. "You could have been an agent, Jacie Kosart."

She shrugged and grimaced. "Not my calling."

"Come on, we're going to my cabin. Hopefully it's still intact. We can figure out the rest of this mess in the morning." Zach shoved Tracie's phone and wallet inside his back pocket.

"Come closer to the door. I'm going to turn out the lights."

Jacie stood against the wall beside the door, aware of Zach's warmth next to her.

Zach switched the overhead light off, plunging them into darkness. "I'm going out first," he whispered against her cheek.

The warm draft of his breath made gooseflesh rise on her arms. He was close enough to kiss.

"Wait until I tell you to come." He touched her hand and then slipped out the door into the night.

Jacie's heart fluttered and she held her breath for what felt like a very long time. Then the door nudged open.

"It's okay, my cabin's untouched." Zach was there

again. He captured her hand in his and led her across to his cabin.

Once inside, Zach closed the shades and pulled the curtains over the windows. Then he switched on the light. "Now let's take care of that wound."

"Earlier…" Jacie stiffened when Zach's fingers reached for the buttons on her blouse. "I can do it." Jacie wasn't sure she could resist him at such close quarters. He drew her like a fly to honey and she was too tired to resist.

He shook his head, his lips firm. "Let me do this. I'm trained in first aid and buddy care."

"My mother taught me enough that I haven't died yet," she argued halfheartedly. Her arm stung and she didn't have the strength to argue. Jacie sighed. "Fine."

He sat on the edge of the bed.

Jacie drew in a deep breath. This was not a good idea. Not when her defenses were down.

Zach stood in front of her and reached for the top button on her shirt. He pushed the button through the hole, then the others, all the way down to where the shirt disappeared into the waistband of her jeans. He tugged the tails free and slid the blouse over her shoulders, easing the fabric over her injured arm.

A quiver of awareness rippled across her skin, and her breasts tightened. Jacie closed her eyes and sucked in a long, steadying breath.

Footsteps sounded, leading into the bathroom. Water ran in the sink and the footsteps returned.

Every one of her senses lit up. With her eyes still closed, she inhaled the scent of Zach, letting it wash away the fear of seeing him fighting two men at once, not being able to help for fear of shooting the wrong man. The way he'd held her the night before, the way she hoped he'd hold her again.

"I'll try to be gentle."

"Just do it," she whispered, praying he would.

CHAPTER TWELVE

ZACH WAS IN over his head on this one, with no way to swim to the top.

Jacie sat with her eyes closed, her hair spilling down her back, the light shining down over her face, neck and breasts, giving her a golden glow.

God, she was beautiful.

His hand shook as he smoothed the damp cloth over her wound.

He would never have suspected her skin would be so soft and silky beneath her tough-gal exterior. She smelled like the Texas wind and herbal shampoo as she sat with her eyes closed, her head tilted back slightly, her breathing shallow, the rise of her chest captivating.

Tempted to steal a kiss from those full, luscious lips, he dragged his focus back to the task at hand, shifting uncomfortably as his groin tightened.

After cleaning the wound, he opened the tube of antiseptic, hoping it would bring him back to his senses with its acrid scent. It didn't.

He applied the cream, his gaze slipping to the swells of her breasts, peeking out from the top of a lacy black bra. Who'd have thought the hunting guide would have such a sexy piece of lingerie in her wardrobe? His thoughts shifted farther south. Did she wear matching panties?

Zach fought the urge to slip the strap over her shoulder and bare one of those delicious orbs. He peeled the backing off a large adhesive bandage and taped it to her skin over the injury. "There—" He cleared his throat. "All done."

She turned to him, her eyes opening, the hunger in them hard to miss. "Now your turn," she said, her voice husky and so sexy Zach thought he might lose control.

Holy cow, how was he supposed to sit while she administered first aid to him? He could barely move, he was so hard.

She rose from the bed and walked toward the bathroom, wearing her bra and her jeans, her hips swaying with every step. Perhaps she'd be appalled at how sexy she looked.

Not Zach. He couldn't tear his gaze away from her rounded bottom. A groan rose up his throat.

Jacie was the job. Making love to her wasn't part of the contract. But when she emerged from the bathroom with a damp cloth, all good intentions flew out the window.

She came to a stop in front of him, hesitated a moment, then straddled his legs and bent down to apply the cloth to the wound on his cheek. Jacie leaned close enough Zach could easily have reached out and touched one of those lace-clad breasts with his lips.

After cleaning the wound, she applied the antiseptic and the bandage, then sighed, straightening. "Am I that homely?" she whispered, then started to step away from him, a frown wrinkling her forehead.

Zach grasped her hips. "What did you say?"

Her cheeks suffused with a pretty pink and she glanced away from him. "Nothing."

"Wrong." He tugged her hips, forcing her to sit on his legs. "Do you know how hard it is to be a gentleman when you're wearing only a bra?" His hands slipped up to the catch at the middle of her back. "When all I want to do is this…." He flicked the hooks open and slipped the straps over her shoulders—gently around her wound. "I just didn't want to cross the line."

She laughed softly, letting the bra fall to the floor. "Don't tell me you're a rule follower. I can't picture you as one."

"Never." He looked up at her, his gaze capturing hers. "You've been through a lot today. Are you sure this is what you want?"

Jacie smoothed a hand over his hair. "I not only want this, I need it." She tugged his ears, dragging him within range of one full, rosy-tipped breast. "Please, don't make me beg."

He couldn't resist the temptation. He sucked her nipple into his mouth, his other hand rising to capture the other breast. His tongue swirled around the tip until it puckered into a tight little bud. He nibbled it and then switched to the other, giving it equal attention.

Jacie's back arched, her bottom squirming against his thighs. They still wore jeans and Zach wanted nothing more than to lie naked beside her and feel all of her against him.

He stood her on her feet and rose from the bed.

She frowned. "Is that it?"

"Not unless you want it to be." He shrugged out of his shirt and slung it to the corner.

"No. I want it all." She grasped the top button of his jeans and forced it through the opening. Then she worked the zipper down until his engorged member sprang free.

Zach let out the breath he'd been holding, the relief only temporary. He pulled his wallet from his back pocket, tossed it onto a pillow, then shucked his jeans.

Her gaze followed the path of the descending denim, her tongue sliding across her lips when he stood naked before her. Fire burned through his veins at the hunger in her expression. Past rational thought, he reached for her waistband, ripped the button open and shoved her jeans down her legs until she could kick free of them.

He scooped her up in his arms and laid her across the comforter and then crawled into the bed over her. "We should be sleeping," he said, pressing a kiss to her lips—sleep the furthest thing from his mind.

Her hands laced around his neck, her mouth turning up in a smile. "Sleep is overrated." She pulled him close, capturing his lips, her tongue slipping between his teeth. For every thrust of that magic tongue, an answering tug hit him low in the groin. If he didn't concentrate, it would be over before he had a chance to pleasure her.

He slid his mouth over her chin and down the long line of her throat to the base, where her pulse beat a ragged staccato against her skin. He tapped his tongue to the tip of one breast and captured the other, pulling it fully into his mouth, where he suckled until her back arched off the mattress.

Jacie's fingers wove through his hair and she tugged, urging him lower still. Her thighs parted, allowing him to lie between them on his journey down to her nether regions.

His fingers led the way, parting her folds buried beneath a light smattering of fluffy dark curls. He slid his tongue across the special bundle of nerves packed into a simple nubbin of flesh.

Jacie bucked beneath him, "Oh, Zach!" She dug her heels into the bed and rose to meet his tongue's every stroke, her fingers digging into his scalp. Her body grew rigid, her thighs tight, her face pinched as she catapulted over the edge.

Zach climbed up her body, rolled to the side and grabbed his wallet from the other pillow, tearing through the contents until his fingers closed around a foil packet. He ripped it open with his teeth.

Jacie pulled the condom free and rolled it down over his swollen member. "Now. Please."

He leveraged himself between her legs and slipped into her warm, wet channel, sliding all the way in. Her muscles contracted around him and he fought for control.

Soon he was thrusting in and out of her, his pace increasing with the intensity of sensations filling his body. The tingling ripped through him from his toes to the tip of his shaft. He rammed home one last time and collapsed on top of her, buried deep inside Jacie's warmth.

Her legs wrapped around his middle, her arms around his neck.

For a long time, he pulsed inside her, the troubles of the world so far away they could have been on an entirely different planet for all he knew.

When his senses finally calmed and he returned to the present, he rolled to his side, taking her with him, their connection unbroken.

She lay with her head pillowed on his arm, her

eyelids drifting to half-mast. "Are you always this intense?" She touched a finger to his lip.

He kissed the tip, giving her the hint of a smile. "Only when it counts."

"Um. I'd say it counted." She draped a leg over his, sliding her calf across his thigh.

"To answer your earlier question, no, you're not homely. You're beautiful." He brushed a kiss across her lips and pulled her closer, resting his chin on the top of her head.

Within seconds, Jacie's breathing slowed and her body relaxed against his as she fell asleep.

Zach lay awake for a long time, sanity crowding in on him with each passing minute.

He'd done exactly what he'd sworn he'd never do again. He'd slept with a woman whom he could very easily fall for. Hell, he was already halfway there.

Jacie was everything he could possibly want in a woman. Tall, gorgeous, open, honest and tough enough to set him in his place. She was loyal and loving and deserved a man who could give her all of himself.

Zach just wasn't that man. After what had happened to his partner, he vowed never to become so emotionally committed to any woman. It hurt too badly when you lost her and he knew his heart wouldn't survive another blow that deep.

An hour later, Zach slid his arm from beneath Jacie's neck and climbed out of the bed. He pulled on a pair of jeans, grabbed his cell phone and let himself out of the cabin.

Clouds had moved in to block the moon. Except for the porch lights on the tiny cabins and the security lights on the lodge, everything was shrouded in inky, black darkness.

Zach sat on the porch steps and checked his phone. He'd been so wrapped up in everything that had happened since he'd gone into the canyon to find Los Lobos hideout, then Jacie...he hadn't checked his calls and messages. Only one call had come in. It was from his friend James Coslowski, and he'd left a message.

Zach's heartbeat picked up as he hit the play button.

"Dude, what the hell have you gotten into? Apparently this Kosart woman was working without authority on a case that wasn't assigned to her. The whole bureau is in an uproar and the big bosses are threatening to roll a few heads. Call me when you get this message and I'll fill you in."

Zach dialed James.

"Do you know any other time of the day than middle of the night?" James answered in a whisper. "Let me get somewhere that I won't wake my pregnant wife so I can talk."

A moment later, he spoke in a normal tone. "So you got my message."

"I did. Why is the bureau all up in arms?"

"Classic case of the right hand not knowing what the left hand was doing. DEA supposedly was working the Big Bend area when your Tracie Kosart wandered in and got herself kidnapped and the agents killed. Any luck finding her?"

"None so far."

"It's a shame. I didn't find anything on Tracie. She checks out as a good agent, follows the rules—until now—and keeps her nose clean. Have it on file that she and Agent Bruce Masterson are in a relationship.

I'm guessing you already know that since he's been assigned to the team responsible for finding Agent Kosart."

"He's here."

"One of the FBI big dogs, Grant Lehmann, has also
assigned himself as overseer of the operation to retrieve
the Kosart woman."

"I guess with the two agencies involved, they felt it
necessary to have adult supervision?"

"Probably. I found it interesting that one of Bruce
Masterson's past assignments was to infiltrate a drug
ring in the San Antonio area. He pulled in a pretty
major leader on that case and got all kinds of kudos
and awards for his work."

"Seems like he needed to be a little farther west."

"Yeah, but the ringleader has connections to people
in your area."

Zach sat up straighter. "Names?"

"Let me find my notes." The sound of papers being
turned crackled in Zach's ear before James said, "Here
it is. The file only listed one, Enrique Sanchez. Lives in
a trailer six miles south of Wild Oak Canyon. The notes
in the file indicate he makes frequent trips to Mexico
and has been seen with members of La Familia Diablos on the Mexican side of the border."

"Anything else?"

"That's all so far. I'll let you know as soon as I dig
up anything else."

"Thanks, cos."

"Keep your head down, buddy. It's likely to blow
up even bigger than you think. What with two agencies fighting over jurisdiction and blaming each other
for everything that's gone wrong."

"Trust me, I'm here. I know." Zach clicked off his cell phone, his heart pumping, sleep so far from his mind he couldn't stay still.

He had to get to Enrique Sanchez. If he was a member of La Familia, he might know what happened to Tracie. Trouble was that he couldn't leave Jacie alone. Not after her cabin had been ransacked. Since whoever had tossed her home had tried to break in while she was there, they weren't concerned about being seen by her. Meaning they would have either taken her or killed her.

Zach would have to wait until Jacie awoke. He'd get the cell phone to Hank's team and let them hack into it for any information they might find. For safekeeping, he'd leave Jacie with Hank and check out Sanchez.

From that point on, Zach spent time cleaning and checking his weapons. He couldn't afford to have one jam on him when he needed it most. And if Sanchez proved to be a member of La Familia, it wouldn't be an easy task to convince him to talk.

SOMETHING BRUSHED JACIE'S LIPS, tickling her awake in the predawn of morning. She rolled onto her back and blinked open her eyes.

Zach leaned over her, dressed only in jeans and looking so handsome he hurt her eyes.

"Go away," she grumbled, slinging an arm over her face. She probably looked like hell.

"We have work to do. I got a lead."

Jacie sat up straight, forgetting for a moment that she was completely naked. Her face heated and she grabbed the sheet, dragging it up to her chin. "What lead?"

Zach's lips quirked upward, his gaze traveling over

her. "The name of a man who could be connected to La Familia."

Jacie flung the sheet back and leaped out of the bed, all sleepiness forgotten. "Where are my jeans? I need a shirt. Why didn't you wake me earlier? Why are you just standing there?"

He shook his head, unable to hide his smile. "You're beautiful." Zach stepped up to her and finger-combed her hair back off her forehead, his brown eyes darkening to near black.

Jacie's body responded to his light touch. "Not fair. You have all your clothes on."

"I can fix that."

"What about the man from La Familia?"

"It's still dark outside. It can wait until light." Zach wrapped his hands around her waist and pulled her against him, the hardness of his erection pressing into her belly, telling the truth. He wanted her as much as she wanted him.

She circled her arms around his neck and pressed her naked breasts into his chest. "Then what are you waiting for?" Jacie slid her calf up the back of his leg.

Zach kissed her as he cupped her bottom and lifted her, wrapping her legs around his waist and backing her against the wall.

He reached beneath her to unfasten his jeans. His member sprang free and nudged her opening.

"Are you always this hard in the morning?" she asked.

"Always."

She sucked in a deep breath, so ready for him to come inside her, but not too far gone to be stupid about it. "What about protection?" She kissed his cheek, then his eyelid, trailing her lips across to the other eye.

Zach carried her across to the bed and dumped her on the mattress.

"Hey. That's not very romantic," she protested.

"Shut up and hand me my wallet," he said through gritted teeth.

She found the leather billfold and pulled out a package similar to the one they'd used the night before. "Last one." She waved it at him. "Better make this count."

"Oh, I will." He dove for it.

Jacie dodged him and held it out of his reach. "Not yet."

"What do you mean, not yet?"

"As you eloquently put it, shut up, and let me show you." Her lips curled in a wicked smile. She pressed her palms to his chest, forcing him onto his back. "I hope you're not one of those men who thinks foreplay is overrated."

"I am."

"Then prepare to be proved wrong." She straddled his jean-clad hips, lowering herself enough to touch his hard shaft, but not enough for him to enter her. At the same time, she kissed him full on the mouth, taking his tongue with hers in long, sexy strokes.

Oh, yeah, she liked touching him and could see herself doing it a lot more. If he'd let her.

"Hell, Jacie, I'm about to explode. Could you hurry it up?"

Her lips slid across his chin and down to his chest, where she nibbled on the tight little brown nipples. Jacie wasn't a virgin, but she'd never played with a man before Zach. She liked it a lot. Her trail led her lower, bumping over the taut ripples of the muscles of his abdomen to the thatch of curls at the base of his shaft.

She wrapped her fingers around his hard, thick member. "Is this fast enough?"

"Hell, no." He leaned up on his elbows, his eyes widening as Jacie touched her lips to the tip and swirled her tongue around the circumference.

Zach dropped to his back and sucked in a deep gulp of air. "Wow."

"Like that?" She did it again, this time followed by slipping his shaft into her mouth and applying a little suction.

He groaned, his hands lacing through her hair. "I can't take much more."

She gave it to him anyway, going down on him until he filled her mouth.

Her blood sang, the fire burning low in her belly flaring, crying out for her to get on with it and take him inside her. Now.

Unable to hold out any longer, Jacie sat up, rolled the condom down over him and mounted, easing down over him.

Zach wrapped his hands around her hips and guided her up and down. "That's nice." Then he flipped her onto her back and thrust into her. "But this is better."

Jacie had to agree as he rocked in and out, the friction sending her to the edge and over.

At the same time as her body exploded in a tingling burst of sensations, Zach hit home one more time and remained buried deep inside.

Minutes later, they both drifted back to earth and

the reality of the sunshine edging around the side of the curtains.

Zach rolled to the side, slapped her bottom and smiled. "Get up. We have work to do."

"How can you move after that?" Her body still vibrating with her release, she lay for a moment longer, basking in the afterglow. She moaned and sat up. Today they had to find her sister. "I'll be ready in five minutes." And she dashed for the bathroom.

Inside she stared at the stranger in the mirror. Her face was flushed, her lips bruised, her hair all over the place. Jacie had never felt more alive and desirable than she did at that moment.

She found a plastic-wrapped toothbrush beneath the sink, scrubbed her teeth and finger-combed her hair. With nothing to tie it back with, she was forced to leave it down. Then she splashed her face with water and was finally ready to dress. That's when she remembered all her clothes were in the other room and she'd have to parade once more in her birthday suit in front of Zach.

So much for modesty. But then they'd made love twice. Why should it matter? With a deep breath, she threw back her shoulders and marched out.

Zach held her jeans and one of his T-shirts. "Yours was torn and bloody."

When she held out her hand for them, he raised them out of reach, his gaze panning her body from top to toe. "If only we had more time."

His heated gaze made her body burn. "If only my sister wasn't still missing." She wiggled her fingers, wishing she had the luxury of lying around in bed with Zach all day. "Your T-shirt will fit me like a dress."

"It'll look better on you than it does on me." Zach

handed over the clothes, his fingers dropping to tweak her naked breast before he sighed and stepped away. "I called Hank. He's expecting us in thirty minutes."

"Then we'd better get going." She slipped her arms into his T-shirt and pulled it over her body.

Zach's gaze followed the fabric all the way down.

"Eyes up here, cowboy." Jacie pointed to her own eyes and laughed.

"Can't help it. You have a great body."

Her cheeks heated again. "Let's find my sister and you can tell me more about it." Jacie pulled her jeans up over her legs and zipped them, deciding going commando wasn't so bad after all. Once she had her boots on, she glanced around the room. "You have my sister's phone?"

Zach patted his pocket. "I do."

"Then let's go."

At the door Zach pulled her back and into his arms. "You know I leave after this job is over."

Jacie swallowed hard, pasting a smile on her face. "I know. I'm just in this for the sex," she shot back at him as flippant as she could make it sound.

Then she pushed through the door, her chin held high, her heart sitting like a lead weight in her belly. Hell, she'd known from the start that Zach was on assignment from Hank's talent pool. He'd move on to the next job once they found Tracie. Jacie had known the ending of their story from the start, and she'd chosen to have sex with Zach anyway.

Still, the thought of Zach leaving made her day duller and darker than the rain-laden skies. Finding her sister would be bittersweet, but it had to happen.

CHAPTER THIRTEEN

ZACH DROPPED THE cell phone on Hank's desk. "Can you have someone hack into this and see if there are any numbers or information Tracie might have been using to go after the DEA agents?"

"Will do. My tech guy, Brandon Pendley, just got in and I had him working on hacking into the FBI database." Hank stood with the phone in his hand. "I'm sure this will be a piece of cake for him."

"While you're with Pendley, I need information on Enrique Sanchez. Anything you can find out. His address, family, friends. Anything. As soon as you can get it."

Hank's gaze moved from Zach to Jacie. "Someone we should be aware of?"

"I got word that he's connected with La Familia. Jacie and I will hit the diner and see if we can find out anything else about him. Then I'm going to pay him a little visit."

"I'll get Pendley right on it." Hank frowned. "If you think you need backup, I can have three other CCI men in less than an hour—including me."

Zach nodded. "I'll let you know. Have Pendley call or text the information as soon as he has anything."

"Will do." Hank nodded toward the window. "The joint operations team is expanding their search, supposedly sending feelers out to the other side of the border to see if they can locate Tracie. The FBI regional director is an old friend of mine, Grant Lehmann. He said he was giving the search top priority."

Jacie inhaled and closed her eyes for a moment. "It just seems so pointless. Is anyone actually going to find her?"

Zach slipped an arm around her and hugged her close. "Yes. And we're going to start by following the leads to Enrique."

"Let me get Brandon on this phone and the information you need to find Enrique. Then before you go, let me arm you with a few things you might need in your efforts. I should have given them to you before, but I wasn't sure if you'd actually employ them." Hank waved them to the back of the house and down the steps to a reinforced basement.

The first room they entered had computer screens lining the desks and larger screens affixed to the walls.

A young man wearing blue jeans, his hair hanging down to his collar and a single earring on one ear, glanced up. "Hey, Hank, who've you got with you?"

"Brandon, meet Zach Adams and Jacie Kosart."

Brandon stood and held out his hand to Jacie. "You're the twin?"

Jacie shook his hand. "That's right. I'm Tracie Kosart's sibling."

"Sorry about your sister."

"Don't be, just help me find her."

"On it." Brandon shook hands with Zach. "Nice to finally meet you in person."

"Actually," Hank added, "it was Brandon that found you and recommended I hire you."

Zach grinned. "Thanks. I think."

"Hank's a good man. You'll like working with him."

Zach made note of the fact that Brandon had said working with Hank, not for him. That indicated a level of teamwork and trust, reinforcing Zach's decision to go to work for Hank.

Hank handed the cell phone to Brandon. "Tracie Kosart's cell. Hack it for any information you can get out of it. But before you start, locate Enrique Sanchez for us."

Brandon gave a mock salute. "On it." He dropped back into his chair, and his fingers flew over the keyboard, his concentration fully on the screen in front of him.

"Brandon will have information about Enrique before you leave the ranch." Hank swept his hand to the back of the room. "Now, if you'll follow me."

Zach wondered how large the basement actually was as he followed Hank deeper into the maze.

Hank stopped at a steel, reinforced door and clicked numbers into a keypad. The door slid open and he stepped aside and gestured for them to follow. "Please."

Inside, the walls were painted a stark white and lined with racks filled with every kind of weapon imaginable.

Jacie spun in a circle, her eyes wide. "Holy crap, Hank, where'd you get all these?"

"Some of them I bought, others I had manufactured in one of my plants." He pulled a canvas bag off a hanger and handed it to Zach. One by one, he plucked armament off the shelves. "You might be able to use these incendiary grenades if you need to create a diversion." He tucked the grenade into the canvas bag and moved to the next shelf labeled CS Gas. "If you need to get the enemy out of a reinforced location, these come in handy. Here, you might need these, as well." Hank handed him a pair of night-vision goggles.

"Hank." Zach shook his head. "I'd be scared if I wasn't convinced you were one of the good guys."

"I wanted my operatives to be prepared for any event."

Zach held up his hand as Hank prepared to shove more into the canvas bag. "I'd never get past the gauntlet of the joint ops team outside with much more than I have in here now. I could use nine-millimeter ammo and a couple tracking devices."

"Got it." Hank handed Zach several clips and boxes of rounds and a web belt with straps that would hold clips and grenades. "And take this." He handed him a shiny SIG Sauer Pro. "In case you need a backup."

Zach stuffed it all into the canvas bag. "That should about cover a small war."

"You're in cartel territory," Hank reminded him. "They have far more firepower than that." The older man handed him three small disks. "Keep one somewhere on your person at all times. Tuck it in your underwear or shoes, just don't let it out of your reach. If you get into trouble, I'll be able to locate you."

"Sounds like you expect big trouble." Jacie shivered.

Zach wished he could shield her from all this, but she was smack dab in the middle and might as well be mentally as well as physically prepared with major hardware. "When we locate your sister, she's likely being held in a guarded compound. Getting in might not be a problem. Getting out with your sister will prove more challenging."

Jacie's chin tipped upward, though her face had paled several shades. "I'm not afraid."

Hank stared hard at her. "You should be. The cartels are ruthless."

Zach nodded. "He's right. I've seen what they can do to a captured woman. It's not pretty." He closed his eyes as memories of Toni's torture washed over him. "On second thought, Jacie, you should stay here with Hank. You'd be better off here monitoring efforts than getting caught up with the cartel."

"You know how well I stay put. Take me with you now or I'll follow you anyway."

Hank chuckled. "I might have to hire you onto my team. I hear you're a good shot."

Jacie nodded. "I am. But I'm not interested. I like my job. Getting shot at by a negligent hunter isn't nearly as scary as getting shot at by an angry cartel member."

Hank shrugged. "The offer's there if you change your mind."

Zach hooked Jacie's arm. "If you're done negotiating, let's get out and find your sister."

Jacie shook her arm loose as she exited Hank's armory. "What? You don't like the idea of me playing undercover cowboy?" Her eyes narrowed. "Why?"

"It's too dangerous."

"And it's not as dangerous for you?" She flipped her ponytail over her shoulder. "Sounds a bit chauvinistic to me."

At that moment, they passed Brandon's desk. "Give it up, dude. You'll never win."

Zach growled, his gut in a knot at the thought of Jacie being in harm's way every day. She made a good point about double standards, but he couldn't help it. His instinct to protect her was strong and he was struggling to get past it. If he could tie her up at Hank's and be assured she wouldn't find a way loose, he'd have left her rather than take her with him to interrogate Enrique.

Brandon gave Zach a sticky note. "That's Enrique's home address. It's just outside town. Be careful, the man has a police record of assault and battery. He's a mean dude."

"Thanks." Zach tucked the note in his pocket and placed his hand on the small of Jacie's back, guiding her toward the stairs.

"For the record, take the job if you like. It's your life."

Jacie paused with one foot on the step. "That's right. It is my life. And you're not staying around anyway, so why should it bother you?"

His gut clenched. He'd told her that he'd be out of there as soon as the case was over. Why it hurt hearing this from her, he didn't know, but it did. Zach had to remind himself not to get attached, although he feared it was too late. "Now that we're agreed, keep moving or we'll be here all day." He slapped her bottom as she climbed the steps out of the basement.

"My, my, we're grumpy, aren't we?" She threw a twisted smile over her shoulder at him. "Didn't get enough sleep?"

Her teasing wink only made him want to spank her again, or kiss her. Either would have been just as satisfying at that point, but not nearly enough. He wanted to take her back to bed and make love to her.

Unfortunately now was not the time or place.

"Here, hold this, it will look less conspicuous than if I walked out carrying it." He handed the canvas bag to Jacie before they left the ranch house and crossed to where he'd parked his truck. He glanced up at the steely gray skies, glad for the added darkness, yet hoping the rain would hold off until he had a chat with Enrique.

Bruce Masterson emerged from the operations tent and waved at them. "Jacie!"

"Just keep going," Zach urged.

Jacie placed a hand on Zach's arm and brought him to a stop. "What if he has information about Tracie?"

Zach smiled down at her and spoke between clenched teeth. "You're carrying weapons that aren't necessarily legal for civilians to own."

"Oh." Jacie hiked the bag higher on her shoulder. "Now's a good time to tell me."

"Just make it short." Zach turned to face the FBI agent and nodded, his arm slipping around Jacie, pressing her and the bag against his side. "Masterson."

"Adams." Bruce nodded curtly toward Zach and turned his attention to Jacie. "We got a possible lead on your sister's location."

Jacie's eyes widened and she started to take a step forward.

Zach held her firmly in place, schooling his face to give away nothing. If the FBI truly had a lead, good. In the meantime, they had their own information to follow up on. But he'd hear the agent out.

"Where is she?" Jacie asked. "Is she okay?"

Bruce raised his hand and snorted. "Not so fast. It's a lead, not yet confirmed. I sent agents across the border to check it out. I'll let you know as soon as I find out anything."

"Oh, thank you." She touched Masterson's arm.

"Where will you be? Do you have a number I can reach you at?"

Jacie hesitated.

"You can leave word at the Big Elk Lodge," Zach offered. "Giddings will pass the message on."

"Right." Jacie gave the man a stiff smile. "I'll be busy working outside, away from my phone and out of decent reception."

"Okay, then." Bruce clapped his hands together. "I feel good about this, so don't go too far out of touch in case we bring her back. I'm sure Tracie will want to see you."

Jacie sighed. "Just bring her back alive."

"We will." Bruce spun on his heel and returned to the tent.

Zach turned Jacie toward his truck.

"Why did you tell him to call the lodge?" Jacie asked. "I'll have my phone on me."

"I'd just as soon not give him the number. You don't know who in that operations tent is on our side. Remember there's a mole inside either the FBI or the DEA. We're not sure which, but I'm not willing to take chances."

"Right." Jacie nodded. "And phones can be traced through the global positioning system."

Zach handed her up into the truck and closed the door before climbing into the driver's seat.

They accomplished the drive to town in silence. As soon as they headed back out of town on the other end, Zach's fingers tightened on the wheel. "I'm not going to drive right up into Enrique's yard."

Jacie turned toward him. "I'm listening."

"I'll park the truck back about half a mile from his place, hide it in the brush and hike in on foot. I'm going to pretend I broke down. That way they don't start shooting right away."

"Sounds good so far."

He breathed in and let it out, then continued, knowing exactly what her reaction would be to his next words. "I want you to stay with the truck and watch for other vehicles that might enter or leave."

"In other words, you're not taking me in." She crossed her arms. "You know how I feel about that."

"I need live backup. By staying back, if you hear gunfire, get the hell back to town, where you'll have cell phone reception and can get Hank's help."

She shook her head. "Not getting any better. Why can't I come with you and we pretend we're the happy, lost couple?"

"Because Enrique might know you or recognize your face if he had anything to do with Tracie's disappearance. It would be like waving a red flag in the bull's face."

Jacie sat back against her seat, her gaze riveted on his. Finally she sighed, her shoulders sagging. "I hate it when you make sense. Okay, I'll stay put, but I'm not going to like it."

"Thanks." He pulled off the highway and onto the side of the road, bumping across the uneven terrain, fitting the truck in the middle of a clump of scrubby juniper trees.

Cedar scent filled the interior of the truck.

Zach switched the engine off and faced Jacie. "I also didn't want to worry about you." He leaned across the seat, cupped the back of her neck and kissed her soundly on the lips. "Damn it, you're growing on me and it scares the crap out of me."

A lump formed in Jacie's throat. "Goes the same for me."

Zach climbed out of the truck and struck out across the scrubby terrain without a backward glance.

The sky rumbled in the distance, and a single raindrop hit the windshield. Jacie hoped the rain would hold off a little longer until Zach came back.

ZACH RAN PARALLEL to the highway until he reached the dirt track leading into Enrique's place. Old cars littered the front yard, some with the hoods lifted, others jacked up, the tires long gone.

Though he knew he'd be a big target, Zach stepped out in the open, pretending to be a motorist whose car had broken down on the highway.

"Hello. Anyone home?" Zach called out. No one answered.

The flutter of a curtain in a window of the house caught his attention. A woman's face appeared, then disappeared.

A child cried inside and was quickly hushed.

"Hello." Zach walked closer. "My truck broke down. I need to use a telephone."

The front door opened and a short, round, Hispanic woman peered out. She waved her hands as if to shoo him away, speaking in rapid-fire Spanish, almost too fast for Zach to understand.

He caught the gist of what she was saying, something about leaving before her husband returned.

"I'm sorry." Zach held his hands palms up. "I don't speak Spanish. Do you speak English?"

"No," the woman said.

"She doesn't, but I do." A man appeared around

the side of the house, carrying an semiautomatic rifle. "What do you want?"

"My truck broke down on the road and I need to use a telephone."

"We don't have a telephone." He tipped the rifle. "Leave."

"You don't happen to have a tire iron, do you?" Zach moved closer, pretending to be unaffected by the presence of the rifle. "My tire went flat and I can't get the lug nuts loose."

"You can't stay here. Leave now." The man pointed the rifle at him.

"Hey, it's okay." Zach raised his hands. "I just need a tire iron with a lug wrench on it and I'll be out of your hair." He walked around the side of the house.

The man Zach suspected was Enrique followed. "You can't stay."

Once he'd rounded to the back, Zach noted a truck standing with doors wide open. Boxes and furniture had been thrown into the bed as if in a hurry. "Going somewhere, Enrique?"

Zach spun and lunged for the rifle before the man had a chance to fire. He grabbed the barrel, jammed the nose down and the butt up, hitting the guy in the face, causing his hands to loosen enough that Zach ripped the weapon out of his hands and flung it to the side. He yanked the man's arm around to his back and drove it up between his shoulder blades. "Enrique Sanchez, I understand you're a member of La Familia."

"I don't know what you're talking about." He stood on his toes, his face creased in pain.

"Really?" Zach twisted the arm tighter until the man cried out. "Wanna rethink that response?"

"*Sí, sí,*" Enrique squeaked. "I am. So? What do you want?"

"Answers." The clock was ticking on Tracie's life, and Zach had let it go on for too long.

"I don't know anything," Enrique insisted.

"Were you there when the DEA agents were murdered in Wild Horse Canyon?" Zach bore upward on the arm.

"*Sí, sí. Madre de Dios!*"

"Who murdered the DEA agents?"

Enrique didn't answer.

Zach hated doing it, but he ratcheted the man's arm tighter. "Who killed the DEA agents?"

"*Aya!* Go ahead, break it! Nothing you can do to me will be as bad as what La Familia will do if they get to me first. So go ahead. Kill me. I am a dead man already."

"Why?"

"I was supposed to meet *mi compadres,* but when I got there, they were dead. La Familia will blame me."

"Did you see who killed them?" Zach loosened his hold, finally letting go.

"No." Enrique dropped to his knees. "I don't know."

"Did you see who took the woman?"

"No." Enrique struggled to his feet. "I have to leave. I have to get my family out before—"

"Zach, look out!"

A shot rang out and Enrique jerked forward, slamming into Zach, his eyes wide, blood oozing from the wound in his gut.

Zach staggered backward as Enrique slid to the ground, his eyes wide and vacant. The man was dead.

CHAPTER FOURTEEN

JACIE SAT FOR as long as she could stand before she flung the door open and dropped down out of the truck. Zach had been gone too long, as far as she was concerned. He could be in trouble.

She grabbed her rifle and tucked her nine-millimeter in her waistband, then set off in the same direction as Zach had minutes earlier. Staying low, she used the available vegetation for concealment as she'd seen Zach do, moving parallel with the highway. When she came to the dirt track leading into Enrique's place, she stopped and listened, then turned and worked her way slowly toward the house.

Nothing stirred out front, so she circled wide, around the back of the house and the workshop behind it.

Voices carried to her, urgent and angry.

One belonged to Zach.

Her heartbeat fluttered and her palms sweat as she eased around the back of the workshop to get a better view, her rifle in front of her, in the ready position.

Zach stood with his back to her.

A man, who Jacie assumed was Enrique, was on his knees in front of Zach, struggling to stand. With only the one man in sight, Jacie gathered that Zach had everything under control. She had started to back away when she saw a movement from the corner of the house.

The barrel of a military-style rifle poked out.

"Zach, look out!" she yelled.

A shot rang out. Enrique, who'd managed to stand, dropped to the ground.

As a man stepped away from the side of the house, Jacie crouched to a kneeling position, aimed for the man's chest and pulled the trigger.

The shooter dropped to the ground before he could fire off another round.

Jacie's pulse pounded so hard the blood thrummed against her eardrums. She didn't hear the footsteps behind her until too late. A rock skittered by her, her first indication she was not alone.

Jacie rolled to her back, holding her rifle to her chest. Before she could aim and fire, a boot punted the rifle out of her hands.

A bulky, dark-haired, barrel-chested man grabbed the front of her shirt and yanked her to her feet.

Jacie kicked and fought to get free.

The bulk of a man spun her around like a rag doll, pinned her arms behind her and pulled the pistol from her waistband, tossing it to the side. He shoved her forward into the clearing.

Zach crouched, holding his weapon in front of him. When he spotted Jacie, his eyes widened. "Jacie."

"I'm sorry," Jacie said. "I thought you were in trouble."

"Drop the gun," the man holding Jacie demanded in a heavy accent.

"Don't hurt her." Zach tossed his pistol to the ground and raised his hands.

Another man came running around the side of the house, cursing as he leaped over the body of his dead *compadre*. He ran straight up to Zach and hit him hard with the butt of his high-powered rifle.

Zach dropped to the ground and didn't move.

Jacie cried out and lunged forward.

Meaty hands squeezed her arms so hard that pain shot up into her shoulders.

The two men spoke Spanish so fast Jacie couldn't begin to translate with her own rudimentary skills in the language. By their urgent tone and the way they kept looking over their shoulders, they were anxious to leave.

One of the men ran for the workshop.

Jacie stared at Zach, willing him to get up.

He lay so still, a gash on his forehead where the thug had hit him with the rifle.

Jacie struggled again, fighting past the pain of having her arms pulled back so hard.

Her captor loosened his hold long enough to punch her in the side of the head.

Pain rattled around her head, and fog tinged the edges of her vision.

The other guy emerged from the workshop carrying a roll of duct tape.

Pushing past her fuzzy-headedness, Jacie kicked and bucked, trying to twist loose of the hands holding her like steel clamps. If they got the duct tape around her wrists and ankles, she wouldn't have a chance.

She dug her booted heel into the man's instep and backed into him, ramming her elbow into his gut.

He yelled and hit her again.

Jacie fought the pain, struggling to stay upright and

losing. This time, the gray fog won, shutting out the sunshine and dragging Jacie into darkness.

LIGHT EDGED BENEATH Zach's eyelids, and the soft keening wail of a woman crying stirred him to wake. He opened his eyes and winced at the harsh light shining straight into his face from the setting sun. His head ached as he fought to regain his senses.

The crying continued and a baby's whimpers added to the sadness.

Zach turned his head in the direction of the sound, and a bolt of pain shot through his temple, clouding his vision.

A woman knelt in the dirt beside a man's body, a baby clutched to her chest. She rocked back and forth, tears coursing down her cheeks.

Enrique. The cloud over his brain lifted and Zach jerked to a sitting position. He swayed and braced his hands against the earth to keep from falling over.

The woman cried out and scooted away, holding the baby tightly.

Zach raised his hands, then pressed one to his temple where a knot had formed. He winced. "I'm not going to hurt you." He closed his eyes and fought a bout of nausea, then pushed to his feet, his mind coming alive. His first thought was Jacie.

Everything came back to him in a rush. He dug in his pocket for his cell phone and hit the speed dial for Hank. No service.

"Do you have a phone?" he asked the woman on the ground, holding up his cell phone at the same time.

She shook her head, her tears flowing faster.

"Sorry, I can't stick around to help. I'll send someone out." He didn't know if the woman understood what he'd said, but he didn't have time to translate.

He jogged around the house and workshop, his first instinct relief that he hadn't found Jacie's body. His second, dread at what she would be subjected to. He had to get to her before the cartel carried her back across the border and did what they'd done to Toni.

A lead weight settled hard in his gut. He pushed aside the negative thoughts and sprinted back down the road and out to the highway. Once he found his truck, he raced back to town.

As soon as he came close, he checked his service and dialed Hank.

"Zach, where have you been? I've been trying to get in touch with you for the past hour."

"La Familia has Jacie."

"Any idea where they took her?"

"None." That lead weight flipped over in his belly. With no leads, no inkling of where they'd have taken her, he had nothing. Jacie would suffer. "I need you to get Pendley to bring up the tracking devices. If she still has hers on her, we have a chance."

"Pendley hacked into Tracie's phone. Other than Juan Alvarez's number and Bruce Masterson's, there weren't any others leading anywhere."

"And how is that helping me?" Zach drove through town faster than the posted speed limits.

"Pendley checked Bruce Masterson out and found several calls to a Humberto Hernandez at the Big Elk Ranch."

"Isn't he the other guide that works with Jacie?"

"He's the one."

"Did you question Bruce?"

"Haven't seen him in the past three hours. The other agents manning the ops tent said he took off saying he was checking on a lead. I called Richard Giddings and asked him to keep an eye on Humberto until you got there. He called me just a moment ago to say Humberto is saddling a horse and that he'd try to stall him, but he didn't know how without letting on that he's now a person of interest."

"I'll be at the Big Elk in ten minutes. In the meantime, find Jacie's tracker." Zach pressed his foot down hard on the accelerator as his truck headed out of town on the highway leading to the Big Elk Ranch. With Humberto being his only lead, he had to get to him before the guide took off.

The ten minutes might as well have been ten hours. Topping speeds of over one hundred miles an hour, he reached the ranch gate in eight minutes. His truck bed spun around as he turned onto the gravel road to the lodge. Zach straightened the wheels and kicked up a cloud of dust all the way to the lodge. Without stopping, he drove around the big cedar and rock building, skidding to a halt in front of the barn.

Zach grabbed his Glock, dove out of the truck and raced for the barn.

Richard Giddings stood to the side of the door and pointed toward the interior.

With his Glock leading the way, Zach ducked around the door and into the shadows. He paused for a moment to allow his sight to adjust to the limited lighting in the barn's interior.

"I know you're there." Humberto cinched the girth around the gelding he had saddled and dropped the stirrup into place. "Don't try to stop me. I have to make things right."

Zach stepped out of the shadows into the beam of light from an overhead bulb. He pointed his pistol at Humberto's chest. "If you want to make things right, start by telling me where you're going."

"After Masterson."

"Why?"

The man bowed his head for a moment, then raised it and stared at Zach. "I made a mistake."

Zach drew in a frustrated breath. "Could you be a little clearer?"

"I trusted Masterson. He told me I was helping with an undercover operation." Humberto slid a bridle over the horse's nose. "We had a routine. He'd call and let me know when an agent was coming through the Big Elk to pass information on to their undercover operative in La Familia. I got them to the canyon, they passed the information and I made sure they got out of the canyon. Until two days ago."

"What happened two days ago?" Zach stepped closer, his heartbeat kicking up a notch.

"You know what happened. Those DEA agents were murdered and Jacie's sister was taken."

"Why is that your responsibility?"

"Masterson told me to guide different hunters, but they canceled at the last minute. I was supposed to guide the guests going south, but Jacie insisted on taking them. If I'd known they were agents, I would have been prepared for the attack. Instead Jacie and her sister took the hit and the men were killed." Humberto's lips thinned. "I tried to tell myself Masterson had been mistaken. But the more I thought about it, the more I realized Masterson had been using me.

"The men he'd set up to make the drop backed out when they discovered DEA agents were onto them. Afterward I found out Jacie's sister was an FBI agent. That's when I knew something wasn't right." The man's hands shook as he adjusted the straps on the bridle.

Zach's gut told him Humberto was telling the truth. "Where are you going?"

"I asked one of my cousins to snoop around and find out where La Familia would hole up when things got hot. I know where to start. There's an abandoned ranch house south of here, close to the border. They could be holding Tracie there." He gathered the reins and stepped toward Zach. "I have to make this right."

Zach grabbed the man's arm. "You can't do it alone."

"I feel as responsible for those DEA agents' deaths as if I'd pulled the trigger myself. And if I had been there instead of Jacie and her sister, her sister wouldn't be missing. I have to do this."

"Not without me," Zach said. "I'm going with you."

"I'm going too." Richard Giddings entered the barn.

"No." Humberto raised a hand. "You both need to stay with Jacie and make sure nothing happens to her."

Zach's chest tightened. "It already has."

Humberto closed his eyes and muttered a curse in Spanish.

Richard closed the distance between them. "What's happened to Jacie? Where is she?"

Zach told them what had occurred at Enrique's place and that as far as he could tell, Jacie had been gone nearly three hours. Plenty of time to get far away.

"They wouldn't try to cross the border during the

daylight." Humberto glanced at the barn door where sunlight streamed in, casting long shadows. "It will be dark soon."

Zach's cell phone vibrated in his pocket. He dug it out and noted Hank's number. "Did you find her?"

"Yes, south of here, near the border. I'm not sure what's out there, but we have a GPS coordinate on her. Based on the county map, it's an abandoned ranch house. Do you want me to let the joint operations folks know?"

Zach's fingers tightened around the phone. "Not yet. They might try to fly in with a chopper. There's little enough vegetation to hide a chopper, and they'd hear it long before it got close. Wait two hours and then send them in. That should give us enough time to get down there on horseback and scope out the situation. I don't want La Familia to get spooked and shoot their witnesses." His heart pinched at the thought of what might happen if the cartel got wind that they'd been discovered.

"Us?" Hank asked. "How many of you are headed out?"

"Three." Zach stared at the men beside him, realizing he was going into a tight situation with two men untrained in special operations. But he had to take what he had and get down there. If nothing else, they could shoot and provide cover for him.

"I can have myself and three other men available in the next hour," Hank offered.

"We can't wait. Send the others in only if they can get there before you notify Joint Operations. You'll need to stay and make sure the FBI and DEA launch on time." Zach checked his watch. "It should be dark in one hour. That gives us another hour to get close and locate Tracie and Jacie."

"Godspeed, Zach." Hank ended the call.

"You should take Thunder. He's one of my fastest horses and he's surefooted in the dark." Richard Giddings headed for a stall and lead a black stallion out. "Are you a good rider? This horse can be a bit high-spirited."

"I can handle him." Zach ducked into the tack room and retrieved a saddle and blanket, his pulse hammering, urging him to hurry. The longer it took them to get down there, the more time the cartel had to harm Jacie and her sister.

Richard tied the horse to the stall door and headed for another stall. He led a sorrel gelding out and threw a saddle over his back.

Zach saddled the stallion and slung a bridle over his head. "We'll need saddlebags and scabbards."

Richard nodded to Humberto. "Handle that. I need to duck up to the lodge for a moment."

Humberto retrieved the necessary items, securing the scabbards and saddlebags to the back of Richard's and Zach's horses.

Zach ran out to his truck, gathered the canvas bag, web belt, his rifle and the SIG Sauer Hank had loaned him. He met Richard on the way back to the barn.

The man carried an M110 sniper rifle and had another slung over his shoulder. "Thought we could use some more firepower." His pockets were loaded with boxes of shells and he had two ammo belts looped over his other shoulder. He shrugged. "Our guests like to fire different types of weapons."

Zach smiled grimly. "Glad you cater to them. These will come in handy."

They loaded the magazines, fit the extras into the web belts and tested the weapons. All their preparations took less than fifteen minutes. Fifteen minutes Zach felt they couldn't spare but had to in order to go into cartel-held territory. As the sun sank toward the horizon, the three men mounted and aimed their horses south, setting off at a trot to spare the horses.

Zach prayed they were headed in the right direction and that they wouldn't be too late.

CHAPTER FIFTEEN

"WAKE UP," A MAN'S voice yelled in Jacie's ear.

She wavered in and out of consciousness.

A hard slap to the face jerked Jacie out of the black abyss. She blinked open her eyes. The room around her was dark with one light shining overhead and dust moats floating in and out of its beam.

"Wake up," the deep, intense voice repeated.

Jacie turned to face her nemesis. "What do you want from me?"

"Nothing. It's what I want from her." He pointed to the woman sitting in the shadows, her wrists and feet bound to a chair, her hair drooping in her face.

As the dust motes cleared and Jacie's gaze came into focus, she gasped. "Tracie?"

"Oh, Jacie, I'm so sorry." Her sister's voice cracked. Her face was bruised, her lips split and one eye was swollen shut.

Jacie lunged toward her sister, realizing too late that her own hands and feet were bound with duct tape to the chair in which she sat. The seat toppled and she landed on her side, her head bouncing off a dirty, splintered wooden floor. It was then she noted the windows had been painted black. Even then, no light shone through or around. It could be dark outside for all she knew. How long had she been out? And what had happened to Zach?

Her heart clenched. God, she prayed the men who'd taken her hadn't shot Zach and left him to die as they had Enrique.

"Don't hurt her," Tracie cried. "She doesn't know anything."

"With her here, maybe you'll start talking." He spoke perfect English with no hint of an accent.

Jacie stared at the man with the voice. He wore a black mask over his eyes, and a black bandana covered his hair like an evil Zorro. "Why are we here? What do you want with us?"

"I want your sister to tell me why she came to Wild Horse Canyon. Who sent her?"

"I told you." Tracie shook her head, wincing as if the effort was painful. "No one sent me. I came on my own."

"Why?"

"To visit my sister."

"Lies!" The man pulled Jacie back up, chair and all, and slapped her face hard.

The blow was hard enough that her teeth rattled and her head swam.

"No, don't!" Tracie cried. "She's just a trail guide. Nothing more."

The man stepped away from Jacie and ran a finger along Tracie's face, brushing across her swollen eyes and lips. "But then you aren't, are you? Who in the FBI sent you down here?"

"No one." She heaved a tired sigh. "It's the truth."

"Then why did you come here?" He moved back

to stand beside Jacie, his hand rising. "Tell me now or your sister suffers for you."

"Don't!" Tracie strained against her bonds.

"Your memory returns?" the man asked.

"I came because I read a text on my boyfriend's cell phone. One that asked a man to assist the Big Elk transfer."

"You didn't get orders from your supervisor?"

"No. I was concerned because it was the Big Elk. I wanted to know what it was about since my sister works at the Big Elk Ranch."

"Who did you notify of your search?" he demanded.

"No one."

The hand descended, lashing across Jacie's face with sufficient force to create a resounding echo in the empty room.

Jacie rocked sideways in her chair, her head reeling. "Leave her alone. She came to see me."

"No, Jacie, I came to find out what Bruce was up to." She stared across at Jacie and sighed. "I had a friend trace the text and it went to Humberto Hernandez."

"The Big Elk's guide?" Jacie closed her eyes and opened them, hoping to regain focus. "How does he know Bruce?"

"I don't know. But I couldn't let it go. I had to know what was going on and what danger you might be in on the Big Elk."

"All very touching. Who else knows of Masterson's contact?"

"No one but you, Bruce and Humberto, as far as I know," Tracie answered.

The man raised his hand to hit Jacie again.

She couldn't help it. Jacie flinched back in her chair.

"Then why did you contact Hank Derringer for assistance?" the man demanded, his hand poised to strike.

Tracie leaned forward, constrained by the bindings. "I wasn't sure what I was up against and when it would go down, so I asked him to help me. Only he didn't have anyone available right away. I didn't tell him why I'd come, just that I might need his help."

"So you came to prove your boyfriend was a traitor?"

"I didn't want to believe it, but I had to know." She slumped in her chair, tears trickling down her cheeks.

Jacie's heart bled for her sister. She looked so tired, dirty and defeated. "Let her go. She's telling you the truth."

"Shut up."

Jacie's anger simmered along with her frustration. If only she could get loose.

Then what? The man had the advantage. He was stronger and probably had weapons at his disposal. Jacie might get free, but she wouldn't leave without her sister.

The man waved a finger toward the shadows. "Bring him in."

Jacie's breath lodged in her throat and she braced herself. Who was the masked man referring to? Had they captured Zach? Was he still alive?

Two hulking Hispanics with dragon tattoos on their arms dragged a man into the light.

He slumped between the two men, moaning, his dark hair hanging over his forehead, the shadows cast by the overhead light blocking his features.

Then the henchmen let go.

Their captive slumped to the floor and rolled onto his back. Both eyes were swollen and a large bruise had formed on his jaw. His clothes were torn as if he'd been whipped.

Tracie's eyes widened. "Bruce?"

The figure on the floor moaned, "Tracie."

"Your boyfriend was more forthcoming. It seems he's been busy cutting deals with both the Los Lobos and La Familia." The masked man waved a hand at the men standing nearby. "This makes *mi familia* angry."

The man closest to Bruce kicked him in the side.

Bruce groaned and tried to crawl away from him.

"What are you going to do with us?" Jacie asked, dreading the answer.

"La Familia suffers no traitors." The man stood and walked toward the door. "They're yours. Dispose of them."

It took them longer to get to the abandoned house than they'd anticipated because of the ominous overcast sky stealing the light of the stars and moon. Riding through the night without light proved to be more difficult than originally expected. Thunder rumbled, teasing them with the possibility of a raging storm at any moment. But the rain didn't come, which let them progress through the darkness.

They would have missed the perimeter guard altogether had Zach not slipped on the night-vision goggles when he did. Thankfully the wind had picked up. That and the thunder covered the sound of their horses and the creaking of saddle leather as they dismounted.

"You two stay here until I take care of the outlying guards."

"We can help." Richard pulled a knife from his belt. "I was in the infantry back in the day."

"I appreciate that, but I'm the only one with night-vision goggles and we can't afford to alert the rest of the camp. Once I take this man out, Richard, you move forward to where he was. I'll be circling to the right. Give me five minutes and then Humberto can take up a position a hundred yards to Richard's right. Make sure you have clearance to fire into the compound."

"But we can't see anything," Humberto pointed out.

"Once I have the guards taken care of, I'll start the fireworks. You'll be able to see into the compound and they won't be able to see out. Only fire if you're certain of what you're shooting at. My first order of business is to find the women. When I do, I'm going to create a diversion. Be ready." Zack filled a clip with rounds.

"What kind of diversion?" Richard asked.

"Something with a lot of fire and noise." Zach pressed a hand to the incendiary grenade.

When he found the women, he'd have to distract the guards long enough to free Tracie and Jacie and hopefully get them out.

"Hank's sending out his men and will be notifying the FBI and DEA about now. If they send out their helicopter, we'll have additional firepower should we run into trouble. The main thing is to get the women to safety first."

Richard nodded. "We'll cover you."

Humberto's head hung low. "I'm sorry I got Jacie involved in this."

Zach held up his hand. "Now's not the time for regrets. It's time for action."

"Sí." Humberto squared his shoulders, his lips firming into a straight line. "We're behind you."

Zach checked his web belt one last time, memorizing the location of each item of equipment. With his rifle in hand, he slipped into the night, his night-vision goggles in place.

He made straight for the man on the northern edge of the compound perimeter. As he grew close, he slipped the goggles up on his head and circled around behind the man, dispatching him with a swift, clean stroke with his knife.

One down, still more to go before he could enter the grounds and check for the women.

Zach circled the compound, moving as quickly as he could without making noise. At the western edge of the perimeter, he found one of the compound's sentries fast asleep. The man never knew what happened. He died where he lay.

Another man on the south side was easily taken care of. At least one other remained on the eastern perimeter. The green glow of his body heat registered in Zach's night-vision goggles.

As he eased toward the man, his gaze fixed on his target, Zach didn't see the rock until he kicked it with his toe.

The sound of the stone skittering across the dry soil might as well have been the blaring of a horn.

"Que hay de nuevo?" The man lifted his weapon, aiming toward Zach.

"Es mi," Zach replied with his best Spanish accent; then he slipped around to the side of the man holding the weapon aimed at the spot where Zach had kicked the rock.

"El que?" The man's voice rose.

When Zach was behind the man, he rushed forward and grabbed him from behind.

The guard struggled, his hands still on his rifle. A shot rang out.

Damn. The entire camp would be on alert now.

Zach used his knife to dispatch the man and ran back to the south side of the compound, away from where he'd dropped the last guard and where the others would be headed to discover the source and reason for the gunfire.

With the first shot having been fired, Zach's plan would have to move a little quicker than anticipated.

With only three buildings on the old ranch, Zach snuck up to the back of an old, dilapidated barn that leaned precariously, slats missing from the walls. No light streamed from inside, and a quick scan with the night-vision goggles concluded it was empty. He pushed the goggles up on his forehead. This was the spot, and it was now or never.

Footsteps pounded against the dirt, and a shout rose, followed by more and the clinking of metal against metal as men grabbed weapons and headed toward the perimeter to investigate the shots fired.

Zach pulled the incendiary grenade from the loop holding it on his web harness and yanked the pin. Then he tossed it into the old barn and slipped away in the shadows toward the next building. He threw himself to the ground, covering his ears.

Let's get this party started.

THE GOONS LEFT to "dispose" of Bruce, Tracie and Jacie chuckled as they hiked their rifles up and prepared to follow orders. They spoke to each other in Spanish, pointing first at Tracie, then Jacie and finally Bruce.

Jacie held her breath. With her hands duct-taped behind her, she was helpless to stop what was about to happen. She twisted her wrists, hoping to stretch the tape and allow enough room to pull her hands free. But they'd bound her so tightly, her hands had gone numb. She stared across the room at her sister, praying for a miracle.

The La Familia gang members raised their rifles, aimed and—

Jacie braced herself for the carnage, her gaze inexplicably drawn to one man's trigger finger as his finger tightened.

An explosion ripped through the air, shaking the ground beneath Jacie's feet.

The gunman jerked as he pulled the trigger, hitting the other gang member in the knee. The wounded man dropped to the floor, clutching his knee and screaming Spanish obscenities.

The man who'd shot him bent to him, speaking fast, then he ran to the front door and flung it open.

With her back to the door, Jacie craned her neck to see what was happening. A glow filled the night sky, reflected off the low-slung clouds.

The man on the floor struggled to his feet, using his rifle as a makeshift crutch. He hobbled to the door and out onto the porch with the other man.

"Jacie," Tracie called out. "Can you make your way over here?"

"I don't know." Jacie gathered her strength and performed a kind of sitting hop, moving herself a mere inch toward her sister.

"Again." Tracie did the same. With their legs bound to the chair legs, they couldn't get much traction, but with both of them moving forward, the distance shortened.

Her heart pounding in her ears, Jacie hurried until they were almost knee-to-knee. "Pass me on your right."

Tracie hopped past Jacie.

Once behind her, Jacie scooted her chair to the side. "Can you move your fingers at all? They used duct tape on me."

"You might have a better shot at untying me than I would at tearing the tape."

Jacie strained to reach her sister's bindings, leaning forward to tip her chair backward enough to raise her hands.

The men left to kill them were shouting at people running by.

"Wh-what's happening?" Bruce lifted his head and peered through swollen eyes at the room around him.

"We don't know, but help us," Jacie whispered, loud enough for Bruce to hear.

Bruce pushed up to his hands and knees, then collapsed again, facedown on the floor.

The men in the doorway stopped yelling and turned back to the house, guns raised.

"Jacie." Tracie spoke quietly. "We've got trouble."

THE EXPLOSION ROCKED the ground beneath Zach.

Shots rang out in the distance.

Zach prayed the guards hadn't found Richard and Humberto. For a moment, he second-guessed his decision to bring them along. They weren't trained in these kinds of operations.

Pushing aside his concern for the two men, Zach inched around the side of the small building. He stayed in the deep shadows cast by the fire growing in the barn. The grenade did its job and set the building ablaze. It wouldn't take long to burn to the ground. The ancient timbers would be easily consumed.

A man raced by, sporting an M110 similar to the one Zach carried. Where had the man gotten the American weapon?

As soon as he passed, Zach ran to the next building.

A motorcycle revved and took off out of the melee, a man wearing a black bandana and a black mask heading north, lights extinguished.

Above, thunder boomed in the night and the first drops of moisture splattered the earth.

More shots were muffled by the descending clouds.

Behind Zach, the fire grew, undaunted by a few drops of rain and building in heat and intensity. Chaos reigned.

Banking on the confusion, Zach pushed through the door of the small outbuilding. Light shone through the windows from the barn's fire. The building contained boxes and burlap sacks, but no people. With only the ranch house remaining, Zach steeled himself. He quit the smaller outbuilding and raced across the grounds.

As he neared the house, a man leaned out over the deck, his weapon pointed toward Zach. *"Que hay de nuevo?"*

Zach didn't bother answering; he shot the man and dove for the shadows, rolled to his feet and rounded the corner to the back entrance.

Another guard leaped off the back porch, heading straight for Zach.

Zach didn't give him the opportunity to ask who was there. A single bullet pierced the man's chest, downing him where he stood, leaving the back door unprotected. Zach sucked in a deep breath and nudged the door open with the nose of his rifle.

As soon as he pushed through, he dodged to the left, out of the backlight from the burning barn. He'd entered through the kitchen. If they had the women in this house, they'd be in the living room or locked in one of the bedrooms.

Zach moved from room to room. Above the shouts and rumbling of thunder, Zach heard low thumps and scraping sounds. He headed toward the sound, stopping at a corner. There it was again. The bumping, scraping sound.

Crouching low and staying as much in the shadows as he could, Zach peeked around the wall.

Bound to chairs, Tracie and Jacie sat back to back. He recognized Jacie by the clothes she'd been wearing earlier. She faced him. A man lay sprawled across the floor. He looked vaguely like Bruce, only banged up. Standing in the front door was a large Hispanic man, wielding a semiautomatic rifle aimed at Tracie's chest. If he pulled the trigger at this close range, the bullet would cut right through Tracie and lodge in Jacie, killing both women.

His heart skipped several beats and the world whirled around him. Images of a similar style of torture flashed through him. Toni being beaten by the men of Los Lobos while he remained tied to a beam, powerless to help her.

His breathing grew shallow, his hands clammy. The hopeless feeling washing over him made his hands shake, crippling him.

"Let her live," Jacie begged. "Kill me if you must, but let my sister live."

Jacie's words rang out, cutting through the fog of Zach's memories. She wasn't Toni. Zach wasn't helpless this time. His heartbeat settled into a smooth, deadly rhythm, his hands growing steady.

Zach refused to let Jacie die. He wanted more time with the woman who'd brought him back to life— the woman who marched bravely into battle and who wouldn't give up on her sister or on him.

He tipped the nose of his rifle around the corner and lined up the sights.

Jacie's eyes rounded when she spotted him.

Zach pulled the trigger.

CHAPTER SIXTEEN

ANOTHER SHOT RANG OUT.

Bruce jerked on the floor beside Jacie and moaned. Blood pooled on the floor beside him.

A loud thump was followed by a shout from the doorway.

Jacie scooted her chair halfway around so that she could see what was happening.

Zach leaped past her to the front door.

The cartel man with the wounded leg had thrown himself off the front porch into the dirt, yelling at the top of his voice.

More La Familia gang members came running toward the house.

Zach stepped back and closed the door. He yanked a blood-encrusted knife from a scabbard on his thigh.

"Look out, Jacie!" Tracie cried. "He's got a knife."

"It's okay. He's a good guy," Jacie reassured her.

Zach sliced through Jacie's bindings and then Tracie's. "We have to get out of here before they surround us."

Jacie leaped from her chair and steadied herself on Zach's arm.

Tracie was not so fast, having been starved for the days she'd spent in captivity and beaten on multiple occasions. She stumbled to her feet and pitched forward.

Jacie and Zach grabbed for her before she fell to the floor.

Zach looped Tracie's arm over his shoulder, then tossed his pistol to Jacie.

She caught it and aimed it at the front door as Zach half dragged, half led her sister to the rear of the house.

"What about Bruce?" Tracie asked.

"Leave him. He'll slow us down," Zach said.

Jacie hated Bruce for what he'd gotten her sister into, but she knew what his fate would be if they left him with La Familia. "They'll kill him if we leave him."

Jacie followed Zach, inching backward, her gaze trained on the front of the house, torn between helping the man and getting out alive.

At any moment, La Familia Diablos could storm the house to find the people responsible for their buddy's commotion. They'd find Bruce, blame him and finish him off.

"I can't leave him. He's still alive." Jacie stopped backing up.

"He's not worth it," Zach insisted. "He's a traitor to his country."

"Yeah, but let the courts sentence him. Not La Familia." Jacie took a step back the way she'd come.

"No, Jacie! Zach's right. Saving Bruce isn't worth your getting shot." Tracie dug in her heels and stopped herself and Zach.

"Don't, Jacie. If anyone should go back, it should be me." Zach reached out and grabbed her arm. "He'll be heavy. You can't lift him on your own. Get your sister out of here."

Jacie chewed her lip. "No, I can't let you go in there."

"We don't have time to argue about it. Take my gun

and get Tracie out." He looped Tracie's arm over Jacie's shoulder, pressed a kiss to Jacie's lips. "I want a real date when we get back to sanity."

Jacie's heart turned a somersault and she grinned. "You got it. Don't stand me up." Her chest squeezed hard as Zach ducked past her and back into the front room.

Jacie forced herself not to think about what he might be facing. With Tracie leaning heavily on her, she hurried through the house to the back door.

"Wait." Tracie laid her hand on the door, refusing to let Jacie go through. "There could be men outside the door. Check through the windows first."

Jacie propped Tracie against the wall and crossed to the bare window, careful not to stand behind its glass. Although it was dark in the kitchen, she couldn't take the chance of someone seeing her.

She eased her head around the window frame and peered out.

Men gathered in the yard between the barn and the house. Some faced the barn. They were talking and waving their hands at the flames leaping toward the sky, stirred by a strong crosswind.

One man faced the house. He spoke to another and pointed toward Jacie. She ducked back away from the glass, her pulse hammering. Had he seen her? Did it matter? With that many men standing out in the barnyard, they didn't have a chance of sneaking out the back door.

"We have to find another way out." Jacie helped Tracie into one of the bedrooms, eyeing the window on the far wall. It was on one of the house's sides, out of view of the barnyard and the front yard. She checked out the window for movement. That side of the house was shrouded in shadows. She watched for a full thirty seconds. Nothing moved. "Think you can make it out this window?"

"It's either that or die trying." Tracie's chin lifted. "I might need a boost from you."

"You got it." Jacie pushed and shoved the window, the old paint having congealed, sealing it shut. "I can't get it open."

Tracie slipped out of her shirt and handed it to Jacie. Her body was covered in deep purple bruises. "Wrap your arm with my shirt and break the glass."

Jacie swallowed her anger at what the cartel had done to Tracie and did as her sister directed. She kicked the glass away, praying La Familia couldn't hear the noise over the roar of the fire and the thunder of the approaching storm.

Using the shirt, Jacie cleared the glass from the windowsill. When it was safe enough, she shook out Tracie's shirt.

Her sister put it on, wincing as she raised her arms over her head. "Let's get out of here."

"Not without Zach." Jacie ran to the bedroom door, her gaze panning the empty hallway.

What was taking Zach so long? He should have Bruce and be back by now. So far no more shots had been fired close to the ranch house. Still, Jacie was worried.

Given the short amount of time she'd known Zach, she wasn't sure why she was so concerned. Other than that he made her heart beat faster and his kisses curled her toes.

She waited another minute. When he didn't appear in the doorway, Jacie returned to where her sister leaned against the wall. "We're getting you out of here." Jacie stooped to give her a boost.

"That'll be a challenge." Tracie raised her foot and stepped into Jacie's cupped hands.

Jacie sagged under her sister's weight, then pushed up with her knees and shoved Tracie through the opening. Her sister lodged halfway through, moaning as her ribs hit the windowsill.

"Hang on, I'm going to shove you out." Jacie planted one of Tracie's feet against her own shoulder and leaned into her, pushing her over the edge.

Tracie half slid, half rolled out, dropping to the ground onto the broken glass.

Jacie leaned out the window and whispered loud enough that Tracie could hear but the cartel couldn't, "Okay out there?"

"Will be," Tracie grunted, and righted herself, "as soon as you're out here too."

She hated leaving Tracie all alone. Not when her sister was so weak and barely able to hold herself up. "Lie low for a minute. I'll be right back. I'm going to see what's keeping Zach. Stay in the shadows."

"No, Jacie!" she called out.

Jacie ran for the living room. Zach had lifted Bruce off the floor, and struggled to throw him over his shoulder in a fireman's carry.

"What are you doing in here?" Zach staggered under the other man's weight and glared at Jacie. "I told you to get your sister out."

"I did, but I thought you might need help."

"Do you ever do what you're told?"

"Quit arguing, mister. There's a man headed this

way." She held her gun steady. "I've got you covered, first door on the left."

"Yes, ma'am." Zach sagged under Bruce's dead-weight. The man had been beaten to within an inch of his life and had suffered a gunshot wound to his abdomen, but he still had a pulse. Much as he wanted to, Zach couldn't leave him to die at La Familia's hands.

He entered the bedroom.

Jacie entered behind him, closing the door.

Zach peered over the edge of the windowsill. "Tracie, move out of the way." With no time to spare or take it easy on the injured man, Zach shoved Bruce through the window.

Tracie did her best to cushion his fall, ending up knocked to the ground for her efforts.

Then Zach nodded to Jacie. "You next." He scooped her up and stuck her legs through the window. Jacie dropped to the ground as raindrops splattered across her cheeks.

"I think he's dead," Tracie mumbled.

Bruce lay at an awkward angle, his head cradled in her lap.

Jacie crouched beside the man and touched her fingers to his neck, searching for a pulse.

It took a moment before she felt it. But it was there and very weak.

Zach hauled himself through the window and dropped to the ground. He ran to the back corner of the house and then to the front, returning with a sigh. "We're not out of the woods yet."

"Which way?" Jacie asked.

A voice shouted from inside the house, and footsteps pounded across the wooden floors.

"Follow me and you'd better move fast." Zach grabbed Bruce's arms and yanked him up and over his shoulder. Then he ran due east, away from the house.

Jacie wrapped an arm around her sister's waist and followed Zach into the shadows. The farther they moved away from the flames of the burning barn, the less likely anyone would see them.

Unfortunately they didn't move fast enough to avoid detection.

A man called out behind them.

Zach dropped Bruce to the ground and shouted, "Get down!"

Bullets winged past them, kicking up plumes of dry Texas dust.

Jacie fell to a prone position at once, dragging Tracie down with her.

"What do we do now?" she cried. If they got up to run, whoever was shooting at them would have an easy target. But they couldn't stay glued to the ground forever. Soon others of La Familia would join the shooter. It wouldn't be long before Zach, Jacie, Tracie and Bruce were full of lead.

"Now would be a good time for the backups to show," Zach muttered.

"We have backup?" Tracie asked.

"In a perfectly timed world, we would, but given the weather, I'm not sure the FBI and DEA can get the helicopter off the ground."

As if to emphasize Zach's point, the wind whipped across Jacie's face, twisting her hair.

Bruce lay beside Jacie, his eyes blinking open. "Tracie?"

"No, I'm Jacie," Jacie corrected.

"I'm here." Tracie took his hand and held it, tears shimmering in her eyes as she stared into Bruce's face.

"I'm sorry." Bruce coughed, spitting out blood. "Please forgive me."

"For almost getting me and my sister killed?" She shook her head. "I can't."

"I never meant to hurt you."

"Yeah, well, you did." The tears were flowing in earnest by now from swollen, bruised eyes. "I trusted you and you lied to me."

"I wanted out," he whispered. "But I knew too much. You have to believe me."

"You had two DEA agents killed." Tracie's hand smoothed over Bruce's face. "Where was the mercy? I don't even know you anymore."

"I'm still the same person," he insisted.

"You're not the same man I fell in love with."

"I didn't…" Bruce's voice gurgled, as if his lungs were taking on liquid. "I didn't order those two men killed."

"Then who did?" Tracie demanded, leaning up.

The man in the house fired on them, the bullet hitting the dirt in front of Jacie's face, kicking it up into her eyes. She blinked and rubbed the sand out.

Bruce's eyes closed, his breathing growing shallower.

"Don't you die on me." Tracie shook the man, tears flowing freely down her dirt-streaked cheeks. "The least you can do is tell me who is behind all of this."

"He's powerful," Bruce whispered.

"Was he the one interrogating us?" Tracie sucked in a deep breath.

"Yes."

"What's his name?"

"Too dangerous… FBI…can make people disappear."

"What do you mean?" Zach asked.

"Hank's wife and son…" Bruce's body shuddered and he coughed up more blood, and then settled back against the earth, his face creased in a grimace of pain.

"What does he have to do with Hank's family?" Zach demanded.

Bruce inhaled, the gurgling sound more pronounced. "Still alive."

"Where?" Zach grabbed the man by the collar.

Bruce's eyes blinked open, found Tracie's and they closed. "I loved you," he said, the words released on his last breath. His body went slack.

Tracie leaned her face against his chest, her shoulders shaking with silent sobs. "Damn you, Bruce. Damn you for everything."

Jacie's heart ached at her sister's distress.

Bruce had made some big mistakes. He'd betrayed his country and betrayed Tracie, but deep down had never stopped loving her.

Though tears welled in her eyes, Jacie refused to let them fall. She couldn't dwell on Bruce's mistakes, not when they were pinned to the ground, unable to move for fear of being hit.

Shouts rose from the barnyard. Flames climbed higher into the descending clouds.

Zach glanced over his shoulder and sighed. "I believe the cavalry has arrived."

Headlights shone in the distance from half a dozen vehicles. The advancing army had the remaining La Familia members scrambling for motorcycles and jeeps.

The man who'd pinned them apparently didn't know he was being surrounded and kept shooting random shots—some bullets hitting far too close for comfort.

Zach's cavalry pulled in to the ranch compound and skidded to a stop in the gravel. Doors flung open and men wearing flak vests and carrying guns poured out. The remaining cartel thugs were quickly killed or held up their hands in surrender.

As the last man standing, their sniper suddenly stopped shooting and spun, his weapon now aiming for whoever had entered the room behind him.

Two shots were fired. The sniper slammed against the windowsill and tipped out onto the gravel below. Another face appeared in the glassless window. A man wearing a dark cowboy hat instead of the dark gear of the FBI.

"Well, I'll be damned. Hank must have sent in his guys as well as the FBI. If I'm not mistaken, that was Ben." After a moment Zach stood. "I think that was our cue. Come on, let's see if they brought a medic." He reached down to grab Jacie's arm, hauling her to her feet.

Jacie touched her sister's shoulder. "We have to go."

"Go without me," Tracie said, her voice catching on a sob.

"Can't." Jacie shook her head. "You're a part of me. You're my sister. I could never leave you behind."

Tracie slid Bruce's head from her lap and pushed to a kneeling position. "Why did he have to go and be an idiot and play both sides?"

"Who knows what motivates different people?" Jacie answered. "For what it's worth, it sounded like he loved you."

Tracie snorted. "Apparently he loved himself more." She stood, swaying slightly.

"What I want to know is who the hell was the man in the mask?" The beast of a man who'd been so harsh to her sister and herself would forever haunt Jacie.

"I'm done with the bureau." Tracie pushed her hair back from her face, revealing more bruising.

Jacie flinched at all the damage. "What do you mean?" She cast a glance toward the vehicles crowding the compound, hoping they brought medical personnel to treat her sister's wounds.

Tracie's dried, split lips pulled back in a sneer. "What good is it to be an agent when you can't tell the good guys from the bad?"

Zach grabbed her shoulders and forced her to stare into his eyes. "The important thing to remember is that *you* are a good agent and that you are vital to this nation, to our country, to keeping us safe."

She stared into his eyes. "Who are you?"

"I'm Zach Adams." His hands dropped to his sides. "I used to be a special agent like you."

"Why did *you* quit?" Tracie asked.

"I lost hope." Zach faced Jacie. "Someone helped me find it again." He held out his hand to Jacie.

She took it, butterflies storming her belly and gooseflesh rising on her arms. The man definitely turned her inside out.

Tracie turned her bruised and battered face toward Jacie. "I feel like I missed something." She gave the hint of a smile. "Do you two know each other?"

"We didn't. Now we do." Jacie gave a shy smile.

"We can talk later." Zach slipped Tracie's arm over

his shoulder. "Right now we need to have you seen by a doctor."

Jacie looped Tracie's other arm over her shoulders and together, they closed the distance between them and the vehicles parked near the burning barn and outbuilding. Floating embers landed on the house, lighting it like a tinderbox.

As the house burned, Jacie couldn't feel regret for the old structure, not when it held memories of terror and torture. She hoped never to feel that trapped and hopeless again.

ZACH'S PULSE HAD finally returned to normal. After finding Jacie and Tracie tied up and on the verge of being executed, he thought life had come to a standstill. Thank God, he'd arrived just in time. Bringing them out of that house alive had lifted a weight heavier than the current situation from his shoulders.

It was as if now he finally knew the meaning of his life. When he'd been a captive of Los Lobos and they'd tortured Toni to death, he'd asked God why he'd spared him and took her. Seeing Jacie and her sister about to be killed had brought his life back in focus. God had a purpose for him. He'd led him to Hank and this amazing woman. Zach was meant to fight for truth and justice, the fight he thought he'd joined the FBI to accomplish.

As the three staggered into the open, Hank Derringer broke away from a group of agents and cowboys.

"Zach, Jacie!" He took over for Jacie and, with Zach's help, led Tracie to the back of a Hummer. The hatch was open and a man was applying a bandage to Richard Giddings's forehead.

Zach held out a hand. "Thanks for covering me." He glanced around. "Where's Humberto?"

"Already on his way back to the Big Elk."

"Any injuries?" Zach asked.

"Humberto got off without a scratch. I would have too, if I hadn't tripped over my two left feet and landed a face-plant in the gravel." Richard grinned at Jacie. "You don't know how happy I am to see my best field guide on her feet and alive."

"Thanks, Richard." Jacie gave the man a hug, moisture glistening in her eyes.

After a quick once-over, the medic cleaned one of Tracie's facial wounds. "Won't know what else is damaged until we get her back to the county hospital in Wild Oak Canyon and get some X-rays. Might even take her into El Paso for CAT scans."

"The county hospital," Tracie insisted. "And a hot shower, please. Then I think I could sleep for a hundred years."

Hank bundled her into another Hummer. Jacie and Zach climbed in on each side of her. As they pulled away from the ranch compound, Zach's gut clenched as the enormity of the situation hit. He'd almost lost Jacie.

The few raindrops the clouds had released did nothing to extinguish the fire that had completely consumed the house by now. Hank called ahead on his satellite phone and had the local doctor meet them at the county hospital, machines warmed and waiting.

After what seemed an interminable amount of time and X-rays, Tracie was shown to a room where she'd spend the night monitored by a competent staff. Zach insisted that the doctor look over Jacie, as well. Though she protested that she was fine and didn't need a doctor, she went with him.

Throughout Jacie's examination, Zach paced in the waiting room, clenching his fists, frustrated and angry at what Jacie and Tracie had gone through.

When she finally emerged, she smiled. "Told you I was fine. Other than an ugly bruise on my cheekbone and a split lip, I'll survive." The doctor found no signs of concussion or brain trauma from the multiple hits she'd taken at the hands of the mystery interrogator.

"I'm glad you're okay." Zach gathered her in his arms and pressed a gentle kiss to her forehead. "And for the record, you look great."

"Liar." She leaned into him, her arms circling his waist, her forehead pressed to his chest. "I'm glad it's over."

"Me too." He smoothed her hair from her forehead and tucked it behind her ear.

Jacie tipped her cheek into his open palm and pressed a kiss there. "Thank you for coming for us."

Zach's chest tightened as he stared down into her gray-blue eyes. "Wild horses couldn't keep me away."

Her gaze broke from his, her eyelids drifting downward, hiding her emotions. "I want to see my sister."

Zach wanted to take Jacie somewhere they could be alone and hold her until his arms ached and the desperation of the past twenty-four hours abated. Instead he led her to her sister's room.

Tracie lay with her damp hair spread across her pillow, her damaged cheeks wiped clean of dirt and grime. Her eyes were closed, her face relaxed.

Jacie paused with Zach in the doorway. "I'm staying with her tonight," she whispered.

"No, you're not." Tracie's eyes blinked open.

Zach's fists clenched at all the swelling and the purple bruises.

Jacie stepped forward. "I'm not letting you out of my sight for a while."

"Yes, you are." Tracie's lips quirked upward slightly. "I know you want to help, but Hank assured me he'd have someone stand guard throughout the night. And I should be okay to leave the hospital tomorrow. You've done enough and need rest as much as I do."

"Still," Jacie sighed, "I'd feel better knowing you're okay."

"And I won't get any sleep with you hovering over me." Tracie closed her eyes. "Please, I just want to sleep."

Jacie closed the distance between them and gathered her sister's hand in hers. "Are you sure?"

Tracie sighed. "Yes, I'm sure." Her eyes edged open again. "Zach?"

Zach joined Jacie beside the hospital bed, the scents of alcohol and disinfectants making him itch to leave. "Yes."

Tracie disengaged her hand from Jacie's and held it out to Zach. "Thank you for coming to our rescue. I don't want to think about how this day could have ended." She laid his hand over Jacie's. "Now get her out of here. And you'd better be good to her, or you'll have me to contend with."

Zach laughed. "If you're anywhere near as tough as Jacie, I'll be shaking in my boots."

"Got that right." Tracie's eyelids drifted closed as though they weighed a ton. "I'll see you two in the morning."

Zach led Jacie out of the room.

Jacie cast one last glance over her shoulder. "I don't like leaving her."

"You heard her. She wants to sleep." Zach hugged her middle. "Hank assured me that Ben Harding is one of the best ex-cops you'll find. He'll make sure Tracie is safe."

Jacie leaned into Zach. "It's been a helluva day, hasn't it?"

"You were so brave."

"And stupid. If I'd stayed put when you told me to, I wouldn't have been caught."

"And I'd be dead. You saved me." In more ways than one, and he'd spend a lifetime thanking her. "And that tracking device you had in your shoe led us to you and your sister. I'd say it worked out okay." Zach paused for a moment in the hallway of the hospital and touched a thumb to the bruising on her cheek. "I have to admit, though, it was a little too close for comfort." He kissed her cheek, careful not to apply too much pressure. His mouth moved to her lips.

"Ouch." Jacie backed away.

"Sorry." Zach straightened. "Did I tell you I'm really glad you're okay?"

"Yes, you did." She laughed up at him. "Do we have rides back to the Big Elk?"

"Hank let us have use of the Hummer. He'd like to see us tomorrow if you're up to it."

"Ask me tomorrow. Right now I just want to go home to bed." Her hand slipped into his and they walked out of the hospital.

The drive back to the Big Elk Ranch was accomplished in silence.

At first Zach thought Jacie had fallen asleep, she was so quiet. But a glance at her face proved him wrong. Jacie stared straight ahead, her eyes open, her bottom lip captured between her teeth.

When they pulled up in front of her little cottage, Zach leaped down and rounded to the passenger side of the vehicle to help her down. He walked her to her door. "You know, we never did have a chance to put your cabin back together."

Jacie's shoulders sagged. "I'll manage."

"You could stay in mine," he offered, turning her to face him.

Jacie's gaze rose to meet his. "I don't know if I can keep my distance."

"I'm counting on that."

"I don't know if I want to get any closer to you. Now that it's all over, I'm afraid you'll be gone tomorrow." Her eyes filled with moisture, the blue-gray of her irises swimming. "I almost lost you today to a bullet. I'm not strong enough to lose you again."

"You're not going to lose me." He slipped his hands beneath her legs and scooped her up into his arms. "I want that first real date and a lot more after that."

"Are you sure? I thought you didn't want a lasting relationship. And I won't settle for less."

"I was wrong, and for once, we're in agreement." He strode across the yard to his cabin and twisted the key in the doorknob while balancing her in his arms. "A little help here?"

"Not until you answer one question."

"Fire away."

"Do you think you could ever love me like you loved Toni?"

Zach stood still, his gaze captured by hers. Then he shook his head. "No."

Tears welled in Jacie's eyes. "Put me down. I can't do this."

He refused to let her go, his hands tightening around her. "Hear me out."

"I refuse to fall in love with someone who can't love a second time. It's hopeless."

"I don't think so." He laughed, the vibrations of his chest warming her. "I can't love you like I did Toni because you're a different person. Sure, I loved Toni. She was my partner. I'd give anything to have been able to save her life. We were a team."

"See? I can't compete with that. I'm just a trail guide."

"And a very beautiful and courageous one at that." He brushed a kiss across her undamaged cheek. "You never gave up. You taught me that anyone can make a difference, if they care enough."

"I didn't make a difference. *You* saved us." Her brow furrowed. "Put me down. I need to be alone."

He shook his head. "You made the difference, Jacie. You saved me, not only from that gunman at Enrique's place, but from myself." He held her tighter. "I could very well be falling in love with you, something I thought I could never do again."

Her eyes widened. "You're falling in love with me?" She squeaked and grasped his cheeks between her palms, her frown deepening. "But I thought you couldn't love me like you did Toni."

"I can't love you like Toni because you're Jacie. I'm falling in love with you, if you'll give me a chance."

Her eyes filled with tears, and a smile spread across her face. "So what's keeping you?"

He laughed and pushed the door open to the cabin. "I don't want to make any rash decisions when we've known each other less than a week."

"Ever heard of love at first sight?" Jacie tipped her head. "Or in our case, maybe it was second or third sight."

Zach set her on her feet and pulled her into his arms. "Whatever, I want to spend time getting to know you better."

"Now you're talking." Jacie pushed the door closed behind him, shutting the world out and them in.

EPILOGUE

HANK LEANED AGAINST the front of his desk. "Zach, thank you for helping Jacie and Tracie out of a tight situation. I knew you were the right man for the job, and you didn't disappoint."

Zach held tight to Jacie's hand. "I'm glad I could help. Thanks for the opportunity." His gaze was on Jacie, not Hank.

"Although we didn't get the man behind it all, at least we uncovered one of the moles in the FBI."

Tracie sat in a wingback leather chair, her color returning, though her eyes seemed dull and unhappy. "I wish I'd known sooner about Bruce's activities."

"What would you have done that you didn't do once you learned of them?" Jacie asked.

Tracie stared at her hands. "I wouldn't have fallen for all his lies."

"The thing to remember is that you stayed true to your country and your duty as an FBI agent. I commend you on your spirit and desire to seek justice and truth." Hank drew in a deep breath and opened his mouth to go on. "Which brings me to—"

Zach held up his hand. "Don't you think Tracie makes a perfect FBI agent?"

Hank smiled. "I guess you know I was about to offer her a position?"

Tracie shook her head. "Although I'm disappointed that some of our agents are bad, I'm not giving up on the bureau. I still believe in it and what we can do to preserve justice in this country. Between you, Zach and Jacie, you reminded me of what an honor it is to serve."

Hank waved a hand. "If you decide to retire from the bureau, please consider my team."

Tracie smiled and nodded. "You bet I will."

Hank turned to Jacie. "What about you? You're quite a good shot, brave and a seeker of truth and justice—"

Jacie held up her hand. "Though I know I could do the danger thing in a pinch, it's not for me. I like leading hunting parties and promoting the Big Elk Ranch."

Zach squeezed her hand.

Warmth flushed her neck and cheeks at the memories of all the places those hands had been throughout the night and halfway through the morning. "Thanks, but I think I'll stay where I am."

"That leaves you, Zach. I consider the job you did a trial on your part and mine. I'm convinced you will be a valuable asset to this organization. Care to continue?"

Zach nodded. "If Jacie has no objections, I'm in."

Jacie raised her hand. "No objections here, as long as I get to see you between jobs."

"Then that's settled. I have my contacts searching for the leader of the stateside La Familia gang that held you two ladies. Until then, stay on your toes in case he seeks retribution."

"One other thing, Hank," Zach interrupted. "Before Bruce died, he mentioned the man was powerful with connections in the FBI. Bruce said that he could make people disappear. He mentioned your family. He intimated that they may still be alive."

Hank's face blanched and he closed his eyes, dragging in a deep breath. "Any clue as to where he's keeping them?"

"Sorry, Bruce died before he could say more than that. He didn't know a location or in what condition they were."

Zach didn't want to think about what physical state Hank's wife and child would be in. Given the mystery man's propensity for pain, it couldn't be good.

His arm slipped around Jacie's shoulders. "I'll do anything in my power to help you find him and bring him down. After what he did to Jacie and Tracie, the man deserves to die."

Hank rose from his seat, crossed the room and held out his hand to Zach.

Zach stood and gripped the outstretched hand.

"Thank you, Zach," Hank said. "I'll be taking you up on that offer."

* * * * *

We hope you enjoyed reading this
special collection from Harlequin® books.

If you liked reading these stories,
then you will love
Harlequin Intrigue® books!

You crave excitement!
Harlequin Intrigue stories deal in serious
romantic suspense, keeping you on the edge
of your seat as resourceful, true-to-life women
and strong, fearless men fight for survival.

Enjoy six *new* stories from
Harlequin Intrigue every month!

Available wherever books and
ebooks are sold.

THE WORLD IS BETTER WITH

Romance

Harlequin has everything from contemporary, passionate and heartwarming to suspenseful and inspirational stories.

Whatever your mood,
we have a romance just for you!

JUST CAN'T GET ENOUGH?

Join our social communities
and talk to us online.

You will have access to the latest
news on upcoming titles and special
promotions, but most importantly,
you can talk to other fans about your
favorite Harlequin reads.

Harlequin.com/Community

Facebook.com/HarlequinBooks

Twitter.com/HarlequinBooks

Pinterest.com/HarlequinBooks

Love the Harlequin book you just read?

Your opinion matters.

Review this book on your favorite book site, review site, blog or your own social media properties and share your opinion with other readers!

HARLEQUIN®

A *Romance* FOR EVERY MOOD™

Stay up-to-date on all your
romance-reading news with the
Harlequin Shopping Guide,
featuring bestselling authors, exciting new
miniseries, books to watch and more!

The newest issue will be delivered right to you
with our compliments! There are 4 each year.

Signing up is easy.

EMAIL

ShoppingGuide@Harlequin.ca

WRITE TO US

HARLEQUIN BOOKS
Attention: Customer Service Department
P.O. Box 9057, Buffalo, NY 14269-9057

OR PHONE

1-800-873-8635 in the United States
1-888-343-9777 in Canada

Please allow 4-6 weeks for delivery of the first issue by mail.